Thingamajig
and Other Splendelicious Stories

Copyright © 2024 Joan Bullion El Faghloumi

Brilliant Bird Projects

ISBN: 978-1-0686223-0-4

The right of Joan Bullion El Faghloumi to be identified as the Author of the Work has been asserted by her in accordance with the Copyright, Designs and Patents Act 1988.

All rights reserved, including the right to reproduce this book, or portions thereof in any form. No part of this text may be reproduced, transmitted, downloaded, decompiled, reverse engineered, or stored, in any form or introduced into any information storage and retrieval system, in any form or by any means, whether electronic or mechanical without the express written permission of the author.

Cover and layout done by Spiffing Publishing

'By Magic' illustration: tonysimpsonart.com

Thingamajig
and Other Splendelicious Stories

Joan Bullion El Faghloumi

I've decided to include my maiden surname in my author name. I'm proud to be part of the Bullion family – in the 50s and 60s, they were a well-known South-East London family living mainly in New Cross, with our particular branch originating in Methven, a village in Perth, Scotland, with the birth of John William Bullion in 1836. His family line goes back to the 1700s. In 1860 he settled in London and set the wheels in motion.

His eldest son, William John, lived to be 96, passing in 1932. William John owned his own house in Rolt Street, Deptford, something that was unusual at that time for a working-class man. His son, Archibald Noel Bullion, was my granddad – who I never knew. In turn, his eldest son, born in 1919, was named Archibald Henry Cyril – my much-loved Uncle Archie.

We believe that our family name is derived from the aristocratic Boleyn family, well-known from the 16th century Tudor era, with their origins in France, making us descendants. The name Boleyn was spelt in various ways back then, with Bullion being a later version.

With huge thanks to my cousin Janet Setter for researching our Perth connections – which she'd previously discovered on behalf of our family.

For my Dad
Fred Bullion

always my inspiration

and
dedicated to all the Bullion family,
past and present

Contents

Foreword ix
Successes xi

Thingamajig 17
Don't Tell Your Mother 27
Blabbermouth 37
Two-Way 40
Operation Ritz 45
Etiquette and Pretty Ladies 54
Cracked Heart 64
Pops and the Clock Face Weirdos 68
The Man She'd Met 78
At Home with Winnie 86
Cold, Cold Blue 94
Kissed by The Devil 96
Playing the Diamond Game 106
Love in Arabic 117
A Short Glossary 119
    Rabat 120
    Honeymoon 127
    Mish Mash 149
    On the Beach 157
    Beni Ahmed 169

Appealing	177
Desesperado	185
Legal Spies	188
The Lyceum Arms	202
Big Boss	214
Devil of a Day	226
Educating Nadia	237
The Day After	249
The Queen of Spain	255
Sweet Manic Dreams	265
Liberty	279
The Poke Police	296
Proper Love	300
The Devil Did It	314
Spawn	321

An Accidental Woman	324
Losing Him	331
On Mission Oeuf	346
Grade A, Grey Day	363
The Embodying Spirit	371
The Other Me	380
To Know Seville	383
That Crazy Vibe	393
In the Shadows	398
Party Piece	403
By Magic	404
Shiny-Eyed	415

Foreword

I'm delighted to have my first book of short stories published.

Two-thirds of the stories you'll read here have been shortlisted in prestigious international writing competitions, sometimes shortlisted with more than one competition, and three of my stories have been outright winners. I hope you enjoy reading this diverse selection of tales – they're mostly on the dark side, which seems to come naturally to me.

Some of my stories are based on my own life experiences, and for those who know me well, these will be obvious.

At junior school in Deptford, S.E. London, I remember winning the RSPCA short story competition prize two years running. This put me on the path – eventually – to think about becoming a writer, following in the footsteps of my dad, Fred Bullion. In addition to his achievements, and accolades earned, he was a fierce philanthropist, and in the '60s he wrote occasional short 'cosy corner' articles for The Kentish Mercury on local historical figures of the 16th and 17th centuries, such as Sir Walter Raleigh, diarists Samuel Pepys and John Evelyn, and playwright Christopher Marlowe – all connected to Deptford at that time. A century later the Russian Czar Peter The Great travelled to Deptford several times, showing great interest in the Royal Shipyard science of shipbuilding, and working alongside the hired men. My dad was so immersed in local history and loved to find time in his busy schedule to contribute his knowledge.

Thank you so much to all my friends and family who've supported me over the last few years during my writing resurgence; and with special thanks to my friend Norman in Swords, Co. Dublin for all his kindness. I had always wanted to publish a book, and here it is – at last.

Joan
Seaford, East Sussex

Successes

An Accidental Woman –
Aug. 2021 – Globe Soup – *Romance* theme – Hon Mention

Blabbermouth –
Apr. 2015 – Mash Stories Flash Fiction (online) + podcast broadcast – Shortlisted – **Published online**

Devil's Kiss –
Aug. 2019 – Writers' Forum magazine – Shortlisted
Apr. 2020 – Flash 500 Short Story Competition – Shortlisted
New name:
Kissed by The Devil – Jan. 2022 – Globe Soup – *A Christmas Like No Other* theme – Hon Mention

Don't Tell Your Mother –
(formerly '***Shot to Pieces***') Aug. 2015 – Writers' Forum magazine – Shortlisted
June 2018 – Henshaw Short Story Competition – Shortlisted
Last quarter, 2017 – Ink Tears – Longlisted

Etiquette and Pretty Ladies –
May 2022 – Writers' Forum – Shortlisted

Grade A, Grey Day –
June 2020 – Writing Magazine – Shortlisted
Aug. 2020 – Writers' Forum magazine – Shortlisted
March 2024 – Flash 500 Short Story Competition – Shortlisted

In The Shadows –
Oct. 2023 – Writing Magazine – *Villain* theme – Shortlisted

Legal Spies –
Oct. 2018 – Writers' Forum magazine – Shortlisted

Losing Him –
Oct. 2019 – Writers' Forum magazine – Shortlisted
Apr. 2020 – Flash 500 Short Story Competition – Shortlisted

On Mission Oeuf –
June 2017 – Writers' Forum magazine – Shortlisted

Operation Ritz –
July 2017 – Writers' Forum magazine – Shortlisted
First quarter 2018 – Flash 500 Short Story Competition – Longlisted
Apr. 2022 – Globe Soup – *A Twist of Fate* theme – Historical genre **Finalist**

***Proper Love* –**
March 2017 – Writers' Forum magazine – Shortlisted
2016/17 – Flash 500 Short Story Competition – Longlisted

***Shiny-Eyed* –**
Nov. 2021 – Globe Soup – Micro-writing. Theme of Pride – 2ⁿᵈ place Shortlisted

***Sweet Manic Dreams* –**
Jan. 2017 – Writers' Forum magazine – Shortlisted

***The Embodying Spirit* –** formerly *The Spirit*
April 2021 – **Winner** of *Magical Realism* genre category – Globe Soup 7-Day Short Story Competition

***The Man She'd Met* –**
Apr. 2017 – Writing Magazine – 1ˢᵗ Place **Winner – Published**

***Thingamajig* –**
Mar 2019 – Flash 500 Short Story Competition – Long- and Shortlisted
May 2019 – Writers' Forum magazine – 1ˢᵗ Place **Winner – Published**

***To Know Seville* –**
Oct. 2017 – Writers' Forum magazine – Shortlisted

***Two-Way* –**
Jan. 2017 – Writing Magazine – Shortlisted

The Capricious Nature of Human Behaviour

We're all caught in a perpetual cycle
of turmoil, angst and joy.
People's lives, and the predicaments encountered
on their personal journeys – there's nothing more
fascinating than that.

Thingamajig

The volunteer girl has arrived; she's coming through the double doors. Above the din in the hall, I hear the swollen doors clunk behind her, as they always do – but louder this time. Her raspberry hair wafts around her shoulders.
    She looks just as I imagined, and as pale as death.
    She's late. We've been running around ragged. I put down the Beatles tee-shirts I'm pricing-up, and wave an arm. She's looking in every direction except towards me; suddenly she snaps her head the right way.
    'Over here!' I shriek.
    St. Jude's Church Hall's floorboards are groaning beneath the weighty shuffle of feet. Random spotlights from the rafters pick out assortments of items on the trestle tables, and illuminate the tops of punters' heads as they shift and rummage and dig through jumble and bric-a-brac.
    She's elbowing her way through, getting closer.
    'Hi! How you doing?' she shouts, like she's known me all her life. She's very young; wears a large nose-ring, two lip-studs, and who knows what hidden

beneath her black layered get-up. Her mouth, set in that pasty white face, is a livid slash of scarlet; like it's fallen onto a chopper, as my granddad would've said.

We'll see about this one. Could be interesting.

I adopt my usual cheerful stance, smiling and nodding. It'll get me what I want.

She's here, almost nose to nose with me. 'Am I late?'

'I'm Wendy,' I say. 'You must be Sasha.'

She's peering around her, through the gaps in the crowd, at the trestles heaped with clothes, shoes, books, toys, bits and pieces. The loudspeakers suddenly spit and stutter... music blares erratically.

She looks at me in horror. 'You want me to sell... this stuff?'

We'll see. I always get my way.

'That's why you're here,' I say.

She stares at me. 'Stuff like *this*?'

'Strangely, yes.'

'People give money, like, for this... stuff?'

The smile on my face is getting stuck; my jaw twitches. Three occurrences of her saying *stuff* is enough.

She's pulling back the candyfloss hair and standing there, sullen. There's bulky chains on her earlobes.

'You volunteered.'

'Nooo. Someone volunteered me.'

'Sasha— '

'Where's the... bog?' she says, then immediately spots the 'Ladies' door at the far end of the hall. 'Be back in a jiff.'

I see myself at that kind of age: sullen, twitchy, uncooperative – and nervous. This girl isn't unconfident at all; on the contrary. She isn't here to make any kind of contribution. *Born to take, not to make* – one of my mother's sayings. She said I should be civil to others, even if they'd royally pee-ed me off. Make out everything is fine and dandy, always. As the years roll by, with all that I've involved myself in, it's getting increasingly difficult to live by that doctrine. But I try.

I have my own methods to get what I need; and I'm not kidding.

Looking towards the fringes of the bedlam in the hall – all the best buys taken already, I'd say – I pick up on a suspect figure: someone making their way stealthily towards the back of the hall, looking all around; past the array of dusty Moroccan lamps, the Aspidistra in its fractured pot, and the sad, over-stuffed armchair. It's a young man, hoodie up, and carrying a rucksack. What's he up to?

'Oi!' I yell above the racket.

He gathers pace, and I plunge my way across to him. 'What you doing?'

'I'm lookin' for Sasha.'

The Searchers boom out just at that very moment: *'Don't throw your love awaaay... '*

'What d'you want with her?' I say.

Quick as a flash: 'Nothin'.'

I smile at him. He's very young too. 'What's with the rucksack thingamajig?'

'I always 'ave this with me.'

'Looks dodgy. I wasn't born yesterday, sonny.'

He looks horrified, struggling for words. 'What?'

'On the pinch, are you?'

'How... did you know? I mean... '

'Easy-peasy – it's empty. I'm no fool.'

'No... no, just... '

'What do you want with her?'

'She said she'd... uh, get me some stuff. Real legit, like.'

'What kind of stuff?'

'Int'resting stuff.'

I laugh. 'At a steal, eh?'

'What?'

'Sasha's not started working yet. It's still to come,' I say, 'though not sure it's gonna happen, matey, to be honest.'

He clutches his rucksack tighter. 'She said she's up for it,' he whines, looking anguished. 'She said she was, uh... '

'If you have some kind of deal going on,' I say, 'it's alright. If you find something of interest, then you just need to pay. *Nothing* is expensive here – you can see that for yourself.'

I'll be making sure he doesn't nick anything, as well as alerting my helpers.

'Can I... 'ave a look?'

I notice he's spotted some old coins and an assortment of foreign stamps nearby.

'Feel free. And if you want to give me a hand, that's okay too. I might even make you a cuppa.' I smile at him, and he gives me a toothy one in return.

He looks quite wholesome.

Then he shambles off towards the front double doors, the ancient rucksack now hanging from his fingers. I catch a glimpse of tattered *Ban The Bomb!* badges peeling off the flap, vintage in themselves; his dad's, or more likely his granddad's.

Aldermaston.

I was there. Greenham Common too.

'Wendy! You got a minute?'

Doris calls me over to the women's underwear trestle: there's no price tag on the baby-pink silk French Knickers; a missing hook on a nursing bra; a jumble of nylon suspender belts, all tangled together. 'How on earth did *that* happen?' Doris, my best helper, remarks, grumbling as she tries to unscramble them. 'Flippin' Nora. Might 'ave to get the scissors to 'em.'

I pick up a satin boned corset that looks like it has some history. A basque: black, lacy, frayed. Grubby.

'That's some thingamajig, that,' says Doris. 'Gawd knows where that's come from, and what it's seen, eh?'

I smile at her terminology. A thingamajig is whatever you want it to be; sometimes to replace a forgotten word, and other times referring to an object more specifically: something more covert.

The basque is dumped back onto the trestle, sitting atop the skeins of gussets, straps and mangled brassiere cups. I'm usually impervious to the odour of used clothes, and I remain stoic, but a chance whiff of patchouli oil from a nearby trestle makes me gag. It competes with the secondhand vestiges hanging in the air; a sour, pungent mingling of jumbleland tat and random merchandise.

Someone will buy this stuff. It all gets sold.

I go out back to wash my hands, and think of having a cuppa. I wrestle with the vending machine, then give up, find a stray teabag and put the kettle on. I'm too impatient to wait for it to boil, the socket in the wall looks iffy in any case; and, scrabbling through the eyelevel cupboard, I can see there's no kind of acceptable mug with less than two scummy fissures running through it, never mind the inbuilt brown stains. It's all a mess. I abandon the idea altogether and retrace my steps into the hall.

It's heaving. But that's good.

I'll go back to the agency tomorrow – they should know the right kind of people to send to me. It's not rocket science. I like a young person to train, and sometimes to pamper; you could call it grooming.

More than that. I turn them into little warriors.

Ms Candyfloss isn't likely to cut it, unless I can administer a bit of persuasion. Where did they get *her* from?

There's a tussle going on: two women have dug out a garment at the same time, both pulling on it. It's getting heated. Doris intervenes, grasping the thing – a small, colourful item – in the middle; firmly and calmly, akin to the hand of Solomon. Her Sixties wedding ring, dulled by age, and biting through her fleshy finger, suddenly catches the light, winking fitfully.

'Now, now, ladies,' she says. 'Is that really gonna fit you?' she observes, looking each of them in the eye.

'Too tiny for me, and it sure as hell it won't fit you two neither.'

Doris stands her ground. This is why she's so invaluable.

With that, each woman surrenders her end. They pause and then, without looking back, shove their separate ways through the multitude.

I exchange a look with Doris. She crinkles her mouth and goes back to her sorting.

The Searchers again. Another lacklustre track limps its way through – skidding to an abrupt halt in the last chorus. Then, breaking things up, there's a fresh surge of punters coming through the moody double doors.

The place is swarming.

I push my way across to my favourite stall to flick through a few gardening books as I wait, keeping an eye on the hoodie boy, and his limp rucksack. He's talking to one of the helpers: a good sign. I look up at the old British Railways clock on the wall, above the trestle supporting clusters of dried-out cakes on paper plates, and I tut-tut. I finger my phone in my pocket. If I could just move time on... get this girl out of here, or get her working.

If only.

I should look into it. I've achieved similar things.

Anything remotely wacky should be possible these days with a special thingamajig like mine.

'*Needles and Pins*' roars and crackles the length of the hall. A familiar era, it's music that sounds strangely run of the mill now. Stale, and heard a million times. But I'd never divulge that thought to anyone.

Sasha emerges, another layer of what looks like chalk on her face.

'Okay,' I say, going up to her, putting on a smile.

She shrugs.

'D'you want to take a look around?' I say. 'Something might suit you, and then you can get selling. I need the help.'

She sniffs. 'I don't think so.' Her animosity is tangible.

'Loads of retro things. How far back d'you want to go? Fifties?'

She glowers at me.

I clock Rucksack Boy on the *other* side of the ancient toys & games trestle; with his back turned, he's talking earnestly to the stallholder.

I don't want him seeing her.

I want her gone.

'Noisy in here,' I say. 'We better go out the back.'

I turn and push my way through, and she follows me. Past the cracked Butler sink and the propped-up squeezy-mop, sacks of rubbish, the grubby vending machine; then out the backdoor, and into the alleyway behind.

We stand there. Still I don't let my cheeriness slip.

She steps sideways, takes out her iphone, prods it with one purple talon. Slouches, caresses an ear chain. Sniffs loudly.

'Sasha,' I say. 'It's a mix-up then?'

She says nothing. She's still fiddling with her phone. I can see it isn't this year's model, or even last year's: a sign of the times.

'Church hall jumble not your thing?'

'Proper vintage, yeah,' she says. 'Not, like, worth rooting around here. Grannies' junk. It's all crap.'

Vintage!

I'm vintage. I've rubbed shoulders with Emmeline Pankhurst.

'So you're abandoning me.'

'And the *stink*,' she says. 'Disgusting.'

'What stink?' I look suitably affronted. 'No stink here.'

'I'm calling my mum, pick me up. Tried before in the bog.' She pulls a face. 'Can't get a signal.'

I keep smiling. 'Here, let me... ' I take my phone from my pocket, thrust it at her. 'Try this.'

She takes it doubtfully, turning it over and over in her hands.

'Here!' I say, directing her finger. 'You wanna go home? Press there.'

She presses.

Zap!

It does the trick. Sasha disappears... not exactly in a puff of smoke, but she's gone. I always get what I want. I hope she'll be where she needs to be, and safe. I'm still a bit of a novice with this special kind of feature.

But I'm getting there.

I'll catch up with Rucksack Boy; so far, so good with him.

I need him.

I lean down to the gutter and retrieve my special thingamajig, and slip it back into my pocket. I grin.

New technology has come a long way and, curiously, running in sync with the blitz of political muck-ups in recent years.

We live in a fragmented society. It's all a mess.

The rich are getting richer; and the needy are getting desperate.

There's no let-up with the public in their searching, battling even, for a bargain. And a *Make Do and Mend* ethic has filtered back into our lives whether we like it or not.

Food banks are rarely open now.

You should see the frenzy for groceries; the queues really are something else, spiralling off into infinity at times, not seen in this country since the days of WW2 and its aftermath.

I've seen it all.

Not surprising that in these days of escalating austerity, it's hit the younger generation like a battering ram. Walloped them.

Most of them. They had it *so* good before.

My role is to guide those deserving of it.

Come the revolution, the big kick-back, the uprising – we'll need these trained grafters.

You might call me something of a vigilante, and that may be true. Others are out there doing the same; and if you want to know where I come from – never you mind.

I'm as old as the hills; as tough as an army boot.

I go where I'm needed, my rejigged thingamajig to hand.

I draw a breath, and push open the back door. There's work to be done.

Don't Tell Your Mother

When Dad went into the home, it damn well splintered his heart.

He missed his familiar possessions, his own home of 60-odd years, his long, industrious and happy life: the kind of life that a schoolteacher makes, with interests aplenty and a wife by his side.

I hardened up to the situation; I needed to.

I'd told him straight — he absolutely had to go.

He was at the far side of a large bright room in his special chair. Others sat in their own special chairs around the edges of the room; a low wooden bookcase served as a half-way divider, with a widescreen swivel television mounted on top.

I'd have to make my presence known gently.

'Hello Dad,' I said, touching his arm.

'Is that you?'

'It's me, yes.'

'Took your time,' he said, like a wilful child. '*Hate*

it. Take me home.'

'They look after you here,' I said, adjusting the cushion at his back. 'Think of it as a hotel. You get *three* meals a day, and there's entertainment too.'

'I don't want to be entertained.'

'You'd get bored without it.'

'I can't... I can't even read a bloody book now, son,' he said, waving a hand at eye level. 'I don't want to be here. Can't you... can't you take it in turns to come and look after me? At home?'

'Dad— '

'I don't see what the problem is.' He screwed up his face. 'I can't see, I can't walk... but I do bloody have a brain.'

'We've been through all this. We have jobs.'

'Excuses. Again.'

'And, the house is sold – you know that. That's how you can stay in this lovely place.'

'Lovely? My arse.'

'It is. You don't have to worry about a thing.'

'Where's my medals? Eh?'

'They're in your room. Safe. They're where you can see them... and feel them.' I softened my voice. 'Remember I sorted that out with Matron?'

He sat thinking about that one. Then he became agitated:

'Where's my wife? What've you done with her?' He was trying to get up, his face set with determination. 'She... she's gone. Haven't seen her for at least two days.' His voice was rising. 'Where the bloody hell is she?'

'Calm down, Dad.'

One of the carers, Greta, was looking over.

'Dad, you know we lost her last year.'

'Lost her? Where'd she go?'

I rolled my eyes. Sometimes it was best to go along with what he was saying, but we'd agreed this wasn't one of those occasions. 'Dad, she's in heaven. So you're in The Greenleaves, here, to be looked after.'

'No one told *me*.' He was feeling for his stick, the now non-existent stick he hadn't used for over two years. 'You're cold, son. *Cold*.'

He'd been so lost without her. Refused to believe it at the time, and now he didn't remember at all.

A shock to lose her so suddenly.

I still spoke to her; it was the only way to cope. I told her about Dad. She needed to know what was going on.

I let him flail around for a bit. I wasn't sure how to play it. I knew I had to be strong; for him, and for myself.

Greta came over. 'Now, now Mister Lloyd. It's all okay.' She held his arm lightly and spoke soothingly.

From across the room: 'Help! Help!'

Greta half-turned, then caught my eye and smiled. 'He's at it again, that one. He thinks everything is an emergency. Won't be told otherwise.'

'Let's hope it's never a case of the boy calling wolf, if you know what I mean,' I said. 'It must be difficult for you all here.'

She understood.

'What?' said Dad. 'Wolf? *Where?*'

'Mister Lloyd. Now, can I get you a cup of tea?'

'Tea's awful here,' he grumbled. 'Don't have it, son.'

'No – she' asking *you*, Dad,' I said. 'Not me. I'm a visitor.'

'Alright. No bloody sugar then.'

'Help! Help!'

'Him again,' said Greta, not smiling now. 'Terrible shame really. What's going on in his head!' She bustled away. 'Oh!' she said over her shoulder, 'there's entertainment here next Monday evening. Would you like to come?'

'Me?'

'Yes, you could sit with your dad. It'll be a good evening. Marlene Dietrich will be here, doing her thing. He'll like that.'

On Monday I turned up alone; my wife asked for some space – in other words, she wasn't keen on being subjected to 1930s sleaze music as she called it.

There was a murmur of anticipation in the room. Now bathed in the radiance of four or five elaborately chintzed table lamps, each with period tassels, the room looked fit for a film set.

It was packed, the carers standing to one side near the kitchen area.

'Who are you?' he demanded as I touched his arm, as I always did. 'Eh?'

'It's me, Dad,' I said. 'Tom.'

'*Who?*'

'Your son. It's *Tom*.'

He cupped one brown-flecked hand to his ear. 'I don't know you. Speak up.'

Greta appeared from nowhere. 'It's *your son*, Mister Lloyd. Your *son*.'

'Ah. I see. Tommy.' He put out a hand to pat little Tommy on the head but managed to jab me in the groin instead. 'Sorry,' he said, somehow knowing he'd got it wrong.

'It's okay, Dad. I'm grown up now. Look, it's a special evening. Marlene is appearing soon.'

'Who?'

'Marlene Dietrich. You remember her, I'm sure.'

'Marlene?' He looked up, his rimless glasses still on his nose despite his loss of sight. 'Dietrich?'

'That's the one.'

'Ah. Well, of course I know her. She's coming here?'

'Not Marlene exactly – but someone who sings like her.'

'That's *terrific*,' he said, raising both arms and jiggling in his special chair. 'But no one told me.'

'They probably did.'

'No. No one says a thing.'

'Dad— '

'So, son – what will she be singing, this Marlene?'

'You'll know that better than me, Dad.'

'She was an American, y'know. A Yank.'

'No, Dad – she was German.'

'Yes, German. But she was given American citizenship. Didn't know that, did ya!'

'Not sure.'

'She had legs.'

'Of course she had legs.'

'Gorgeous legs. But, y'know, she said: the legs aren't so beautiful... she just knew what to do with 'em.' He wheezed with laughter.

I rubbed my chin. 'Did she say that?'

'Of course. She said a lot of things, son.'

He went quiet, evidently thinking hard. 'Hated making those films, she did,' he said softly. 'Ugh. But she enjoyed nightclub work. She could just be herself, be a bit sleazy.'

'I didn't know that you— '

'I know all about her. She loved to kiss too.'

I grinned. 'Did she! A bit saucy, eh?'

Dad's expression didn't change. 'Huh. They said they had to put a new layer of lipstick on her after every kiss, she kissed so damn hard. Shovelled it on, they did.'

Again: 'Help! Help!'

'That bloody lunatic over there!' Dad was trying to get up. 'Losing my thread here... how can I talk about... about...?'

'It's okay, Dad. Get yourself settled and I'll sit here beside you.' The carers were fiddling with the lamps, the lights were dimming. 'She's just coming on now.'

'Who?'

'Marlene.'

'Never heard of her.'

'Okay. Listen, and you might remember.'

The music came first: a measured, sensuous introduction to a song that sounded familiar, but I couldn't place it. Dad's face registered nothing.

From the shadow of the kitchen area a short figure came into view. She wore a dark tuxedo and a top hat; she brandished a long cigarette holder and moved like a cat – half prowl, half swagger. I expected a purrrrr, but nothing came from her mouth.

'Y'know, son,' said Dad loudly, 'she said a lot, that woman. Made sense.'

'Did she?' I said, grabbing his arm to distract him. 'Dad – here she is... '

'Yep.'

'It'll be good.'

'Y'know, she approved of prostitution she did. A country without whorehouses is like a house without a bathroom.' He wheezed with laughter. 'That's what she said.'

'Shush... Dad.'

Greta looked over from her place by the window. She smiled, putting a finger to her lips.

The whole room went into time-freeze... residents and carers were gazing at the suited figure gliding across the lounge, stopping to caress the wooden bookcase as she slid into position. I could see a tiny microphone nestled near the top button of her shirt. I smiled to myself; all hi tech for The Greenleaves.

Dad had gone quiet now. He probably sensed the suspenseful hush.

'*Where... have all the flowers gone...*' Marlene's voice was perfect.

Dad flinched. 'She always sang that in *German*,' he shrieked. 'What's she *doing!*'

'Now, now Mister Lloyd,' Greta said soothingly, tip-toeing over. 'Give her a chance. She's only just started.'

That seemed to work.

'Describe to me,' said Dad, relaxing, 'what she looks like.'

'Well,' I said, 'she's wearing a top hat and a dark suit – a tuxedo.'

'A what?'

'A *dark* suit, a white shirt, and a top hat. And holding a cigarette holder, of course.'

'Ah.' He lifted his face to the direction of the singing. 'Ah. Marlene.'

Marlene was winding down her song. She dipped languidly to one side, keeping in character – and stood hand on hip for a minute or two as the music was being readied for her next number. Dad was entranced. He didn't move a muscle, he just waited like everyone else in the room.

Our Marlene was a short, plump young woman. Her voice was good, her acting abilities adequate. The tuxedo trousers were a little too tight, they showed off her thick thighs. As she stood waiting she twirled the cigarette holder, wobbling slightly on her chunky high-heeled boots.

The music began, as before. Again, Marlene bided her time before she started her song.

'*Out-side the barr-acks...* '

I knew this one.

'This is a love story,' said Dad.

From across the room: 'Help! Help!'

The carers went into action, wheeling the Help! man out of the room. Maybe it was all too much for him.

'Bloody stupid idiot,' said Dad. 'He should've gone out before.'

Marlene was still singing: *My Lili of the lamplight, my own Lili Mar-leen...* '

'I knew she'd come back,' Dad said. 'I always wanted her to.'

'I know,' I said, making a face.

'I told your mother: never get jealous.'

I could see glistening in the eyes of the elderly women opposite, all against the wall in their special chairs. They would remember those times, of the flickering screens, the movie magazines, the haunting songs. I thought, it's a dying age – all but vanished.

Mum would've enjoyed this too.

'Don't tell your mother,' Dad instructed. 'She don't need to know.'

Lili of the lamplight was finishing.

Marlene paused, then walked across the room, heading in our direction. She took Dad's scaly old hand. He didn't resist.

'May I?' she whispered. Dad's usual pallor had been replaced by blazing cheeks, his glasses on the end of his nose now, his blue eyes wide in anticipation.

The introductory music began.

'Falling... in love again,' she sang. *'Never wanted to...* '

Standing by the window, Greta had her hands to her face.

'*...what am I to do...*'

'*I can't help it...*' finished Dad.

Marlene growled almost inaudibly.

'I knew you'd come back,' he said. 'I knew.' His lips quivered, a tear dripped from his chin. *This cranky old man, in tears...*

My eyes were stinging, ready to brim. I bent down to Dad and adjusted the back of his collar. I took my time.

I swallowed hard, my resolve to be brave in tatters.

I tweaked his cushion for him, accidentally brushing his shoulder. He turned his head and peered up at me, sightless, but with an odd look in his eyes: *She don't need to know.*

No. She doesn't.

My sweet Mum. Not that she'd have been that bothered...

It was one man's fantasy.

And I won't tell. Ever.

Blabbermouth

They stood by the graveside, hanging back slightly, porkpie hats clenched in front of them, heads bowed.

'Happy as hell I am,' Jimmy said. He hissed through his teeth, finishing in a faint whistle.

'Not so loud,' whispered the man next to him. 'We gotta have respect.'

Jimmy slanted his head closer. 'If they only knew,' he said. 'This fella really needed a watery grave, not this charade. No one listened, Frank.'

'Yeah, whatever you say,' said Frank, shifting a fraction, 'but bleedin' Satan is here, d'you know that?'

'What?'

'Satan. There's a crow over there, hopping about like crazy.'

'Oh, Jesus.'

'And, would ya believe, there's a black cat on the prowl, over on the next row of graves.'

Jimmy flinched. 'No! Which direction is it going?'

'It's stalling, just dilly-dallying.'

'*Lordy.*'

The officiating priest paused, looked over, one

shaggy eyebrow out of alignment.

'*Quiet,*' Frank mouthed, nudging Jimmy. 'Use yer noddle.'

Jimmy bowed his head lower, hunched his shoulders, and tightened his grip on his porkpie.

'*May his soul, and the souls of all the faithful departed through the mercy of God, rest in peace.*'

'Amen,' droned the gathering.

The group of mourners dispersed, respectfully, suitably sombre; the priest's attention was taken with the family. It was all over.

'Should've swung him by the ankles,' mumbled Jimmy, putting on his hat. 'Down to Davy Jones, trussed like a chicken, be seen no more. Amen.'

'Yeah. The canal was the answer.'

'Bloodless, my friend.'

'I know.'

'Mourners,' someone said, 'there's tea in the vestry, if you would like to join the family... '

'Better get in there,' observed Frank. 'Need to be seen.'

'Nah, give it a miss. What would we say to them!'

'That he was a blabbermouth... that he had it coming. They'd appreciate that, I'm sure,' Frank snorted, pulling a face and placing his hat on, carefully adjusting the brim.

'Too much blood to mention to anyone,' whispered Jimmy. 'Topped, in his mohair suit, height of fashion they said,' he guffawed. 'Hollered awful, he did – said he'd come back to get us.' He paused to light a cigarette. 'A crooked criminal of his like needed to be with the fishes. No blood, no blame.'

'Yeah, I know. Big mouth. Couldn't have him blabbing.'

'Is that cat still with us?'

Frank wheeled round. 'It's coming towards us... '

'*Christ*. I don't like it. Forget the friggin' pleasantries, let's *go*.'

'It's prancing this way... it's looking at the sky, it's— '

Crows were massing erratically in the nearby trees, their silence broken suddenly by a staccato, multi-throated *caaw caaw*, loud and worrying. Jimmy and Frank, on the pathway, ran for it. The swarm of birds followed, the black cat keeping pace, looking skywards with its mouth open, its teeth bared. *Meoiwww!*

Frank, more informed than Jimmy, had a mad thought. *Didn't they say – a Murder of Crows?* His heart was pounding, sweat breaking out all over.

'True,' said the cat nipping at his heels. 'Murder... by crows. It's at my bidding.'

'Whaat?'

The cat continued: 'Told you I'd get you, didn't I – *and* the others!'

Inspired by the lyrics of *Mack the Knife* – Bobby Darin, 1958

Two-Way

I sit down, get myself comfortable; it could be entertaining, probably chaotic.

This one's the biggest scoundrel of the lot. He's older than the others, he led them all into a sticky situation and ended up carrying the can. He doesn't seem to learn.

An interrogator kicks off the interview. '*Okay. Tell me why you think you've been arrested.*'

The detainee, defiant, jerks his head back.

I sip my hot tea absently. It's perfect, not too milky, not overly strong.

'*We're here to discuss your arrest on suspicion of robbery... armed robbery...*'

He's wearing his ferocious face, arguing with the interrogators... then putting on his stony mug, refusing eye contact just to annoy them further. 'Want your mummy?' the lead guy sneers. The other one laughs – too loudly. They get a bit out of hand at times, my officers. I let them go so far; they know what they're doing, I have to trust them.

He's not being co-operative, not one bit. They

eyeball him as much as they can, craftily catching him off guard. I watch as they wheedle, coax, then feign indifference... until they reach saturation point, all the time trying to conceal their exasperation.

They do well.

They're checking a wristwatch, giving the time of cut-off, abruptly stopping the tape, going through the formalities, and then they disperse quickly. They're going to need a cuppa in the absence of anything stronger.

Someone says, almost regretfully, 'It's time to get his brief in, guys.'

'He didn't want it.'

'He does now.'

I reach for a biscuit, dunk it in my tea.

The detainee sits there, alone. My officers have seen a lot of this one; they could describe the scars on his face and neck without looking at him. He swipes the beaker of water to the floor with his forearm and slumps forward. He's not sure what's coming next, though you'd think he would by now. One moist eye glints in the overhead light, his fingers twitch. Deflated. And he's angry, not just with my officers – he's furious with himself.

Busted.

And he thinks no one's watching.

I'm watching, behind the two-way. I'm studying his mood, his body language. I see the spreading sweat stains under his arms, can almost smell the acrid odour. His thin shirt is pretty much stuck to him, tight on his skinny frame.

He's trapped, he's fearful.

He's ready for a fight.

I finish my tea, reach into my handbag, and replenish my lips with *Dusky Rose*, a quick slick. I feel a pang of pity and try to suppress it; he deserves what's coming to him. No doubt at all.

Nicked.

I know it's his eighty-first birthday tomorrow. He knows it too.

He's led out of the room.

I catch a look at him in the corridor as I go into my office. The damp rings under his armpits are thick. He looks resigned now, stooped and subdued.

He's lucky to have been born when he was – it was only at the time of his teenage years that things began to change with police procedures; he's never known the real cruelty of the past: the beatings, the deprivation of sleep, food and water, or denied use of a toilet. He has it good.

But he's taking this silence tactic too far, it won't wash for much longer. He should know better – god knows, he's had enough experience of what to expect.

I fear for him.

The custody officer approaches, wiping biscuit crumbs from her lips. 'Request to keep him in on a thirty-six hour.'

'Yes. This is a thirty-six hour one, get it going. We'll keep him in. But... treat him well, won't you,' I say. 'Make sure he has some kind of decent meal.'

'Will do.' She paused. 'He spat at them y'know.'

'I know.'

'I asked him if he was warm enough. He looked at me like I was mad.'

'He's good at that,' I say.

Further along the corridor, a commotion. *'Effing good cop, bad cop, is it? You bleeders – get off me!'*

The custody officer raises an eyebrow. 'Charming,' she says. 'From the gutter. But,' she says, flicking a speck of lint from her jacket, 'he's got it about right. They'll crack him.'

'Eventually,' I say.

A fitful gust catches at the half-open window, clanking the old rusting metal fasteners and sending a flow of chill across the room; it uplifts the edges of the papers scattering my desk. Everything stays intact, just about.

It's November already. It'll be Christmas soon.

'Close that, will you?' I say.

I stare at a calendar on the wall, its intense colours intended to be mood-lifting; to lighten the ambience in this noxious working environment.

This month's illustration is a glittering, palm-fringed shoreline on the Costa del Sol.

A hoarding shows : *Esperanza Beach*.

Esperanza. It means *Hope* – and this man needs hope. He needs to co-operate, but that can only come from him; no one else can help on that one, it's his call.

I groan to myself.

I shouldn't be involved – I can't help him.

'Get another cup of tea sorted, will you?' I say. 'For me. More biscuits would be good too.'

'Right you are,' says the young officer. She heads for the door, then turns on her heel. 'I'll get the thirty-six hour order back to you, Ma'am,' she says. 'I'll push. Shouldn't take too long.'

I pick a crumb from under my fingernail and tut-tut at the chipped nail polish. I move towards my desk and sit down heavily. I shrug, reach for a pen. I doodle fitfully on the cover of my notepad. When she returns to wave the document in my face, I'd like to tell her my worries; but I can't. I can tell no one.

It wouldn't do to rock the boat with what I know.

And I have to stay away from the detainee. I can't let him see me.

His agonised stance is still in my head. With years of estrangement from my family, I know how it is to feel defenceless at times.

This black sheep of a man is doing himself no favours. Will he never learn?

The door opens, there's footsteps. 'Here's your tea, Ma'am. Nice an' hot.'

He's too old, too vulnerable.

I have to take a backseat.

How could I, after all this time, tell anyone that this difficult, elderly rogue of a man is my granddad?

Operation Ritz

Dolly caught a late afternoon bus uptown, alighted at Charing Cross Road, and then walked on to Piccadilly Circus.

She stopped and took a deep breath, lit a cigarette, and continued to push through the jubilant crowds; elbowing past American jitterbugging, uniforms and civvies, pretty women in their best outfits. Groups of excited little children were waving Union flags.

With the back of her hand, she brushed away a tear.

It was VE Day: a time for celebration.

She'd heard Mr. Churchill on the wireless earlier, rumbling on with his victory speech, but with a salutary warning: *'There's still toil and effort ahead.'*

That's when she'd started planning. She needed a plan. And today was the best bet.

He'd said: *'The lights went out and the bombs came down.'* Not anymore. The thought of peacetime seemed peculiar after so many years of destruction and fear.

There'd been a rainstorm in the night, but it'd cleared early and the day had been warm and sunny. Dolly knew that would bring crowds of people onto the streets – not that they would need encouraging; this auspicious day in May would go down in history, that's what Mr. Churchill said. She'd wept when she heard the news the day before, and gave her children an extra-special cuddle. But, before she could rejoice in their liberation and get through the coming days, there was something she had to do...

A bus was inching through the crowds on Piccadilly, tooting its hooter, bringing on shouts of good humour and wisecracking. Dolly allowed herself a smile. She heard the intermittent pealing of bells, and watched as toilet paper rolls were unravelled from high windows, cascading through the air. Someone was playing a banjo nearby, people singing *For He's a Jolly Good Fellow*.

As she pushed forwards, a sailor seized her and stole a quick kiss. She didn't react, she walked straight on. People at play, following their hearts, while she was following her head: sticking to the plan.

'No sirens or gunfire stuff today,' she overheard. 'Too much like bloody war, so they ain't allowing it.'

'Quite right an' all,' said someone else. 'Those Lancasters zipping over – they're our own. No worries with *them*. A joy to see.'

'It's gonna be a different world, my friend. No more darkness.'

'And some of the troops are coming home today, that's what they're saying. By plane. Not wasting no time, are they!'

Here and there, couples embraced, kissed lasciviously and fiddled with each other. She thought of her husband. All that remained was a few photos of him, and just the one of their wedding day. He did his bit for his country, and he died. She wanted to spit on a Kraut – if she ever met one, she would.

A burly man jogged her as she squeezed through a group of dancers.

Dolly rubbed her shoulder and carried on, immediately bumping into a cluster of laughing young women wearing red, white and blue hats trailing fancy streamers.

It was getting dark.

Further along Piccadilly the crush was worse.

Erratic snakings of the *Conga* broke up the crowd in places, she had to side-step to avoid colliding with others, but then she'd crash into someone else. No one cared.

A reek of sour sweat filled the air...

A soldier had scaled a lamppost, hanging on with one leg and one arm. He was downing alcohol, singing *God Save The King!* He took no notice of the laughing woman tugging at his leg, but his hold was becoming precarious. A couple of men had climbed on top of a bus shelter, stretching their arms to the sky. Fixed searchlights from above, utilised specially for the day, caught their ecstatic profiles.

Dolly noticed flash photography, and a newsreel crew were struggling through the fray. She didn't want to be seen. She dipped her head, pulled her hat down a fraction. No use bellyaching, she had to carry on. Even with the commotion, Dolly heard the pounding of blood in her ears. She clenched her fists, tight, and thought of her kids at home. She'd come this far, no point in thinking to turn back now.

She was nearly there.

At The Ritz, sandbags were still piled all around the colonnades – getting in the way of trampling boots and women's heeled shoes, already splitting and churning the sacking and contents. Glass bottles rolled between prancing, dancing feet.

She found an entrance and stood just outside. On the other side of the glass door, a large sparkling chandelier was suspended from the high ceiling. Beyond that, she could see a blur of movement. People. As wild inside as it was out.

She bit her lip.

No more black-out. No more darkness.

She stepped back and looked up. Windows in the upper rooms were filled with light; behind them, young people kissed, writhing and contorting, holding champagne glasses, arms flung this way and that.

Very gay. *So* young.

A uniformed doorman stepped forward from the shadows, frowning.

He caught her eye.

She couldn't go in.

Her plan was crushed, undone. *How could she have thought she was welcome in such a place?*

She carried on along Piccadilly, in her head revising her plan as she barged her way. She'd heard rumours:

money for the having that was so simple, as long as you were careful. There were certain areas in the centre of London that were best, and it was easy to be anonymous, especially at the moment. She didn't want to think too hard, just kept on walking... shoving her way through.

The Deepest Shelter in Town had been the most popular song in London. Why could she not get this out of her head? The defiant and saucy Florence Desmond was infamous. She sang about the *neatest*, the *deepest* shelter; and she wore a pink chiffon negligee *gown* (to rhyme with *town*) as she'd plied her trade. It was said that she had a reliable alarm clock too, to ensure her clientele returned to the battlefields in good time.

And Florence said she knew *her stuff*.

Dolly hoped that her own knowledge was adequate.

Could she do it? Could she?

Heart thudding, she was through the park gates. Green Park. The cheering and racket from the street subsided; in the darkness she heard muted sounds, soft talk, and points of glowing red moving in the gloom at low levels: people smoking, stretched on the grass.

Someone approached. 'Hello, pretty lady... '

Dolly took a deep breath.

'How did you know,' the stranger murmured, 'that you'd find me here?' Then he chuckled, holding out his hand.

Between the bushes in Green Park, the euphoria was so great, it wasn't difficult to find willing partners... they were drunk and more than happy to hand over a few shillings, or even a ten bob note. One GI gave her chewing gum along with his dollars; she'd have preferred a pair of nylons, but her kids might enjoy it.

Finally, she crept away to sleep under a shrub, as far away as possible, to curl-up alone. The night was a mix of distant clamour and erratic lights. She covered her face with her hat, and hugged her handbag to her. The grass felt damp. She emptied her consciousness as best she could.

She left in the early hours, walked back to Charing Cross Road to catch a bus, and was lucky to find a seat once they'd reached Parliament Square.

The sky was clear, cloudless, with searchlights still embracing the buildings, and fairy lights strung along window ledges wherever possible. *Fairy lights?* Wartime didn't normally yield anything fancy or frivolous, not for ordinary people.

With one hand, to make herself feel better, she jingled her earnings in the pocket of her gabardine coat, adjusting her hat with the other. She could feed her children now and pay the rent – she'd been skilled enough. But had it really mattered that much?

She had to put it out of her mind.

We've won the war! We're safe.

She knew a man who could get things; he could acquire most commodities on the quiet, but for a price. So they could eat really well for a little while. Her eldest was desperate to taste a banana. Things would be much better in due course; Mr. Churchill had said so.

But her chin trembled. She looked around at the people on the bus, exhausted people with their eyes closed, couples slumped together holding hands, contented. Some were talking quietly, respectful of the calm atmosphere. Dolly turned her face to the window, her breath misting the glass. The sky was lightening; dawn was very near.

The bus gained some speed, its tyres pounding hard on the roads through Lambeth. They swept into The Elephant and Castle, and then they'd be onwards to Camberwell.

Not far now.

She reapplied her lipstick, eyeing what might be going on behind her in the mirror of her little powder compact; she didn't want to be noticed by anyone. She didn't feel anything like Florence Desmond, but then she hadn't expected to.

Her eyes looked tired. Her skin was pale and puffy.

Her head ached.

She slid her lipstick and compact into the empty pocket on the other side of her coat, pushing them right down, checking with her fingers to make sure the lining wasn't ripped anywhere. She wanted them out of sight; they were too much of a reminder.

The children would be wanting something to eat. She hoped they'd slept through and not woken in the night; she'd told them she might be out for some while, and not to worry. There'd been no one to ask for help, not anyone who she could trust. The neighbour downstairs would ask too many questions, she wasn't sure she could dream up a likely set-up of why she needed to be away for some hours, certainly without awkwardness plastered all over her face.

No matter now.

She'd done her best.

Dolly snapped open the clasp on her handbag to find her cigarettes and matches. She lit up, the sulphur from the flame tickling her nose.

She inhaled.

Her head was pounding, her mouth dry, her skin prickling.

She'd be home soon.

'Hope Winnie's wrong with this gloomy stuff,' said the man sitting behind her. 'Once the year's out, we'll be alright... eh? I'm blinkin' sure o' that!'

'He's done his best,' said his wife. 'We'll soon be back on our feet.'

Peace. And no more fear.

Someone further down the bus chimed in: 'I don't see how it can be that easy, mate,' they said. 'London's a bloody wreck. The Blitz saw to that.'

The next stop was hers.

She blinked hard, and ran her fingers over her pocket...

Money. More than she'd ever seen.

Dolly pitched through the open, on-the-latch front door, and paused before taking the long climb up to her two attic rooms and her children.

She clicked open her handbag and fumbled for her key.

Behind the tiny hallway door belonging to her

neighbour, there was a noise. Just a slight sound, nothing loud. Dolly felt her heart leap; she couldn't see if the door was ajar or not. She stood very still, not daring to breathe. She didn't want any trouble: to be sneered at, belittled. Judged for leaving her kids alone. For being a party floozy.

She turned slowly and then trod very carefully up the steep stairs to the top of the house, her lungs bursting. She reached her own front door and turned the key.

Inside, she was safe.

She felt rich. Fate had stepped in – and was on her side. But it didn't feel like that.

She checked on her sleeping children...

Just yesterday she'd been thinking only of schmoozing some fellow for an hour or so; nothing more. For drinks. Just one easy, compliant man – with one chance.

'Dear God,' she said, her hands flying to her face. 'Oh, Lord...'

And the tears came.

Etiquette and Pretty Ladies

'You're not heeding their cultural norms,' I say. 'It's important to honour them, Jack – you know what it's like here.'

'What?'

I tut-tut. 'For example – it's customary not to fill your own glass... '

'How else am I gonna drink?'

'You know exactly what I mean.'

Standing here, in this tachinomiya bar, was meant to be a standing-up novelty, a pleasure. I'm trying hard. A very long counter sweeps along one side, bearing little dishes of deliciousness. My business mate Jack had blanched at the sight of them; especially *Whale Belly*. Looking at them now, I see more little cards propped strategically, for English speakers' benefit of course :

'*FUGU*. Pufferfish liver & other organs – *not the poisonous one*'; and

'Pufferfish Crispy Tails. *Easy Finger Food.*'

That's one to Google for sure.

Our important meet-up isn't going to plan. Not at all what I imagined, it's a strange choice of bar. We're both uneasy.

Jack sweeps his arm, pointing at our host standing further along. I swivel. He's already here! Haruto. We don't know him that well, he'd always been the courteous, polite voice on the other end of the phone over many months.

I groan. My mate is drunk, bladdered, and doesn't care. Dragging me to the bar before our flight in the wee small hours at Heathrow had been a hint on how things would develop.

'No pointing. *Ever*,' I say. Exasperated, I look up at the ceiling... at the huge swirl of smoke, an uncommon thing back in the UK now we're not allowed to light-up indoors in public places. The noise level goes up a notch or two. That shows how packed it is, the Japanese tend to speak evenly, or at least the business types do.

Our host Haruto looks our way. 'You like our tachinomiya?' he mouths, waving, his face so animated, his hand movements so elegant. 'A little *different* type bar, yes?'

'And the chopsticks thing,' I continue, 'it's all part of their etiquette, you know they have to be a certain–' I stop, wave back at Haruto. His dark eyes shine with goodwill. He has a colleague each side of him, the same guys as yesterday, and suited almost identically.

Suits, suits and more suits in every direction. An occasional glimpse of coloured fabric in the crowd means we have some ladies present. Within that sea of dark, well-tended men's hair, there's one or two young rebels to be seen. A flash of green or mauve at the hairline; or a complete, daring shave-off.

Mostly, very corporate.

Last night, we two had the freedom of Tokyo and had no idea of where to go, what to do. Jack found solace in alcohol around the Golden Gai quarter, while I looked at the interiors in some of the posher eateries, sipped beer, and perused restaurant menus. We both watched the Japanese world go by. Not without incident, as it happened.

I met Jimi. Just by accident. We talked for quite a while.

Standing in the corner here in the tachinomiya, a young man in a white apron tries to top-up our glasses; as custom has it, holding the sake bottle with both hands. I politely place my own hand over my glass as a no-thank-you, but not Jack. Then the thought strikes me that refusal of hospitality might be seen as a slur. By Haruto.

Haruto, beaming, is pushing across towards us.

He probably thinks we'd been begging for more alcohol.

Damn bloody Jack.

Haruto, unusually tall for a Japanese man, slaps my shoulder, looking right into my face. 'We so please for meet you and Jack,' he says. 'It be so many months since first we do business. Next time, we come to London for hospitality, with you. Yes?'

'Of course,' I say, with zero conviction. With Jack

out of the picture, I *could* reciprocate. Could I swing that? Jack was, technically, my boss.

'We proud of our city, and Kabukicho here most definite. It's *The Sleepless Town*, this part. I think Jack, he like it.'

'He most certainly does,' I say grimly, wondering where the rest of the evening was going. 'In New York too – y'know, the sleepless thing?'

I wonder if he has any clue on what I'm saying.

Haruto nods benignly, like a much revered uncle.

'We has ladies here, in Kabukicho. Very nice, so pretty.' He pauses. 'Maybe... you might want see this evening? Amusing to see.'

So... *that's the way it's going.*

Jack suddenly pipes up: 'Red Light?' he says, flicking his cigarette. 'Like... Soho, or Amsterdam?' His thin little face blossoms at the thought.

Haruto looks at my glass, observing its emptiness. 'Biiru?' he enquires. Well, that sounds as near to Beer as dammit, so I nod appreciatively hoping I'm right. I should know that by now.

'For Jack also?' he says, moving away.

'Yes. Thank you.' What else can I say? Jack's up for anything.

'This guy never speaks to *me!*' Jack grumbles. 'Why is it always to you?'

'No idea.'

Jack obviously has some kind of complex.

After knocking back our beers, we all leave the bar for the outside world, pushing through the heavy street door, me trying to be polite by letting our colleagues go first. Jack manages to get entangled in two low-hanging white-and-red paper lanterns just outside. Calmly, Haruto deals with it, and I suspect is trying not to laugh.

Time to eat.

Above, red and pink streaks split the skyline, echoing the glitzy neon centre of Tokyo – ten times more in your face than Piccadilly.

It'll be dark soon.

We walk together in an uneven bunch. Further along, dozens of people are lined up at the kerb, waiting to cross the road.

'See *scramble* crossing?' says Haruto. 'With wide roads in Tokyo, this we must have. It's safety for people, never they take a chance by running.'

'The green man on a signpost, he show when you can go,' says one of his colleagues. 'See? Up, up, up… ' He points skywards to the lofty traffic lights construction, the usual three generic colours of red, amber and green horizontally spaced. 'This control the traffic.' I wonder if he thinks we don't have anything that similar back in the U.K. and consider if I should respond to him.

Jack is stumbling hopelessly. Kindly Haruto takes his arm. It doesn't bode well for us. I grit my teeth, thinking on what I could say to diffuse things.

'You two persons, I have to look after you,' Haruto says, his colleagues looking on with interest. 'So, *European Style Interiors* is our baby, for us all. We welcome your trade very much. And– '

'Our baby?' I say. 'Is that what you say here too?'
Somehow, Jack lets go and falls hard...
I flinch, and pull a face.
I don't want to lose our rapport with Haruto, not after all the schmoozing I've done. It's been hard work. Our Dream Team of suited men rush to help Jack up: all five-foot two inches of him.

'Small Jack, he overwhelm with all this. But, no worry, he's the very best salesman ever I know. He not know Japanese custom, but in a strange country he can be excused. You,' – looking at me – 'you worry too much my friend.' He sighs. 'Please, *stop!*'

My heart plummets.

I'm confused.

Now, the people who've scrambled over from the other side of the wide road are swamping the pavement around us, pushing me further away from our group. Haruto, flailing somewhat, looks displeased. Yep – that makes two of us.

I'm fuming now.

You want it Jack, you can have it! *I'm off.*

I fix on a grin, and take a chance. '*Mata ne,*' I call to Haruto, hoping I've hit on the right form of see-you-later. His inscrutable face gives away nothing. He's a man of many layers I think. I try a little wave, a really encouraging smile. I intend to find the Golden Gai again and pray I'll know where I'm going.

I turn, choosing a good time to hurtle across the wide road without observing the *scramble* rule, looking forward to another beer, and a seat somewhere – and they charge plenty of yen for that privilege.

I'm a business woman, with escapist instincts.

I'll follow my instincts tonight; let loose, run free. Haruto, Jack... let them decide how they want things to play out.

If I'm offered a job, again – as I was last night, much to Jack's amusement – I might be persuaded to play along, just for the hell of it. Hilarious. I could become a pretty lady, white woman version.

A bit of fun. Maybe.

What do I have to lose?

I want to explore more of the tiny bars in Golden Gai; there's around two hundred of them it seems, packed into a few narrow alleys. Haphazard, and interestingly rustic. More my kind of thing that's for sure. And I want to examine more brilliant, goggle-eyed, three-toed dragons; silvery-white Koi fish; and red *maneki-neko*, the beckoning cats – all lacquered to within an inch. Talismans to bring luck, good health and prosperity.

Maybe sample some of that whale belly too if it's available.

Looking back across the road, I see a face that I know. A certain smirk, a swagger. Early Elvis greased-back hair. *That guy from yesterday!*

The one that actually caused Jack to laugh.

It's Jimi.

A Japanese Elvis. Not wearing a suit, this one. As before, a blood-red drape jacket and blue jeans – not remotely corporate. He's good at hustling; but I have his measure.

He spots me. *'Hey!'*

Close behind him I see Haruto, head and shoulders above the crowd. He's looking grim, pushing forward as the lights change. There's a huge mass of people in front of him. He's solo, not with his associates – they're probably babysitting Jack.

Both men are fairly close as they cross. Haruto looks relieved now he's seen me, even attempting a modest wave. The Elvis guy, Jimi, is grinning like a maniac – maybe he thinks I've come back to seek him out. He might be right.

Which of them will reach me first?

I plant my hands on my hips and wait. There's a tide of people around me, some obvious tourists, definitely European, and Brits aplenty. The sky is dark now, streaks still visible but almost eclipsed by the haze of the glittering lights of Tokyo's famous Kabukicho. My brain spins with the frenzy of activity and winking colours, the gleaming neon, the throb of the city.

Almost in sync, the two of them wave at me and surge on.

With Haruto slightly ahead, their expressions change into something else as they reach the kerb. This is when they notice each other, stop in their tracks and come almost nose to nose. Pedestrians from behind stream happily around them. Naturally, what these two are saying mostly escapes me, but neither are pleased, and it's very animated. Their eyes flick my way in between bouts of shouting.

Another tide of pedestrians lands on the pavement, ebbing quickly.

It looks like things are easing with the altercation;

they're shrugging, averting their eyes, grimacing. Haruto straightens his tie and brushes his hands over his jacket.

Jimi shouts something...

And then they come to blows.

Howling and grunting.

A tight crowd gathers. I'm standing back.

Jimi has a bloody nose...

He's holding Haruto by the throat...

Haruto yelps pitifully.

The crowd shuffles, murmurs and stares. I hear:

'Yeah – father and son, apparently. Generation gap, bad blood.'

'I hear it's to do with a pretty lady they both know.'

'Really? Hussy! Preying on respectable men.'

'Shameful... so shameful...'

'Look – the police have arrived!'

The shriek of a siren cuts through the ongoing brawl, and the outraged crowd begins to disperse.

Jimi screams an obscenity.

The traffic lights are changing again; a few last-minute walkers are quickening their pace. I'm not imagining it, the remnants of the Dream Team are also pitching themselves across the road, they're only halfway over...

Bleak-faced.

There's Jack too, looking awful, panicky and hobbling.

Bulky, dark-clad police are seconds away from the disorderly scenario of blood-smeared, dishevelled men.

Tears are clouding my eyes.

How has this happened?

I turn away, look out for the next *scramble* crossing further on – and with my heart thumping hard, and legs unexpectedly turning to jelly, head off to Golden Gai, or wherever my feet might take me.

Cracked Heart

His creased ugly mug appeared next to me at the graveside.

I shifted away slightly.

'She's in the best place,' he said, 'but – will she stay there?'

'What d'you mean?'

'They used to bury witches facedown. She's downstairs, in Hades. No doubt at all.'

'Is that so?'

'Happiness is being with God. Her, she'll never be happy.'

The officiator spoke: 'May her soul, and the souls of all the faithful departed through the mercy of God, rest in peace.'

'Amen,' droned the gathering.

'Fat chance,' said Ugly Mug. 'No forgiveness for her.'

The wind was getting up.

'If she's trouble,' Ugly Mug continued, 'you know what they might do?'

'What?'

'They could bring her back up.'

I turned to him. 'Why? And who are these people?'

'They'd take out her evil heart, cut it into four. Then they'd burn one piece at each corner of the village.'

I kept quiet.

'But, before that – first, they'd turn her burial clothes inside-out.' He sighed. 'It's a slog to go the cut-up heart route, you can imagine.'

The drizzle was gaining momentum. Mourners were dispersing.

'Always a last resort,' he added, 'the heart thing.'

'*Refreshments in the vestry, mourners,*' said someone imperiously.

'Why is this woman so evil?' I said, deciding to improvise. The scene needed a bit more meat on its bones.

'She cuckolded me,' he said. 'She deserves everything she gets.'

'Does she?'

'A *bitch!*' His face became a snarling beast. 'And I know who the bloke was. Don't think I *don't*.'

'You're ad-libbing too much, Muggy,' I whispered, eyeballing him.

He kicked at the mud-streaked grass. 'Her heart was cracked. All evil heart, no love for me. The time is right for vengeance.'

'Don't look at *me*,' I said, carefully. I was going hot and cold.

Ugly Mug spoke again. 'So – that's it. I'm out to get him.'

I moved back even more.

'*Cut!*' came from the director.

'We've stopped filming, mate,' I said. 'Get it?'

Muggy shrank away.

'Muggy, man... ' I said, 'we're actors. This isn't real.'

'I put her there myself, it was no accident. She confessed. Her bloke thinks himself so important. Jumped-up twit. Huh!'

'Hey, Muggy!' The director, Lucas, came over. '*Pillock*. You're getting your movie parts mixed-up.'

I'd done my scene. I sauntered off, relieved.

Lucas flicked back his mane of blond hair, then pointed a stern finger. 'Any more of this, and you'll be getting your marching orders. This costs *money* to keep reshooting. Get your act together, or else.'

'You can't fire me.'

'Oh, I can! You've had too many chances already, pal. I've only been keeping you on as a favour.' He smirked. 'Pulling ugly faces doesn't cut it – you're no Laurence Olivier.'

'I know secrets. I know what you're like.'

Cold, hard, slanted rain came in abruptly from nowhere. Was that a thunderclap overhead?

Lucas roared with laughter, throwing his head back, his eyes glittering. He looked so handsome as the rain plastered his crop of hair to his skull, displaying his fine profile as he turned to wink at his assistant Bob.

'Such drama!' said Bob, grinning, ambling over. 'Sure eclipses the original plot.'

Scowling, Ugly Mug fumbled in an inside pocket – producing a knife.

That wasn't part of the script.

'Did you think you'd be forgiven?' he hissed, waving the sharp blade around. His eyes swept over us all. 'Thieving what didn't belong to you? Rudolph Valentino, eh? *Eh?!*'

I sussed we were still rolling.

He spat on the grave.

Nobody moved.

Lucas hollered: 'Drop that, *now!*'

Someone shouted 'Cut! For godsake, *cut!*'

The bedraggled, horrified cameramen backed away from their equipment.

Lucas looked scared. Bloody scared. '*Someone do something!*'

Without a word, Ugly Mug moved in. As Bob turned to run, the knife was plunged into his back, then twisted – and within seconds he was on the ground, smeared with mud and spurting an enormous amount of what most definitely wasn't the usual cinematic mix of diluted cranberry sauce.

Pops and the Clock Face Weirdos

The walnut grandfather clock in our hallway had always been a fixture of the house over many generations. I barely noticed it tucked away in the alcove, except when it chimed throughout the day at weekends when I was home.

I was unhooking my coat from the coat stand when Big Will struck his first irritant of the day – making me flinch.

'Damn you, clock!'

'Oi!' said my grandpa behind me, coming down the stairs.

'Morning, Pops.'

The clock always struck on the quarter hour; then held its tongue during the night hours until 7:15 a.m. Pops said that could be adjusted – he loved tinkering – but we all agreed that a quarter past seven in the morning was early enough. There was a moon movement dial at the top, above the clock face, bearing an enamel lunar illustration, very fairy-tale; primary blue and yellow. My wife Nancy had said it made her think of the owl and the pussycat. She'd loved Edward Lear, and so did I.

And I still do.

Then things changed.

I'll never get over her leaving me and the kids after her breakdown. She said this house spooked her, that I irritated her.

She said she had to go. Said she felt betrayed. She implied she'd get back at me in some way – but I thought it was the meds talking.

Mum had never taken to Nancy, but she was so upset for me and the kids.

But what had I *done?* Maybe just not enough. She'd moved a long way from our neighbourhood, getting in with a crowd she'd met during her treatment; some kind of alternative way of living. I hoped it would make her happy.

Dad had said he prayed she wouldn't be putting a hex on us all, but I'd shushed him. Nasty talk.

'Don't make jokes,' I said.

'Only kidding.'

We didn't need that kind of wisecrack.

I shrugged into my coat.

'Mum's not well, y'know,' I said. 'I'm worried.'

'I'll keep an eye on her.'

'Good.'

'See... it's an eight-day movement,' he said. 'Best to wind every five or six days before the weights drop too low.'

I knew it'd been a mistake to abuse his clock, even in jest. He loved the flaming thing.

'Why should that matter?' I'd asked this in the past but had never taken in his answer.

'Because we can't see them, lad,' he said. 'I want to know they're okay.'

I unlocked our front door, about to go on a three-day business meeting.

'Yeah, Pops.' I crinkled my mouth at him, picking up my holdall.

'It's time for a rewind,' he muttered, his smooth pate gleaming under the hall lights.

'I'll leave you with Big Will,' I said.

It was raining, cold, and barely daylight. I stepped back into the hallway to pick up my big brolly from the stand. I didn't want to leave the house at all, but it wasn't possible to pull out now.

'A good William Webster,' he said, reaching for the crank key hanging on a hook at the back; to keep safe from generations of children's prying fingers. 'Seventeen Twenty – thereabouts.'

'What?'

'I'm saying... made in the early eighteenth century. Our *Will* – from William's name, of course.' He was releasing the clock face cover, carefully easing out the hinged glass, and then poking his precious crank key into the left-hand arbour – a mini ratchet, the kind of implement, he said, that vintage cars were cranked with.

'I'd better go.'

How many times had he told me Big Will was

a William Webster! Back in the day, it drove Nancy barmy. How many times, in recent years, had I thought his beloved grandfather clock should be anchored to the wall, maybe just loosely? The kids could be rowdy.

I'd need to make sure that got fixed; we shouldn't risk it.

He fiddled with the clock's hands, a fingertip placed delicately to adjust the minute hand by just a fraction, the tip of his tongue poked out in concentration.

'See you later, Pops. Look after Mum, okay?'

He grunted, which meant yes.

This conversation stayed with me on the train, running through my head almost as a background comforter.

Tick-tock-tick. Tick-tock-tick.

Pops and his clock.

Tick-tock-tick... the reverberation on the track seeming to echo that cadence; I found myself listening to the rhythm, musing on how it felt like time ticking away, slipping through all our fingers...

Tick-tock-tick... click-clack... clickety-clack...

I thought of Mum.

Clickety-clack...

Mum-not-well... Mum-not-well...

It was a worry.

And Nancy. Six months since she left.

Where was she now? I felt that painful pang of regret, of confusion.

I buried my nose in my newspaper. Travelling to Cardiff was a long journey, and all for a few short meetings. I went into a doze, newspaper drifting to my lap; ten minutes or so later I resurfaced, gathering up my paper and looked to see where we were.

The tick-tocking had stopped. So had the clickety-clack.

We were stationary just outside Winchester; I'd need to change train soon.

Twenty minutes ticked by. We weren't moving.

A broken, crackly voice from somewhere informed us that we'd be moving shortly but I knew that, short of a miracle, I'd missed my connection.

We passengers were finally off the train at Winchester. I headed for the right platform and the nearest coffee outlet, pushing through the crowd, past an overflowing rubbish bin, avoiding cases-on-wheels.

Forty-five minutes to wait for my next connection at 10:00 hrs.

I'd need to phone through to the guys at the Cardiff office.

Bloody ten o'clock train!

Next to the coffee and cupcakes counter was a plain door with a laminated notice pinned on: *'Books for Sale – please come in'*. With a latte in my hand, I found myself in a small room lined with low bookcases. A metal cashbox was cemented-in at one end with *Please Give Generously*, listing two charities I'd never heard of.

I browsed.

A slim book with a brown and red spine was crammed in between two large volumes. I prised it out. It was in good condition. On the front cover, a stylised picture of a red pitch-fork surrounded by lurid flames. I flicked through... warnings and significance of: bats, broken mirrors, brooms, candles, cats, crows... ladders, lightning, owls, playing cards, salt, sparrows – and of course horseshoes if hung the wrong way up.

I pushed a £2 coin into the slot and pocketed *'Invitation to Omens'*. It might keep me occupied.

Back on the platform, I skimmed the index of my new book, and then read the preface:

```
Early man believed that every phenomenon
   of nature was the work of a spirit
        or devil. All filled him with
               fearful dread.
```

An old book, with musty yellow pages, from the 1920s maybe. Scant info. I couldn't see an edition or date on the first pages. I flipped to a random page... Clocks. Clocks, again!

Clocks: Should a clock strike thirteen, this means...

My phone shrilled. I answered.

'Dad,' said a young, frightened voice. 'It's *Pops!* Come home – *please.*' Then Mum came on the line: 'He's collapsed, Tony. Just come back now. We're so *worried.*'

It was four minutes before ten o'clock – my train, still some way off, was approaching the platform; but I rushed over the footbridge to the return platform, and frantically scanned the electronic board for departure times. Luck was on my side, I leaped on a train back to Clapham Junction right away.

By the time I was home, Pops was out of hospital. He'd had a funny turn, nothing too sinister. One of the kids heard Pops shriek when he fell.

Dad had driven him there and back.

'Nothing to do with the clock?' I asked.

'What?' Dad looked at me, his mouth open.

'The clock. I left him this morning as he was winding it up.'

'Funny, that. He was standing next to it.'

'Was it chiming?'

'No. But he had the clock face glass open... '

The hinged glass was still half-open, the big, latticed clock hands missing from the face, all scattered on the floor by my feet.

'There's something odd with this clock at the moment,' I said, stooping to pick them up. 'Let's get Big Will fixed to the wall – soon.'

Dad eyed me strangely. 'What's up, son?'

Mum stood by his side looking grim, her skin waxy, her eyes puffy. 'I felt even worse after you'd gone, Tony,' she whispered.

'Mum, please go back to bed. I'll bring you some soup, or whatever you fancy.'

I was up early the next morning. I checked on Pops, who was sleeping soundly; then Mum. Downstairs, I crept into the hallway. I hadn't yet heard a chime from Big Will, and it was gone a quarter past seven.

I shivered.

The clock face was blank again. No hands. It didn't make sense, I'd locked the hinged glass cover, and there it was, open again. The beautiful hands were splayed on the hall carpet just as before.

'That bloody clock,' said a voice on the stairs. It was Dad, his hair standing up at all angles. 'What's up now?'

'The hands. They've come off again.'

'Get the superglue out,' he said, exasperated.

'There's no reason why these hands should come off,' I said. 'I'm stumped. I screwed those hands in really tight, locked that glass with the little key in the lock.'

I carefully picked up the strewn-around hands. 'I'll remove the key,' I said. 'I'll put it somewhere safe.'

'Are the kids...er, playing games?' asked Dad.

'Of course not!'

But I *could* talk to them.

'And there's no chimes,' I added, though Dad was already going back upstairs.

Sitting at the dining table, I was following the next meeting in Cardiff on my laptop.

The house was quiet.

As a contentious issue was raised, I thought I heard the postman come – something dropped onto the carpet in the hall with a clatter. A moment later, Pops walked in.

'Feeling okay?' I asked, still looking at my screen. 'Want a cup of tea?'

'Lad – it's happened again,' he said. 'Clock hands all over the carpet.'

'*No.*'

'Big Will is going crazy. This is what sent me into a spin yesterday. Bloody things fell off in my hands.'

I felt for the small key in my trousers pocket. It was still there.

I reached for my jacket. I found the brown and red book. It fell open at C.

'Clocks.' I skipped the bit about thirteen chimes, and read out-loud: 'With missing hands, this signifies man's powerlessness to control his own fate... *within one specific daylight hour to the next.*'

Twenty-four hours.

Tick-tock-tick.

'Glad you're here at home, lad,' said Pops. 'Radio news – a bad train crash just outside of Winchester yesterday, mid-morning. Just before ten o'clock.'

My scheduled train; the one I'd been waiting for.

In the hallway, Big Will was chiming. I held my breath. Ten chimes.

Ten o'clock.

I raced into the hall, Pops following on.

Tick-tock-tick.

We looked down, then up.

I gawped at Pops, and he at me.

Big Will was intact; glass closed, both hands safely back in place.

Tick-tock-tick.

I caught... I felt... a resonance of Nancy's throaty laugh in our hallway...

How could that be?

Pops heard it too. The look on his face squeezed my heart

'Moved to the dark side,' mumbled Pops, his mouth twisting. '*Bitch.*'

'You mean...?'

'New life, dodgy bunch of weirdos.'

Her threat... toying with us...

'Jesus, Pops!'

'I know, lad.'

Then footsteps on the stairs.

'I'm back to normal,' said Mum, grinning as she reached us, her dressing gown flying behind her. 'I was having the most ridiculous dreams, darling,' she said. 'Awful! And... I thought I was going to lose you, Tony.'

How could I begin to explain!

'Mum,' I said, 'it's all okay. No more bad dreams.'

'I really hope not, sweetheart,' she said, flapping a hand and turning to go back upstairs. 'Just some kind of stupid virus, wasn't it...'

The Man She'd Met

I felt uneasy, and a quiver went up my spine as she talked about the man she'd met. I tried to maintain the same interested look as I drew in breath, slowly, and my innards somersaulted. She would never have clocked my reaction, she was too glittery-eyed, too immersed in lust to notice anything at all.

'He's tall and fit, ex-sailor, cropped blond hair. Treats me great.'

'Please don't see him again,' I said. The words were out, vibrating on my tongue, before I knew it. I couldn't help it.

She looked at me in disbelief. 'Have you not been listening to a word I've said?'

'I sense these things,' I said, as evenly as I could. 'See, I knew my uncle was gonna die. He wasn't ill. Please, Bella – I've always had that gift. I *feel* it.'

I'd never told her about this awareness before. I didn't tell many people.

'So,' she said, hands on her hips, 'what do you sense about this beautiful man? Uh?'

I felt cold.

'Go on,' she urged, 'what've you got to say?' Her eyes shone with tears, or rage; I wasn't sure which.

'Just trust me, Bella,' I managed. 'I have a bad feeling.' I moved away, feigning haste. 'I'm sorry, I... '

'Telepathic, are you?' she sneered. 'Think of me with this gorgeous man tonight. We'll order a gigantic pizza, have a few beers. Nice sloppy kisses. Think he might corrupt me?'

She sure had the love bug.

'Lust away,' I said. 'Just take care of yourself.'

'Jealousy will get you nowhere, Sharon,' she yelled after me as I headed for the Tube. 'Thinking about what *you're* doing tonight, are you? With your dodgy bloke?'

That hit home. Wish I'd never told her anything about him.

I'd never said a lot.

She wasn't to know we'd split up. I wanted to keep that to myself for the moment; I knew from the start he was a wrong 'un but you know how it is. I gave him chances.

I was envious of her cosy evening, but I knew what I knew. I feared it wouldn't stay snug with him for long... maybe not tonight, but soon; it'd all come apart at the seams in a very ugly way. Somehow. The feeling I'd had was exceptionally strong... it'd knocked me sideways.

My 'gift' ruled my life, got in the way of how I lived. If challenged, I'd be hard pressed to describe how the damn thing works. Sometimes I doubted myself... was it a symptom of paranoia? But I knew my instincts were good. With people I didn't know, the signals were weak, and mainly I managed to ignore them. With people I knew it was a different matter.

I made myself a meal, something small. I didn't have much of an appetite. I knew I had Bella's number but resisted calling her. She'd be in the middle of something with the man I knew to be... *what?* He was much more than just a bad 'un, that one. My senses were always reliable.

Losing my uncle was hard. I begged him not to go on that holiday. My family thought I was nuts; Uncle Joe was going on a long hiking trip, something he'd wanted to do since he was a young man. *But he's going with his club members*, Mum said. *How can you possibly think he's in danger? Really, Darling, you're taking it a bit far.*

She frowned at me.

I'd had a rush of light-headedness, a wave of nausea. I felt ill, really unwell, for a few moments.

She couldn't talk to me when we heard he'd been hit by a lorry in the Lake District. Everyone avoided me. It was almost as if they blamed me, that I'd been at fault. The driver was drunk. A man who'd taken a different route to his usual; a man who subsequently raged that a gaggle of walkers had been in his way as he'd rounded a bend on the wrong side of the road. It was their fault.

And it was my fault.

I should bury my talent; ignore it, all of the time. It's a curse.

By the morning, I resolved to keep my nose out of everything weird in future. I kept my head down as I walked to the Tube, focused on what was ahead for me that day.

I changed at Oxford Circus, just two stops onward for Holborn.

I didn't see who it was at first as a person zig-zagged between scuttling commuters on the crowded platform. It was Bella; her hoodie was pulled right up, her hands plunged into her pockets. Her shoulder bag jumped around wildly as she careered along, as if she was being chased.

I think she'd spotted me first.

I kept track of her.

Once I'd struggled through the surge of people, I could see she was on the parallel up-escalator, almost level with me. I watched as she fiddled with her bag, caught a glimpse of her face as a current of air caught the edge of her hoodie, lifting it from her head for a second or two. Maybe I was looking for it... but it was clear to me that she was hiding something from the world: on her cheek was a dark blotch. She'd probably dabbed concealer on it, but it was too fresh a mark, too puffy, to properly disguise.

I knew it would happen. I *knew* it.

The escalators were packed with people; the usual grim-faced, passionless lot.

She wouldn't thank me if I scurried after her once we'd reached the top of the escalator, if that was even possible.

I wasn't sure what to do.

Fate brought us together in the exit area. I was almost shoulder to shoulder with her as we shuffled forwards. She was looking straight ahead.

'*Evil* bastard,' she hissed. She turned to look at me. '*Your* fault.'

'Mine?'

She found an opening in the crowd somehow, elbowed her way through, and fled.

I left work a little later than normal that day and travelled by Tube to Notting Hill Gate. Once there, I took a wrong turn at Holland Park Avenue then walked back the way I'd come. I finally found the terrace of large Victorian houses I was looking for, and walked to the very end.

I felt edgy.

I approached the front door.

Five bell-pushes, each against a corroded mini-holder containing a name.

I rang a bell tentatively... I didn't know what to expect, and I didn't want to risk any antagonism. I knew I had the correct bell – next to it I could see a sliver of grubby white card poked into the mini-holder. It didn't fit; it was jammed-in badly. Bella's name was there, scrawled in deep red ink.

It jarred with me. The letters jiggled and danced.

I took a deep breath.

Behind the door, footfalls on carpet. Measured steps.

I was still staring at Bella's name. The ink was blurred, I put a hand to my forehead; my legs trembled.

The door rattled and opened with a jolt. I dragged my eyes from the piece of card. At the door, through the opening, half a face was visible. *'Help me!'*

The door opened wider.

I stepped through the doorway, closed the door behind me. There was a sticky smear of red on the handle.

I followed on, unsteady, as Bella ahead of me was shaking and sobbing.

She turned. 'I confronted him,' she said. 'Told him I heard he was no good.'

I blanched. *My fault.*

I saw blood on her fingers.

'He hurt me,' she said. 'I'm going to the police... but not just... yet.'

Her face was swollen, her eyes half-closed.

'Why?' I said, stupidly. I knew why, but why the delay?

'I've just had, y'know... another peep. Touched him.'

'What's happened, Bella?' I said, something tightening in my chest, my heart slamming like a sledgehammer. 'What's gone on here?' I went to touch her shoulder, but she shrank away.

'He had it coming. *No one* treats me like that.'

'Where...?'

'In here. He's in here.'

She led me into her living room. Sprawled awkwardly in a corner was a man, a large-framed guy. He wasn't moving.

'He was still breathing last night, and this

morning,' she said. 'Not now.' She moved across the dark room and jabbed his arm, kicked at one of his legs. 'I killed him. Don't know what to do. I need— '

'*Stop!*' I moved in closer. I took in the remains of pizza strewn across the dining table, the cardboard box still there, gaping open, containing chunks of tomato-smeared crust and stained, crumpled kitchen paper. Nestling inside was a knife.

My eyes slid back to the corner. I could make out large tan boots, short blond hair, and a face that I recognised, even in repose...

The hammering in my chest carried on with its steady *bang, bang,* and a cold sweat prickled my skin. I'd assumed he'd found someone else, and I was glad to be rid of him...

But not like this.

There was a thick dark area beneath his body...

Nausea hit me. Saliva flooded my mouth.

She'd asked for help...

'Bella,' I said. 'You need... you need... ' I couldn't finish. I turned and shot out of the room, hurtled through the hallway, grappled with the smeary handle on the inside of the door, and ran into the road, blinded with fear.

It was my fault. *It was.*

But she'd killed him.

I stumbled back towards Notting Hill Gate Underground, turning back and forth, hopelessly lost. Finally, I knew where I was, and took the Tube home, my heart beating crazily all the way. It was then I noticed blood on *my* fingers.

It seemed a very long journey.

I locked my front door, heaved a heavy trunk against it.

I collapsed on my settee, shaking.

Then back up on my feet, into the kitchen.

I found a bottle of vodka and sank a few. *What would she do?*

What *could* she do?

I phoned Bella, but there was no answer.

I tried again and again.

Never any answer.

At Home with Winnie

'We'd better skedaddle,' Elsie said, giving one last skim of her duster as she passed a large Moorcroft vase near the door. 'They'll be in the corridor before we know it.'

'I know,' said Ruby. 'So bloody particular, ain't they. Better get a move on.'

'Get going – quick, quick, quick... '

In the corridor, two men appeared at the far-end just as the two chambermaids drifted off in the opposite direction. These men knew exactly where they were going, with the portly gentleman leading on. With a flick of his wrist, the heavy door was open and he marched across to his favourite chintz armchair. He watched as an assemblage of young men followed on into the room to set things up.

'Slippery buggers,' he said, lighting up a fat cigar. 'Where's the drinks?'

'I take it you don't mean tea?' His companion smiled. 'No, of course you don't.'

'Tea at The Ritz? No. Not today.'

'Wouldn't it be dreadful to live in a country where

they didn't have tea? The workers will be having it – cake too, no doubt.'

'No time for all that,' said Winston, 'we have a fair bit of discussion needed and, you know, all that jazz.' He took a long draw on his Havana, then exhaled – flooding the polished room with an acrid cloud or two. 'I like it here, it feels safe. Too many bloody people, always – and especially in the Palm Court area.'

'Do you always ask for the Marie Antoinette Suite?' Noel was pouring drinks, remembering Winston never had water with his whisky. Or did he?

'You bet I do. Well, my girl does. I have a good one at the moment – incredibly fast typist and bright. Needs to keep up with all my bunkum, of course, eh!'

'I see perfectly.' Noel grinned, bringing the glasses over. It was a large, airy room – one of the best, with a spiffing view over Green Park. The snow was beginning to thaw, leaving a jigsaw of pale green patches of grass.

'Down in the basement bar,' Winston said, slowly, 'there's quite a mêlée of people socialising still. No one's put a stop to it, and quite right too. A person's sexuality is their own business I say. The authorities thought it was getting too notorious, did you know? All's well currently.'

Noel raised his glass. 'Let's drink to the hope that one day this country of ours, to which we owe so much, will find dignity and greatness and peace again.'

'To Hope!'

Noel smirked. 'And I have, of course, said that before.'

'I know. Your party piece.' Winston gulped at

his whisky; Noel sipped delicately. It was still early evening, and he had work to do later.

'Look at the wood panelling.' Winston indicated with his glass, his arm outstretched. 'Lovely. Beautiful in here. See that gorgeous Majolica dish over there? Those colours inspire my paintings – blues… turquoise, sea-green, jade. Gives the heart a lift.' And he thumped his heart with his other hand, laughing. 'I hope we can survive another bombing raid here. Those bloody jerrycans, that's nine times we've been hit all told in this hotel. If it was a cat, it'd be the end of its nine lives, what!' He roared with laughter, cigar ash spilling onto the expensive, immaculate carpet. 'How's the writing chappies doing?'

Noel continued to smile. 'That crazy chap, Orwell – George, the writer, has started a novel that I think will be very unsettling. He's thinking in terms of the future, nineteen eighty-four specifically, when the world will be very different. Or around that time.'

'Oh, really?'

'Once we get over this war of course. He's dithering with the title – wants *The Last Man in Europe*… so he says. Sounds more like a flaming disaster, what! An Armageddon.' He took another sip of whisky. 'He says it's a long way off being finished. He needs to think about it.'

'Ah, yes. Best not to go toying with the future – we have enough on our plates currently. But, you know, things will have to change, Noel. Once this country is settled and we're over the worst, of course we'll need to recruit help from our allies, especially those that didn't want to get involved with all the blood and sweat in the first place. Rebuilding, strong trade deals. The Scandinavian countries. I've couched it already, but no one– '

'Too soon to think of that yet Winnie. At least the Arts will be up and running again, properly – a bit of a lift to those whose lives are grey and meaningless after– '

'The Arts? All well and good, but they'll need bread, butter, better health and a few bob in their pockets. And some kind of work, and Jesus Christ, we'll need– '

There was a *crash!* from a far corner of the room – loud enough for Winston to jerk in his armchair as he held his empty glass out for a refill. He was damned if he was going to struggle up and get it.

'Golly gumdrops!' Noel, always unflappable and poised, took Winston's glass and headed back to the walnut pedestal table serving as their personal bar. 'What the *hell* are they doing?'

A voice: 'Sorry, Mr Coward. It's these wires, cables... oh, yes, apologies Mr Churchill too. It won't be much longer.'

'You mean, the war?' said Winston. 'Optimistic, but you might be right.'

Noel laughed out loud. 'It's exactly what we're supposed to be discussing,' he said. 'Just chit-chat so far. Amusing though.'

'We're at the beginning of nineteen forty-five,' Winston said. 'This war? Surely not too much longer, you think? We're doing our bloody best. Those Yanks have, as they'd say, come up trumps.' He paused. 'You know I've had Eisenhower in here, along with de Gaulle? Interesting talks on manoeuvres. One man, dammit, quite formidable. That's Ike. The other, kind of tricky, which was to be expected. Difficult.'

'Oh.'

'Yes. Clemmie had her own opinions, of course.'

'No doubt.'

'How's your latest play doing?' said Winston, accepting the fresh glass of whisky. '*Still Life*, isn't it?'

'It's done so well in theatres. And you know I was minded to get a film made? Based on that play, an adaptation. It's been a devil to set-up that's for sure. What with the blackout and restrictions with everything, travelling all around the country to shoot.' He paused to extract his silver holder, and lit a cigarette. 'But the premiere should be later this year. We're all very excited.'

'With what we're putting up with, that's marvellous. No end to your talents, eh, Noel. What's it called? The same?'

'*Brief Encounter*. The best we could come up with. And that's exactly what it is – an encounter that should never have been, but DID happen briefly, causing untold misery for the lead players.'

'Sounds like wartime.'

'It does.'

'Did your actors fall in love?'

'No, they didn't. All the negative signs were there, not much connection at all. We'd have known. But all credit to their acting, they played their parts very well.'

'Glad to hear it.'

At that point, a door at the far end of the room opened abruptly. More young men strode in shaking their heads. Raised voices, then silence.

'My dear boy,' said Noel. 'What the hell's going on now?'

'Seems to be a lot of equipment there,' said Winston. 'Bulky too.'

'Too much. New-fangled stuff no doubt. They don't need all of that. I should know.'

Winston stubbed out his Havana, growling. 'This will not do at all. Not at all. Waste of time. Keep buggering on, as I always say.'

'Or *plodding* on, if in the presence of a lady.'

'Well… to hell with that.' Winston choked with laughter again. 'What are these chaps playing at? I'm ready to leave, aren't you? Time for some dinner.'

'Bottoms up!'

Clink… clink…

'Likewise!'

'That equipment, that stuff. Just imagine… if you can,' said Noel, standing up. 'One day, maybe one day, we could have our own private notebook, telephone, encyclopaedia, all of our own in one. Not dependent on anyone else. Something for the future.'

Winston looked thoughtful. 'Remember the doubt about having a wireless, back in the Twenties? Some thought it could speak back at us, like a telephone. That frightened the life out of 'em too, if you remember. Sweaty fingers on the dial, then: *Hello! Hello! HELLO!*'

'Mr Churchill!' came a voice. 'We think we're ready for you now.'

'You think?'

'We... know. But we have been filming too, though we're not sure how well it has turned out. Zoomed in, to catch the... intimacy, if you know what I mean. Possible troubles with the sound system. Trial run, sort of.'

'Well, chappy – in that case, CUT!! Not sure I'd want my private conversation with Mr Coward to be on celluloid.'

The young man licked his lips nervously. 'We think... it might hang well. A kind of *At Home with Winnie* presentation. *Pathe News* might like it.'

Winston spluttered. 'With Winnie? With WINNIE?! Remember, I am your Prime Minister. And this is not my home, though it might damn well feel like it at times!' He struggled to get out of the armchair.

Noel smiled beatifically.

'Sorry, Prime Minister Churchill,' said a louder, much more confident voice. 'We'd like to use what we have, with your permission of course.'

Winston stood stony-faced, one hand on the armchair back. His face was flushed.

'Are you the idiot in charge?'

The voice faltered. 'Well... I mean, maybe certain chosen parts of it. Sorry. And... any chance of a quote from you? You have some good ones. Before you leave us?'

Winston puffed in exasperation. He mused for a minute or two. 'Alright. *The business of life is the acquisition of memories. In the end, that's all there is.'*

'Thank you. That's jolly good of you.'

'Make sure you get it right. And, before I travel the length of this room and give you a bloody nose – CUT!! For godsake, CUT that camera now!'

'Best move along now, fellows,' said Noel. 'Get that equipment out, and through the back door please.' He turned to scoop up his overcoat. 'Good man. Sorry it didn't work out.'

Winston huffed some more. He moved to face the man in charge. 'Let me tell you – if that filming ends up *with Pathe News…* I'll be on to you before you can say *Heil Hitler!* And, remember – that's a joke!'

'He's only gone and left a ten-bob note!' Ruby said. 'Look – in the big blue dish over there. *Weeee!*'

'That'll be the *other* one,' said Elsie. 'The toff.'

'You think so? Hmm, Elsie, I'm not so sure. My dad says Winnie is just like us really. He might come over all la-di-da and grumpy – but he's alright, honest. Dad saw him in an Underground train carriage a few years back, talking to a load of people, asking them what they thought about this flamin' war.'

'If you say so.'

Ruby swiped the ten-bob note and tucked it into her overall pocket. 'He really cares, he does.'

Cold, Cold Blue

Morning
Pink streaks, blue-grey sky
Azure, silver-tinged sea
A blue oasis
They're on the beach, hand-in-hand
Creamy coffee and buttery croissants
Warm white sand, flickering patterns beneath waving fronds

Afternoon
Blistering heat, bustling insects, lush green palms
Chilled, thirst-quenching beers
Toasted cheese served with olives and seared peppers
Skin lotion applied with tender, loving hands
Ice cream speared with melt-in-the mouth wafers
Gulls soaring with crazed, fractured calls

Evening… All dressed up
Cute diamante earrings, spangly necklace
Macho gold on strong wrists, chest and sturdy fingers
Clinking flutes, champagne bubbles
Tinkling laughter, hearty hilarity
Juicy green herby salad with sizzling, spicy brochettes
Sparkling horizon, near midnight blue

Bedroom drinks…
So cool, Miles Davis' sultry pitch
Above, beyond the palms, there's still a kind of blue
Crimson sunset, rustling breeze
At the window, fluttering curtains
Time for bed…
And hot love

Harsh words…
Shattered glass
Rasping hostility, rage
Bruising… whimpering fear
The crash of a door
Despair. Tears.

Regret and guilt in the cool morning light
And, this time, reluctant redemption
Cold, cold blue…

Kissed by The Devil

It was Simon who suggested another night out.

Smart git.

We'd had an epic piss-up the weekend before. He said, let's take it easy this time, Crimble is coming up in two days. Just a little celebration.

I thought, fat chance of that.

Someone new, a sort called Mary, was coming – or she was going to be hanging around; we don't allow females in the 'inner enclaves', as Simon puts it. Full of amazing shit, him. If any babes come along, they can't get too involved. No heavy drinking. And he'll make sure they get home.

Simon's rules.

He says they're too soft to stay the course.

We started at *The King's Head*.

Shimmery Christmas crap decorated the bar.

We're not always welcome there, it depends on who's behind the bar. We'd thrown some manky chips around the last time we'd gone in.

After the first round, this geezer comes out, the

guvnor: paunchy, wearing a leather jerkin and a straw trilby, overgrown mutton chops, and a corned beef complexion travelling all the way down his neck.

He obviously recognised us. I had to admire his expletives – impressed, I was.

So we kicked a few chairs over, marauded through the bar, and out the back door where the murky toilets are. The babes followed on, giggling. I noticed Mary, she was different: dark eyes, dark hair tied up in a sexy knot. Nice.

We went round the corner to *The Griffin Inn*.

Pints of Pils, with strong chasers. It was my shout, and I made a show of it. The babes, all in a gaggle at the bar, were on pink Prosecco. *Jingle Bells* tinkled away somewhere. Reminded me of being really young.

Everyone noticed me in there.

I kind of upped the ante, if you know the expression. Flash, like.

Simon winked. Not sure what that meant. Encouraging; or keep your filthy hands off her? Meaning, with Mary.

Never sure with him.

Was she someone's sister?

The jukebox belted out *Another One Bites The Dust*. We stomped our way through it all, crashing our glasses on the bar top. Simon told us to stop, Pete was getting the next round and wanted to be sure of getting them in. So we obeyed, like good boys.

Then the double doors opened and a swarm of people surged in.

Looked like too many prissy Sloane Rangers,

glittery boas around their necks, holding onto their slick Hooray Henrys. All the Henrys were wearing white shirts and well-fitting, tailored trousers. One or two were wearing Santa hats. Idiots.

What's the betting a few of them were real live Henrys in any case? Henry being a typical Hooray name and all that.

Was this some kind of Yuletide charabanc outing from London? Wa! Wa!

They were already two-deep at the bar, crowding the place out.

I was set to pick some kind of fight, but Simon flashed me a look. He knows me so well. He always says, you might have steel-caps, but you don't need to use 'em.

Wise words.

'Stay in your own posh boozers, matey,' I said to the Henry next to me. 'Ain't you got enough up there in Chelsea to get on with?' His mouth opened like a sea creature struggling for breath; but the Henry the other side of him caught my eye, scowled, and began to roll up the sleeve on his right arm, meanwhile jostling his fellow Henrys...

Time to go.

I drained my lager and looked around for Mary.

Simon pulled us all out real quick. He's in the wrong flippin' job, he is, being a postman.

Next stop, staggerable distance, was the *Royal Sovereign*. Almost empty. An enormous pine tree stood by the fireplace; almost bare, perhaps forgotten. Ugly posters all over the walls, old wooden floorboards, too many poncy real ale pumps. All we needed was sodding sawdust on the floor. We'd missed the live music, and the strippers wouldn't be in until the next night. Or was that a joke? Simon was laughing.

The fruit machines were crashing, banging, whirling. Blinding strobes, then rays of red, green and blue shot around the place, flitting weirdly across people's faces. In the corner, Mary stood with Simon, talking seriously.

About what?

One of the two chunky babes was buzzing around Pete, and he wasn't having any of it. She sat down on his lap, heavily, her wine sloshing around in her glass.

'Get off! Don't use me as a fuckin' chair!'

'*Pete...*'

'You just get yer ass off me, girl. Only smarm round me if you really mean it, not if you're off yer fuckin' 'ead!'

'But– '

'This ain't your throne. It's bloody *mine!*' he said, beginning to see the funny side of it. He thrust one beefy, well-inked arm in the air, making a victory salute. Then he pushed her off.

I knew they'd cause trouble.

I was glad it wasn't Mary. She looked far too composed for that kind of stunt. Serene, even. Like some kind of princess she was. *My* babe.

We stayed a while. The string of reindeer cavorting above the bar bothered me. I remember buying another round. Then some bright spark suggested *The Tudor Arms* – a pub with wicked food. It was a few streets away, so we needed to leg it down there. Some of the babes had fallen by the wayside, including the drunken lap-snatcher, but Mary was still with us, talking to Pete. I intended to knock back my drink and get over there, break it up.

But I didn't.

It was more than a tad lairy by then, but I do remember we were starving. Someone ordered samosas, and some extra spicy stuff, flaming hot, was sitting on the bar. It probably ended up on the floor. I just don't know.

I looked around for Mary, but no sign of her. I'd played it wrong. Again.

Simon and Pete had vamooshed. And the others. I was climbing the flint wall outside, shredding my knees, ripping my hands to bits.

So why climb it? Because it was there.

And I fell off – I'm pretty bloody sure of that. And then they all came back, ear-splitting noise, someone wiping the blood off my hands and forehead. That was Simon.

Definitely Simon.

'I love you, mate,' I said.

'Yeah, yeah. We've got to get you 'ome.'

'It was Henry,' I said. 'He took a swing. Effing city prat.'

'No Henrys around here,' he said, draping me over his shoulder.

There's a continuous soundtrack, a definite *thump-thump*.

It's warm... and it's cramped. And I can't move.
What a hell of a bloody dream. Weird.
I try stretching a leg. I still can't move.
I'll blink a couple of times and it'll go away. I'll save it in my brain cells so that I can recall it later, and tell the lads what a nonce of a dream I had.
Still stuck. Am I ill?
Am I *dead?*
I feel that surge of panic usually reserved for the chased-by-a-demon nightmare; or where you're falling, falling... waiting for the crash to earth, *splat!* And it never comes. That's when you wake up.
When will I wake up!
Jesus!
Everything's buckling... walls pulling back, then closing in...
What was the last thing I was doing – before I crashed out? I think hard.
Okay, how much alcohol? Any drugs?
Yep, probably the usual bit o' this, bit o' that. I was high as a kite, staggering on that dodgy flint wall.
It's all coming back to me.
'Come and get me!' I'd bawled, snorting with laughter.
Simon threw me his worried look.
Brainy, him. He once gave me a book to read – he said it'd give me some clues on how to clean up my act, live a better life. He said it was adapted from something else.
The book was creepy. *'Lessons for Life',* lecturing horribly, and listing all kinds of stuff to avoid: *Lust of*

the Flesh... yeah, chance would be a fine thing; *Lust of the Eyes...* like fancying something beyond your means. Yep – that's me, all the flaming time, you poxy loon writer. Aren't we all like that?

I've had a shit life. I could write a book about my pissing childhood.

Then there's *No Cussing*. Ha! Fuck that.

I recollect *Abstinence from Alcohol* too. No booze! *Crap*. If I can't have a drink when I want it, what kind of life is that! The only way to get rid of temptation – some important geezer said, sometime, years ago – is to yield to it.

Even if it does mean getting a kiss from the bleedin' devil.

'Go easy, mate,' said Simon, edging towards me, his arms outstretched. 'Be safe. It's not worth it, pal.'

'Pillock!' How I laughed! 'All is good, dude,' I said. 'No worries.'

Crazy twonk. Too cautious for his own good.

That's when I fell off the wall.

And Simon wiped away the blood.

I told him I loved him.

Whoa! There's movement here now...

What the fuck? I'm being sucked out of bed.

Am I *in* a bed?

I'm an evil sod. What the hell did I take?

Or maybe I got spiked. I remember Bloody Marys sitting on the bar, laced with scorching piri-piri. Red hot. Lethal.

I'd yelled: Bloody Mary, Bloody Mary! Ha! I lapped it up.

Where was the lovely Mary? My babe. The one I didn't get anywhere near?

Where did she go?

Whoa! Things are speeding up.

Wake up, and quick!

Moisture... sticky. A violent jolt.

I shriek.

I'm out. Squirming.

Shit!

I need another drink. It's too bloody real.

Simon, I'll be coming to get ya! This is your fault – it has to be your fault.

'Her Serene Highness the Queen Catalina de Aragón,' a man reports. 'Thine child, a living daughter. Praise be to God.'

'Prithee, inform the King,' the woman says wearily.

She whimpers.

I sense hands on me. I'm carried somewhere and wrapped in a cloth.

My head and face are wiped.

What's going on! Wake up, man!

''Tis pity it is not the son so desired,' he continues.

'Your Majesty,' whispers a different woman, moving back across the room with me in her arms. 'Hither, thy daughter. A new Tudor, of robust health.'

'Thank thee, Mistress Pole.'

I'm handed over to her. I struggle to open my eyes, try to shove my arms up.

I cry out!

I'll pissing well thump Simon once I get out of this nightmare.

Simon and his clever brain, his kindness – and that shit book.

I'll slaughter him.

I'm a complete dick. And so is he.

'Pray, be rested, little daughter. Thou art here, and living, and of fine health. King Henry, he will bid thee well come, yet thou be not the son he so desired.' She sighs. 'Not this time.'

Her words wash over me.

Henry?

I scream bloody murder. *Let me wake up!*

Wicked bastard! Who spiked those bleedin' drinks?

'Mary Tudor, my beautiful. Well come. *Hush!*' she croons, rocking me in her arms. 'What ails thee? My seer quoth great woe, such *bloody* times for thee ahead. Nay. Methinks he be a simpleton! Ha!' She chuckles. 'Wither goest thou? Perchance to become Queen?'

I scream again.

'My Mary.' She strokes my cheek. 'Dearest child, let thou life be ever blessed.'

Okay, Simon – enough's enough. Explain this.

This... Mary?

Tudor stuff? And, Queen!

So – I'm kissed by the devil... and wrecked by the devil.

Seems he has his own agenda and does what he likes.

I've now changed sex, Simon. And I'm reborn. Ha!

And babe Mary. We're one and the same, locked together?

With a gruesome future ahead...

Bloody hell. Not quite what I had in mind for Christmas this year.

You'll need everything you got – all your twonking, screwball knowledge for this one, mate.

Nightmare of a dream.

It *is* a dream – isn't it? *Simon?*

Playing the Diamond Game

The only way to survive is obvious: play the game, as others do.

No choice.

Those huge figures towering over our world, determining what came next, had to be observed carefully. I say *our* world, there's a few of us, though they're unknown to me. We don't communicate. I just play the game, doing my best. Surviving.

Another world. This came to me out of the blue – yes, a cliché, but it's true. My own life had been plodding along, nothing too extraordinary happening; semi-retired from journalism – up at the Dog & Duck for a pie and pint two or three times a week, sorting out the world with Bill and Ted, keeping up with world news, and *this* happens. Whisked away to this other world, part of a perpetual game, trying to survive. No food needed, no sleep required, no spoken words possible, and no idea of timeframe. How long have I been here?

A month? A year? A decade?

Trapped.

It's freezing. *Really* freezing. Above, a riot of fake stars as our whole world moves onwards towards something ominous. Loud shouts as the enormous figures above get excited – they push and bang and shove, our glass ceiling juddering. This is a new setup, very popular with the ever-shifting crowd of figures fixated on us and the stage-setting around us. Recently, in a different cabinet, we were part of a jungle playfield – hot, hot, *hot* – it was not pleasant at all. Now we're plunged into this icy terrain, surrounded by clamour and uncertainty.

I'm always on the lookout here. I don't miss a thing.

When I have time to think, I wonder what I was doing before this astonishing change. Was I reading, watching television, talking to someone?

Hit by a bus?

Loitering by the pool table, with a pint? That sounds quite feasible. Balls. Rolling balls…

Whatever, it caused this damn ridiculous change in my life. Being optimistic, maybe I'll wake up soon, so I'm best not to worry too much; it's wasted time.

We're nearing midnight. The stretched inky sky is tranquil.

Engines churning, random discharges.

Vast shadows sliding across our scenario.

I hear the shrill of fiddle music and stomping. The Irish are having a céilí.

Crash!!

The ship shudders.
Stillness, then harsh voices, pounding footfalls.
Distorted sounds of the ship's horn, mournful, alarming.
'SOS! We have struck ice and require immediate assistance!'
Things were livening up.
More thick-toned horn noises.
'Where's the Captain?'
Bawling. Screaming.
The death of a ship. A four-funnelled very famous vessel on her maiden voyage.

The gathering above is lapping it up. Down here, we'd heard it all before, standing there ready to take our orders. It's going to hurt. These figures really are fully humanoid, not some kind of mutation or offshoot.
I'd had my doubts.
The boy playing the game draws back the metal spring-loaded plunger, launches the ball, and off it goes, someone-contained-as-a-ball spins around the whole bloody set-up, clackety-clack, aiming to settle in a place where he, the boy above us, has choices.
'Hoping for the flamin' captain,' he says, kicking a leg of the pinball cabinet. 'It's all *his* fault after all.'
The wireless operator speaks calmly. 'RMS Carpathia – come at once. We have struck a berg. It's a CQD, old man. Get here as soon as you can.'
Customary Quick Despatch.
In other words – Acute Distress. *Danger.*
Then, alarm bells. The water-tight doors had,

famously, failed. The gash on the hull has been substantial.

Around, around, around... flippers working madly to redirect.

The ball disappears into a pocket. The backbox shows:

Save a mother who has a baby

'Eff!!' he shouts. '*Not* what I wanted.'

'My turn,' says the lad shoulder to shoulder with him. 'I want to save 'im, it's only fair.'

'Cool it, Daddy-O!'

'See this knuckle sandwich, dork?'

Now, the usual jostling, thumping on the reinforced glass surface. Only one measly ball per game doesn't help. That's because the rewards are unusual. Life-changing – or so they think.

Unless, of course, I'm the one out of step.

They were lucky not to have a TILT warning. These boys get so worked up. Nothing new of course. It's that kind of age, and not that long since the end of war (for now) with a new, shiny rock 'n' roll era to enjoy, and at last the end of rationing in their world. They've no idea of what to expect in the future – and that's no bad thing. Meanwhile, they're still hooked on the past.

Strains of Little Richard's *Tutti Frutti* wails from a jukebox somewhere, now sounding hackneyed to my twenty-first century ears, but somehow reassuring; it confirms the existence of this off-kilter parallel world.

I knew I was right.

Someone inserts a coin, sending it hurtling down into the depths of the cabinet with a *thud*.

The next ball isn't yet in position. More thumping and shoving of the pinball cabinet. I know it's my fellow ball's acute anticipation of the huge wallop that will send him UP and then spinning around and around. I feel his fear.

With years of being shoved and thumped, the cabinet is becoming unsteady and splintering in places. Maybe woodworm too. Due for repair, no doubt.

I'm third in the queue.

A voice bellows from the wheelhouse: '*RMS Carpathia in transit!*'

It's the wireless operator again. His job is thankless.

'Huh. Cap'n Edward Smith can't be saved, dweeb,' said one bright spark. 'It'd change history just *too* much. Can't be done.'

'Aw, he's ancient anyway,' said someone else. 'He deserves to pay the price.'

'It was actually Robert Hichens at the wheel,' said the first guy. 'If anyone's to blame, it's him.'

'Bighead, ain't ya?'

A chorus of voices.

Squabbling begins on what to do.

I took no heed.

Our overall setup is faltering in these damn North Atlantic icefields, just as it's programmed to. How miserable for those on that fated ship. I reckon the gods are laughing at me, being in the thick of what would've been a sensational scoop for me back in my old world, had I lived in 1912.

Broken in two, mid-ship. Hours since the iceberg incident. So many people afloat on whatever they could find, freezing to death in the perishing sea, or in a lifeboat if they're very lucky.

I'm now second in the queue.

The latest ball has come to rest. On the backbox, there's a choice this time:

Execute a quicker response from the Carpathia
Find the looter's Gladstone bag before anyone else does

Looting jewellery? Not sure the timing is correct with that; folk in the 50s knew far less of the bones of this icy, miserable disaster. Oh – to be able to use my knowledge to get out of this horror.

The boys are mulling over their choices. They're not sure what a Gladstone bag is. They *really* think they can change history! In their era, anything seems possible. They believe they'll be kept informed of the outcome.

Dumb?

Around 1:45 a.m: 'Come as quickly as possible, old man – the engine room is filling up to the boilers.'

'All our boats were ready and we're coming as hard as we *could* come.'

'Alright. Look out for our signal rockets.'

But three minutes later, the distressed ship disappears under the freezing water.

The *Carpathia* is on the horizon. Our ship sank an hour and a half ago. There should be loud cheers from the floating survivors, but all we have is some faint murmuring, and one or two weak whistle blasts from men in charge of lifeboats. It feels subzero.

Below, grouped in line, we all are freezing cold in the pits of the cabinet. Wretched. A tremor runs through our queue of six. Number six ball was still out of sorts from his recent jaunt around the playfield. He arrives with a smart, steely *click-clack* and a sigh.

Another coin goes in. *Ker-plonk!*

A two-second pause.

Twaakkk!!

The ball ahead of me is now journeying.

He's ricocheting around from bumper to bumper – these are 'dead', inactive ones. There's nothing sophisticated with this setup yet.

Someone has triggered the TILT warning on the backbox. Flashing lights, beeping sounds. Pivoting diamonds. All this makes the game more immersive. With one more warning, it'll be game over. When in play, a slight body-nudge to the cabinet can assist the ball's journey; those who are astute enough, do it without incurring a warning and might go on to get the ball where it's really wanted.

The ball falls out at the bottom, down to the pits to join us.

The player this time is unlucky. Probably a very young kid. He's soon shoved out of the way. And guess who's next to make an appearance?

Me.

And there's a new kid in the crowd. He's cocky.

The spring-loaded plunger hurt, as always. However any of us contorted ourselves, it got us in the small of the back – at least, that's how it felt.

Circling of the playfield begins. I've been misfired, clumsily, so my progress is sluggish, out of control.

I'm spinning wildly.

Body-nudges from all sides. Shouts of profanity, enough to make anyone but a journalist's ears bleed.

I spin against a bumper and then… a fluke – I go into a pocket and disappear from view. A riot goes on overhead, and a voiceover:

'*I'll never let go, Jack. I promise.*'

'What?'

'That's new.'

'Hey, not heard *that*… '

Proper words spoken! Confusing.

Before another word can be uttered, the new choices are shown on the backbox. With arms slung over mates' shoulders, they stand gazing at it:

Rescue more of the Irish in Steerage
Discover the whereabouts of the diamond rose-gold and silver bracelet

It's getting a bit complex.

I'm as puzzled as everyone else.

Weird. But it's all wrong. They've gaffed. Someone has made an error…

There's definitely info there that this world would not have known.

I've been waiting for a chink in this world's armour. I need to act now.

The gang moves inwards, wondering what the hell to do. 'Bloody *diamonds*, chum!' says one, 'I'll have myself some of those.' Some light fags while they ponder, the smoke spiralling high above their silly young heads.

I'm thinking hard. There's a bracelet in the mix; in the *real* story. The 1997 movie touched on a brilliant blue diamond necklace that the character Rose kept… until, as a very elderly woman, she slipped it over the edge of the 1985 investigative ship; back into the foamy ocean and down, down to the depths to rejoin Jack in the decaying sepulchres.

All a load of Tinseltown tosh, of course.

Since that real-life 1985 discovery mission, my generation knows more. We know about the Gladstone bag bulging with pilfered jewellery – of course we do. Found on the sunken wreck, or nearby. The diamond rose-gold and silver bracelet was a rare piece. Not difficult to see how it cleverly transformed into a precious blue diamond necklace in a mega-budget Hollywood flick.

The bracelet belonged to a woman called Amy, her name encrusted in diamonds. Records showed that only two women bore that name on the ship, one of whom had been travelling in third-class.

Amy is my wife's name. She'd love a diamond or two.

From one of the boys: 'Somebody's life is about to change. Ha Ha.'

He's talking about diamonds – and I'm *thinking* about them.

Taking off my journalist's hat, figuratively, I muster the spirit to act. Seeing the weakness in the cabinet around me, I launch myself against the side, the part that's badly splintered, and burst out.

There was a sudden shout: 'Oops. Bloody ball escaping… '

You bet I am. I surge forwards, glad now of those days at the gym getting my body the best it could be. Now a ball with muscle.

I've nothing to lose.

The belief is strong. I'll try some of that naivety, gullibility – or magic.

The museum of artifacts would have those diamonds, somewhere. That's where I'm going. In my head? Something to strive for, to live for.

Ted spotted me first. 'Here's Jack!'

Bill ordered me a pint. 'Where've you been, you old sod?'

'You wouldn't believe me,' I said. 'Here and there, y'know.'

'You look thin, mate,' said Ted.

'Yeah. Maybe.'

'Things getting tight for you?'

'Not really. Rather good now, to be honest.'

Bill laughed out loud. 'Won on the horses?'

'Better than that.'

'Ah. Sweet.'

I'd committed a crime; not sure how safe I'd be if the cops got involved. My alibi was watertight.

'Keep it under your hat then, Jack,' said Bill, sauntering over to the pool table, casually thwacking a ball – the cue ball, the white one. 'We wouldn't have told a soul.'

I pulled a face.

'Fancy a game, mate?' he boomed, glugging at his pint. 'Eh?'

He was so close to the pool table, one hip just grazing it.

'No, not at the moment,' I said, sitting down hard. 'Feeling a bit drained, pal.' I rubbed my eyes.

'Aw, come on… '

'*No*. I've just told you,' I said, irritated.

A pause.

'I could tell you a diamond of a story, though,' I said. 'But I won't.'

'Huh! You will, but not *yet*. Give it a bit of time.'

The pool table was beginning to vibrate…

I knew it! I'd been right.

'Probably never,' I said, turning to get up and run. 'If I were you, mate, I'd get away from there… '

Love in Arabic

A Novella

A Tale of
Discovery, Mismatch and Misunderstanding

Morocco

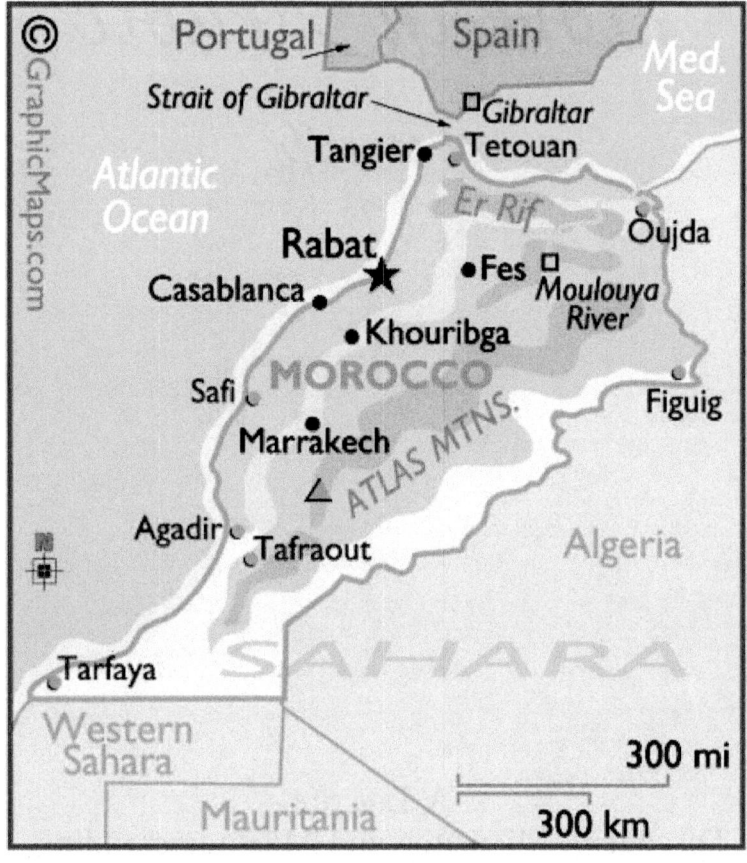

A Short Glossary

Aiwa!	An emphatic Yes (*Yeah!*)
Arwah!	Come on!
B'slemah!	Goodbye!
Chokraan	Thank you
Cuul	Eat
Floos	Money
In Sha'Allah	God Willing
Labas	How are you? / Welcome
Luh	No
Na'am	Yes
Salaam	Hello / Welcome
Wuh huh	Okay (in agreement)

Rabat

Morocco
June 1990

Out of the heat, and into the cool reception area.

We took a breather before we walked towards the glass swing-door.

I'd felt more confident this time because I had engineered this meeting; but once inside the Consulate I had a niggling worry that things might not be easy.

We moved forward, through the door, and approached the reception counter.

'Hello. We have an appointment with Mr Fairburn,' I said. Youssef was chiming in, saying the same in Arabic. The receptionist looked doubtful.

'The *Consul*,' I added. 'I made an appointment for this morning, eleven o'clock.'

'Really?'

Youssef looked alarmed.

The receptionist seemed doubtful. But I knew how easy it could be to overlook something written down that's staring you in the face; I'd done it so often myself.

'I phoned from England a few weeks back and spoke to him personally – no one else,' I expanded.

The receptionist, ignoring the bulky computer to her left, was leafing through an appointments book, backward and forward, from day to day. She looked puzzled.

No, no...

Checking dates, rechecking pages; running a finger along indecipherable handwriting written in various shades of biro.

Please...

'I don't think so,' she said finally. 'I can't see any sign of appointments made with him for today, or any time this week. He wouldn't normally be seeing— '

She didn't finish her sentence. 'Jack – have you got a minute?' She walked away to speak to a male colleague who was examining papers at the back of the large reception area. They spoke quietly, glancing our way once or twice. Youssef shifted uncomfortably, clenching and unclenching his fists. Jack disappeared briefly and came back with a slim, hard-back notebook. A diary?

The receptionist returned.

'I'm very sorry, but he isn't here. All appointments had to be cancelled.'

'But— '

'He's been called away. We have his private diary here. Seems that we couldn't find a contact number for you, so couldn't let you know. How long are you in Rabat?'

'We were going back to Tangier today. Later on.

But we could stay for tomorrow?' I gave Youssef a swift look to see how this was going with him. 'Is that any good?'

'I'm afraid not. He isn't back till next week. I'm very sorry.'

Youssef came out of his silence. 'It not good! We come here for... meeting, expect to be seen. Why not you tell us this first we come in?'

'I said I was sorry. Look, I'm standing in for someone else, I didn't know about this.' She met Youssef's glower with one of her own. 'Not sure there's anything else we can do. Phone another time and make a new appointment? It'll take a while.'

I turned on my heel, fighting back tears. Youssef walked alongside me, his face a picture of misery. We headed for the door, out to the heat and oppressiveness.

There was a shout from the reception counter.

'Wait!'

We stopped in our tracks.

'Come back!' It was the receptionist's male colleague, Jack, who had taken over her position at the counter, by the half-turned, flickering computer screen; a piece of technology possibly new to them, it looked on display rather than being a functional part of their workplace. 'I remember you two. I might be able to...'

Youssef and I looked over our shoulders and turned.

We retraced our steps.

'You were here before, I remember. And refused entry to the UK?'

'Yes,' I said. 'That's right, he was.'

'Are you married?' Jack asked.

'No. We tried this week, going to government departments, but it's more difficult than we thought.'

'Why?'

'Oh, the red tape. All kinds of other stuff.' I leant on the counter. 'Having to be here for ten days, all that.'

'Aha,' he said. 'But, you know, there *is* an easier way.'

'There is?'

'Maybe I shouldn't be telling you, but... you could get married in Gib.'

'Where?'

'Gib. Gibraltar.'

'Oh.'

'You'd need a visa to get over there, young man. Not difficult.' He rubbed his shiny bald head pensively. 'There's lots of Moroccans there.'

'I know,' Youssef said. 'My uncle, he works there. He come back to Morocco for see family when he can, an' he sends money.'

'Anyway... just apply for a visa now and you shouldn't have any trouble. When would you need it?'

'Er... not sure,' I said. 'When, Youssef? I'm confused now.'

'It'll take a while to be approved,' said Jack.

'I suppose I could go in October,' I said. 'It gives me time to get back to work for a while before I go away again. It keeps the peace in the office.'

'Maybe September, Jeannie... '

'It needs to be October, Youssef. And too bad if it

isn't to anyone's liking at work,' I said. 'Let's *do* it.'

'Shall we say,' Jack said, 'a two-week visa for Gib? Last week in September, first in October? That way you're covered, just in case.'

'Perfect,' I said.

'*Perfecto*,' Youssef echoed.

'Go for it?' Jack had his pen poised.

'Yes please.'

Jack tossed the pen aside, narrowed his eyes theatrically and wagged a finger. 'Remember... this advice is strictly off the record. *I didn't tell you.*'

A short *taksi* ride from Rabat Bus Station took us back to Youssef's uncle's house in the less salubrious part of the city, Ben Slimane.

'*Escorpion* house again, Jeannie. Hope that thing has gone now.'

'It's having a siesta behind those walls.'

I was trying to forget the scorpion in the bathroom walls from earlier that day. It'd scuttled out from behind a badly broken tile. At first sight, it looked like a small frilly lobster. The encounter soon concluded, with me calling out to Youssef, and with just a cotton towel between me and possible death...

On a scrubby dust track, we were nearing the front door. 'They'll be getting some food ready for us. They do their best. Remember to eat, Jeannie – take all they give you this time.'

It was a square, modest house full of adults and small silent children with big eyes. There was a warm fug of cooking coming from the tiny galley kitchen. Those people who before had looked like Youssef's parents, and Uncle Aziz, Aunt Safia, and Youssef's granny who we called Ya Ya, now took on more of their own identity. But I was despairing. I gritted my teeth, trying to smile, knowing we were there for only one more night.

Like Youssef's parents' home in the Rif mountains, the house had no mains water; unlike the mountains abode, they had electricity – they were in a town after all, and part of the city of Rabat.

We walked through to the back.

The family sat on fabric-draped couches in the cool, windowless room. Taking off my shoes, I tip-toed in bare feet across the concrete floor haphazardly strewn with a mix of small ethnic rugs, and one covered in pink rosebuds. The two low tables, surrounded by very squat stools, were draped with lace cloths of beige plastic. One table bore the customary silver teapot and assorted gold-edged glasses on a tray, ready for pouring heavily-sugared mint tea. I'd tried to always accept their hospitality.

'That's it then,' said Youssef, sitting down, and cracking his knuckles one by one – his way of de-stressing. 'We go to Tangier, back to the hotel tomorrow. Go to Gibraltar later this year – get marry. Very long time to wait!'

I grimaced. 'My wedding dress has travelled far.'

'You get 'nother dress for October?'

'Oh, no. This one will do.'

A wedding dress, of sorts, now creased to hell – it'd

need a good steaming and an iron.

He went on to translate for the family, who looked intrigued, their gazes sliding across to where I was sitting. I knew I was the first European person they'd ever set eyes on in their own home.

It's a strange thing to be scrutinised so thoroughly by so many people and not have a clue about the thinking behind it. It was evident that I was a good few years older than their adored nephew – but I was to go on to find that didn't bother Moroccans in the slightest. Maturity meant a lot.

Honeymoon

Gibraltar
October 1990

Above the navy blue sea the sky was darkening, festooned with thin strips of silvery cloud and banners of red.

The end of an extraordinary day.

It was now much later in the day than we'd wanted. We needed to go.

Pablo's battered white van was parked outside the *Hotel Margarita*, one sliding door pushed back to receive us and our luggage. We scuttled down the steps of the hotel, Youssef ahead of me as usual, and he pushed each piece as far back inside the van as he could. A pair of hands from the depths dragged it out of sight.

We prepared to scramble in.

'Bye bye, La Linea,' Youssef muttered.

La Linea, a kind of no man's land, with half a foot planted in Gibraltar, and more than tinged with Moroccan influence. We were heading for the frontier and on to Andalucia's Costa del Sol. Gibraltar had served a purpose. Now we were ready for our honeymoon.

Youssef jogged my arm. 'Pablo say, you the bride, so sit in chair big.'

'Big chair? This one?' I said, throwing myself into a bulky armchair with wooden arms which stood well forward of the back of the spacious van. Two low Moroccan leather pouffés squatted just behind and Youssef hurled himself down onto one of these. Pablo's sister Carmen sat hugging her knees tightly on the other. Her boyfriend lounged right at the back on a carpeted section, surrounded by our luggage and various bits and pieces of Pablo's craft ware business. I caught a glimpse of huge, bright conch shells threaded onto cord, badly broken, tangled with glass-beaded door hangings. A large oiled wooden Don Quixote, one arm missing, stood sternly to one side.

Pablo's sister Carmen was keeping up a rapid discussion with him, words like scabrous gunshot pouring from her lips like nothing I'd heard before. When she laughed, her cheekbones became slanting razors in a heart-shaped face.

'Do anything, she. Jump off cliff, drive motorbike like... *devil*,' Youssef said. 'Crazy.'

She wore ripped blue jeans and a tight floral top which showed off her curvy figure. My knee-length mauve outfit didn't compare.

'The devil!' I said. 'I'm surprised you mention *him*.'

'Mummy, she says, devil – he get you if he want you,' he said airily. 'If he don't get you first time, he get you later.'

'*Tsss!*' With a swing of her head Carmen swept back the tangle of dark curly hair hanging in her face.

'You, lady, have *luna de miel* good one,' she shot at me, like an instruction. I smiled back at her.

Ana, Pablo's girlfriend, sat up at the front beside him. She was more soberly dressed in loose pastel clothes.

'*Vamanos!*' shouted Pablo as the van lurched forward.

Let's go!

Pablo, also in jeans, was head and shoulders above everyone; Rasputin-like with his mane of collarbone length hair, liquid eyes and rough beard.

'I feel like the queen,' I said.

'You *are* queen,' replied Youssef, holding with both hands the rim of his pouffé as Pablo took a sharp corner.

'I'm wallowing in queen-ness,' I said, crossing my legs with decorum, knowing I was still under the influence of the sparkling wine we'd had after the wedding.

'Uh, Jeannie?'

'Hey – is Pablo okay driving? He took that last turn— '

'He drink a lot black coffee and water two litre. His belly, it turn to... *river* now. If listen careful, we hear water it go swish swish.'

'Don't make me laugh...'

'*Ehhh*, Pablo— !' Youssef, pleased with himself, repeated his observation in Spanish and Pablo's hands left the steering wheel for too long as he choked with laughter.

I bellowed too. I felt I needed to shout to be taken

notice of. 'Please, Pablo, don't laugh too much!'

Pablo grunted.

'Pablo, he good driver,' said Youssef. 'He knows what to do.'

We'd nearly reached the frontier. Pablo slowed down and the Spanish police approached. We had to produce our passports. I had mine and Youssef's ready in my handbag.

'Better give quick, Jeannie. They not like keep wait.'

'They're here, I've got them. Keep yer 'air on.'

'Uh?'

I passed our passports to Pablo, who handed them over. A broad, tight-lipped policeman began scrutinising each one in turn, then handed it to his partner. Youssef's and mine were the last to be scrutinised.

He leaned into our van.

Rapid words were exchanged with Pablo.

Youssef's green Moroccan passport was flapped around by the policeman as if it was something not very pleasing.

My heart lurched.

'He say I not be allow go in, Jeannie.'

'Yes, I realise that. *Christ.*'

'Pablo, he try to say that I now marry to European, so should be allow go into Spain.'

'Oh *God.*'

The policeman was looking through the open window at Youssef sitting apprehensively on his pouffé towards the back. His beaky nose suddenly thrust further into the van – he was having a very good look at our rogue Moroccan. I turned to look too, I wanted to know what was so fascinating about Mr. Youssef Mohammed El Mamechi sitting there. I gazed overtly. One-armed Don Quixote, sporting a similar look to the policeman, and propped next to Carmen's boyfriend, stared grimly ahead.

'No. No es possible,' said Beaky Nose. 'No.' He shuffled the passports, putting the green one on top, and handed them back to Pablo.

There was a frozen silence. Even Carmen had shut up.

'Jeannie, you get out and speak. You have certificate of wedding? You need— '

'Okay,' I said. 'Okay. Looks like it's our only chance.'

I stumbled out of the van in my high heels and approached Beaky Nose, who'd backed away and now stood warily with his partner.

'*Por favor*,' I said. '*Este papel es... el certificado de Boda, de hoy.*'

I gave him our certificate.

'*Si?*' He was giving it a good look and I indicated both our names with my forefinger – first mine, and then Youssef's. '*Es el primero dia de nuestro vida juntos.*'

I looked him in the eye. '*Entiendes?* Our first day,' I said. '*Youssef, el es mi marido. Por favor...* '

I knew he understood me. My Spanish wasn't perfect, but it was adequate.

'*No, Señora. No es possible. No visa, no entrada.*' He gave the certificate back to me.

'*Por favor...*' I was marching up and down in my heels, getting into the spirit of the moment. '*Pero, el es mi marido!*'

But he is my husband!

I was back, standing beside him, waving the certificate under his nose. '*Yo, estoy Inglesa. Mi marido tienes... en justicia, estar con migo.*'

Youssef had the *right to be with me*... that was all I was left with; all I had.

Beaky looked at me silently. I was now groping for Spanish words, having exhausted my reserve.

'He has the right to be with me,' I added for good measure. 'He's my husband.'

'No. Señora— '

'Jeannie, maybe it best stop. He getting... angry.' It was Ana. She had climbed down from her perch next to Pablo. She smiled politely at the police and took my hand in hers, leading me back to the van. I let her take me, but I was despairing.

What would we do now?

We reversed. Beaky and his mate watched us turn the van around to drive back to where we'd come from. They smirked at each other, shook their heads and walked back to their covered area.

'*Bastard!*' Youssef spat out. 'What I do bad in Spain? *Eh?*'

I was speechless. Numb.

My new husband gave me a mournful look. 'Pablo, he take us back to hotel. We stay there tonight.'

'What happens after that?' I asked.

Youssef shrugged. 'What 'appen, 'appen.'

I handed over our passports. 'Is it possible to have the same room as before? Room 121?'

'No, it taken now. We has someone that want that room.'

'Well, *we* wanted it too.' I knew I was being rude.

The hollow-eyed receptionist threw back a lock of springy hair and looked exasperated. 'It gone.'

'Already?'

'Yes.'

'But— '

'*Tsss!* I 'as Room 413. Take it?'

I pulled a face. 'Okay. Room 413 it is.' I signed us in.

I stooped to pick up my case. 'Thank you.'

'Why, Jeannie? Why— ?'

'I can't believe someone's taken our room.'

'But— '

'It doesn't matter – we're tired. Let's just get some sleep.'

'*What* happen with our room?'

'Someone's bloody got it.'

'Already they have?'

'Already.'

Youssef shrugged. 'It not really matter. Room is jus' room.'

'No, it not really matter,' I said, parrot-fashion, mimicking him. 'Let's get in that lift and get up to our new room.' I sighed. 'Bloody *hell*.'

He took the key and rolled his eyes at the receptionist.

'Sleepy time,' I said, trying to lighten the mood.

'That right.' He looked directly at me. 'We share name same now, no?'

'We do. Strange, eh?' I picked a pink paper horseshoe off his shirt collar.

'Very strange.' He mused for a second. 'You not *look* like El Mamechi. It take time get use for this.'

'You're telling *me*.'

'Uh?'

We stumbled into the lift. Once inside, tiredness overwhelmed me. I waited quietly for the lift to stop at the fourth floor. Youssef supported our luggage by anchoring his long legs around the cases.

At the first floor the doors opened to let in a stocky middle-aged man. He smiled nervously at us as the door closed.

'Going down?'

'Going up,' I said.

'I'll go with you. Not much choice really, is there,' he murmured.

'Uh?' Youssef said.

I kept my gaze fixed to the floor of the lift.

'Well, hey, it looks like you got married today.'

Youssef eyed him. 'How you know?'

'Confetti?' His gaze focused on the top of our heads. Youssef had a smattering trapped in his dark curls.

'It's still in our hair, Youssef. In fact, I think it's everywhere, in places— '

'Pablo, he put it hard down my neck.'

'Congratulations!' our man said. 'You're on your honeymoon now, then?' A brief pause. 'You don't look too happy though.'

'True,' Youssef muttered. 'It doesn't go way it mean for be. We— '

'Problems? Can I— ?'

'Nothing much anyone can do really,' I said. 'We can't get into Spain for the honeymoon so we've come back here.'

Youssef scowled. 'We check-out an' come back. Feel silly really. Spain, it not want me.'

'*And* we lost our room,' I added, still feeling peeved.

'What's the problem? No visa?'

The lift had reached the fourth floor and we all got out, Youssef dragging our luggage.

'We tried to get him in by saying he was now married to a European – *me*,' I said. 'But they, the police, didn't want to know. We had no choice but to— '

'Look, my name's Tim— '

We were standing in the corridor. Youssef was jumpy, gazing around, scanning door numbers close by.

'—I come and go a lot over the border. I'm on business and I'm going back into Spain tomorrow. What if— '

'Jeannie, our room it's at end, right at— '

'Hold on, Youssef. Just a minute.'

'What if you two come in my car with me? I can flash three European passports at the border. I have my wife's with me, as it happens, and that should do it.'

My mouth was hanging open. 'That sounds— '

'Jeannie, it be along here, this way. I'm *tired*.'

'The frontier police know me, I'm always backwards and forwards.'

I cupped my hands to my mouth. 'Youssef, come back and listen a minute. Yes... I'm tired too, but this is... important.'

'What?' He dragged himself back, leaving the luggage in the corridor. '*What?*'

'Tim here, he says he could help us. If we go with him tomorrow... ' Youssef immediately looked suspicious.

'Don't worry mate, I'm kosher. I was just suggesting that, if you meet me downstairs at, say, nine, tomorrow morning, we could take a trip over the border easy. I have my wife's passport.'

I left Youssef and Tim to thrash it out. Youssef was taking on the look of an enlightened man. I took the key from his hand, found the door to our new room at the end of the corridor and let myself in.

I went back for our luggage and dragged my case to the end of the corridor to prop the door open, returning for Youssef's carrier bags, the remaining bottle of sparkling wine chinking as I dropped the bag hard against the door of the room. Youssef was still in conversation with Tim, looking like he couldn't believe his luck. His whole body language had changed.

I left the door propped open. Once I emerged from the bathroom Youssef had at last made it to our room.

He was lolling on the bed, looking around.

'Youssef – let's get to bed now. I'm knackered.'

'Me, I knacker too. Got to get up, have breakfast

an' meet that man in the morning. He's good man I think, Gibraltar man. You know he go Spain all the time?'

'I know. He told me.'

I was getting into one side of the bed, my head throbbing.

'He have passport of wife, an'— '

'I know. He told me.'

'Uh? Well, I'm happy now, Jeannie. I get a good sleep I think.'

'We both will. Good night.' I jogged him slightly with my under-the-cover leg, and then a firm push to his arm.

At last, he got up from the bed, stretching both his arms above his head.

'True. I go to bathroom now.' He slammed the bathroom door shut as he spoke, then opened it again in a heartbeat.

'Happy Day of Wedding, Jeannie,' he said. 'It a good day, most?'

'*Very* good day – mostly,' I said. Youssef closed the door again.

I was thinking about Tim. He was taking a big chance by helping us.

It was going to be risky, and we didn't know this man.

By the time Youssef reappeared and threw himself into his side of the bed, I was nearly asleep. In no time Youssef was snoring. Unusual for him.

Images of the day's faces and events emerged from the shadows, rotating in my head... the bright room where we were married, the open register, flowers and passports spread out on the table in front of us; then sitting in clanky metal chairs drinking plonk and eating omelette and chips in the sunshine.

I closed my eyes tightly.

Carmen, and our Good Samaritan Tim, loomed large.

And Beaky Nose. I'd never forget his snooping face.

Youssef continued to snore. My heart was beating hard; I could not switch off.

A nerve throbbed in my stomach and I felt a sudden surge of dread; I stared into the darkness of the room, imagining shadowy unfamiliar shapes moving, shifting... coming towards me, rising to the ceiling. The ugly drone of snoring contributed fitting acoustics.

I was lying there a long time before I gave up and looked at my travel clock on the bedside table: One thirty... Two forty-five... Four fifteen...

'What if the police remember us?'

'No problem, Jeannie. The police change today.'

'It'll be a different shift,' said Tim. 'There's no chance of them being the same guys.'

'I really hope you're right,' I said.

We were approaching the frontier in Tim's car, and there were the obligatory two policemen standing on guard. I looked hard and could see they weren't the same men. I didn't remember seeing a moustachioed man previously, and one of these officers was wearing very light coloured trousers with his police jacket.

No sign of Beaky Nose.

Relieved, I looked sideways at Youssef seated in the back with me. He seemed shrunken, sitting motionless and looking straight ahead.

We slowed down as we neared the police, one of whom strode up to the car. I cast a nervous glance. Tim was giving a vague smile, holding up three red passports like a hand of winning cards; relaxed and nonchalant, one hand still on the steering wheel.

Our car was waved on, and we pulled away.

'Phew, Jeannie. We do it.'

'My god,' I said. 'It was *Tim*.' I touched Tim's shoulder. 'Thank you.'

Youssef sneaked a look back at the policeman now returning to his own area. 'Yes, we thank you so much.'

'No problem. Glad to help.'

'*Phewww*. We go to Spain now, Jeannie, for *luna de miel*.'

'Unbelievable,' I said, shaking my head. 'I just can't believe we've got away with it. James Bond, eat your heart— '

'Ja-mez Bond? I feel I be *him*.'

'Here's your passport back,' said Tim, handing it to me over his shoulder as he drove on. 'Drop you at Algeciras? There's a bus— '

'That right,' Youssef interrupted. 'We wait maybe one hour, an' then get bus to Nerja. I need coffee! You, Jeannie?'

I was examining the passport, just to be sure it was mine. 'Silly question.'

'It helps with being shaky, no? Coffee?'

'Would you like a coffee with us, Tim?' I said.

'No, I have to keep going. Thanks all the same.'

'We give you champagne,' Youssef announced, digging around in his carrier bag. ''ere! It remind you of us, Tim. We have bottle remain 'ere, for you. We give it.'

'Thank you. That's very kind.'

Tim struck me as being more of a champagne man than a quaffer of discount store plonk; but the thought was there.

We shook hands with Tim when he dropped us off at Algeciras Bus Station. Youssef handed over the sparkling wine like he was giving away the Crown Jewels and, picking up our luggage, we looked for the nearest *cafétéria*, always plenty to choose from.

I looked back as Tim got into his car, noting the bulk of his frame and the air of calm about him. I wondered what he thought of me and Youssef, and what he did for a living. I hadn't asked and, although he seemed very open, he hadn't offered the information.

'Strange be in Spain again, Jeannie.'

'Yeah. Gib's not one thing or the other, is it.'

'Big coffee?' he asked.

'Big coffee, yes. We'll need pesetas. Got any?'

'I have, but... ' Youssef was burrowing in his pockets.

'I have some. I always have some,' I said.

We found a table quickly.

'You... you seem sleepy, Jeannie. Tired.'

'There was a monster in the bedroom last night,' I said. 'All night.'

'Uh?'

'Making noises. Rumbling all night.'

He cocked his head to one side. 'Devil, he not be allowed come to us.'

I assumed he knew what I meant. I was never sure.

Youssef had caught the eye of a waitress and now pointed at the coffee cups on the table next to us and held up two fingers, luckily as in the Victory sign rather than a rude display.

'Pablo, he says he'll give party for us when we get there.'

'*If* we get there. It didn't look likely, did it.'

'Uh?'

'It didn't look like we would *get* to Spain. You know, the police— '

'I *know* we get to Spain. I know it. All luck bad, it's gone now, Jeannie.'

He looked around the *cafétería*, smiling. The sun was glinting through the open doorway casting long chair-leg shadows across the pale tiled floor. On the next table I noticed the sun shining through a dimpled glass, jagged and rosy faces forming; phizogs with crazy profiles, ever-changing with the sizzle of the *agua con gaz* keeping them dancing and alive. I closed my tired eyes and could still sense those swaying beings; mouths opening and closing... somehow poignant, spooky.

Our coffees arrived and Youssef asked for a sticky bun to share.

Frugal, as always.

'Thing they go better now. I know it. Our time, it

be 'ere – at last.'

'*Felicidades, Youssef y Juanita! Felicidades!*'

'Just look at the cake, Youssef! There's you and me on the top.'

'Uh?'

'*Wehhhh! Felicidades!*' In the gloom there were at least a dozen faces around us, smiling mouths working in synchronised congratulation. Only two or three people looked familiar to me.

'Where?' Youssef had his nose buried in a glass of champagne. More plonk. 'Where, Jeannie?'

'Look – the little man with the top hat, carrying his bride. See?' Youssef shifted his gaze. 'See them? There? Wonder where they got that from!'

'Ah! I see. I not know what it is. It us?'

'Yes, it us.'

He swept an arm. 'Never I think it be in basement in Spain. Me, I imagine get marry in Morocco, with all thing I know.'

I looked up. Most of the smiling faces had melted away already.

Pablo was still there. He nodded in my direction, scooped the cake from the top of the bar and came to present it to me. I took it carefully, placing both hands underneath, grateful it had a firm base. I noted the carefully placed glacé cherries studding the top of the white goo surrounding the teetering bride and groom. The groom's foothold was precarious. How much longer could he hold the bride, and how long before they both fell flat on their faces?

Pablo brushed his wet lips across my cheek and signalled to Youssef to take my camera from the bar top and take a photo of him and me holding the cake. Youssef took the camera, clutching it doubtfully. I grinned; Pablo grimaced, pointing at the bride and groom with a bony forefinger. Youssef pressed the button. Then, immediately after the blinding flash, his long legs moving uncertainly, Pablo left me holding their touching gift and shambled across the bar towards a small group of drinkers.

''e drunk,' observed Youssef. ''e take something *bad* too.'

'Oh? What's that?' I asked, placing the cake back on the bar. Youssef gave me a look.

'You enjoy, Jeannie?'

'Enjoy what?'

'This,' he said, sweeping his arm again, expressively. 'All this party.'

'Let's stay a while longer and then slide off. Pablo won't know we've gone.'

'Ah, Pablo. He know everything it 'appen. He see *everything*.'

'Really?'

'Really. It true.'

Someone was approaching; with no suggestion of a preamble, a young Spanish girl seized Youssef and hugged him fiercely.

'Carlota! *Que tal?*'

They obviously knew each other very well. They spoke animatedly, barely drawing breath. Pouty Lips Carlota shrieked as he lifted her into the air, her legs flailing as he held her under the armpits, her breasts pressed against his face.

I wasn't the only one who noticed.

I moved away to speak to Ana, who was sitting alone at the bar. She poured me another glass of champagne. She could see I was irritated, but said nothing.

'When you go 'ome, Jeannie?'

'Soon, I think. After this glass of champers.'

'No – I mean, when you go England?'

'Oh. Well, the day after tomorrow.' I took a gulp of champagne and tried not to make a face as its acidity hit the back of my tongue.

I turned to her. 'Not a very long honeymoon, is it.'

'No. Can you not stay in Spain more long?'

'Not really.' I was watching Youssef having a drinking competition with Carlota. They were grappling with a Yard of Ale, or the Spanish equivalent – the ale being replaced by red wine. I'd never seen Youssef so lively.

He looked my way. 'Come drink *vino* with me, Jeannie!'

'At least he knows I'm still around, Ana. That's something.'

'Sorry?' she said.

She didn't understand me. I expanded: 'He can do it without me. I'd much rather sit here.'

'*Jeannie!*' roared Youssef. 'Come! It *good*. Never I do before!'

'That's obvious.'

'Sorry, Jeannie?' asked Ana, looking worried.

Someone had grabbed my camera and was busy finishing off the rest of the film.

Half amused, half annoyed, I looked at Ana, who had her own problems to deal with. We could see that Pablo was half-crouched on the floor, propped up against the side of the bar. His head bent forward, he was vomiting. Ana tut-tutted. He looked up suddenly, his hair wild, his wide-open eyes swivelling in their sockets.

Ana turned away shaking her head.

'How long it take you travel from Algeciras today?' she said.

'Oh... four, five hours.'

'And you return same way?'

'Yes. Bus, then I fly from Gib.'

'And Youssef?'

'He gets the boat back. To Morocco of course.'

'Yes?'

'Then I write to the Home Office, enclosing our marriage certificate.' I shrugged.

'Long time be on bus,' she said, throwing back her curls, giving a smile showing acres of teeth and gums. 'Arrive today, go back— '

'Look!' I interrupted. 'The cake's on the floor!'

It was late.

'Why you let me drink?' Youssef demanded, stumbling along Post Office Street. 'Why let me— '

'Who was I to stop you?'

'Too many champagne, too many wine. Too many *everythin'*.'

'Our party. That's what parties are about.'

'I feel *terrible,* Jeannie. I want go 'ome early, but you not want.'

'Hold on a minute – don't blame *me*. We agreed we would go, but there you were, being chatted up by that girl with the tits, and next thing I know you're drinking the red stuff like... like— '

'Uh?'

'—like there's no bloody tomorrow. Let's just get home.'

'Wish it be bit more near. Long way to— ' He stubbed his toe on a step and I caught his arm as he lurched towards me.

'*Mierda!*'

'Ha! Mind how you go.'

'I not really want drink like *that* 'gain.'

'Good party though,' I said. 'Hey – remember the cake throwing? Who threw it first, you or Pablo?'

'Uh? *Our* cake?'

'Our cake. Someone threw it.'

'I not remember... Oh, yes. It was Pablo. I pick up from floor an' throw back, an'... '

'What a terrible ending to our lovely cake,' I said. 'And what has become of the bride and groom on top?'

'Uh?'

'The little man with his wife – *them.*'

'It us! *Shame.* They gone, for *ever...* '

'Gone forever. Unless, of course, someone picked them up,' I said, 'rescued them.'

'No, no one do that. It too many mess in there, an' every person they drunk.'

'Maybe someone did,' I said, patting my handbag as I tottered along, the clip-clop of my heels echoing in the silence; being a good wife, carefully holding onto Youssef's arm to steady him. I'd unearth them later, our doppelgangers. Good souvenirs, a reminder of a sweet yet curious time in our lives. Unique.

People would find it hard to believe. Too bizarre.

Clip-clopping some more, and then... I heard an almighty crash from behind us. My skin tingled with shock. It sounded like a car had driven into a brick wall; but there were no cars around. The street was deserted except for we two drunken people hobbling home.

I froze, my heart leaping in my breast; then looked back cautiously.

'Christ!'

There was a heap of rubble on the pavement, four or five doorways from where we stood. Then I looked up. I could see that part of a concrete overhang had disintegrated. Suddenly, with no warning. I felt that cold drop, that *plummet* inside my belly; the realisation of what could have happened to us a few seconds earlier. I was trembling.

Newly married – almost killed.

'*Jesus*, Youssef. We could've been walking underneath.'

'Uh?' He was just ahead now, craning round, oblivious.

'That roof thing collapsed! *Look!*'

'Oh.'

'Five seconds ago we were *there*.'

'Let's get home, Jeannie. I *so* tired.'

'No one's come out to have a look... '

How had it happened? It was like something malevolent was playing games.

'Don't you think that's strange?' I said.

'No one they worry, they use to this.' He gave the heap of concrete a cursory look, turned away and carried on walking unsteadily, his feet colliding. 'Nothing for do with devil.'

'Weird day,' I said.

'Never he find us here, him.'

'He can travel... '

'Let's get *home*.'

'That's where we're going. Keep walking.'

'Uh?'

'Too much talk of the devil.'

'Me, I want honeymoon be perfect, Jeannie,' he said, wiping his brow with the back of his hand. 'Bit dodgy so far, no?'

'Dodgy, yes,' I said. 'In every way.'

'It get better,' he said, 'by tomorrow.'

'Hope so.'

I was looking ahead at a man at the very end of the street; he'd just appeared. He was tall and bulky, walking steadily. As he came nearer, under the lamplight – I was still looking intently – I had a good view of his face. He had a long beaky nose and appeared to be hurrying towards us...

Surely not?

Mish Mash

Tangier
April 1991

The centre of Tangier was just a short walk from the Hotel *Solazur*. As we left the main entrance, bowed out by a smiling fez-topped commissionaire, we were set upon by a gaggle of dirty faced, ragged little boys; maybe three or four.

'*Pen*, Monsieur. Madame, *pen*,' pleaded two of them in unison, both making wiggly, writing gestures in the air.

'*Dirham?*' A sad face with enormous eyes looked up at me, a thin little hand creeping my way. Youssef looked straight ahead, ignoring them, walking smartly along the boulevard, dragging me with him.

'They look like they could do with a bit of help.'

'Ignore, Jeannie. They keeping beg if you look.'

'*Dirham*! Monsieur, *dirham*!' They were beginning to realise we were something of a challenge.

The boys kept good pace with us – jigging mostly alongside Youssef, who continued to ignore them. There was chanting now:

'*Dirham.. Dirham.. Dirham.. Dirham..* et pen, Madame? Plume?... *Plume?*'

'Francais?' The tallest boy, alongside Youssef, touched his arm – just a light touch, intended to get his attention and evoke sympathy. Monsieur exploded. He discharged the most vicious sounding Arabic and, in a mad scramble, the boys ran off full pelt, one or two looking behind them in disbelief.

'They think I'm French. *Tourist.*'

'I know... Monsieur!'

I laughed. Youssef half laughed, taking my hand and squeezing it, at the same time quickening his pace.

We headed towards the row of little shops coming up on our left, selling ceramics, rugs and souvenirs. This side of the coast road was well developed – shops elbow-to-elbow, with large and lavish hotels rubbing shoulders with others just as grand. The Hotel Rif, further along, I knew was famous.

A row of robed, alert owners sat on rickety chairs outside their premises, smiling benignly at likely customers as they approached. Youssef was weighing it up; where to go first.

We moved forward. The shop owner's face became instantly alive at our appearance. His mouth broke into a smile, the emergence of his black, badly broken teeth remodelling his amiable face into something that suddenly was not.

'Welcome to my bizi-ness. Nice price for you. Very nice.'

Again, Youssef was thought of as a foreigner.

He, enjoying the anonymity, was going to leave it as long as he could before he had to speak to the man. He picked up a large leather handbag, turning it over and over, aware that the man's eyes were on him.

'For lady?' said the shop owner. 'Nice price.' Youssef abruptly dropped the bag back on the display and walked to the other end of the shop near to where I was examining some corroded jewellery.

'For lady?' I echoed, pleased that he might be thinking of buying me something. 'For me?'

'Wait, Jeannie,' he said, flashing me a look. 'Not now.' And he went back to his game, picking up something else, with sideways glances at the approaching shop owner.

When Youssef did speak it was in French. The shop owner immediately responded in the same tongue.

I wandered off to examine the clutter of chipped and dusty ceramics. Some of the pieces were beautiful but had not been looked after. I imagined large cardboard boxes or crates, stuffed with perhaps straw, packed with ceramics... being tossed around from place to place.

I was listening with half an ear to what was going on at the front of the shop. I picked up a little blue and yellow pot, thick with dust, and nearly dropped the ill-fitting lid. I replaced the pot quickly. I could hear that Youssef had finally reverted to his own language:

'...*floos...floos...*'

This word, *floos*, must have been one of the first Arabic words I was aware of. *Floos* cropped up again and again in the guttural and rasping, yet strangely attractive, conversations in Arabic all around me. *Floos* means money. It seemed to me to be their main topic of conversation – the making of money, and the letting go of it; and quite probably the lack of it.

I gave up examining dusty ceramics, nothing appealed. We weren't buying anything.

Youssef told me later he was given a blow by blow account of the history of the shop and what he thought about the Government. Youssef, though always interested in these things, had trouble extricating himself from the man – who remembered, too late, that we were potential customers, and swiftly halved the price of everything in his shop, calling for us to come back, then running after us...

'I give you nice price, very nice price!'

But we'd gone.

'Not nice things in there, Jeannie.'

'I know. What a mish mash!'

'Uh? Mish mash is *Arabic* word!'

'Is it?'

'What means it, in English?'

'When everything is all over the place.' I demonstrated, tumbling my fingers. 'A mess. A muddle.'

'There's mish mash in the market.' He took my hand and pulled me along, past the remainder of the parade of shops. 'I show you. Wait see what mish mash it is.'

I'd learnt that bread was *hobs*-something-or-other, and okay was *wuh-huh*.

It was a start.

And his family thought the Queen of England was married to John Major.

Youssef's long legs managed much longer strides than mine ever could. The sun was high in the sky and without mercy.

Beyond the other side of the road lay a long stretch of unspoilt smooth beach, fringed by clusters of palm trees at the roadside as well as along the central island of the boulevard. Groups of low square buildings sat erratically on the nearside of the beach, serving as beach restaurants, though there was no immediate indication outside that they were. I missed Spain's flamboyant advertising, the in-your-face-ness of that country's approach. I had been wrong to think that Morocco was going to be similar.

I was an innocent abroad.

Morocco certainly was a foreign country.

We reached Rue Touahin, turning sharp right into Rue Semmarin.

The Street of Gold.

'Easy peasy get 'ere,' Youssef said triumphantly. 'We not need your map book.'

'It's handy to have, just in case.'

His eyes were shining. 'Nice things buy 'ere.'

'It's got forty-four jewellery shops, this street,' I said, patting my shoulder bag. 'I looked it up.'

'Good gold. It all you need know.'

We took a look inside, intending to be very quick.

I fancied a *Hand of Fatima*, a very simple version without the all-seeing eye in the centre. I knew it was for good fortune, and I felt we could do with some of that. Youssef took far too long sorting out his small change to pay for it. He seemed so reluctant. Eventually, he handed over a palmful of change.

I slipped Fatima's hand into a pocket.

'Why does she have two thumbs?'

He didn't answer.

I found the souk a jolt after the relative calm of the boulevard on the seafront, and we attracted our share of attention: more wide-eyed grubby children begging for biros; insistent, vociferous traders; an unexpected brazen interest in my bare legs.

I glimpsed stray rubber gloves reaching towards cauliflowers; packs of scouring pads nestling next to sheer nylon knickers; and streamers of colourful headscarves overflowing into basins of loose brown tea leaves. There were plenty of clothes rails, mottled with rust, packed tight with garish, embroidered kaftans. Nearby, a tiny, filthy ginger kitten sat quietly on a piece of sacking in the gutter.

An amplified *Muezzin* blared suddenly from the local mosque, calling Muslims to prayer – just as we'd reached olives on trestle tables – cleverly built into pyramids, glistening on enormous platters: pinky hues mixed with chopped garlic, black olives with chilli seeds, and *olive*-green olives. A delicious sharp, tangy aroma. Curly chillies and lemon wedges embellished the bases. One trader seized a handful and offered them in his knotty hand. His cloudy eyes locked with mine,

so I had to stop to sample them.
    I said 'Buy some?'
    'Not now. Another time.'

Cutting through a side street, we were in Rue de la Plage, the road which would take us back to the Hotel *Solazur*, but Youssef changed course and we were again walking through cobbled streets into the *petit socco*.
    'So – where's your mish mash?'
    'Just wait.'
    My anticipation grew. A gift?
    His tarpaulin spread before him, there sat the denture trader; snug at his feet, sets of teeth grouped artistically, the outside ones facing inwards, almost like a stage set. A full mint tea glass stood steaming to one side. Some of the teeth looked broken and blackened, but Youssef, getting impatient, assured me someone would want to buy them.
    'Where does he get them?'
    'Where you think?'
    The man picked up a full set to make them chatter in his hand. We laughed, and walked on to the nearby fruit and vegetables quarter.
    'Wait 'ere… '
    I grinned.
    Bananas. It had to be. His favourite, hanging in huge bunches from metal hooks. I remembered how he'd been so pleased to buy them cheap in Woolwich market, hoarding them in the fridge at home. I could make out a heap of smooth-skinned avocados – *my*

favourite. But, no, he was reaching for something else. His broad back hid from me what he was doing, and soon he clinched the deal with the stallholder.

'See, Jeannie.' He turned towards me. ''ere – mish mash!' he said triumphantly, holding up a bulging transparent bag of rosy apricots. 'We say *mushamash.*'

'*Oh.*'

'Daddy and Mummy, this they like,' he said. '*Lovely* present – but will have to give to Aunt Safia this time. Very nice for her!'

On the Beach

Tangier
April 1991

The afternoon before we were due to leave Tangier, we had a ramble along the seafront boulevard to the shops. Youssef picked out three kaftans he thought might be suitable for me. Red with green panels? Orange with purple stitching? Grey edged with turquoise? I dismissed the first two straight away, and the third was far too small.

Simple blues caught my eye. I tried on a sky-blue cotton kaftan which fitted perfectly. It had white looped stitching round the scoop neck, also on the edges of the loose short raglan sleeves, and all around the hem, which was split an inch or two at each side.

'Just enough room to get into it, but now, *well...*' I grumbled, struggling to take it off over my head. Youssef's arms were draped over the changing room curtain rail helping me ease off the kaftan, tugging away, not caring that he was causing a minor stir in the shop.

'I'll have to stop eating for a while. I blame the

cous cous.'

'You strungle, Jeannie. Really, need zip.'

Back in the hotel room Youssef tut-tutted. 'You look like a waiter, Jeannie.'

'What?' I twirled and preened in the mirror wearing my new blue kaftan. It would help me blend in.

'You think... hair *up* looks better?' I asked, still twisting and turning, flipping my hair up with one arm.

'It same as waiter wear here in 'otel.'

'What?'

'This kaftan you have.' He tugged at the fabric. 'Same as *waiter*, exact same.' He sighed in exasperation.

'*No!*'

'We call *kandura*, this thing. Exact same as waiter– '

'Well, it can't be helped. I won't look like a waiter back in England though, will I?'

'You wear this in England?'

'Of course. Nice and cool during the summer, if we have one this year.'

'*Aiwa*. England too bloody much rain, yes.'

From behind Youssef came closer to me, so close he was breathing on my neck. 'Jeannie,' he said slyly, 'if I give you tray, you go get dinner for me?'

'Get away with you!' I made out to cuff him around the head. 'At least I'm not wearing baggy trousers with it, am I, like the waiters.'

'Uh? Oh, trouser. You want some?'

'No! But, let me tell you, I'd give anything for a coffee.'

We went down to the beach that afternoon. I couldn't wait to spread out my beach paraphernalia, relax, and feel the sun on my skin.

It didn't take long to scramble out of my canary yellow mini skirt and take off the matching midriff-baring tee-shirt. I felt slightly self-conscious. In a new blue cotton bikini, I sat on my large multi-coloured Spanish towel, my face held to the sun. I ran the fine grains of sand through my fingers, thinking back to my childhood beach holidays on the south coast of England. And, later, the beaches in Spain.

I'd never been on an African beach before. I looked from side to side, taking in what was going on around us. There wasn't much remarkable to see. I remembered reading that the Krays had spent time in Tangier in the early '60s, enjoying the climate, the drug scene and back-alley fleshpots. The thought sent a shiver through me. A long forgotten grainy black & white photo I'd seen in a book came to mind: The Twins on Tangier beach with their retinue.

I lay down on my towel, digging a hollow in the sand with my backside to get comfortable, wriggling around to the extent I disturbed a slumbering Youssef lying on his towel next to me.

'How can you drop off to sleep so easily in a public place?'

'What?'

I sat up and looked along the sweep of the beach.

'Have you ever heard of the Kray Twins?'

'Uh?'

I knew he hadn't. How *could* he.

I could imagine this being the area where the Krays and entourage lounged, laughed and chilled out, getting drunk on whisky; perhaps this very spot of the sandy beach, Ronnie and Reggie plotting and scheming and making treacherous deals.

I heard a torrent of Arabic from somewhere along the beach. Looking sidelong again, I could see a group of men larking around. The shouting came nearer, from behind – angry, agitated. My skin tingled; I felt the present-day danger of Morocco, and Tangier in particular, and was glad to be there with one of its own.

'What you think, Jeannie? What in your head?' Youssef was lying on his side looking at me.

'It's no place for foreign women. That's what I'm thinking.' I lay back down on the sand, positioning myself on my towel with care.

'In Morocco?'

'Yes, Morocco.'

'True.'

No use mentioning my musings to Youssef; he hadn't heard of Marilyn Monroe or John F. Kennedy, let alone the Kray Twins. He did know about Elvis though, but possibly only because one of his cousins had been told he looked so much like him, or so he claimed.

'Uh, Jeannie? Nothing more?'

'Nothing much. Just... glad to be here.'

'I glad you be here too.' He laid his hand briefly on mine and then quickly withdrew, back to his rucked-up towel on the sand to lie down again. I examined his profile as he lay soaking up the sun's rays. His nose was shiny, his cheeks rosy.

His eyes opened. He lunged at me, taking me by surprise, then quickly flopped back down onto his towel feigning exhaustion.

I stretched my arms out to the sun, slowly easing my back off the sand. The heat was intense.

'It hot, Jeannie. Not touch it.'

'Uh?' I said, surprised *that* word was coming out of my mouth. 'Touch what?'

'Sun. Not to touch.' He laughed at his own joke. I found his schoolboy quips funny and endearing; I was hoping the next interviewer in Rabat would think the same when he returned – or, at least he'd be more in control this time.

Youssef was still grinning at his words. Again, I looked at his profile. He swatted a fly as it buzzed around his mouth and he suddenly scratched his nose vigorously.

'You thirsty, Jeannie?' He was restless now, suddenly sitting up on his towel, closely examining the skin on his arms with that familiar totally engrossed look, brow creased into deep furrows.

A water seller walked by, shouting and whistling. He was wearing a large tassel-edged hat made of leather, and had skin that looked much the same. Youssef was on his feet instantly. He closely inspected the seal on the chilled two-litre bottle he was buying, making sure it was intact, taking his time before he handed over his money.

'They thief, these people. They put water from tap an' sell. I make sure every time is okay.' He snapped open the bottle, putting it to his lips greedily, guzzling, the water flowing onto his bare chest.

'Moroccans on the cheat, eh? *Water* cheats.' I had to smile.

Youssef offered me the bottle. I took it.

'What *would* I do without you?' I said, putting the bottle to my mouth.

'You not last long here, Jeannie – not for two minute. Really. Get poisoned by somethin' quick, I'm sure.'

'It's not the water, it's the people who would worry me. I wouldn't know who to trust.'

'Trust no person.' He took the bottle back, taking another long swig from it, his lips, chin and chest glistening with water. I took the bottle from him, screwed on the cap and put it in the shade of my floppy straw beach bag. He rubbed vigorously at his chest with the palm of his hand, flicked water from his chin, grunted, gave a cursory tweak to his crumpled towel and settled back down.

I laughed.

'Why you laugh at me?'

'No reason.' I backtracked, aware of the possibility of denting his dignity. 'Well... really, it's just so nice to be here on the beach at last. Something I'll remember.'

We were travelling to Beni Ahmed the next day to see Mummy and Daddy. I'd met them only once before, in Tangier, when we'd first travelled to Morocco to keep our appointment at the Consulate. I had bad memories of the interviews there; and mixed feelings about that initial onslaught of *people* and cultural norms. So difficult to be composed, to keep a smiling face. So much a stranger in a strange land.

We stayed on the beach too long. My skin was beginning to tighten and I feared the after-effects. 'I don't want to end up really burnt.'

'Not me. I not go red.'

'You're looking red to me. Cooked. We both are.' I reached for my tee-shirt. 'Even with the sun cream it gets to you eventually. Better get out of it now.'

'He got to his feet and picked up his towel, shaking it out in my direction. 'We go anyway. Need eat. *Arwah!*' Then he paused. 'What matter with you, Jeannie?'

'*Sand!* All over me. Why d'you do that?'

As I gathered up my beach gear, Youssef had a thought and rushed off in the direction of a café set further back on the beach. He reappeared minutes later, speeding across the hot sand with what looked like a large green beach ball. He tossed it high into the air, catching it deftly each time. However, as he neared me, he lost his concentration and the ball fell with a thud to the sand.

'For eat. An' for skin.'

The green ball was a watermelon and it had split. It was very ripe. Youssef yanked it apart, then tore it into rough segments with his hands. He put one slice to his mouth, noisily sucking and chewing on the pink flesh, eating the pips. He lowered what was left of it, looking very satisfied, with pips and shreds of pink melon round his mouth, nose and chin. I laughed out loud.

'Why you laugh?'

'Well, it *is* funny. You can't see yourself.'

He wasn't happy with me but was intent on carrying on with his plan. He took another wedge of melon, moved over behind me and started to rub my bare back with it. Briskly.

'*Ouch!*' I moved away.

'For skin. Good for skin, after being in sun.'

'Not when that skin is covered in sand! It *scratches. Jesus!*'

I struggled into my new kaftan. My head took a long time to appear through the top opening, my arms flailing about to get through the armholes. I could feel my face burning with the sun, and with annoyance and frustration. 'It bloody *hurt*, Youssef!' My lower back twinged badly again, stopping me momentarily as I pulled the fabric down over my legs.

He was standing in the same spot, looking at me, genuinely puzzled. 'What?'

'See you later,' I said.

I finished gathering up my things and walked away.

Dinner was being served in the hotel restaurant. We sat at a table in the corner in silence. Opposite me Youssef shifted in his seat; his leg swung across under the table, kicking me hard in the knee. I flinched. He carried on eating.

'You just kicked me.'

'No.'

'Didn't you notice? You *must've* realised.'

'*No*. Well... it not matter. Just my leg.'

'It *does* matter. Jesus *Christ*.'

'Jeannie— '

'I have never, ever heard you say sorry for anything. D'you know that?'

'It's nothing. It's only me, Youssef.'

'Nothing? Is this how you treat women, like they don't matter?'

But by now he'd gone into one of his sulks, his face turned away, head down, fiddling with his fingernails. Shuttered. I stared at him. He'd caught a lot of sun and looked sore. I felt slighted, angry, confused.

I fled.

Later, I tracked Youssef down to our room. He was sitting on the edge of the bed, his head in his hands. He wouldn't respond to my cajoling, and just as I was about to walk out he muttered something through his fingers...

'You... you not try be part of my country... '

'I do my best! Let's face it, you don't always let me know what's *happening*.'

'Uh?'

'*Do* you!'

Youssef leapt to his feet, waving his arms dramatically, his eyes blazing. I stood my ground, feeling wretched and aware of how ridiculous, and precarious, the situation was. He raised an arm towards me and I flinched. I backed off but he turned away, shaking his head.

'For God's *sake*, Youssef.'

'You don't *try!*'

'How can you *say* that! Remember how you were in *London? Eh?*'

'I was okay in London. You... you think you be my *teacher!*'

'There was so much you needed to know! You didn't want to listen – I did my *best*.'

'I try to listen... '

'You ignore me here, so much. Patronising when you do bother to speak. I know you get sick of translating... but what can I do? That's not *on*. Bloody lack of respect.'

'You not trying hard enough here. You laugh at my culture... Hand of Fatima, she's special. You think it's just a little... little... '

'I asked you about her – about Fatima. Didn't you hear? I had to read up to find out for myself.'

He gawked at me.

'You were bloody hopeless in London, awkward, insulting, insensitive... Not *trying!*'

London... Morocco. Morocco... London...

Backwards and forwards the insults flew. Like two dogs with a meaty bone, we to'ed and fro'ed with caustic accusations. Finally, we slumped onto the side of the bed and burst into tears, with Youssef sobbing harder than I was, tears streaking his face and dripping from his chin.

'Never I think it be like this, Jeannie. I think we be

okay. I bring you here an' you make... trouble. I'm *sick* of translation all the time...'

'*Trouble!*' I yelled. 'You look after me, but only when you want to. I feel stranded so much of the time... and you do strange *things!*' I grimaced. 'Did you notice I'm a grown *woman?*'

'Let's not fight. Please, no more.' He grabbed my hand.

'No more,' I whispered. Using my free hand, I wiped away his tears with my fingertips, feeling surprised and touched by this sudden vulnerability.

We lay huddled on the bed, hot and clammy. I reached up to turn off the overhead light and we lay in each other's arms, exhausted. Youssef was soon asleep but I lay thinking. Why should it be so difficult, this relationship?

This couldn't go on.

When I did extricate myself from his grasp to get up to go to the bathroom, my back was hurting so much I gasped with pain. It was difficult to straighten up. What rigid Moroccan beds had started, the stresses of that day had finished off. My back felt like a mass of knotted muscle. I fumbled for painkillers and searched for my bottle of water.

'Oh *God*,' I moaned. '*Please.*'

I climbed slowly back into the bed, desolate.

Continuing flashes of pain in my lower back. Outside I could hear the sounds of shouting and laughter. It wasn't that late but it felt like it could have been in the middle of the night. I wanted to blot out what had happened and wake up to a brand new day.

Youssef murmured in his sleep, laughing softly at something in his dreams. While I, on the other side of the bed – the two single beds we had pushed together – had settled into a foetal position, hugging myself for comfort, willing the pain to subside so that I could get some sleep.

Sleep evaded me. At dawn I lay motionless as the *Muezzin* began his call to the people of Tangier. I looked across the expanse to where Youssef remained so still, and edged slowly across, inch by inch, to put my arms around him. He mumbled quietly and slept on.

Beni Ahmed

A rural commune
in the Rif Mountains
April 1991

From the *Blue City* of Chefchaouen – known locally as Chaouen – it took the best part of an hour in a *taksi* to reach Beni Ahmed.

I'd kept a keen eye on the views from the mountain passes, with layer after layer of craggy yet verdant landscape unfolding in our wake as we climbed higher and higher. Earlier, the *taksi* from Tangier to Chaouen, shared with other travellers, took forever; fortunately, this was the last lap.

Our *taksi* became oven-like as we reached the heights, and this with the windows rolled down. Our driver, half his limp body hanging out of his open window, grunted as we skidded to a halt in a cloud of dust.

Youssef looked alert.

'Is this it?' I asked.

'This Beni Ahmed.' Youssef winked. 'But not yet.'

'What?'

'It as far as *taksi* it go, Jeannie.'

The driver grinned, holding his hand out for payment. 'Beni Ahmed!' he announced, a mix of mirth and, I thought, scorn.

God forsaken place?

Youssef paid him and leapt out, seizing our bags from the boot.

The dust track gave way to bumpy ground. Luckily, I'd abandoned any shoes with heels. My new Moroccan sandals were holding out well.

Youssef guided me. 'Careful, Jeannie. Careful. It bit jerky here.'

He looked up and suddenly waved an arm. There was Daddy, skullcap clamped on, his grey and brown striped *djellabah* billowing out behind him as he strode across the rough terrain to greet us. His eyes shone, hands already extended to take ours into his.

'Daddy! Daddy!' Youssef looked at me to see if I was smiling. 'He don't know *what* I say... but he don't care, just he know it's us. See? See he smiles, Jeannie?'

Daddy reached us.

After a long embrace, Youssef and Daddy exchanged a few words of formal greeting, touching hands in a brief grip, then using the elegant gesture that always held my attention, brushing the palm of the right hand over the chest to show sincerity, from the heart.

Daddy then embraced me enthusiastically.

'Daddy, he not know what time we come, so he stand here for three hours to wait.'

'Three *hours?*'

'He don't want to miss us. He's so pleased we decide to come.'

'I can see that. He's bursting with it.'

It was quite a walk to the house, and as we three passed through brambly bushes and over unexpected dips and hillocks, Youssef and Daddy lifted me along between them as if I was a child or an invalid. I squealed and gasped from time to time when the going got rough.

'Daddy, he say we should have think for family 'orse. 'orse can carry you easy.'

In the near distance, as if part of a film episode, Mummy was standing at an open door, hands on hips, squinting in the sun. A low stone wall separated us from the house and we had to change course to get to the opening. Suddenly we were in the front yard. Before we could reach her, a swarm of chickens advanced.

'These birds, they think we have dinner for them.'

'It's always the way with chickens.'

'Ignore, Jeannie. Don't be scared.'

'I'm not scared of them. They're funny.'

The chickens collected in a gaggle at our feet, their sharp little eyes watching us, heads flicking this way and that, busy fluffing up their back feathers and flexing their wings. Daddy and Youssef strode through them. As I, too, passed they looked puzzled, or disappointed we had no food for them. Or perhaps that was just my imagination.

The house was a basic, low building which had been added to over the years. The outside had a rough, uneven surface, whitewashed, and was topped by corrugated metal sheets with brick and straw padding packed in beneath. We stepped inside, through the heavily painted blue door, Mummy leading the way. We passed a room on the right and I sneaked a quick look; the interior walls were painted a deep turquoise – large brush strokes still apparent, going in every direction. Chunky, low beams were painted a darker shade of turquoise. The overall impression was cave-like, but curiously cosy; in homage to the blue-painted houses in Chaouen no doubt.

There was a circular table placed in front of the usual low fabric couches. A large colour photo in a yellow circular frame was mounted on the main wall: Youssef, smouldering over his shoulder at the camera like Brando or James Dean. Strange that he'd never heard of either of them.

Mummy led us out to the back into the yard, which had a clothesline running across diagonally. Several pairs of pantaloons hung limply; and three pairs of socks, individually pegged, dripped vigorously.

'Jeannie, there's no toilet here. Must go up the mountain outside.'

'Oh? A bit chilly at times, I bet.'

'Yes. And best climb high, go away from house.'

'I'll have to make sure I've got tissues, or even that loo roll we have in the bags.'

'English woman, they soft Jeannie. Them, they want everythin', need nothin'.'

'That's harsh.'

'Well, it not be needed. People who live here, they're okay.'

'That's just *it*, isn't it? They're used to it. It's a different way of life.'

'You here now, so you must get used for these things.'

I tried to keep a pleasant look on my face. Mummy was looking worried. I turned back to him: 'Why doesn't Daddy build a toilet? A little shed, outside?'

'He thinks to do that. But, all bloody neighbours, they want use too, so no good.'

I laughed, imagining an orderly queue of the locals in Daddy's yard. The thought had obviously occurred to Youssef too and his mouth crinkled, ready to slide into a smile. He put his arm around me briefly, squeezing my shoulder.

Youssef turned to face his parents, suddenly very formal. 'Mummy Soudia an' Daddy Ahmed – here's Jeannie,' he said, smiling. 'Of course, you seen before.'

Both beamed as they heard their names.

'Daddy is one of the chief persons here. All others respect him.'

They were tall. Mummy, swathed in three headscarves, was in all white, and broken teeth showed through her nervous gummy smile. Her face broke into a thousand creases. Daddy was an older version of his son but without Youssef's head of dark curls. There was a skullcap on his shiny balding head and unexpectedly he had eyes that looked in different directions.

I moved forward and embraced them in turn, exchanging the customary three kisses on the cheeks. Daddy took my hand, holding it in his for a few seconds; he released it at just the point where it could seem impolite not to.

'How did they meet?'

'They know themselves all their lives. They're cousins.'

Mummy scuttled away to make the mint tea.

'Ya Ya knows we're here,' Youssef added.

'Does she?'

'She sends her regards. She wants to know everything. She never leave Chaouen very often, just get the bus to Tangier to see other lot of family.' He laughed. 'She little bit jealous you're here – but she approves you. She thinks you make good wife, strong – not skinny like some women she see in European magazines.'

'That's a relief.'

'She thinks you'll really, really look after her boy... that's me, of course. I'm special, she thinks.'

'Well... of course I will,' I said. 'I'll do my best.'

I remembered encountering Ya Ya on my first trip to Tangier to meet the family over two years before – a tiny, shrunken old lady with a knitted brow; she'd fixed her deep-set chocolate eyes on mine, the deep lines around her eyes runny with melted kohl.

She seemed fierce. But I knew that a hard life had left its mark on her.

Ya Ya had stroked my hand, squinting to see my engagement ring paired with a plain gold band, sitting rather insignificantly on my left hand, suddenly laughable in its British high street lacklustre.

We sat on rickety chairs and debated the dilemma of the Queen of England being married to John Major. Daddy wanted to know why Mr Major hadn't stepped in and claimed the top job for himself. It should've been a simple explanation but it wasn't at all – even Youssef was baffled.

'Do you think,' I said 'they thought that the word *Major* meant something to them, like it's an Army term and he's an important person?'

'Never they know this word, Jeannie. It mean nothing to them. All they know is that the Queen of England has a husband an' they think it's John Major.'

'Of course,' I said. 'What was I *thinking*.'

We moved on to other things.

'Jeannie, I ask them if they hear of Nelson Mandela. They say, of course.'

'How?'

'On radio, when they were in Chaouen, and photos in newspapers. All the world know.'

'I see.'

'I said, that man looks like our King Hassan, you think? Like *brothers!* They agree, and Mummy says it's for a reason. Always it's for some kind of reason. Good, or bad. Both these man are here to be important. Mummy says, that's all we need to know.'

Youssef made it clear with his body language that the conversation was now at an end. He didn't want me to try to pursue it further; and he was probably sick of translating back and forth.

The afternoon was drawing on.

We climbed open whitewashed steps – with no safety-rail – going up to the quite bare, cool bedrooms. We'd been instructed to get some rest before dinner. We slept for not much more than an hour and woke just as the sun was setting. Their oil lamps would be lit very soon.

In the very blue dining room, I was expecting more cous cous, but the meal Mummy Soudia cooked was delicious juicy chicken with vegetables and a bowl of olives to dip into. Hunks of dry bread were arranged on a piece of paper.

'*Chokraan*, Mummy,' I said.

Thanking Mummy for the meal was really heartfelt. I explained that all the fresh air was making me extra hungry.

Youssef translated the part about the stimulating fresh air.

Mummy piped up with a shrill response immediately.

'She choose the fattest chicken here to cook, Jeannie,' said Youssef. 'They want you to really enjoy your meal with us today – they bit disappointed when you don't eat much in Tangier, that time at Aunt Safia's daughter's house. You need to try more hard.'

Appealing

Denton, East Sussex
May 1991

The kettle was just beginning to boil. I stood and watched the steam rising, the vapour going into a swirling mist before the kettle snapped itself off. I remained where I was, hands clasped together, unable to focus or think.

I was a robot with no purpose or expectation.

I felt the house had barely been lived in as yet. Moving down from London to the seaside had been a great idea, and it happened quickly... and just before Youssef needed to get back to Morocco in compliance with his six-month UK tourist visa the year before. He'd spent barely a fortnight in our squat end-of-terrace red-brick; he'd loved the proper garden wrapping around on three sides, with a grassy slope going up to an uneven wooded area and onto The Sussex Downs. He'd immediately named the wood *The Jungle*.

The phone rang suddenly making me jump. It was Youssef. 'You phoned at exactly the right time. I'm feeling... terrible.'

His voice was low. 'You know how I feel I, Jeannie. I don't need say.'

'You know how I feel too. Tearing my hair out. It's so strange here without you.'

'Everything strange.'

'Where are you?'

'Tangier.'

'I know. But whereabouts?'

'Outside Marco Polo, the agent for travel. Remember where?'

'Of course.'

'It takes me *ages* for get through, this phone it keep take money.'

I pulled a face to myself.

'You see me waving? On step, at *hotel*?'

'I did.' I'd never forget how choked up I felt. Another parting.

'I watch your coach go an' I go speak to a man about buy new mint teapot for Daddy.'

'Does he need a new one?'

'No. But always it good have new.'

A pause as I smiled.

'You gone back to work today, Jeannie?'

'Yes, I did. Took forever to get home. There was a cow on the line.'

'A... what?'

'A cow on the line, at Southease and Rodmell. You know, just this side of Lewes Station.'

'Cow?'

'Yes, a cow. Crazy, eh?'

There was a slight thump. I thought we'd been disconnected.

'Youssef?'

'Jeannie?'

'Did something happen your end?'

'Me, I change ear Jeannie. There's a queue here... behind me... '

'I see.'

'Yes, better go. This phone eats many money. All family, they send regards also. And, Jeannie— ' This time we really were cut off.

I'd been home for two days and couldn't shake off the feeling of hopelessness that I had. It seemed that I had brought the good weather back with me but that was no comfort at all, it was far too hot to travel, and to work in a sweaty office. My blue kaftan was still waiting to be unpacked, I had washing to do, the garden was desperate for attention – those veggies Youssef had planted wouldn't survive – but my heart wasn't in doing anything.

I couldn't sleep.

Too often the sentiment of a silly pop song on the radio had a special poignancy for me – painful, love-struck lyrics stopping me in my tracks, words that I had never listened to before.

It hurt.

All those years of quite happily living alone and now it seemed to be the worst possible scenario. I hadn't had time, or perhaps the inclination, to tell Youssef how my first day back at work had been.

Maybe the cow on the track, when I was travelling home, could be blamed for early morning troubles on the line too. Had the animal been wandering on the railway all day? Or was it a different cow? The consequence was, whatever had happened, I was nearly half an hour late for work.

The sight of the boss's stony face and thick blubbery lips was enough to send a shudder through me. My heart stood heavy in my chest. After the interrogation he gave me, he softened somewhat. He hadn't of course known Youssef couldn't return with me.

Again.

The failed visa application interview in Rabat, long ago last year, had gone *so* badly it was embarrassing. Naïve Youssef… giving the most inappropriate answers possible. He wanted 'his papers', he'd said, without thinking ahead to what was the best tactic when speaking to consulate officers. It seems he'd practically *demanded* his papers, he wanted to be married to me. He'd argued, he'd shouted. A black mark instantly, a red flag waving throughout. He'd had no idea of diplomacy. And the interview was conducted in his own language, so there really was no excuse.

My interview was apparently fine. I was genuine – but my young fiancé, as he was then, wasn't.

I put on some music. Joni Mitchell sang about deprivation of her man; colliding with *them lonesome blues*. And the bed's too big, the frying pan's too wide…

What I wouldn't give to have Youssef in the kitchen making cous cous, creating a terrible mess, clattering pans and shouting out to me to lay the table.

By my second week back I was becoming more reconciled to being temporarily alone once more. I was getting through the huge container of olives quickly. The threaded dried figs were still on the kitchen work surface where I'd left them, abandoned like huge beige necklaces, looking alien now alongside the English breadbin and glass cruet set.

I'd made a few decisions; there was a trip to the Home Office booked for the following week. I'd decided to lodge an appeal to try to reverse the Consulate's decision, which might mean another interview with Youssef in Rabat.

Second time lucky maybe.

I knew exactly how I was going to word the appeal. Mention of things like how good Youssef's family background was should count for a lot. I knew his paternal grandfather had been the equivalent of Mayor of Chaouen. He was the one who'd had three wives, with Youssef's Ya Ya being the youngest – but, alas, she gave him no children. I knew how to do it, how to lay on the pathos and the disruption to our lives, and how good Youssef's intentions were in wanting to come to the UK. They weren't going to be that interested in the love angle, broken hearts, I knew that much. It was all to do with Youssef's intentions. But when I looked over what I'd typed it appeared so lame and lacking.

It took a lot of ingenuity and creativity to get it right.

I triple-checked what I was doing with the email before I pinged it off to the Consulate.

Once I'd lodged the appeal I had to play the waiting game.

I had a thumping heart, a dry mouth and moist palms when I arrived at Lunar House; and an added extra, a splitting head, once I was ushered into a side office. Impossibly bare and impersonal. But my Home Office contact, Mr Blake, looked more concerned than I could have imagined.

'Sit down, please.'

'Here's the case number,' I said, 'and my report to the Consulate. And here's the letter from my MP, writing in support. Here's... '

He took the papers I offered him. 'You really do want this man back, don't you.'

'Of course! I'm getting to the stage where... where I'd consider handcuffing myself to Buckingham Palace railings.'

'Don't do that. I wouldn't recommend it.' He laughed.

'Being married in Gibraltar... we thought that might ease things through, but it didn't work out quite like that.'

'A good wedding?'

'Oh yes! Very memorable.'

'It'll help, I can assure you.'

'Really... I just don't know what to do next. Trouble is, once they think you're an *undesirable*... '

'That's true. It's difficult to shake off. I've seen it before.'

I unclenched my hands and tried to relax. I took a deep breath. 'I'm going to Morocco later on this summer if the appeal doesn't work. I want to make an appointment to see the Consul again,' I said. 'If *he* can look into it— '

'Yes. That's definitely the next move.' He smiled encouragingly.

'Well... Youssef has a few influential relatives, so maybe it'd be fairly easy. It's all in my report.'

I looked down at my clammy fingers twisting in my lap.

He started to get up. 'That's it then. I wish you the best of luck. We'll get him back. Don't hesitate to get in touch, will you? I have your case under my wing and I'll contact Rabat as well.' He smiled.

'Thank you so much Mr Blake. I really appreciate you looking into this. It's been... terrible.'

I was on the verge of tears of gratitude.

'I'm pleased to help you, Jean. You're obviously committed to... ' – he looked swiftly at the top paper in the wodge I'd given him – '... Youssef... so— '

'Definitely. I won't let it go – until he's back.'

'You'll be an expert on all matters of immigration before too long,' he said, gathering up his files from the desk. 'Good luck.'

'Thank you again Mr Blake.'

I shook his outstretched hand and turned, leaving the office, and walked back down the corridor. I clutched my remaining papers to me and allowed myself to smile. My heart felt lighter than it had for months.

The following week Youssef phoned again. 'I get a letter now, Jeannie. I'll see someone in July, a different woman.'

'Please don't lose your temper this time. Stay *cool*.'

'I try.'

'We've got to get you back this time. The garden is going wild, and— '

'Ya Ya, she sends regards. She so 'ot she not know what she do.'

I laughed. 'And how's Mummy?'

'She okay. She not well last week, but get better soon. I worry for her.'

He paused. 'How you do for money, Jeannie?'

'Not good. The mortgage's sky high, just goes up and up.'

'Why they can do that?'

'They can. It's out of our hands.'

'I been sent you money, Jeannie. Last week. I put in a packet, with lot of paper wrapped round, so postman he not see and go steal.'

'*Wheee!*'

'It two note. Two twenty pound.'

'Two twenty pound notes?'

'That it. What I said.'

'Why… ?'

'Cos I know you need. Easy peasy here, all family look after me. Where I go, always I take olives, or coffee, and they give me a meal.'

'Wish I was there with you… '

'Soon, Jeannie. Soon. *In Sha'Allah*.'

Desesperado

Denton, East Sussex
July 1991

'They refuse me.'
'*Again!*'
'They not believe I... I'm... '
'Genuine?'
'That big fat woman, really horrible to me.'
'That was the Deputy Consul?'
'Maybe.'
'*Bitch!*' I spat out.
'So, what I do now, Jeannie? Eh?'
'We go and see the Consul again. It's time we did.'
'I can't believe this. I say to Daddy, I need go Spain now, find job, make money.'
'Don't go to Spain!'
'Daddy, he won't let me go. He say, you listen to your wife, she knows what is best.'
'That's right. Best to stay where you are.'
'In Beni Ahmed?'
'Not necessarily there, but for God's sake stay in Morocco.'

'But... I don't know what to do. Bored! I'm *desesperado*, Jeannie!'

'You think I'm not desperate too! I'll get things going. Don't you worry.'

'I don't want be without you.'

'I should bloody well hope not,' I said. 'Listen, keep your cool.'

'I trust you. I know you try to do best. Daddy, he says this too.'

'Tell Daddy he's a wise man. He understands.'

My mind was racing. I was furious – with Rabat, with the fat woman, with Youssef, and with myself. Tears sprang to my eyes and I brushed them away angrily.

I had to be strong. And motivated.

We needed that trip to see the damn Consul. Thwarted before – but I was determined to get there and be heard.

'You know,' Youssef said, 'if I'd stayed in England, like I said, we not have all this stuff going on. It's your fault – you *know* that. I tell you this in London.'

'*What!*'

'I didn't need to go back to Morocco. In London, I met a man who— '

'*No.* Absolutely not.'

'Never you listen to me! *Never* you— '

'Do anything illegally, you'll end up in real trouble.'

'Jeannie— '

'No.' I replaced the phone.

Twice refused.

Continuing aggravation.

Was the cosmos against me?

'What are you doing, bringing a young foreign man to London, Jeannie?' Zoë had asked. *'Good luck matey – but watch out!'*

'You sly one,' said Marta. *'Smugglin' him back – no chance for the rest of us now! We liked looking at 'im.'* So said my close friend at work, Zoë, the would-be lawyer; and then my crazy Polish pal Marta in Spain – each with a different take on it.

I sat for a while thinking, with a heavy dragging in my heart as I grappled with my emotions. Youssef didn't phone back.

Legal Spies

Croydon and East Sussex
March 1992

'Thank you, Mr Blake,' I said. 'Thank you so much.'

I replaced the phone on its cradle.

The office was quiet; it was lunchtime.

I swivelled half-way round on my typist's chair and gazed out of the window. Lincoln's Inn redbrick buildings stood imposing and invincible, the scene sprinkled with neat, mature trees just about to burst into blossom. I moved to pick up a biro then let it fall clattering back onto the desk. Refocusing, I tried to look at the paperwork tucked neatly by the side of my keyboard; with my thumb I flicked at the edge of the pages.

I could hear voices at the far end of the office, but nothing made sense, words hung in the air. The muscles around my mouth were numb, and my hands didn't know what to do; I could see my fingers quivering as I spread them over the keys, poised to carry on typing. I couldn't find words to speak, and I couldn't type, not just yet.

Breathe. Take in air... huge gulps.

Once I could speak, I couldn't stop, and word got around quickly. By the time I had let the news properly sink in and had picked up the phone to leave a message for Youssef to call me later at home, a bottle of pink champagne appeared on my desk from a well-wisher. It was from someone who worked in a different department altogether, two floors down.

The train journey home to Sussex took its normal course, three changes, though I was barely paying attention.

I shed a few silent tears.

I needed to snap out of it.

I scarcely had time to shrug my coat off when Youssef phoned.

'Youssef! Where are you?'

'Chaouen, of course. My cousin, he rush to Ya Ya and say news good!'

'So you got my message!'

'Well... it very good, Jeannie,' he said, his voice sounding strangled. 'What that man he say to you?'

'He said... *You'll be very pleased to know, Jeannie, that your husband Youssef now has leave to stay in the U.K., approved by the Home Secretary. I'm delighted for you.*'

'*Delight-ed*? What's that mean?'

'Happy. Over the moon. *Overjoyed!*'

'Oh.'

'So, the Consul in Rabat didn't have the last word after all, but at least he got things moving.'

'I see.'

Youssef didn't *really* see, but the main thing was that he was coming home.

'Hooray for Mr Blake, eh?'

'Good man, yes.'

'When're you coming back?'

'I not know yet, Jeannie. I think go to Spain, see my uncle – you know, Big Boss. He's there at moment.'

'*Spain.* Hang on, you can come home here now.'

'I know. I need come back to England from Spain. Flight, it's too expensive from Morocco, you not believe how much.'

'Youssef... '

'Just a few days, Jeannie.'

'Well... we have a bottle of champagne to drink. *Pink.* I can't drink it all on my own.'

'Champagne?'

'It was a present from someone at work. They were so pleased to hear the news.'

'Who? Which person this?'

'Jane. You don't know her. She's been very sympathetic all along, gave me good advice.'

'*Tsss!* Long time. An' I not there yet.'

I bit my lip... disappointed...

'*Uh*... I must go, someone want to use phone.'

'Okay. 'Bye then. Phone again soon?'

'Spain. From Spain.' And he was gone.

I hadn't mentioned what Jane said as she placed the champagne on my desk. 'They'll be watching you,' she cautioned, 'at the airport.'

'You think so?'

'The spies'll be there to check him out – to make sure he's, you know, *legit*. I know about this stuff.'

'Really?'

'If he makes a move in the wrong direction, they'll be after him.'

'Why should he?' I asked.

'Of course, he *won't*. Just thought it worth mentioning.'

'But... he has permission for entry now.'

'Exactly. They want to be sure he's genuine.'

'My *god*, Jane.'

'Well, you would've had that before, when he first came over, at Heathrow. You wouldn't have known. They're always there.'

'Legal spies... '

'Yeah, right. That's it.'

The night before Youssef was due to appear at Gatwick, I dreamt of his arrival. He was bringing Ya Ya with him and she trundled along despondently, holding her travel bag close to her; and a shadowy figure appeared from nowhere as they both approached Passport Control: Uncle Big Boss. He was tapping Youssef on the shoulder... 'You good?' he asked him.

Youssef cowered, ready to run.

'You has permission for entry? You sure you be legit?'

I unlocked the front door, stepping straight into the conservatory, its inner double doors wide open leading into the rest of the house.

'What this, Jeannie?'

I closed the door behind me and turned to see a banner fixed above the double doors. I was as surprised as Youssef was.

Welcome Home, Youssef!

'Those kids!'

'Uh?'

'A neighbour's kids. They've been in here.'

'When they do that?'

'Search *me*. They've come in and fixed it while I've been gone meeting you.' I laughed. 'What a lovely thing for them to do.'

'How they get in?'

'They've got a key, haven't they. Remember, someone has to keep an eye on things when I go away, when I've gone over to Morocco.'

Youssef was having a closer look. 'What all that stuff?'

'It's... shooting stars, glitter, and— '

'Nice.'

'Now, enough questions. Where's that bottle and those glasses? I feel drained.'

'What these olives here?' He was looking at the little dishes of food I'd put out.

I pulled a face. 'Not as nice as Moroccan olives, I know, but they'll do.'

Youssef looked around him. 'House look just same.' He walked into the kitchen, opened the fridge and took out the pink champagne. He wedged the bottle between his thighs, grappling to open it.

I joined him. 'Well, it's not going to look any different, is it?'

'I imagine thing it change.'

Suddenly it struck me; he had the air of a man just out of prison.

The champagne exploded with a POP! The foaming liquid stopped just short of the top of the bottle.

He turned, his back to me. He tried three cupboards before he found the glasses; I had meant to put them out, ready. He glanced out of the window. 'Some yellow flowers coming soon – they *daff* thing, no?'

'Yes, they are,' I said, studying the set of his shoulders and the curve of his cheek in profile.

He put out the celebratory flutes I'd been given as a wedding present from work, poured, and handed me my glass, grinning. 'Lot of stuff in fridge!'

'It took all my money to stock up. It's really chokka.'

'It... full?'

'It full.'

'I get some plant from Beni Ahmed some time, for the garden. They're nice. They can come on holiday here an' stay forever.'

I laughed. 'Sounds good.'

He turned awkwardly, staring out of the window again.

It was almost like starting all over again with him. I hadn't expected it.

'Garden. I can do that for you, I'm back now. We need veggies.'

I hugged him hard and gave him a peck on the cheek. He smelt of garlic, of lemon – and his own tang: the scent of a man.

The front doorbell chimed.

Youssef looked startled. His head jerked round. 'Some person at our door!'

'Open it then.'

'Er— '

'Don't worry. It's the neighbours from next door. Just popping in.'

'But I not know 'em!'

'You soon will. I invited them in to say hello to you.'

I knew the couple next door quite well now. They were in their twenties and looked like two little mice. The young wife, petite, with a piercing voice, tried to wear the trousers but never with success; her husband just laughed at her.

'We heard you nattering earlier... ' she trilled as I opened the door.

'Come in, Tess!' I said. Teddy was hanging back. 'Come on, you,' I said, ushering him in. 'Come and meet the returning hubby.'

Youssef extended his hand. He didn't look happy.

'We've heard so much about you,' said Tess, her tiny chin quivering. Youssef did look formidable and seemed enormous next to these two little people.

'Champagne?' I said brightly, going off to find another couple of suitable glasses.

'Never I really see you,' Youssef explained politely. 'We move here for few weeks only before we go to Morocco.' He sighed. 'I be away long time.'

'I know,' Tess said. 'I saw you in the garden once. I was hanging out my undies.'

'Uh?'

'My... underwear, on the clothesline outside. I remember, it was all my black stuff.'

'Yeah,' said Teddy. 'All her lacy bras and stockings; all that seems to get washed in one big swoop. Dunno why.'

'Uh?' Youssef was looking baffled as I came back in holding their brimming glasses. They took them gratefully.

'Well, it was a *black* wash, Ted,' she remonstrated. 'I wouldn't go putting it in with the *whites*, would I?' I looked at Tess' slight frame and wondered how she might look wearing all her sexy gear. I couldn't envisage it.

'I can't believe how many suspender belts I have,' she said. 'And I've got a few g-strings now, but they're not very comfortable.'

Teddy snorted. His nose was well into his glass of champagne. He said something about cheese cutters but it was very indistinct.

'Sit down, sit down,' I urged, pushing nuts, olives and the bowl of crisps towards them as they perched on the smaller of our two ill-matched settees, the closing-down sale pink-striped one.

'Have you come far?' I said, as a joke. They immediately got it and chortled. Youssef looked blank.

'Ugh!' Tess said, dragging an olive out of her mouth. 'I thought they were *grapes*. *Yuk*, can't stand these things.'

Youssef's incomprehension turned into indignation, but he said nothing.

'We can't all like the same things,' I trotted out. Such a cliché. But I didn't believe my own words. Never good to be dismissive of things so easily.

Did my new Moroccan family think that of *me*? In Chaouen and Tangier – the problems I had with inedible meals, those little pieces of oily grey meat and hunks of stale bread; the thick, over-sweet mint tea. The cultural norms.

The language.

I believed they did. I didn't fit in.

'Anything foreign,' Tess continued, 'I find tricky to get on with. We know you can't beat good ol' Engl— '

Teddy stopped her with a look and a muttered aside about mouths running away with themselves.

It was obvious that Youssef found it difficult to keep up with them, and for these little English people to be comfortable with him.

It was early days yet.

And good to have decent neighbours next door.

I opened a bottle of Spanish red to supplement the champagne.

Twenty minutes later, to supplement the red, I asked Youssef to open a bottle of white. He put a hand over his own glass when I went to pour. 'In Islam, not really good for have alcohol. I do this just for you, Jeannie.'

I suspected it was Ramadan time but I didn't ask.

And after that, the little people and I started on the liqueurs.

As back-up to the story behind the pink champagne, I told the tale of the possibility of legal spies lurking at Gatwick.

'So if you'd made a run for it... ' Teddy said.

Youssef looked at him vacantly.

'*I* could be a spy,' Tess said. 'I'm so little I can worm in anywhere. What's more, I can lay on the charm and stuff.' She stretched out one of her miniature legs and lurched slightly towards Teddy, who quickly steadied her. 'Easy, girl.'

'And you have the black sexy knicker,' Youssef agreed. He was half-cut but still alert enough to try a bit of sarcasm. He raised an eyebrow at me as I stood in the doorway – I was wondering how we'd reached this point in a comparatively short space of time.

'The spies my friend was talking about,' I said, 'were ordinary people, officers, not Mata Hari or anything. But trained, obviously, to spot— '

Youssef wrinkled his brow. 'Mata? *Mata*, Jeannie? What that?'

'Oh, a famous wartime *puta*. She worked as a spy for the Germans, and the French. Did a bit of sexy dancing too it seems, then got herself shot.'

'I can dance!' shrilled Tess. 'Can't I, Ted?'

'How you know this stuff?' Youssef asked, swaying noticeably as he got up. 'She be wife to that man 'itler or— ?'

'No, No!' Teddy responded. 'Wrong war.'

'That's right,' I said. 'How d'you know of Hitler?' I was talking to Youssef; as far as I knew he wasn't aware of any twentieth century historical figures.

Youssef tapped his nose, then said: 'Big Boss, my uncle, he speak of him. Big Boss, he knows everythin'.'

Teddy winked. 'Big Boss, eh.'

'He tell me, Youssef you going to country where maybe it be different if German they go there after war it end. Would be culture different and language different too.'

'Too true,' Teddy observed.

'When did he say this?' I asked.

'In Spain, couple days back.'

'German *sausage*!' shrieked Tess. She laughed, throwing her mousey head backwards, mouth open showing sharp little teeth. 'That's another kind of thing I can't stand, all those herbs and spicy bits and lumps of fat. *Ugh!*'

'When did you try German sausage?' Teddy asked. All Tess could do was laugh, batting her pale eyelashes.

'I give up,' Teddy said. 'You need to get home.'

'We could cut an archway in the wall, just here…' she said, nodding towards the wall above the larger settee, 'and walk backwards and forwards— '

'I don't think so,' said Teddy. 'Come on, *home*.'

'What you mean?' Youssef asked, wrinkling his brow.

'Our houses are joined here,' I explained, leaning over and patting the dividing wall covered with the despised for-now pink flowery wallpaper. 'Didn't you notice? Just the fronts. The backs are kind of staggered.'

'We could spy on each other!' Tess was screeching. 'We could— '

'Ah!' Youssef said. 'I see.' He looked absorbed. 'Maybe we could buy 'ouse, both?'

'Buy both houses?' I said. 'I don't think our neighbours would want to do that.' I felt mildly embarrassed.

'Depends on how much you want to pay,' said Teddy, picking a spot on his chin and keeping an eye on Tess.

'Me, I has no money,' Youssef said truthfully. 'Not yet. I do good soon, I make money for our future, Jeannie an' me.'

'Yeah,' Teddy said. 'I've heard about all that oil in Arab countries. I'm quite clued-up.'

'Oil? Don't look at *him*,' I said to Teddy, suddenly feeling I'd had enough of the evening. 'He's a poor church... *mouse*.'

The mouse word was out of my mouth.

Teddy said nothing but gave a look that I couldn't decipher.

'More drink, Teddy?' Youssef asked.

'No... I'm alright, thanks. Had enough really.'

'Nice wine,' said Tess. 'Scrummy.'

'We'd better go,' Teddy said, patting Tess' backside and pulling her towards the door. 'Thank you for the drinks.'

'Nice to meet you,' Tess managed, not really looking at anyone, wobbling in her kitten heels.

'Church?' Youssef asked, finally, narrowing his

eyes. '*Church?*'

'And thank you for the laughs,' I said to Teddy, wanting the evening to end on a good note. 'We're all going to have bad heads tomorrow.'

'I see you maybe in garden,' Youssef said. 'When you put black sex—'

I cut in. ''Bye Teddy... 'bye Tess! Sleep well.'

They were through our front door, outside, and approaching our squeaky gate. I heard it growl and clank as they staggered through, banging it shut behind them.

'Forget church,' I said. 'It meant nothing. I'll explain.'

'Uh?'

Then... a key in their front door lock – loud, as if they were putting a key into *our* lock. Our front doors were very close.

'*I could be Mata Hari,*' I heard.

'Yeah, yeah.'

'Was she an Arab?'

'No. Look, mind as you go in. Don't fall over the—'

'Not such a bad fella, is he?' she was saying. 'I think he liked me.'

I breezed over to our front door, eavesdropping. I sniggered against the glass.

'You think so?' Teddy said. 'I'll be keeping an eye on *him*.'

'What d'you mean?'

'Spies an' all that. I'll be on the lookout. We're living next door to an unknown.'

'But— '

'Who is he? This country is stuffed with foreigners enough as it is.'

I flattened my ear to the glass door...

'Did you notice his shifty eyes? We need to be on our guard, missus... *Watch* it!... that's it, just step *over*... that's it. Yeah. We don't want types like that here. I've got the phone number for the Home Office. One foot wrong, and... '

No... No... I closed my eyes...

'Just hold me, Teddy... '

'Right. Got you.'

'You'd be a *spy*... ' she slurred.

'Someone has to be.'

The Lyceum Arms

London
April 1992

Coming down from The Strand I walked past the top of Villiers Street, then turned into Charing Cross Station, battling through the Friday night rush hour crowds. I arrived on the concourse at exactly a quarter to six.

The arrangement was to meet Youssef under the clock; he was already there, looking ill at ease and still in his work clothes. We embraced and kissed hastily, conscious of the swarm of people around us.

'Who we meet?' he asked, taking my hand into his as we pushed through the masses; we were going against the tide. Everyone else seemed to be on their way home.

'The people I work with.'

'Uh?'

'You know that. They keep asking about meeting you.'

'I know this. But what their name?'

'Well... there's Maureen and Keith. They're a

couple, they met at work. Maureen's very pretty, very sweet.'

'Pretty? Make bit of change, so much girl they be ugly here.'

'You think so?'

'I think, yes. Too much makeup and stuff. Moroccan girl, they suit have kohl on eye and lip red. English girl, she look like tart.'

'Okay, if you think so.'

'So, what people go to pub?' He looked concerned.

'Okay... there's Eugene, our odd job man – he's Jamaican, a real character, you'll like him. A few other good friends. And then there's Zoë.'

'Zoë?'

'She's the one who warned me I might be biting off more than I could chew,' I said, grimacing.

'Uh? What she mean?'

'If you remember, she wasn't sure if... well, if I was doing the right thing. She said: *How well d'you really know him?* I said: *Well enough. And, anyway Zo,* I said: *you've done a few daft things in your time, so don't...* '

'I don't understand Jeannie. What you mean?'

'Well, she meant bringing this wild Moroccan man back here to England.'

'Uh?'

'Who else is wild and Moroccan?'

He looked bewildered.

'Let's get to the pub.'

I shouldn't have started all that. It was rocky ground.

We continued walking up The Strand, my high heels clicking on the pavement. We left the rush hour swarm for the most part behind us. My hair was swept back by the chill easterly wind and I shivered.

'*Where* this pub?'

'Right at the top end of this road, on the left. Not too far to go.'

'It most all shop and pub in this road?'

'Mostly. There's a few restaurants, *and* a McDonald's. It's back there, we've just gone past it.'

'McDonal'! I see lot of them, every place.'

'We're getting close to The Savoy, a very famous hotel. All the rich people stay there.'

'Savoy? Never I hear of that.'

'It's like... The Ritz, in Paris. Places like that.'

Youssef gave me a blank look. 'So... what pub it be called?'

'The pub? Oh, The Lyceum Arms. Funny really, it's right next door to a butcher shop.'

'Uh?'

'You know, the shop where they sell meat.' I pondered for a moment or two. 'I must tell you, Youssef – a little story coming up.' I paused, then bit the bullet. 'I was walking along here to work one morning, and— '

'We go to butcher?'

'No. Just that the pub is next *door* to the butcher's shop.'

'Oh.'

'So, anyway... I was walking along, on the other side of the road from here, and I could see the butcher inside, standing near his window, talking to someone. He was leaning— '

'Who?'

'The butcher. Quite an old guy with lots of whiskers.'

Youssef nodded.

'He was leaning... well, his *hand* was leaning... on a pig's head on a slab next to him. I really would've liked to've had a camera with me, it was such an unusual shot, and funny!'

'Uh?'

'But not much fun for the pig of course. Really, I can't see that shop staying open in this area.'

'Pig, it alive?'

'*No.* It was just his *head.* You know we don't have live animals in butcher shops here.'

'No, s'pose no.'

'I'm saying, I can't see that butcher's shop surviving long in this area of London now. It'll be taken over by some wealthy— '

'Is *that* shop you mean?' Youssef asked, pointing diagonally across the road.

'It is. The very one. Closed for the day now of course.'

Youssef narrowed his eyes, staring through the traffic to the butcher shop. 'Not see *pig*. Where it be?'

'*No.* It's long gone. I'm talking about two years ago, something like that.'

'That our *pub*, next to it?'

'That's the one.'

'We go there now? Really, I not sure about drink,

Jeannie. I drink sometime in Spain, but now we be here in London... '

'It's a *celebration,* Youssef. You don't have to drink if you don't want to, but it *would* be nice. Just a few.'

'Who that? Person over *there*? She wave at you...'

'Where? Oh, it's Zo.'

'Zo?'

'Zoë.'

'Why she carry bottle?'

I waved back to Zoë vigorously. Her shock of punk platinum hair was blowing about crazily in the wind, though still keeping its shape, and I could see her bright red lipstick as clearly as if I were standing next to her.

'That's Zo, the way she is. *Every* day is an excuse to celebrate for her.' I waved again.

'But, she has— '

'I know. I worry about her.'

We started to weave our way through the streaming traffic, disregarding the pedestrian crossing not very far away.

'Zo! *Yoo hoo!*'

'Careful, Jeannie. Careful!' Youssef's hands were on my shoulders.

I reached Zoë's side feeling out of breath, with Youssef close behind me.

'How's it going?' she said, taking a dainty swig through tightly pursed lips from her bottle of *Pils.*

'Great. And, yes, *here* he is!' I said, throwing out a triumphant arm in Youssef's direction. 'He *does* exist.'

Zoë beamed, then handed me her bottle of beer

and flung herself into Youssef's arms, burying her scarlet lips into his cheek. 'He certainly does,' she said, standing back and reclaiming her drink. 'I've heard a lot about you, young man. Just look after my friend Jeannie, won't you?' She wobbled in her high heels. '*Oops.*'

Youssef, expressionless, extended his right hand. Zoë ignored it. 'She's done a lot for you. Don't let her down,' she said. She reached out to wipe lipstick from his cheek with her fingers, then she shrieked with laughter and took my hand to drag me into *The Lyceum Arms*.

I managed to glance round quickly before disappearing through the double swing doors. Looking bemused, Youssef was following on.

Eugene, his hips swivelling ever so slightly, was propping up the bar. He had gravitated towards Youssef early on, and he now placed a hand on his shoulder as he spoke:

'So, brother!' he said. 'What kinda moosic you like, eh?'

'Uh?' Youssef was wide-eyed with apprehension.

'Moosic?'

'*Musica*? Me, I like Moroccan music. And Spanish.'

'No, no, no. When I say *moosic*, I mean modern stuff. From the real world.'

'Er... '

'Madonna? Rock? Love songs?'

'Boh-yomm,' Youssef replied after a few seconds of hesitation.

'Eh? Wussat, bro?' asked Eugene, scratching at his tight curly hair, his brow furrowing as if in pain. 'Didn't quite geddit.'

'Don't let him bore you with Bob Marley stuff,' Zoë shouted, getting out her purse and squeezing her way through to the bar.

'Boh-yomm,' Youssef repeated. 'And Ro-Stuuu.'

'Ro-Stuuu? Give us a song, then. Then we'll know.'

Youssef, having had two halves of *Stella*, was up for the challenge.

'I yam sailin', I yam *sailin'*... '

'Ah. Rod Stewart. Well, each to their own.' He smiled wryly. 'I go for proper *lurve* songs. Know whadduh mean? And Reggae, 'course. Can't beat Da Man, Bob. Uhhh, 'e wuz the biz.'

'Uh?'

'And... Mister Barry White, George Benson, Marvin Gaye. Legends. They got *soul*, these guys.'

'Never I hear of these person,' Youssef whispered to me.

'Who's Boh-yomm then?' Eugene persisted.

'You must hear of 'im sometime,' Youssef said.

Eugene scratched his head again. 'Well, no. I can't quite figure it out bro. Say it again?'

'Boh-yomm?'

'American or English?' enquired Eugene.

'Er... 'merican, I think.'

'Say it again bro.'

Standing beside him, I saw Youssef's eye flicker. I sensed his frustration.

Several in our crowd were eavesdropping.

'Could it be Bono?' someone asked.

Youssef looked baffled.

'Goddit!' Eugene shouted. 'It's Bony M!'

'Who zat?' Youssef asked.

'Obviously not Bony M then,' I said, feeling increasingly worried for him.

'Again?' prompted Zoë.

Youssef was getting irritated. 'Boh-*yommg*!'

'Could you sing something of this person?' Eugene was jigging around on the spot, grinning. He was enjoying the suspense.

Youssef turned his back. He began to sing:

'Wherever... I... mmm my-yat, dat my 'ome.' He was very red in the face. I took his arm as he turned back round.

'Paul Young!' Eugene was overjoyed to recognise the song. He punched Youssef lightly on the shoulder. 'Paul Young! Paul *Young*!'

'Yes, Boh-*Yommg*!'

Everyone looked pleased and turned away, back to their previous chit-chat.

Eugene had an expectant look about him. There was no doubt. His glass was empty and so was mine.

'Youssef,' I said. 'How about another drink? It's your— '

'No. I not want,' he said emphatically.

'But *I'd* like a drink.'

'No, I have enough. Jeannie, I want go home soon.'

'But... oh, okay,' I said, finding my purse and opening it.

Youssef was then distracted by Keith standing the

other side of him. I heard Paul Young mentioned again.

I pushed my way to the bar.

'Not too quick with his wallet, is he?' said Zoë, wiggling her hips, dancing on the spot opposite Eugene. 'Hey, *you* already got one earlier, Jeannie.'

'I know,' I said. 'He's not into all this pubbing.'

'Yeah. Looks like it.'

'He'll learn later on.'

'You hope.'

'Yes, I hope. Bottle of *Pils*, Zo?'

'Yeah. Ta.'

'I want small water, Jeannie!' Youssef shouted over.

'Better go further up the bar,' Zoë pointed out. 'It's too packed here, you'll never get served.'

'Help me with the drinks?'

'Nah. I'm *dancing*!' she said, moving across to sidle up to Eugene. 'Get Mister Meanie to help.'

Eugene wasn't finished with Youssef. 'I hear you two got caught up at the border in Spain. A bit of bother.'

Youssef glanced at me nervously.

'It's in the past now, Eug,' I said. 'We want to forget.'

But he pushed: 'You loved telling us that story,' he said. 'What a laugh! Ha! I could *imagine* it...'

I touched his arm. 'Not something we want to broadcast, really.'

Eugene's face clouded and he turned away.

Youssef shoved my arm. I didn't meet his eye.

'Forget it,' I said. 'Beaky Nose is never going to find you here.' I wanted to laugh but it wasn't the right time.

I finished my half pint, placed the glass on the bar, just as Youssef, pulling on his jacket, began to head for the door. He looked like he couldn't wait to get out. I struggled into my coat and gathered up my belongings quickly.

'Bye, everyone!' I shouted from the doorway. 'We're off.'

A few people looked up from their conversations.

'We're going.'

I'd get feedback in the office on Monday, and I knew it wouldn't be good.

Standing behind me, Youssef waved absently and was gone. I moved through the double doors to follow him, pausing for a few seconds just outside. There was a gap where the doors hadn't closed properly; I could hear Eugene reprimanding Zoë.

'Get off! Don't use me as a fuckin' chair!'

'Eugene…'

'You just get yer ass off me girl! Only smarm round me if you really mean it, not if yer off yer fuckin' 'ead!'

'Well, Eug matey – all I can say is *fuck you too*!'

I suspected Zoë wouldn't remember any of it.

I pulled up my coat collar and we turned right, past the butcher shop, walking back down the The Strand towards Charing Cross Station, then on to Victoria.

'So we go home.'

'Yes. Quite an early night.'

'Uh? What?'

'Why didn't you get changed into something decent, Youssef?'

'Uh?'

'You're in those smelly work clothes. I thought you were taking a change of clothes in with you. Tee-shirt, at least.'

'I think of it, but I not be bother. It only for go for drink.'

'You smell of cooking. Onions.'

Youssef shrugged. 'It not matter, it's my job. And, anyway, it for only spend bit of time with you and them people in pub.'

'Did you see how nicely dressed they were?'

He shrugged again. 'They not worth. *Tsss*!' He turned to me. 'See how drunk your friend she be, one who look bit like *puta*?'

'She's always that way.'

'Then, me, always I be this way. I like be like this, not nearly fall down cos of alco'ol.'

I gave him a cool look, though his turn of phrase amused me. 'Have you forgotten about the yard of vino in Nerja?'

'I not like see woman she drink like this.'

'I just wanted you to meet my friends tonight.'

'And she girl who say maybe you not do right thing, no? When first you meet me?'

'Well, Zoë was kind of *worried*.'

'So what *she* know!' He spat out the words.

'I'm trying to tell you! She was worried for me. All my friends were.'

'My family, they worry for me when I say I come here. Drug and stuff in London, they think— '

'Really? No more here than anywhere else.' I glared at him. 'And let's face it, you're fascinated by the whole drug thing, aren't you!'

'Uh?'

We walked on. 'I'm exasperated,' I said, sighing. 'Why is it always like this? Why is there always a bloody problem?'

He flinched. 'Not *swear*, Jeannie.' He waved an arm. 'And why you tell that man about what happen in Gibraltar? And stuff happen after that! No one need to know!'

We walked on in silence for a few minutes.

I turned my head to look at Youssef's hurt, indignant profile. He plodded on down The Strand by my side, hands stuffed into his jacket. Unexpectedly a wave of affection swept over me and, as we crossed the road, I linked my arm with his, tucking my cold hand into his warm pocket. He didn't draw away.

Big Boss

Rabat
July 1992

Youssef smiled broadly. 'This is Big Boss, Jeannie. My uncle.'

'Ah. I've heard– '

'I tell you before about him.'

'I'm very pleased to meet you,' I said, shaking Big Boss' hand.

'Welcome. Are you good?'

'I'm... fine, thank you.'

I didn't know his name. What I did know was that he was an important man in local government, and looked it. His handshake was a bone crusher but his smile was friendly and genuine.

'You 'as journey well?'

'Yes, thank you.'

He continued to smile at me. I was impressed with the way he looked – a tall, well-made man, thickly moustached, with a good head of black hair combed straight back. Youssef stood next to him, grinning, in his grubby jeans and creased tee-shirt, in sharp contrast to his well-to-do uncle. Big Boss was smartly dressed, in a crisp short sleeved pastel shirt and tailored camel trousers.

We walked away from Rabat Bus Station to Big Boss's awaiting car; it was a big shiny Jaguar. We'd suffered a long, hot journey from Chaouen's dirt-yard turnaround clearing.

'Okay, Jeannie?'
'What happens now?'
'*Cuul.*'
'We eat? What a good idea.'
'Made by their servant.'
'A *servant?*'
'*Na'am.* House it nice, very, Jeannie. You'll like it. I seen it already when the workmen were here, building.'

I gave him an impressed look. I *was* impressed.

'If I'd known how important Big Boss is, I'd have mentioned him in my appeal to get you home,' I said. 'But we cracked it anyway.'

'Me, I want house this same thing one day. I want to do good, Jeannie, here an' in England. I work hard until I get all things I want.' He had a look about him that validated his words and I didn't doubt his determination at all; but I did wonder, mindful of his lack of qualifications, how on earth Youssef would do it. His aim was to have his own restaurant in Brighton. Meanwhile, he still slogged it out in Burger King – rising to become a supervisor almost immediately after starting. He loved having authority.

Big Boss's Jag purred along the beach road. Spiky palm trees lined the way, their tiered gnarled trunks uniform as each tree stood equidistant along that long smooth stretch.

We slowed down, approaching the house by way of a curved driveway. The exterior of the house loomed. It was pure white with enormous windows and a large, impressive Spanish style light-wood front door. There was a gravel frontage with shrubbery, small flower beds and lawn going round to the back.

'Big Boss, he says they not here long, so they not get garden finished yet.'

'It's beautiful, Youssef.'

Mrs Big Boss came to the door, a slim and elegant woman wearing what looked like a silk dress, colourful and discreetly patterned. The dress was knee length with a matching tie belt, and she wore strappy low sandals. She was quite dark skinned, with a large, thin nose, her smooth dark hair worn in a chignon.

She ushered us in. We entered a huge, high-ceilinged room with an ornate coloured glass chandelier suspended from the centre, and three stylish gold fabric couches grouped around the ubiquitous low, circular table – brass, inlaid with wood. The walls were white, with the lower half tiled in soft blues and greens. Large vases of lilies and roses were dotted around the room on spindly pedestal tables.

'They not got thing right yet. More furniture, it come soon,' Youssef explained. 'Bedrooms, not much there. You see later.'

'It's gorgeous. Can we move in?'

'We here, Jeannie, for a few days.'

'No – I mean, can we move in forever?'

Youssef laughed. Big Boss laughed too, he had picked up enough to understand what I'd said, and was now busy conveying what had been said to his wife.

'You to sit. Please, to sit,' commanded Big Boss.

'Sit on chair there,' Youssef suggested, pointing to one of the settees. 'They give our dinner now.'

We were served chicken tagine, cooked with plums and pine nuts. We had the usual hunks of bread and the finely chopped salad Moroccans seemed to serve with everything. The cook, who was serving us, smiled shyly. She wore a white ruffled robe reminiscent of Youssef's two female cousins in Tangier.

The tagine came on the customary huge platter but we were all given individual plates should we prefer to eat Western style. No one did.

Once her job was done, the cook retreated from the room. I heard clattering and splashing noises from the kitchen for a while and then the *bang* of the back door as she left to go home.

'Strange thing that. Big Boss, he says usually she come in for say goodbye.' There was a slight hush and then something was said between them all and it was decided what the reason was.

'She's shy, Jeannie. Shy of meet you, an' not want be here if family they has company.'

'Oh.'

Big Boss spoke, Youssef interpreted. 'He wants to know how it go with the Consul when we came here last year – he could maybe help us then.'

'Well... it was crazy, wasn't it. He was so nice. Surprising, too... what he said about me.' I paused.

'That was a total shock.'

Youssef chuckled. 'I'll tell him what that man he said to you… '

'It's kind of embarrassing… '

I watched as the two men chewed over what was said in the Consulate. Mrs Big Boss looked on in surprise, and then delight. I was the focus of attention – again; not unusual during my trips to Morocco.

'Big Boss he says how nice that man say that. You're older, yes… but you could be snap-up by any man who meet you… he must've quite fancy you, Jeannie, for himself… '

I took a breath. 'Yes… but that shouldn't be what determines you, or anyone, entry to the UK – should it? We were lucky. S'pose I'd looked like the back of a rubbish lorry?'

'Who cares? We *were* lucky.'

Just as we were finishing the meal, Fatima came home; the girl who'd previously been earmarked as a bride for Youssef. She looked like her mother – swarthy, slim, and with bone-thin legs. She had a cloud of long curly hair tied back with a ribbon and was dressed in shorts and a white blouse.

'She student still, at university. Clever, she.'

Fatima was introduced to me and I felt her wariness. She gave Youssef a cursory greeting, seeming to avoid his eye. Soon after her two younger brothers trailed in. They were suitably courteous initially and then couldn't help behaving like young boys with a lot of space to lark around in. Big Boss took control and they were chastised gently but firmly.

'We go upstairs, see our bedroom now.'
'Is it alright just to... go?'
''Course. Big Boss, he don't mind.'
As we left the table, Big Boss looked across, smiling benignly. It was obvious he didn't care. I turned and thanked him and his wife for the meal and they both nodded back amiably.

Five medium sized bedrooms were waiting to be filled upstairs. In the quite small bathroom there was a European toilet as well as the usual tiled-around hole in the floor.

'They not use,' Youssef said disdainfully, looking at the toilet. 'A waste really, they not need this. No Moroccan he needs this.'

Before I could say anything, Youssef took me by the hand to guide me back downstairs to show me the cloakroom with a shower, and also a study tucked round the back. The kitchen, also at the rear of the house, was surprisingly small and basic.

'This is odd in such a big house.'

'Uh?'

'This kitchen – not very big.'

Youssef shrugged. 'They get what they want. No need have big kitchen. No one lives in a kitchen.'

'Would Mummy like this?'

'No. Too posh.'

'Would she ever come here?' I asked.

'No, Mummy wouldn't like. It's too big. An' you know she's a mountain woman, she don't like be by sea. I tell you this before.'

'I can imagine. She'd be unhappy.'

'Daddy, yes! He would like. But not sure ever he ever be invited for come.'

'It's gorgeous.'

'We stay a day, or two, then get bus back to Chaouen. Go on to Tetouan, see Mohammed. We can meet his lady – she'll be there, but only visiting. Very young, only eighteen. Should really have someone with her, but the family trust Mohammed.'

'Oh!'

'They're getting engaged sometime soon.'

On the beach at Rabat, unexpectedly I bonded with Fatima. Her English was quite good. She'd left the beach while I wasn't looking, and I was sitting up scanning the busy café area behind where we'd made camp.

I spotted her. She was trudging back over the hot sand with her arms laden.

I watched her as she came closer. 'I buy ice cream an' drink cold for us,' she said, collapsing on her towel.

'Thank you, Fatima,' I said. 'Can we give you some money?'

'Not to worry, is my father money, not mine money.' She handed me a lolly in the shape of a spaceship.

'Thank you!'

'This, first time I use my English, to a English person. I feel— '

'Strange?' prompted Youssef, reclining on his red and yellow Flamenco Dancer towel.

'No, 'appy. 'appy to use.'

She reached over to hand him a red devil ice lolly covered with chocolate chips. He pulled a face once her back was turned.

'Me, I not need devil,' he whispered. 'But 'im, I eat!' He took a huge bite, somehow severing the devil's head clean from his chocolaty body. Youssef's cheeks bulged as he shifted the huge chunk of ice from place to place in his mouth.

We sat contentedly in the sun for an hour or so, and then it was time to go back to the house for dinner. It was late afternoon. We had come from a boiling hot Sussex that summer and were well weathered. As we were getting our beach things together, I compared my skin to Youssef's and Fatima's.

'I don't feel I'm the pallid foreigner.'

'Uh?'

'I'm equal to you and Fatima, yes?'

'You right, Jeannie.' He yawned suddenly, stretching his arms above his head. '*Ahhh*, this beach, it's *wonderfool*.'

'A shame to leave it.'

'Well, we got to go now. Cook, she makes cous cous for you this evening.'

'Oh?'

'Fatima, she tell me.'

Fatima nodded vigorously, her spirally hair bobbing up and down.

'*More* cous cous,' announced Youssef, almost regretfully.

'That's alright,' I said. 'There's cous cous – and then there's *cous cous*.'

'Uh?'

The cous cous we were served was unlike any I'd sampled before. The spiced lamb and vegetables had been wrapped in cabbage leaves and steamed. Once the cabbage leaves had been broken into by Big Boss, the first of us to begin eating, it was the usual story with the spicy innards being pushed my way, but this time I didn't mind. Using our bread hunks, the large platter was soon wiped clean.

'You like, Jeannie?'

'I like.'

'Big Boss, he say we has fruits now.'

'Oranges?'

'No, different one. Lot different fruits.'

A huge bowl of chopped fruit was brought to the table. It was no ordinary fruit. Big Boss doled it out into individual gold rimmed soup bowls and passed them round. An ornate dish of natural yoghurt also appeared and was placed next to the fruit bowl. A small silver spoon sprouted from one side.

'You like mango?' asked Youssef, spearing slippery fruit with a fork then giving up and using his fingers.

'Yes, I do.'

'Pineapple here too, an'... kiwi. An' strawberry. You like strawberry?'

'I like all fruit.'

'Fruits white here, I not know name.'

'It's Lychee. Chinese.'

'Uh? Lychee? Name strange.'

'Well, it's Chinese.'

Youssef tucked into his bowl of fruit, juice dribbling from the corners of his mouth.

'You like Big Boss special fruits?'

'Of course I do.'

'Me, I love fruits. I be fruits monster.' He made a quick monster face at me, bulging his eyes and stretching his mouth, then carried on eating.

'You'll stay like it.'

'Uh?'

Later that evening we settled in our bedroom, our paraphernalia scattered all around the room. Youssef was busy stuffing soft Egyptian blankets between my sheet and the hard mattress on my bed. I went to him and hugged him from behind.

'Gedoff!!' he roared, turning and pouncing on me.

I laughed, disentangled myself and padded over to the light wood dressing table under the window. 'Why were we invited here?'

'Uh?'

'Here.'

'Oh – they want to meet you.'

'Curious were they?'

'Never they meet English person before. Not properly.'

I laughed. 'Now they have.'

'You different from what they think.'

I didn't ask what their opinion might be.

'Do you have any other rich family?' I asked, tissuing off what remained of my makeup.

Youssef gave the made-up bed a thump with his fist. 'That finish now.' Then he paused, looking amused. 'Only my gran'father. he rich – but he's dead now. Remember, he have three wife. But he never own house like this.'

'I suppose he was a different type of man.'

'Uh? *Na'am*. he not need big house – Chaouen an' Beni Ahmed good enough for him.'

'You could've married Fatima and lived like this y'know. Big Boss would've made sure you were comfortable.'

'No, Jeannie, I not want. I want make my own life.'

'That's *good*, Youssef. Shows you're genuine.'

He busied himself with his own bed. 'Fatima, it seems maybe she get marry to a cousin in England.'

'Yes, you said.'

'He live with his brother an' family, they have chicken an' chip shop some place away from London, not sure where.' He sighed. 'We need go see them sometime.'

'And she's a university student? That would be a shame.'

'Uh?'

'Well, she's spent time having a good education and then— '

'Then she be go cook chicken?'

'Well, yeah.'

'Yes, shame. But they think for her future. They think England be good, get away from Morocco an' have life new. If this happens, Big Boss would give money for business for help of course.'

'How does she feel about it?'

He spread his fingers, moving them this way and that. 'Well... she's not sure. Maybe, maybe not.'

'She needs to know what to expect. Poor girl.' I paused – I had to say it: 'You know, I think she still wants you, Youssef.'

'No... not now. Maybe before.'

'You sure? All the signs are there.'

'No.' He sighed. 'Anyway, Jeannie. Fatima is nice – but me, I not like leg skinny.'

'That's *nasty*.'

We laughed just a little too loudly.

Then we heard footsteps.

Someone outside on the bare landing was coming back from the bathroom; the footsteps stopped at our door.

'Goodnight, you people!' called Fatima. 'Sleep good!'

Devil of a Day

Tetouan
October 1992

'Look over there,' Youssef whispered, indicating to his left as subtly as he could. 'But not too much look.' I craned my neck. I could see the glint of a large blade; a curved blade, reflecting the afternoon sun.

Immediately I felt a surge of fear. I could taste it; my tongue tingled, my teeth crackled. The muscles on the back of my neck were tightening. I felt shaky, disorientated, and reached for his arm. Youssef looked worried, and yet he must have seen this kind of thing dozens of times before in Morocco's towns.

'He idiot, Jeannie.'

'*My God...*'

'Tetouan be place strange.'

'*Seems* to be,' I whispered. I licked my dry lips and felt that cold plunge in the belly, the fright thing.

'Drink your coffee an' we go,' Youssef said. 'But not yet. We stay a while, wait see what happen.'

My heart began a slow intense pounding.

'*Stay?*' I said, leaning forward, narrowing my eyes and again taking in the cluster of young men two tables down from us on the terrace. One especially, the guy holding the knife, shouting and wild-eyed. Unkempt. 'Jesus. He could do *anything!*'

The palms of my hands were beginning to sweat. I had to fight the instinct to get up and run.

'We not get up yet, Jeannie. I think he's with people who keep look out for him. They know he bit stupid, try keep thing safe for all. Don't worry.'

'How... how... often...?' I could barely speak.

'Uh? Oh, it happen sometimes. Usual it be idiot, like him. No need worry much.'

But Youssef did look anxious.

'He's... he's bloody waving it around now!' I grabbed his hand.

'I know. Stay, for a moment.'

Every second ticking by tautened my nerves. All I could hear was the *thud thud* of my heart. I fidgeted, yet I was numb, frozen.

At last: 'We go, Jeannie.'

Nothing much had happened. Some of the crowd had melted away; the heat had intensified; rampant flies continued to tickle my ankles and feet. With a scrape of chair legs, we arose and walked away, Youssef whistling between his teeth. And although I didn't look back, the scenario we were leaving behind was brutally etched on my mind, along with relief – and a curious exhilaration that I didn't ever remember experiencing before.

Youssef's cousin Mohammed pulled a face when we told him what had happened in the town centre.

'You not go out without *me* another time,' he said. 'I protect. You be on holidays and not need 'ave problems.' For a few seconds I took him seriously, then I noticed as he walked away his shoulders were shaking with silent laughter.

'Always he makes joke, Jeannie. Never I be sure which way it go. But I think if he be with us, he would take it serious also.'

'I've never seen anything like this in *Tangier,* Youssef,' I said, 'or anywhere else here.'

'It could happen anywhere. In places like London, Jeannie, too. *Tsss!*' He waved his hands around. 'No place safe, nowhere.'

I was packing my clothes and bits and pieces and seemed to have far more than when we'd arrived. I grappled with the zip. We were travelling back to Tangier early the next morning before flying home to London.

I wanted to move away from the knife episode. 'This week has gone so fast. We've been everywhere. Next stop – Rome?'

'Uh?'

'Just a joke, Rome.'

'Oh. You be joke person too, like Mohammed.' He paused, looking grim. 'Jeannie, I speak with Mummy on phone. She not happy really, but she want come to England sometime. We get doctor look at her. You know she's ill.'

'That surprises me,' I said. 'Leaving Morocco, I mean.'

'She not want leave Morocco, or Daddy. She's

afraid. But I tell her, she must. Get devil away from her.'

'Devil? *Him* again.'

'Remember – it's the devil who bring bad thing to her.'

'Yes, I do remember.' I tried to hide my smile.

'Make him go, that ol' devil. That's all she need.'

'She's a good woman,' I said. 'Why would the devil come to her?'

'She have this bad feel for a long time now, she expect it to come.' His face softened. 'It come an' it go. She says, devil, it get to her, make her ill.'

I felt my smile broaden.

'Jeannie, there's things here you don't understand,' he said curtly.

From the passageway, Mohammed called us, right on cue. He'd made mint tea.

We made our way to his small back room, the one that served as a kitchen, television room, and dining room. I walked bare-footed across the concrete floor strewn with the usual mix of small ethnic rugs. We settled down on squat stools around a low table draped with a real lace cloth. In the middle was Mohammed's silver teapot, and three dumpy glass tea tumblers circled on a round silver tray.

'Jeannie,' he said, pouring a high arc of tea into the first glass to test for colour. He frowned, opened the flip top lid of the pot and swirled the bunch of mint around with his fingers, licked them, then gave the mint a good squeeze before he flipped the lid down again. 'I listen to what you both say, about Mummy. In

England, you have devil? Is he there too?'

I wasn't sure if this was another joke. Mohammed was an educated man, but I knew how much the devil is feared in Moroccan folklore. Just how far did it go?

This time when he poured the tea, it was right. The colour was as it should be.

It was hot in the cramped room. I felt a trickle of perspiration begin its journey down my back. Youssef swiftly changed the subject, and suggested that, after our tea, we go for a trip out of the city in Mohammed's Jeep. Mohammed was very happy to spend some more time with us before we left him the next day. He wanted distraction, he was awaiting his engagement to a local girl, a girl twenty years his junior. He knew he'd struck lucky. But, as was the custom, he couldn't spend time with her without a chaperone.

We climbed into Mohammed's Jeep. Youssef took the wheel, but he didn't look happy as our driver. Impatiently he swung the Jeep from side to side trying to overtake a lorry – a ramshackle carrier crammed with two tiers of goats. Several tufty heads poked out at different points, golden devils' eyes surveying the passing scenery. As we passed, Youssef made snickering noises, but looked despondent.

'Nice goats there, but me, I have trouble with this one,' he said, unused to a left-hand drive. He'd learnt to drive in England, a different kind of experience altogether. He stopped the Jeep in a flurry of dust, and Mohammed, grinning, switched places with him.

We travelled on, past conflicting landscapes:

shacks on the road's edge and eateries with extravagant architecturally designed frontages; and further away, gleaming mosques, soaring minarets spiking the deep blue, stretched sky.

Beggars sat by the roadside amid verges dotted with scorched, spindly trees; growing in agony it seemed, twisted, with their roots protruding through the scant soil like lumpy devils' fingers. Little boys played in rock fragments and dust, and men leaned against walls for no apparent reason. As we slowed down at a crossing, semi-veiled women carrying their market shopping in the ever-present thin plastic bags – *plasticas* – scuttled out of sight, their eyes furtive and worried: a sure sign we were out of the centre of Tetouan.

Further on, we stopped for refreshments. Mohammed was thirsty.

We approached an ice cream kiosk next door to a run-down cafe. The seller reached out to hand Youssef an ice lolly, indistinct in shape, but then I could see it was a red devil with a scattering of chocolate chips. We'd met with him before, on the beach in Rabat. Youssef made a face as we walked back to the Jeep, Mohammed grappling with two cardboard beakers of coke and a hot tea.

'Him, I eat!' Youssef, mouth wide open, took a bite, again severing the devil's head clean from his chocolaty frozen body. Youssef flinched as the ice hit his throat.

'That devil, he *die!*'

As we drove away, I looked back. The name of the café appeared boldly on a large rough fascia. *Café des Jeunes.*

'Young,' I said.

'Uh?'

'Young,' I repeated. 'Back there – it's a place for the young.' I laughed. On the small terrace outside, all in a row, sat several old men, similarly grizzled-faced, jaws working away, each in his own world but ever-alert, watching, watching...

'They look like evil ol' men,' Youssef observed. 'But, really, normal persons.'

Mohammed, at the wheel, threw his head back, his face erupting into laughter lines. 'Maybe they in actual fact be *very* wicked,' he roared, enjoying his remark. 'You think so, Jeannie?'

'Who knows,' I said.

I smiled to myself. *It's been a devil of a day.* I knew it unwise to voice my private quip, it might not have been well received.

Back in Mohammed's flat we had a surprise. A few moments after we returned, a young woman came knocking at his door. Her name was Nadia. Mohammed ushered her in, kissing her cheek.

She smiled and greeted us both in the traditional way.

Nadia seemed very confident and mature to me. Youssef's eyes swept over her appearance, top to toe. She had jaw-length hennaed hair, wore a grey sweater and a grey skirt, thick tan tights and black clumpy shoes. She was taller than me. Mohammed explained that she had chosen to wear European clothes to meet her prospective European cousin-in-law and his English wife.

'Jeannie, it makes her look... old,' whispered Youssef. 'She's a girl young. Better she wear traditional stuff, much more pretty. This makes her look... not right. You think?'

I nodded in agreement.

Nadia moved away to make mint tea and left us to sit in the elegant living room, expensive drapes at the large, high windows, thick rugs, gold brocade settees – obviously a room reserved for Mohammed to receive his visitors.

'She lives a couple street away. Never she here normally with Mohammed on her own. Her father, he knows we come here, so he allow, say she can stay.'

'Stay?'

'Only for hour or li'le bit. She'll go home later.'

'Nice girl,' I said. 'She looks a bit... oriental.'

'Uh?'

'Chinese-y, you know.'

'Yes, she has beautiful eyes,' Youssef admitted, suddenly beginning his knuckle-cracking habit.

I gave him a look, but it fell flat.

'They have to be careful before they marry. Have to get engaged first. All very Moroccan, not like *our* wedding, Jeannie.'

That night, we bedded down for one last time, on the carpeted floor in Mohammed's posh living room, our luggage stacked neatly in a corner. I gazed up at the ornate crystal chandelier looming menacingly in the gloom; I'd positioned myself to one side of where it might fall if it was so minded. I hadn't mentioned what'd been going on in my head, I knew it'd be received with derision, or laughter. I had an inherent instinct for self-preservation, and particularly in a country like Morocco. I was wary of its dark underbelly, even when sharing its environs with one of its own.

Sudden light was streaming in from the street: a car's headlights.

I looked around the spacious room, musing that I'd never properly taken it in before. Its walls were scattered with incongruous gilt-framed prints; I caught glimpses of archaic characters grouped in dusty streets; an expanse of daffodils and crocuses in a cottage garden; and a heavily framed tableau of lush fruit in a crystal bowl. Long, elaborate drapes framed the tall windows, thick gold tassels dangling from each side; all this at odds with the heavy graffiti decorating the grimy, rundown exterior of the building.

'Home tomorrow,' Youssef murmured. 'Glad to go. I miss it.'

Swathed in soft Egyptian blankets, I lay listening to the sounds of the night: the grating departure of the car, a dog's mournful howl, and somewhere in the neighbourhood a winch was being drawn in a teeth-juddering way – and then I realised it was just some old donkey braying his heart out.

'You hear that?' Youssef laughed, and rolled across the floor from his blanket cocoon, pulled my blanket back, and grabbed me, kissing me with an abandon I hadn't known for quite a while. Then he straddled me, grinning.

'Quick thing only, yes?' Without waiting for an answer, he removed my cotton nightie and began to make unrestrained love to me.

'Ssssh!' I protested, 'not... so *loud*.' He was laughing noisily. I clamped a hand over his mouth and then suppressed a giggle myself.

'Me, always I love kiss you,' he murmured, swiftly tearing my hand away from his face, pinning my arm down and putting in even more effort. 'I love have you, Jeannie.'

'Ssssh... '

This was an occasion where I was never going to be riding the crest of a wave with him; but I enjoyed the intimacy and the feel of his broad back and smooth skin. With my free hand I found the curly hair at the nape of his neck. His moist mouth came back to plant a kiss wherever it found me.

He was yelling now.

'*Ssssh... !*'

'I... I *stab* you. See?' And he reached the point of climax. I managed to cover his mouth again; at the same time I sensed something outside, through the open door, in the passageway. I froze. *Someone was there.*

Youssef had moved away and was already crawling back to his own nest, breathing heavily. He pulled his blanket around him, disappearing underneath, still trying to catch his breath.

'Night, Jeannie,' he whispered. 'Have sweet dreams.'

Youssef's brief words of passion came back to me.

Stab. He'd used that word. The knife incident that day was obviously still with him, as much as it was with me. Fear could be a turn-on; it's the adrenalin.

I sat up, wrapping my arms across my breasts, and looked back to the open door, blinking, still not sure of what I'd seen. I could feel my heart beating fast. Maybe it'd been a trick of the light; fingers of brightness were thrown across the dark tiled floor from a source unknown, possibly a high window at the far end of the passageway. That had to be it.

Or was it?

I eyed the provocative chandelier way above, then struggled into my nightie, settling down again, pulling the soft top blanket up to my neck. I was avoiding looking towards the doorway now; I felt spooked.

Something had happened. Possibly the devil, playing his own tricks, gets his chance in those unguarded moments of lust. Or maybe I was totally wrong, was being hopelessly poetic and dramatic, and there *had* been someone outside: *Mohammed!* Cousin Mohammed… possibly curious to know what all the shouting was about. Or perhaps, more likely… understanding only too well.

Educating Nadia

Denton, East Sussex
August 1993

Our slow spring had developed into a fine summer and the temperature soared.

The jungle, up and beyond Youssef's breeze-block built Moroccan wall sprang to life, with white blossom on the trees in late June and wild roses weaving their way through the creeping ivy. On the peripheries, fragrant golden honeysuckle stems entwined with serpent-like bindweed coiling its way into our flowerbeds below. And Youssef's Beni Ahmed plants flourished all over the garden; they didn't seem to adhere to any particular season.

The jungle and garden were alive with birdsong throughout the day – raucous shrieking at dawn, waning to something more melodious at dusk. Neighbourhood cats leapt up the grassy slope, prowling through the encroaching ivy and further up into the jungle, forming a beaten trail through the grass and foliage. We called it Cat Mountain. The occasional fox showed its snout – their harsh barking at night kept me awake sometimes, but Youssef could sleep through anything.

Towards the end of the blistering summer, Mohammed and Nadia arrived unexpectedly at Gatwick one Tuesday evening. They phoned us as we were halfway through our dinner. Youssef drove like a mad man to pick them up and, in his haste, he also managed to pick up a speeding ticket.

Fresh from Spain, the honeymooners arrived in Denton full of smiles and kisses.

'How you do, Missus Jean? You are good?'

'Very well Mohammed. Welcome. Great to see you.'

Nadia stood slightly behind her husband, looking around her, kohl-lined eyes stretched, observing the unfamiliar.

'It not like España,' she said. 'It bit different. But, it beau-ti-ful.' She linked the fingers of her newly hennaed hands expressively. Then she spotted our budgies and froze. Youssef gave me a warning look.

Luckily, at that moment, Mohammed spoke, giving us news of Aunt Safia. He looked at me. 'She at home now. In an' out hospital lot of time, but… ' and he shook his head mournfully, 'she not good. She try laugh, but… '

I could see Youssef's eyes welling up. 'Look at hand of Nadia, Jeannie,' he said, changing the subject swiftly. 'See special… picture? It was done for her day of wedding.'

'I noticed. It's beautiful,' I said. 'Lovely patterns.'

'It means she have lot of baby, she *'ope*, some day. Luck. An' stuff other traditional.'

With Youssef's encouragement, Mohammed and Nadia went upstairs to see where they would be sleeping; in the back bedroom. Luckily the bed was made up and fresh.

'We've got nothing much in to eat for them,' I said. 'Just some French bread left over and cheese biscuits, and some olives.'

'I have good look now, see what we have.'

'I've already looked.'

'They okay, they eat on plane. It's late Jeannie.'

Mohammed came down first. 'I sorry you get *billete* for drive car fast,' he murmured. 'I happy get taxi for travel to your house today, this you know.'

'No,' Youssef insisted, 'this house is bit difficult for find an' I not let you have look for taxi from airport. Me, I'm here for look after you, like you has always in Tetouan, for always.'

It sounded like something Biblical. I wanted to laugh.

Youssef looked at me. 'Jeannie an' me, we want it be easy for you.'

An hour or so passed.

'We have to leave house for half past six in the morning – so better get sleep soon.'

'Why this?' asked Mohammed.

'Work.'

Nadia looked aghast.

'*Tsss*! Better we get to bed, Youssef.' Mohammed

patted my arm. He got up, throwing a sharp look at Nadia as she lingered on the settee examining her hennaed hands. 'Nadia! Come. *Arwah!*'

Before climbing the stairs Youssef gave Mohammed a set of keys to the house so that they could do as they pleased the following day.

'Better get some food in tomorrow,' I said as we closed our bedroom door. 'It would've been nice to have some warning.'

'Uh?'

'They could've let us know *sooner* when they were coming.'

'Yeah. What we can give 'em? Omelette? Salad? I don't know no more.'

We had been in bed for ten minutes trying to unwind when the phone rang downstairs. Someone flew out of the next-door bedroom and galloped down the stairs. Then Nadia's excited voice rang through the house as she spoke rapid Arabic.

Youssef looked grim. He got out of bed, pulled on his jeans, yanked open our door and stomped purposefully downstairs. I heard the termination of the phone call within a matter of seconds, then Youssef's loud voice. Mohammed's feet thumped down the stairs as he, too, went to join in the discussion. I kept a bleary eye on the clock. After fifteen minutes everyone came back upstairs and the back bedroom door was closed abruptly.

'It was her mum, Jeannie,' Youssef muttered, getting into bed. 'She want know how thing it go – an' then, her sister, she want to talk.'

'Bloody hell, Youssef. I know she's just married, but— '

'We work long day, Jeannie.' He switched off his bedside lamp. 'Nadia, never she work in her life.'

'Well, she is practically a schoolgirl still, isn't she.'

'Uh? Well, let's get some sleep now. Look at the time!'

'Don't tell me what time it is… ' As I spoke Nadia shrieked with laughter next door and there was a thump and some giggling.

'What this wall it made of?'

'Not brick, that's for sure. Plasterboard probably.'

Within minutes, Youssef was snoring gently.

It was too hot. The murmuring next door seemed to go on and on. I envied them their carefree existence, and their glow of newly married bliss.

Nothing lasts forever.

Because I was desperate for sleep, I wasn't feeling very charitable. And I was probably a bit jealous.

Paradise Park was always a pleasure, an Aladdin's Cave of delights that were mostly unattainable. Some small pots and plants for me and packets of vegetable seeds for Youssef were usually as much as we could afford.

On Saturday morning we walked along the aisles with Mohammed and Nadia; aisles lined with everything a British gardener could wish for. Along with the usual wheelbarrows, shovels, forks, trowels and compost came ornate, state-of-the-art barbecues and the accompanying paraphernalia arranged on a green felt setting in an area all to itself. Next came ceramic and clay pots and rosy faced gnomes. Picnic sets, rattan furniture; on pine shelves large glossy tomes on anything remotely horticultural, recipe books, dinosaur manuals, and a mass of indoor plants oozing colour on large trestle tables, flourishing in every possible hue, shape and size. Outside was a vast area containing sheds, wendy houses, bedding plants, shrubs and small trees.

Our guests looked impassive.

'They're not interested, Jeannie. All this... ' he waved a hand, 'it mean nothing for them.'

'Nothing?'

'Well, they don't have garden.'

'You don't have to have a garden to— '

'Just not argue, Jeannie. They not want stay.'

'Okay. Bit bloody rude though.'

'Okay Jeannie.'

'What about lunch?' We were standing near the glass doors to the eating area outside. As I spoke, around a leafy corner a miniature train whizzed by full of grinning children. Someone ding-dinged a bell as they passed. The train then disappeared out of sight around the next bend.

Nadia clapped her hands together; one of those excited, fast little claps... *Tap-tap-tap-tap*. She agreed immediately she would like to stay for lunch. We took brown plastic trays in the self-service cafeteria and queued for fish and chips.

Feeding four people was a very different matter from catering for two. Our guests weren't shy, they helped themselves to anything they fancied. What I considered to be a well-stocked fridge one day after they arrived was now more or less empty after only two days.

Later that day we drove to Sainsbury's to stock up.

'Me, I to pay for these food,' Mohammed announced. 'I likes do to 'elp.' He produced a huge wadge of twenty pound notes from his wallet. Youssef looked on greedily.

'Well, they *are* eating us out of house and home,' I said.

'Uh? *Sssh*, Jeannie.'

We dallied a long time in Sainsbury's. Each packet and carton picked up was examined for its ingredients – their three heads huddled together as they stood in the aisles, peering, turning, prodding.

Youssef looked towards me. 'They not want *cerdo*, Jeannie. Pig. They're not sure what be in these things.'

'You should know by now what you like. Beef sausages, stuff like that.'

'I need be sure. Them, they don't know – lot problem in Spain they have, thing like pig kebab nearly they eat.'

'Yes, they like their pork in Spain.'

'Uh?'

'Spaniards. They like pork. And *jamon*.'

'*Ugh*.' He pushed out his tongue. 'That's the thing about Spain I not like.'

Nadia had changed from her jeans into a mustard yellow mini-skirt with a pleated front, teamed with a pink strappy top. The outfit showed off her slim waist but wasn't so kind to her stocky legs.

'This we buy in España,' said Mohammed proudly. 'My wife, she want look European. I 'elp choose.'

The plan was to go dancing in Brighton.

'I'd be happy just to sit at home with a beer,' I whispered to Youssef. 'Any chance?'

'We have to take 'em, Jeannie. Mohammed, always he look after guest at his house.'

'Shall we take a taxi then? It means you can relax and have a drink.'

Youssef pondered. 'Best to do, yes. You phone, speak to taxi place?'

'Okay. But be *ready*.'

'We'll be ready in twenty minute.'

It took half an hour along the coast road to reach Brighton. On the way we admired a marbled red sky over a smooth, hushed sea, and flocks of starlings wheeling and spinning between the two Piers. Palace Pier, populated and bustling still; West Pier, enigmatic in silhouette, stark and aloof in the background. Youssef, looking at his watch every few minutes, quietly kept note of the time we spent in the taxi and I felt his resentment that we would be paying a high fare.

'There are *four* of us, Youssef,' I whispered, with a quick laugh.

'Uh?'

'If you were having to pay just for yourself, I could understand it. It's a night out, for the four of us. Taking Mohammed out and about, yeah? Like you wanted?'

He'd twigged, and scowled. 'Also, Jeannie, we need

come home this way. It gets a bit much.'

When we arrived at *Paradox* in West Street there was a long queue snaking its way back up the incline towards the Clock Tower. But it didn't take too long for us to reach the doorway where the bouncers stood. One brick-built young man in a dinner suit barred Mohammed's way.

'Can't let you in, Sir. *Jeans*.'

'Uh? What he say, Jeannie?' Youssef asked.

'He's saying Mohammed can't go in cos he's wearing jeans.'

Mohammed spread his arms and rolled his eyes, saying nothing.

'You not let my cousin go in?' Youssef had his angry face on.

Mohammed intervened quickly. 'I on 'oliday,' he explained to Dinner Suit. 'I not know this 'bout jean. I with my wife.' He wrapped an arm around Nadia and squeezed her to him and she grinned sheepishly.

'He's not going to cause any trouble,' I said. 'He didn't know about the dress code – well, none of us realised.'

The bouncer looked doubtful.

'Please? He's on his honeymoon.'

The Suit conferred with his mate. His mate had a sneery face, one of those faces that appears to exude perpetual disdain. They both scrutinised Mohammed from head to foot. Mohammed smiled back at them, wide-eyed, playing the innocent.

I tried again. 'Please?'

The Suit's mate, Sneery Face, looking less smart in

his creased DJ, made a decision. 'Alright, Sir, you can come in – *this* time. 'nother time you need to be better dressed.'

'Thank you, thank you... Sir,' Mohammed replied. 'You good man, you be reward for be so good.'

I ushered everyone in before the bouncers changed their minds. They watched us suspiciously as we went through the double doors and into the foyer to pay our entrance fee. Nadia and I stood to one side, leaving it to the men to sort out their small change, unwittingly holding up the uneasy queue forming behind them.

Youssef hated breaking into a bank note. I gritted my teeth and smiled at Nadia. We then went straight to the bar. Nadia had a sweet Martini with lemonade and the rest of us had a pint of lager each.

'Never I 'ave see thin' like these before,' Nadia said, gazing first at the flashiness and clamour of the bar and then at the illuminated, crowded dance area, cigarette smoke forming in a fug overhead. She glowed with pleasure, clutching her alcoholic drink, and dragged me through the crowd, down sweeping carpeted steps and onto the packed floor. We squeezed in sideways.

The bass of the loud music thudded through my body, setting my heart beating faster. Around us the mass of heaving bodies gyrated in unison to Techno. Coloured lights flitted across Nadia's elated face as she danced madly.

After a few minutes Youssef and Mohammed joined us, both still holding their half-consumed pints. Heavy perspiration stood out on their brows.

Nadia, in her mustard mini-skirt and skimpy pink

top, two sets of shoulder straps dangling, danced on and on. We left her to it, returning to the raised area by the side of the dance floor to keep an eye on her and tried to get our breath back. It was too noisy to attempt much talking. We ordered more beer.

We stumbled down the inner steps leading to the main doorway of *Paradox* then stood for a few minutes outside to breathe in the fresh night air.

'Look, Jeannie, nearly it two o'clock now. Time to go home.' Youssef rushed off towards the Clock tower to find a taxi.

I looked at Mohammed and Nadia and spread my hands. We could be waiting for quite a while.

'I 'ungry,' Mohammed said and a few shop fronts down joined a queue for doner kebabs. Nadia stood behind him, looking sulky. I waited outside, half-sitting on the narrow window ledge. I needed the air; I felt exhausted and shaky.

When Youssef finally reappeared, Mohammed and Nadia were standing on the pavement having words. Mohammed spat Arabic at her as she wagged a finger in his face. In a rage he hurled his half-eaten kebab to one side, narrowly missing a passerby. Youssef reached me and looked in disbelief at his cousin bickering with his young wife.

'What 'appen, Mohammed?' he shouted. 'Taxi, it's here! It waiting for us.'

Mohammed's body was tense. Suddenly he lashed out and caught Nadia on the side of the head. She yelped.

'There no *need!*' Youssef yelled. 'You should not hurt woman, Mohammed!'

Mohammed turned towards Youssef, his stance cool, but his eyes were blazing. He spoke in Arabic. Clearly, he was still furious.

Several people had stopped in their tracks for a second or two. They could've been waiting for a repeat performance. Nadia looked dazed, but suddenly moved away; she ran down a side street with Youssef soon in pursuit.

Mohammed stood next to me, silent, his expression stony. He shrugged and lit up a cigarette.

The Day After

Denton, East Sussex
August 1993

I'd pulled the bedroom curtains shut to keep out the morning light. We were wide awake, exhausted and headachy.

'It's because she whinges, Jeannie,' Youssef explained, taking a large gulp of hot coffee. 'She don't want queue for kebab, she always want have thing her way she like it.'

'Still no need for him to hit her.'

'Exactly, Jeannie. But Nadia, she drives Mohammed crazy. 'e not sure how they do for future now. Marry *only* one week.' He tutted.

'They'll be okay. They just need to adjust.'

'He's not so sure. She's spoilt. Mohammed, he tell 'er... *You dance for four hour nearly, an' still you not happy. Youssef an' wife, they take us for drink an' dance an' you be like li'le child.*'

'Well, really, she is, isn't she.'

'She just doesn't know how be wife yet.'

Next door we could hear rumblings and muffled

conversation. Mohammed was talking very insistently and seemed to be striding around the bedroom. The floorboards creaked tortuously.

'Maybe they sort out this thing now,' Youssef went on. 'I hope.' He got up and dragged on his jeans. 'I make mint tea. They expect this for breakfast. It helps I think.'

Later we all sat on the back patio, Nadia and I still in our nightclothes. We had toast, fruit, coffee and fizzy cold water on the white plastic picnic table. The kitchen radio churned out back-to-back chart music and a new cat sat at a safe distance in the garden, watching. Youssef had been nurturing this cat but wasn't having much success.

We laughed at our tired faces and total lethargy. The sun was already high in the sky and warming our bare arms. I noticed Nadia had rinsed through her clothes from the night before and spread them over the hydrangeas planted methodically along the top of Youssef's Moroccan Wall; that explained the smeary, dented washing-up liquid bottle I'd found in the bathroom earlier.

'I ache all over,' I said. 'And everything stinks of cigarettes. That place last night, everyone smoking... '

'Ah, cigarette,' observed Mohammed, lighting up. He passed the cigarette to Nadia, who took it in surprise.

'Me, I want Nadia experience *all*,' he announced. 'She need learn, for be... grown-up lady.' Nadia nodded in agreement, drawing on the cigarette, meanwhile watching out of the corner of one Cleopatra eye for our reaction. She inhaled deeply and immediately doubled-up with a shattering cough. We all laughed.

'Don't bother, Nadia,' I said. 'It's not worth it.'

'You like?' asked Mohammed looking at Nadia.

'I... *no* like!' she replied, trying to stub out the cigarette on the plastic table edge. Frowning, Mohammed quickly retrieved it.

'You like... alco'ol?' he enquired. 'That dring you 'as last evenin'? Martini?'

'Oh yes,' she responded. 'It... *very* good.'

Youssef tut-tutted. 'But it take four hours you drink it.'

'No matter,' she said. 'This dring, it good.'

Wood pigeons flapped loudly in the treetops of the jungle, *whoo-whooing*. Nadia flinched.

'I want Nadia 'ave this... experience,' Mohammed went on, putting the damaged cigarette to his lips and drawing on it heavily. 'In Brighton we 'ave pig burger in Burger King, day other.'

'You *did*?'

'We try them. We not in Morocco, so it possible for try. It not matter, we not cook it.'

'You really *did*?' I asked again, surprised – and thinking back to our visit to Sainsbury's.

Youssef looked over, nodding. 'It cos they not have cook this, Jeannie. It bit different then.'

'Is it?'

'It be just one time only,' Mohammed explained, wagging a finger in the air. 'Never we do 'gain. It for *experience*.'

'I see,' I said. 'A pork burger then. In Burger King.'

'An', Nadia... ' Mohammed continued, 'I want 'er study English. Get perfec'.'

'I *speak* English,' Nadia snorted.

'No, you to speak more better,' Mohammed remonstrated, 'before we get baby.'

'Oh,' she said, pouting. 'Baby, yes. We can... to practise also for this, yes?'

'Really, my wife Nadia, she funny,' Mohammed said, grinning and reaching across the table for her hand. 'She good lady sometime.'

Youssef cleared the plates and glasses, smiling to himself and humming to the radio.

'An' you, Missus Jean,' said Mohammed. ''ow go baby?'

'Not good,' I said.

He shot his wife a look, and Nadia went into the kitchen to help Youssef.

He leaned towards me.

''ow I can be sure Nadia she 'as baby?' he asked rubbing vigorously at his cropped, bristly moustache.

'Well... '

'What mean I, really – a... *inspection* for make sure she can for 'ave? Doctor, 'e can tell if possibles?'

'Best to wait and see. She's young so she's probably not going to have any problems.'

'An', Youssef... '

'Yes?'

'I worry to 'im.'

'Why?' My heart sank. I didn't want to pursue the baby thing.

''e need 'ave... *operation*?'

There was a crash from the kitchen. Nadia shrieked. She had dropped a glass.

'For... a baby?' I asked. 'Well, no— '

'No, Missus Jean. I mean... Youssef, 'e 'as eye bad. I notice this. People from *Sahara* in our country, they 'as eye bad this way.'

'Do they?'

'Yes. *Especial* there, in that place. 'ot an' dust, this be what 'appen for them.'

'I see.'

'An' Youssef?'

'Oh. Well, he's had an operation already. A cataract. It didn't seem to go well, but we're not sure— '

'Why this?'

'He'll need to go back. At least, *I* think he should.'

Mohammed looked puzzled.

'Back to the doctor,' I said.

'This 'e should to do, Missus Jean. If 'e be fathers, 'e need for 'ave good eye. 'e need be strong – as possibles.'

'That's true.'

Youssef appeared at the back doorway, his hands wet. I could see he wanted to laugh too. 'Me, I'm strong,' he said. 'But not much strong today. I hope okay with you, but I go back to bed for li'le time.'

'You tired, Hubby?'

Mohammed had a hint of a smile on his lips as he looked enquiringly up at him.

Youssef yawned. 'Jeannie, I get too old for dance an' alco'ol.'

Mohammed laughed openly, roaring, tilting back on his chair and getting up to slap Youssef's arm.

Youssef yawned loudly. 'Really, Mohammed, it's too much.'

'You be man young, my cousin. You be *young*.'

'No. I be *knacker!*'

The Queen of Spain

Nerja, Spain
May/June 1994

Spring of 1994 was very late in showing its face. Buds huddled, stunted, on tree limbs, and a cold wind blew. Tree tops in the jungle, up from our grassy slope, juddered desolately in the gales, with bare branches held up in expectation of better times.

'D'you fancy a week in Spain?' I asked Youssef.

'No, you know I not bother go back there,' he replied. 'You go.'

'You're sure?'

'You go. You know I have lot of friends here now, so I never be lonely.'

Time on my own seemed a good idea. But before I booked my flight, I needed to check with Youssef that no creature would be harmed on our back patio in my absence. 'Your *Eid* Lamb Day is coming up soon, is that right? How about I write a notice and pin it up somewhere?' I asked wryly. 'No killing. What d'you think?'

'I could do nothing like that now. Jeannie, I look

into animal's eyes... '

'That's good. I was hoping you'd say that.'

'*Aiwa*. Yes, it's true.' He sighed. 'I'd never be any good for Daddy now on Lamb Day, ever. Always at *Bakrid* time I did this for the family, I'm Daddy's first son.'

'Good.'

'When you going?'

'Probably mid-June.'

'You don't need to worry. Lamb Day comes up around twentieth May. I won't be doing anything like that. But a bit of celebration, of course.'

'That's double good.'

'It your fault, you English. Never I think I go like this.'

'Like what?'

'Soft.'

I flew to Malaga in the third week of June, arriving just in time for the festival of *San Juan*. My own tiny apartment in Nerja, still limping on, was on a long term let so I had rented a little studio apartment in *Edificio Torresol*, right on the beach. I overlooked not only the *Torresol* beach, but also the beach bar of the same name, serviced by two short-in-stature waiters we had christened the No-Necks.

The No-Necks' name came about because of their hunched look, brought on presumably by years of waiting at tables. Antonio and Miguel – I was never sure which was which, as they seemed to respond to both names, or the ubiquitous *Tssss!*

My Polish-roots cockney friend Marta, on hearing where I was going to stay, suggested that if I played my cards right, I could get a pulley rigged up from the Torresol Beach Bar to my balcony and therefore get my drinks without having to leave the premises.

'Why would I want to do that?' I asked her over the phone.

'Too 'ot,' she replied. 'Too 'ot to trot.'

In the heat I scaled Avenida Castilla Perez, the curved main road rising steeply from the beachfront into the centre of town. I soon found Marta outside one of the many cafeterias on the *Balcon de Europa*, sitting with a group of her friends. She kissed me on both cheeks.

'You'll find a few changes, Juanita,' she said, dragging a chair over for me. 'This place is shifting towards disaster all the time.'

'*Juanita?*' someone asked.

'It's 'er Spanish name,' she explained, patting my arm and passing a bottle of San Miguel to me. She introduced me to everyone there, which brought a few nods of laid-back acknowledgment. 'She married an Arab,' she said to no one in particular. 'So she's gone decent. But then she was always quite a lady anyway.'

This statement was met with a few inquisitive stares.

I felt the hot sun on my face and savoured the pleasure of being back in Spain. Soon it was almost as if I'd never been away. Flies tickled our lower legs and I gave up swiping at them fairly quickly.

We sat in companionable inane chit-chat for the

next two hours. At quarter-hour intervals the church clock of Santa Maria del Carmen in Plaza Cavana thundered its presence.

Marta passed me another bottle. 'You seen those No-Necks yet?'

'Not yet. Soon enough I'm sure.'

'I 'eard Miguel's fed up. 'e's leaving to set up 'is own bar.'

'Oh yeah?'

'Believe that and you'd believe *anythink*.'

The crescendo to the ritual of *San Juan* is, traditionally, rushing into the sea at midnight alongside friends or family to get thoroughly wet; all this after a vast consumption of alcohol on the beach. By drenching the body, good luck would come your way for the following year. Of course, Marta and I decided to go down to the beach that night, but to give the bathing side of it a miss.

'We'll go on our own. The others'll just bog us down with all their touristy wittering. Anyway, they never stay the course.'

'But will I? Will I stay the course?'

'You always do.'

On *San Juan* Night on Burriana Beach there was chaos – firecrackers sounding like bombs, a huge roaring bonfire with effigies atop, frenzied music, trestle stalls selling fast food and fizzy drinks. And there was a carousel, whirling around crazily on a section of the hard-standing area, shiny coloured horses bobbing up and down, round and round, their fixed unwavering stares distinctly startled.

'It's getting worse year after year y'know,' Marta remarked. 'Bloody shame if you ask me. Sodding spoilt, all of it.'

All the wicker-canopied restaurants were doing a roaring trade. Just about the whole population of the town was on the beach; tourists too if they latched on and were not still in town eating and drinking as they would be normally.

'Right, Juanita – we're off to see what's occurring.'

Marta managed to wheedle a couple of bottles of beer for us from one of the many locals she knew and we trudged along the beach amid the mayhem. She led on as usual, her short almost bandy legs strong and tanned beneath her khaki shorts.

'Ayo's still here, is he?'

'Ayo? 'course! Still wears that greasy bit o' bandage round 'is 'ead, still stirring the ol' paella, still raking it in. My god, people love that place.'

'Well, he's an old gypsy. He'll never change.'

'A *rich* ol' gypsy. But he does still employ some tasty little darlings! I go for regular inspections, of course.'

'Of course.'

We lapsed into silence for two or three minutes, heading away from the main part of Burriana.

'Remember, Juanita... those early years? We could wander down 'ere and sit with the locals? We'd 'ave free beer all night, always. And free sardines— '

'Ugh!'

'—and none of this bloody carry-on we've got now.'

We sauntered down to the sea. I could feel the lap-and-slap of the cool seawater across my feet as I walked the water's edge, the ooze of sand between my toes.

We were now away from the more frenzied area. There were small fires burning all over the beach, fronting the locals in their small tents where they squatted by the front flap, cooking top-to-tail sardines on a grill in the embers. I could smell the fishy tang in the air.

Flames cast flickering movement on the tent sides, wisps of smoke drifting up and into the enveloping darkness of a sultry June sky. Looking up high enough I could see the sprinkling of tiny stars against a velvet-black backdrop. Just enough light was thrown by the column lampposts at the back of the beach, and from hand-held torches, which beamed erratically across the beach like Martian rays.

'Nice, innit?' Marta said, her mouth curling into a characteristic grimace. 'Remember that time they put you on a throne down 'ere? How many years back was that?'

'I'd rather not think about it.'

'Aw, that was funny. You didn't know how to take it, did you, Juanita!'

'What could I do? I just sat there... drunk.'

'Yeah, pissed as a fart you were. Missus Respectable now. 'ow is the young man?'

'Youssef? He's okay.'

'Just okay? Don't you miss 'im?'

'Of course I do. I met him *here*, remember.' I

kicked at a large smooth stone in my way. 'But, Queenie, it's only been one day away from Sussex so far.'

''e not keen on coming back then?'

'Seems not. He's more interested in Morocco and doing well in England.'

'Surprised you're 'ere at all. I expect we'll lose you eventually.'

'I hope not. I really hope not.'

We passed some small tents. I could hear murmuring from inside one of them; through the canvas the slow moving, shadowy occupants looked like they were making ready for bed.

'Too early for sleep,' Marta remarked. 'They got a bit more drinking and craziness to put up with yet.'

A sporadic *Andaluz* shout went up from somewhere further along. A group of *chicos* a little way off were toasting the Queen. They had put a *chica*, a young woman, on a beat-up chair and positioned both chair and occupant on a tufty, sandy hillock. They placed a beer in her hand.

'Eh! That looks familiar,' said Marta looking at me.

'Tenemos *La Reina*...' they proclaimed, raising their bottles in deference. 'La Reina!'

The Queen of the Beach sat demurely on her throne reigning supreme, resigned and smiling. In the background, Ayo, the local entrepreneur, bandana-swathed as always, sprawled with a group of friends. He cackled, waving a hand, joining in.

'That was *you!*' Marta sniggered, bashing my upper arm with her fist. 'Wonder if it's the same little darlings doing it this time?'

'Maybe. It's not that many years ago.'

'I need to check 'em out,' she said, heading towards them. '*Holaaa!*' she shrieked, disappearing into the gloom.

I stood and took a breather.

Further along little groups of sardine eaters sat in the sand enjoying a joke. A bone-thin dog strolled by, pawing the sand, pausing, sniffing, nose momentarily buried, tail wagging; and then he turned to lope towards the sea.

I sat down in the sand on my own. Too many beers that day had taken their toll. My head throbbed, my eyes felt gritty and sore. I ran the fine sand through my fingers and thought about what to do. I gave her ten minutes.

When Marta didn't reappear after fifteen minutes, I found my way off the beach and headed for home. I passed bars off the *Balcon* and into Avenida Castilla Perez, spotting familiar faces through the open windows. I could probably have joined their little groups, but I'd had enough for one day.

As I trudged on, Rosa from Cordoba came to mind from nowhere; Rosa the Tarot reader, Youssef's ex, the one whose heart he had broken. I had heard from Marta in one of her letters that she had recently reappeared in Nerja, reclaiming her pitch on the *Balcon*. She said she looked different, her short dark hair gone now, replaced by lots of long blonde curls. A new beginning? I made a mental note to look out for her.

I pushed through the main door of my apartment block and climbed the concrete stairs, walking on to my studio apartment at the end of a long corridor. It was deserted and deathly quiet. I wasn't comfortable until I'd unlocked the door, gone in, and bolted it behind me.

I looked at my watch. Half past one. An early night by one-time standards, especially at fiesta time. I sat down on the bed. I hadn't spent a night apart from Youssef since I had reeled him back from Morocco. And here I was, on my own, potentially throwing myself back into a life that I had long left behind. I had a week of freedom and I could do anything I liked. *Anything.*

I lay down on the bed, rolling over onto my side, catching hold of and winding the bed sheet around my fingers. *Tight.* Tears crept into my eyes. Alone I could be honest with myself. This town was where it had all begun with Youssef. I didn't miss him, not yet; just his physical presence was missing. All we'd been through initially, the trauma and the frustrations with Immigration. Enough to truly bind a couple together.

But, forever?

So often, the misunderstandings, his lack of finesse, his inexperience, his youth.

His foreignness.

Why had it all come as a shock?

I had to face it: I wasn't sure if what I had with Youssef had enough staying power for us to have a future together. It wasn't a *proper* love. I'd always known that.

And what of my actions? I'd never forget the

awfulness, early on, of trying to speak some Arabic – how Youssef had chastised me when I couldn't say *B'slemah* as goodbye when surrounded by a circle of hopeful family; it'd come out as *Bee-Slammer*.

'Maybe you should not come here.' He'd looked stern. 'You must do thing that happen in country you are in.'

I'd felt myself go hot, and thoroughly scrutinised.

'You know this, Jeannie.'

He'd gazed at my burning, stricken face.

I wanted to say *Yeah, like you did in London?*

I felt awkward and powerless. I was in danger of welling up and disgracing myself. I really did want to shout, to remind him how he'd reacted in London, the way everything fazed him, how inept he'd been. But we'd already been that way before, some years back with that huge argument in a hotel room.

In the U.K. he was still the boy from the mountains, but not when he was on his own turf.

I rolled onto my back, settling myself to gaze up at what appeared to be a water stain on the ceiling. Perhaps I was being overly dramatic. Marta would think so – she'd laugh and pull an ironic face.

I'd have to sleep on it.

In my tired, half drunken state I wasn't really sure of anything.

Disappointed.

Not that I was going to admit that to anyone.

Sweet Manic Dreams

Nerja, Spain
June 1994

We were sitting in Robert's bar, just off Avenida Castilla Perez, perched on bar stools at the far end; Marta in her faded khaki shorts, me in my most flattering purple mini-skirt. Yesterday I'd applied fake tan to my legs, something I never thought I'd need to do.

Flamenco blared from a cluttered sound system behind us, battered speakers and gear heaped on a low podium. It all sat amid chaotic cabling, stacked music albums, and scattered rolls of grey fluff... just as it had the last time I'd been in there.

I shifted around on the stool, a little edgy. Dazed. I tucked my legs under me, wrapping them around the spindly metal supports. I still felt like a tourist, as if I didn't quite belong, though I was on familiar ground; my holiday time in Nerja stretched back a good, semi-dissolute decade.

Marta too looked jittery, but then she always did.

'*Jesus*, Juanita. It'll be that Blues stuff next...'

she said, jogging me with her elbow. '*Goddup this MORning... da da da... duh...*'

'Right,' I said, laughing. 'He loves the Blues, does Robert.'

Some people drifted in from the street and found seats. They settled at the door end of the bar where, above the large brick fireplace, hung a brown and orange framed print of Spanish fighting bulls, entitled *El Toro Bravo*; another of Robert's nods to Spanish cultural trappings. A large double window stood wide open onto the gathering nightlife outside.

Star-shaped, brightly coloured stickers, giving names and prices of cocktails, spattered the wall at that area of the bar. In front stood Robert, stroking his bristly beard, waiting for orders. 'English beer too – if you want it,' he announced. It also housed the toasted sandwich section. Earlier, I'd read the stickers aimlessly... Daiquiri, Tequila Sunrise, Sex on The Beach, and a new one, Shepherd's Pie.

'Bet that goes down a storm,' Marta had observed. 'Some tourist will ask for it. Then he'll ask if they want peas with it or maybe chips. That'll cause confusion.'

There was another slight flurry at the door. One or two heads turned.

Long-limbed black Africans roamed the beaches by day and the bars by night, arms draped with multiple goodies – trailing strands of coloured beads, cheap glitzy watches, glow-in-the-dark lighters on a cord, and miniature Buddhas carved from wood or onyx.

'Lookeee, lookeee...'

'Oh God!' said Marta, flinching. 'Here one comes.

Wish they'd bugger off back to—'

'Don't be so hard on them,' I said. 'You're jumpy at the moment. You don't have to talk to them.'

'Yeah, but they talk to *us*.' She scrabbled in her handbag, extracted what she needed, and lit up a *Fortuna*. 'If I get offered another one of those crap watches, or a flippin' grinning Buddha...'

'Ma-dam?' A slender hand dipped into a canvas shoulder bag to produce... 'Ele-phaant. Nice ele-phaant, for you? Nice price.' He placed a dark and oily looking, crudely carved specimen on the bar. 'Very nice ele-phaant.'

'*Very* nice,' observed Marta, looking the other way and blowing smoke through her nose. 'But *just* bug—'

'Go easy,' I said.

Our African stood by quietly. He was not giving up. '*Wife* ele-phaant, and many baby...' he said, gently positioning a smaller elephant, followed by five diminutive versions decreasing in size, along the bar top. 'Very nice price. How much pesetas you give me? Special price for you.'

'Nothin',' Marta muttered.

'Another drink, Queenie?' I asked her, flapping my hand at Robert, who stood chatting at the other end of the bar, hands on hips, in front of his coloured star-shaped stickers.

'Might as well. And don't call me that.'

'You *are* the Queen of Spain,' I said.

'Get lost.'

I shouted : 'Same again, Robert. Two *Tinto de Verano*.' It was 'spring' wine, though we were into the summer. Nerja's streets were crowded and sizzling hot.

'Coming up,' Robert called.

I touched her shoulder. 'Alright?'

'Mm.'

'Things more or less the same here?'

'More or less.'

'How's the teaching?'

Her face became animated. 'Yeah. Little buggers – those students – call me *Abuela*, you know, *granny*. Bloody cheek really.' She tightened her lips. 'But it's fine... fine.'

'So it's all going well at the *Escuela*. Getting properly paid?'

'Yeah, yeah. I see them out an' about, you know— '

'Who?'

'My *students*. Who else? Juanita, if you graced us with your presence more often... '

'Yeah,' I said, doing something like jazz hands at her. 'Hubby? Flights? Work commitments?' I pulled a face.

Robert slammed our drinks down on the bar top.

Our African was still there. His teeth gleamed. 'Ma-dam?'

A giraffe appeared on the bar top, followed by a carved sword. Then, a smirking coiled cat.

'Pain, aren't they?' she said, taking her *Tinto de Verano* from the bar top for a quick sip.

'The Lookee Men?'

'D'you know, they speak five or six languages. That's clever.'

'So you do have a heart.'

'Buried somewhere. Pickled by alcohol probably,' she said, flashing a swift smile, her mouth crinkling at the corners. I felt I was suddenly back in the saddle, like I'd never been away; I should've known it wouldn't take long.

Two brass containers appeared on the bar top.

Mister Lookee waited.

'I heard everything they earn is sent back to their families in Senegal,' I whispered, gazing at the soft ruby liquid inside my glass and swirling the straws around to make the ice jiggle and clink.

She snorted. 'Who told you that?'

'Hubby, when he was here. He used to talk to them.'

A row of dull silver rings, their glass insets winking under the overhead lights, were laid out for us beside the brass pots. Marta gave them a cursory look.

'*Very* good price for you.'

'I'll 'ave one,' she said.

'You choose which one, Ma-dam?'

'You choose. I'm tired,' she said, grinning.

Mister Lookee looked startled. 'You sure?'

'I'm sure.'

He looked her in the eyes, and selected a green-stoned ring. He began to wrap it carefully in a shred of tissue paper.

'No. I'll wear it.'

He moved forward, easing it smoothly onto the third finger of her left hand.

'We're married!' She laughed.

'We marry!' he responded. 'When we go 'oliday?'

She coyly withdrew her hand. 'Cheeky bugger,' she said. 'Get away with you!' Scrabbling in her purse, she paid him.

Pleased with his one sale our African, tiny bells jingling, left us.

'Here, Juanita,' said Marta. 'Green's not my colour. It's yours.' She thrust the ring into my hand. Before I had a chance to say anything, she was off again...

'Look at 'im!' she said, nodding towards Robert. 'You'd think he'd have a bit more pride. Every time I've seen that bloke he's wearing that grimy vest.'

'Seems to be his trademark,' I said.

She scowled. 'I don't come in here that often, but every time I do – there's that bloody ol' vest standing there. Really, the English have gone to the dogs.' She dug around in her handbag again. 'Keep the ring, it's yours.'

I was laughing. 'Thanks. And don't say that too loudly, there's a few of 'em in here. The English, I mean.'

'And look at that mess behind us,' she said, wincing as the music reached some kind of crescendo. 'Spaghetti junction gone berserk.'

She found her lighter. 'They're an embarrassment here in Spain. And not just because they want bloody Daddy's Sauce and expect everyone to speak English.'

She picked up her cigarettes from the bar top.

'He was looking into your eyes,' I said, 'to see what colour they are.'

'Vesty?'

'No. You know who I mean.'

'I'm sick of it here.'

'Spain? Not sure I believe that.'

'You know,' said Marta, lighting up another *Fortuna*, 'I'm thinking of going back.' She threw her lighter down. 'Going back to London, that is.'

'Oh?'

'This place is wearing me out.'

'You do look tired, even with your tan.'

'It's this bleedin' life. Go, Go, Go. Everyone's afraid to get off the social treadmill.'

'I thought you'd risen above it?'

'I tried. I've always burnt the candle, but this place... well, this place, it's knackering me.'

She blew a smoke ring away from me. In profile her face was drawn. There were dark smudges under her eyes and I noticed a new clutch of lines spidering from her mouth.

'I've never heard you speak this way before.'

'I don't know... ' She took a deep draw then stubbed her cigarette viciously in a white china *Cruzcampo* ashtray. 'Ever since my dad died, I've felt... this need to really live. You know, *use* every *second*. But... is *this* living? You're the sensible one, Juanita. You always were.'

'Am I?'

'Flippin' manic 'ere.'

'I know.'

'Look, I've got to get back to the apartment. Some silly cow is coming round for a Spanish lesson soon.' She looked at her watch. 'I *ask* yer – the day after *San Juan!*'

'*Silly* cow,' I agreed, knowing how frantic the festival always is, how it engulfed the town, swamped the beaches.

'She can't get her head around *bebida* and *bebé*; all to do with my scary tuition I think.'

'Yeah?'

'Yeah, maybe. I had to laugh, she kept coming out with... she would like to have... a *baby*, not a *drink*. I said, you'll be in big trouble if you go into a bar and start saying somethin' like that!'

I sniggered.

'I need to get these private bits of work though, at home. I have to take it. I advertise in all the English pubs here.' She sighed. 'Stupid gits.'

We looked at each other and laughed like two crazy women.

'Drink-up, Juanita. *Vamanos*. Let's go.'

We slithered from our high stools and walked to the other end of the bar, barging our way through. The bar was beginning to fill up, and Flamenco had switched to something Bluesy. Sounded like B.B. King.

'I'm staying,' I said, patting her arm. 'You'd better get off then. Maybe you can get some rest after.'

'A rest? How can I rest while you're here?'

'Relax while you can. You're... overwrought.'

'Overwrought? That's a good word.'

'Just go. I'll see you tomorrow.'

'Once I've sorted out my punter I'll hit the sack... or I might come back here, drag you over to Riverboat an' hit them slammers.'

'Slammers?'

'B52's, Juanita. Keep up.'

She chuckled, clutching her pack of *Fortuna* as she moved to the door. 'Watch out for those bloody Lookee Men.'

'They're no trouble.'

She stood at the open doorway. '*Buenas noches*, Juanita. *Sueños dulces!*' For a second or two, still holding onto her cigarette pack, she positioned her head sideways on her flat hands as if in sleep.

'Sweet dreams to you too, you silly cow,' I replied.

I watched Marta through the large double window as she paused outside to dip into her handbag, just as a slim brown hand slid over her shoulder. She turned, confused, but immediately crinkled a smile. I caught a glimpse of dangling turquoise and amber beads; heard the soft jingle and clink of miniature cowbells. Within a few moments she and her admirer walked away and, I noticed, in the opposite direction to her flat on Avenida Castilla Perez.

She was off to do some living.

The church clock struck one o'clock as I strolled along the *Balcon*. The sun was hot but a cool breeze had sprung up. My aim was to meet Marta, and I knew where to find her.

As I pushed through the crowds in the market area, Rosa from Seville came to mind from nowhere; Rosa the Tarot reader, my husband Youssef's ex, the one whose heart he had broken when he lived here.

'*Rosa, she say I 'as life long, an' many luck,*' he'd said.

Marta mentioned in an email that this girl had recently reappeared in Nerja, reclaiming her pitch on the *Balcon*. She said her short dark hair was gone now, replaced by long blonde curls.

I'd look out for her.

I spotted Marta sitting alone outside Café Jimenez under a red parasol, the movement of the overhead fabric throwing dark shadows onto her face. She was still in her shorts, a café solo held to her lips, a small bottle of *agua con gaz* handy nearby.

'Sorry for not coming back,' she said. Her green eyes were half-closed with exhaustion, her short hair standing on end. 'And how's hubby today?'

'Haven't phoned him yet. He'll be at work.'

'Give him my love.'

'I think I saw Rosa the Tarot girl this morning on the *Balcon*,' I said, fibbing.

'Yeah? Blonde girl?'

'I've never met her, just saw a blurry photo once. It had to be her though.'

'People come and go in this place. I don't know meself. You know I spied her the other day.'

'Yeah.'

'She did my cards once. Load of crap, all of it.'

'Good crap things?'

She shrugged.

'I'm guessing not,' I concluded.

'*Tsss!* To hell with her, she's bad news.'

I felt a pang as I responded. 'She might still be nursing a broken heart.'

'She made a lot of enemies here, wasn't liked at all.

Vicious cow, her. No wonder she's gone and bleached-up her hair.'

'Needs to be incognito?'

'*She beat someone up once!* So, yeah,' she said. 'I'm off home soon... knackered. See you later?'

I hired a sun lounger down on El Salon Beach and snoozed in the afternoon sun. Seagulls wheeled overhead and the tide slapped and agitated at the shingle on the water's edge. I drifted off, dreaming of Youssef – out of the blue, holding a photo – and of Marta's tired, worried face. Somehow all this connected in a dream that made perfect sense.

That evening, I went back to Robert's bar. I ordered a Frigiliana wine that was so strong I had to dilute it with soda. It was still light outside and the day's heat had now dissipated. Occasional loud Spanish cat-calls rang out along the narrow street outside, and traffic hummed and belched from Avenida Castilla Perez.

As I took a taste, Marta slid onto the bar stool next to mine. 'Sacrilege, watering that down!' she instructed.

'I know.'

'Well, here we are again.'

'Feeling better?'

She ignored my question. 'Here we are, on our own. No ties... well, you 'ave – ol' hubby, El Moro.'

I shot her a look. Youssef wouldn't approve of being called The Arab, and she knew it.

Thigh to thigh, Marta still in her khaki Bermudas, me in loose trousers, we watched Robert working the bar in his signature vest. I recognised a stain on the back from the night before.

'Mister Vesty,' she said. 'Look at 'im – does he think he's fuckin' George Michael, or has he forgotten to shave for days on end?'

'Who knows.'

'Bartender!' she said. 'Bacardi an' coke, ice, no lemon.'

Robert nodded.

'I got somethin' to report,' Marta said. She knocked ash off her cigarette.

'What's that?'

'Went on the *Balcon* earlier with Mister Lookee,' she said. 'Had a good look at our resident witch, the lovely Rosa. *He* knows her too. Knows everyone an' *everything*, 'im.'

Something somersaulted inside. I turned to look at Marta. 'What?' I asked, slightly irked that she hadn't already spat it out.

'Yeah. Took my time – and still wasn't sure.'

I felt my mouth twitch in annoyance.

'Does she know about you?' she asked suddenly.

'Course she does. Word got back to her immediately Youssef left for London to live with me. She was well pissed-off.'

'Yeah?' She picked up her drink pensively. 'Well, there I was, on the *Balcon*. I stood, just wondering... *Oh!* – I told Mister Lookee about you, y'know.'

'*Did* you!'

'Yeah, I did. Anyway, Rosa had gone into charm mode with some punter. Then some ol' dear in the crowd piped up: *Oiga!*'

'Oh?'

'Yeah. She poked a finger at her and asked what'd happened to Rosa.'

'I'm confused,' I said.

Marta grinned. 'You won't be.'

'Eh?'

'Rosa wasn't happy, she was involved with her punter. She shot her a look – I had a really good shoofty at her then, at Rosa.'

'Yeah? But— '

'Listen to this. *What – my sister?* she said.'

'Sister?'

'Yeah. Turns out the blonde is Rosa's sister. She's taken over the Tarot stuff from her.'

'Ah.'

'So that accounts for her looking so much like her, but not being her at all!' Marta exploded into laughter. Tears gathered in her eyes and trickled down her thin face. She wiped them away with the back of her hand.

'As you would say, *steady on girl*,' I said. I reached out to hold her arm.

'Aah well, Juanita,' she said, looking for a tissue. 'That's the end of that mystery. We can breathe easy now, be sure not to be gettin' a sharp knife between the shoulder blades any time soon!'

She laughed all over again. 'Well... *you*, anyway,' she spluttered. 'You would've been the victim, not me.'

'Unless the sister is here at her bidding,' I blurted, trying to see the funny side of it. 'She might be tracking me. I'd better keep an eye out.'

'Too true!' she said grimly. 'Make a good film,

this,' she said. 'I can play you, an' you can play Rosa – and her sister.'

'Yeah, why not,' I said.

'Nah. On second thoughts, not such a good idea.' She slurped on her drink, choking. 'I don't fancy the idea of... fuckin' cold steel creeping up on *me*.' And she laughed one more time before rummaging in her handbag again. 'Good job you're flying home soon.'

I had sudden suspicions about the sister scenario. I felt freaked.

'Sweet dreams later, matey... ' said Marta, grinning. 'I'm off soon, meeting my Lookee Man.'

Someone had gone into a heavy whisper at the doorway. There was a little gaggle of people grouped there, but no familiar faces.

The back of my head tingled.

I looked furtively over my shoulder, scanned the bar...

'Be worried, Juanita,' Marta joked. 'Rosa's revenge, eh!'

The thump of my heart rose to my throat.

Mister Lookee. He knew everyone.

He knew *everything*.

She knows where to find me...

Liberty

Denton, East Sussex
July 1995

I heard the gate squeak.

I exchanged a look with Mummy and quickly moved into the conservatory to investigate. At the very same moment Youssef crashed in through the front door with a shout and a smirk. Mohammed and Nadia followed on smiling broadly, looking immediately at home as they, after the customary shared bear-hugs, settled into the small pink settee.

Mohammed's eyes flickered about our living room.

'Nothin' it change,' he said. 'Furnitures, they in differents place, but same more-less.'

Nadia grinned and made a huge fuss of Mummy, who looked like she wanted to run away. Mohammed bellowed good-humouredly, looking around, swivelling his head this way and that, his arms and legs jerking about like a demented marionette. He and Youssef seemed to be sharing a private joke; there was a lot of laughter.

'Bit of trouble at airport, Jeannie.'

'Oh?'

'Person on flight, he have luggage same thing as Mohammed. He takes wrong one, we have to find him for do changeover.'

'Really? You were lucky he hadn't already left the airport.'

'Who?'

'The person who took Mohammed's case.'

'Case?'

'Luggage, then.'

'Oh. Yes. It very strange, but we find him quick, it be okay.'

'Change luggage easy,' said Mohammed. 'We know where find him, this person.'

Abruptly, Youssef marched off to the kitchen. Nadia took my hand: 'Missus Jweenie, it good be here again. Nice, like when time before.'

'You're welcome, Nadia,' I said, trying to look sincere and with a slight pang of guilt. I followed Mohammed as he joined Youssef in the kitchen. Youssef was making mint tea.

'Aah, Youssef. Yous eye, it look betters.'

'Uh?'

'Yous eye, it looks terribles before. You 'ave *operacion*?'

Youssef burst into Arabic to explain while bringing the silver-gilded tray bearing Moroccan pot and tea glasses into the living room. Mohammed nodded. 'Ah! So doctor for eye, 'e do this. That is good, yes Missus Jean?'

'It was Mister Liu, the surgeon,' I said. 'Thank God

for him. He sorted it out eventually in Brighton Eye Hospital.'

'Mister Loo?' Mohammed asked.

'*Na'am*, Mister Loo,' Youssef responded, pouring a high arc of mint tea into the first glass to test for colour. 'He make normal again. A cataract. I pleased it all over now.'

'We can rise our glass… ' Mohammed announced, surveying Youssef's hesitant tea-pouring '… to Mister Loo. 'e take good care for my cousin an' alway be we 'appy now.'

'That's right,' I said. 'Long live Mister Loo.'

Mohammed roared back, taking over the tea-pouring and grunting with satisfaction at the darker colour now decanting smoothly into the first glass.

I should have known that all would not be rosy. Mummy didn't want them there. She'd already been with us for a month and had settled in quite nicely.

Very soon came the phone calls with shouted conversations to and from Tetouan at all times of the day and night; or so it seemed. Youssef rolled his eyes at me knowing there was not a lot he could do about it. We knew they were concerned for their baby daughter, they'd never left her with anyone before.

Youssef tried to distract me: 'Mummy, she look li'le bit quiet. I think it be nice if we do something for her.'

I thought for a moment. 'Remember I suggested we buy her some new teeth?'

'Yes, that she would like.'

'I'll book an appointment at the dentist in Seaford.'

'What she'd really like is to get that ol' devil away from her... '

'I know. If we could only get her well, find something to make her feel better. She's flown all this way... '

The car ride into Seaford with Mummy took ten minutes. As we passed the Victorian terraces overlooking the sea Mummy commented on the rust on the ironwork and how it all needed a lick of paint, just as Youssef had remarked years before.

'She glad she not go to Brighton. Remember the Pier there? She hate it. She don't like walk on bit where she can see water go under.'

'Looking down through the gaps? Yes, I remember. They've been there a very long time those boards.'

'That's what she worry about,' Youssef muttered, turning a sharp left, causing Mummy in the back and me in the front to lurch sideways in our seats. 'She thinks they go fall down and she go down with 'em into sea.'

'Tell her she could be a mermaid.'

We arrived at the dentist's surgery. Mummy looked nervous and was hanging back.

'Relax, relax Mrs El Ma...Ma...er... '

'El Mamechi,' I said, only too aware of our difficult name.

The dentist helped her to lie down on his reclining chair and moved to look into her open mouth. Without prompting she fished her dentures out with one hand. I could see they were totally worn down.

'All her teeth were taken out when she was quite young,' I explained.

He ran his rubber-gloved finger lightly around her gums. 'These dentures are so old they're making her mouth sore.' He sniffed. 'I don't know how she's coping. They don't fit properly at all.' He was staring into Mummy's wide-open mouth.

I suspected her teeth may have come from the market in Tangier and I had a brief flash before my eyes of the trader with his sets of teeth on a blanket on the ground, all carefully arranged as if on stage.

'I can sort her out, no problem,' said the dentist, running his finger around her mouth again. 'You'll have to wait about a fortnight for the next appointment, the impressions would need to be taken and then go off to our laboratory.'

Youssef nodded.

There was a pause of a few seconds.

'I'd say you'd need to pay five or six hundred, maybe a bit more. If you wanted porcelain, it'd be— '

'Six 'undred!' Youssef whistled through his teeth. '*Tsss!*'

'That's the cheapest you'd get,' said the dentist disparagingly.

'It's a lot of money, Jeannie.'

In silence we left the treatment room and over my shoulder I gave the dentist what I hoped was an apologetic look.

We three had a meal to ourselves that evening.

Mohammed and Nadia, now knowing quite well how to get around, had gone to London by train that morning.

We agreed it was nice to be back to the way we were for a while.

Mohammed had been excited and eager to go; he wanted to buy some cheap shirts in the summer sales, and Nadia wanted clothes and makeup as well as toys for their daughter Yasmina. They talked about going to Liberty which they thought was more famous than Harrods. I didn't argue.

Mummy switched on the television. She was getting interested in EastEnders and could recognise the characters now, claiming to know what was, more or less, going on.

'Grant Mitchell, he's her favourite. She says, Grant he look like good, strong man.'

'Strong... but I don't know about good.'

'Mummy say, he have face nice. She like.'

'Don't tell Daddy.'

Youssef laughed and so did Mummy. I didn't know how much she had understood, it was always hard to tell. We watched the usual cliff-hanger episode of Mummy's favourite dysfunctional families in action in the East End; I suspected Youssef enjoyed it more than he would admit to.

By ten o'clock Youssef and I decided to take advantage of the calm in the house and go to bed to catch up on some sleep.

As we said goodnight to Mummy, Youssef looked at his watch. 'Mohammed, he late.' He screwed up his face in the way he did when he was worried, the lines on his forehead prominent. 'I not think he want to be out so late as this.'

Upstairs was stifling, even with the windows open.

Mummy sat up watching television waiting for Mohammed and Nadia to come home. I slept fitfully, bathed in a film of sweat, aware of the blare of the television from downstairs and subconsciously listening out for footsteps and voices which would mean our guests were safely home with us.

I must have gone into a heavy sleep; Youssef was shaking me awake.

'Jeannie! Jeannie! Mummy she's up here... Nadia, she come home.'

'Nadia? What... ?'

'Just she come home from station, on her own. She walked. She's clever, she remember how to get here.'

'So... where's Mohammed?'

'She doesn't know. He lost. She wait an' wait.' He threw an arm in the air dramatically. 'He not come back!'

I was sitting on the edge of the bed by now. I felt groggy with sleep. I pulled on my cotton dressing gown and went downstairs with Youssef. Nadia sat scrunched up on the pink settee sipping some black tea. Mummy was standing up looking shocked.

'You need to phone police, Jeannie.'

'Of course.' I put an arm round Nadia who looked near to tears.

'We be... in Liberty,' she explained. 'Shop big,

London.'

'Nadia, she's very brave,' Youssef went on. 'I can't believe she find our house like this on her own. She catch train correct from London, change at Lewes – an' before that she have to find Victoria in London.'

I rummaged in our pile of directories, then picked up the phone to call Newhaven Police.

'I'd like to report a missing person,' I found myself saying. 'His name is Mohammed El Mamechi. He's... '

'Thirty-nine!' prompted Youssef.

'... Moroccan. He's been in this country a week. *Mm?* Oh, last seen in Liberty... Regent Street, London. When? Today – well, yesterday now.'

Youssef was signalling frantically. I ignored him.

'His wife lost him and had to find her way home, back to us. She's here now.'

Youssef was now staring at me hard, his brow rucked up into its usual set of worry lines.

'We're in Denton. Yes, it's our house.'

I caught a glimpse of Mummy wringing her hands, twisting her wedding ring round and round.

'He's my husband's cousin. He's thirty-nine. Sorry? What d'you mean, too early? He's a stranger in this country.'

'What he say, Jeannie?'

'Just a minute Youssef... Okay, okay. Thanks.' I put down the phone and turned to face him.

'*What he tell you?*'

'They say it's too early to report him. He may've gone somewhere for his... own reasons. *Oh, Christ...* ' I broke off. Something had crept into my head.

'What they *mean*?'

'They said... if we don't hear from him by tomorrow, we should phone again.'

'But... *Nadia*, she was with him. He not go off an' leave her, not in a place like London!'

'Well, that's what they *said*. I suppose it's best to wait by the phone to see if he calls. We can take it to bed with us.'

'Bed? Sleep? It not happen tonight, Jeannie.'

'It's all we can do. I know it's bloody crazy, but what else d'you suggest?'

I was thinking back to the mysterious mix-up of luggage at Heathrow. It'd felt strange. And, knowing of Mohammed's dealings on the side in Tetouan, I couldn't help but wonder if there was some kind of connection.

I shivered, pulling my lightweight robe around me.

Shrugging off such thoughts I looked at the wall clock. It was ten past one. Nadia sobbed and Mummy stood motionless with a tear in her eye.

'He's dead,' Youssef muttered. 'I know he's dead.' He leaned across to place a hand on Nadia's trembling shoulder, but was looking at me. 'What else can it be?'

We didn't sleep. Not a wink.

Dawn had long broken. Tired of lying in bed, each with our separate thoughts, we got up at the same time. Youssef pulled on his jeans and headed for the open bedroom door. 'Jeannie, we not hear nothin'. He's dead, must be.'

Mummy and Nadia were downstairs where we had

left them, both hollow eyed and silent.

I phoned work at nine o'clock and left a message to say I wouldn't be in because of family problems. I phoned the police again and they took more details. This time they said they would pass the information around to London and South East region police stations. Did we have a photo? Youssef immediately rummaged in a drawer then leapt into the car with a photo of Mohammed to take to Newhaven police station.

When Youssef returned, he decided to mow the lawn to keep busy. Mummy put a heap of tomatoes into a pan of boiling water to begin a tagine for later. Nadia made the decision not to phone Tetouan, she didn't want to worry the family there. She slumped on the settee and I made more coffee.

While in the kitchen I kept an eye on Youssef outside. He was so sure that Mohammed was dead. His agony was etched on his face and apparent in his jerky movements. I watched as he manoeuvred the Flymo – and had a sudden surge of sympathy for him. He had been so looking forward to having family around, and now this. I placed my hand on the door handle, ready now to go outside to ask why he was so convinced; I might learn something. But Nadia appeared like a ghost by my side. I jumped.

'Where be Soudia?' she asked, looking nervous. 'She gone?'

'Gone for wee wee I should think.'

'Wee wee? There no person in bathroom.'

'She's gone to her own bathroom,' I said, pointing

out of the window to the grassy slope beyond Youssef's ugly breeze-block wall. 'Up there.'

'She not like toilet,' Youssef added, coming in through the back. 'It not feel right. Always she go there, to the jungle.'

Nadia tried to smile.

Youssef groaned. 'I not know where I be at the moment. I'm all over place. This thing, Jeannie, it's terrible.'

'I know.'

At just after eleven o'clock the phone rang. Youssef and I exchanged a stunned look and, as I was nearest, I picked up the phone.

It was Zoë, my pubbing friend from the office. 'What's up?' she asked. 'I hear there's trouble down there.'

'Hello Zo.'

'I'm worried about you. What's happened, Jeannie?'

'Well... it's bad. Mohammed, Youssef's cousin, has gone missing.'

'*What?*'

'Yeah. Doesn't sound good. We're still waiting to hear.'

'Oh God.'

'Yeah.'

There was a few seconds' silence. 'Give me the details. What happened?'

I told her the basics, dragging the words out parrot-fashion now.

'Leave it with me,' she said. 'Remember, I have connections. Studying law comes in handy sometimes. I'll come back to you.'

I replaced the phone wondering what she meant.

By twelve-thirty she'd phoned back.

'I've found him,' she said. '*Silly* sod.'

'*What?*'

'I've been phoning round all the London police stations. He's been detained. Appeared at Bow Street Magistrates this morning.'

'Bow Street?'

'Caught shoplifting. They didn't want to tell me, but I insisted. Said I was a close friend.'

'Shoplifting? But he's *loaded*, why should he—?'

'It goes that way sometimes. You know, something for nothing.'

'Where's he now?'

'Waiting.'

'Waiting for what?'

Youssef crashed down on the settee by my side, craning to hear what was being said.

'To know what's coming next. He's paid his fine.'

Youssef was pressed up against me.

'Look, here's Youssef. Please could you talk to him? Tell him— '

He seized the phone, speechless for a second or two, his eyes popping from their sockets.

I looked at the two women in the room who gazed at me in silence. 'He's okay! Mohammed's okay!' I mouthed, giving a double thumbs-up sign. Nadia had tears in her eyes and clapped her hands together hard. Mummy slumped onto a chair. Neither of them said a word.

Youssef contacted one of his Moroccan pals, Hamid, who lived locally and agreed to drive up to London.

'I'm not fit for driving, Jeannie. I'd get lost anyway. We need take Nadia too.'

'All organised?'

'All organised. Nadia, she not can *wait*.'

Nadia was ready and hovering, twitchy, wearing elaborate makeup and her best drop earrings.

'Thing I don't understand, Jeannie,' Youssef remarked as he got into Hamid's car, 'why Mohammed didn't make phone call? An' he knows Nadia she's waiting.'

'I know.'

'An', why... steal stuff? I don't understand.' He shook his head. 'Really, Jeannie, first I think maybe it's a worse sort of thing he do.'

'I know you did.'

Nadia quickly got into the back.

'We'll find out exactly what happened later on,' I said, slamming the car door shut. 'Give him our love.'

Mummy was standing behind me, her hands to her face. As Hamid's car pulled away, she waved frantically, then linked arms with me to walk back to the house, patting the trunk of one of the trees growing on the bank of grass above the car park, the one nearest the path which led to the squeaky gate. She had claimed that tree as ours although it was well away from our property.

Zoë phoned me again, this time from home. 'Alright?'

'Yes, alright. They've gone off to collect him. My God, Zo, thank you so much.'

'Glad to be of help. And I reckon he owes me a drink.'

'He certainly does. A whole crate's worth.'

'*Jesus*, Jeannie. Don't they think about the consequences ever? Silly git.'

I didn't know what to say.

Zoë broke the silence. 'Talking of drink, when're you coming out with us again? It's been ages.'

'I know. Tied up with this lot.'

'Just see that you do. Don't let all that lot change you. You were always up for a drink, and now... '

'I know. Things change.'

The ten o'clock news was coming on when they arrived home. Youssef looked glum, Nadia was quiet and Mohammed looked very disorientated. He wanted to go through his story all over again when we sat down to eat. No one was really hungry.

'I *not* be thief.'

'We believe you,' I said, not really sure what I believed.

'The police, I pays what they asks... in court...but what can do I?'

'What happened in Liberty, Mohammed?'

'I leave Nadia... she takes tea in café part of shop, an'... I say I not be long... '

Nadia nodded, confirming this. 'Liberty,' she said, 'be shop big. With stripe, black... an' white, all over.' She demonstrated how the downward stripes went with the flat of her hands.

Mohammed continued. 'I see style shirt I like an' go look for more colour. I put this on my arm, an' across my... soldier... '

'*Shoulder*,' Youssef prompted, without changing his expression.

'My shoulder, yes. Then I see nice jacket. Also, little jacket, too, for our baby. I forget time.'

Mummy sat listening, twiddling the cord of the long Indian skirt we'd bought her, to look more in keeping on the streets – we'd realised her swathed traditional garb might not be the best thing to be seen in.

Youssef translated for her, looking as anguished as Mohammed as he sat telling his tale.

'I look at watch, an' go look for Nadia. She not there. I... get worry, rush from shop. I go into street... '

'Oh dear,' I said. 'Oh *dear*.'

Nadia touched my arm: 'I wait an' wait Jweenie, get worry, then go out to street, look for Mohammed... ' she said quietly. 'I walk in street, go into shop different... I keep look for 'im. 'e no place!'

'Still I 'ave shirt,' Mohammed continued, 'all colour different, on my arm. I shout: *Nadia!* I shout 'er name... one, two time. Then, man, 'e comes an' force me go with 'im. Big man. Police, they arrives, an'... '

Nadia burst into tears. Mohammed took her hand tenderly. 'I tell them, I 'ave my wife wait for me. She not in café, she be I not knows where.'

'What did they say to that, Mohammed?' I asked.

'They not believe me. They say I tell lie.'

'That's terrible, Mohammed. And they didn't let you make a call to us? That's really diabolical.'

'And Nadia, she so brave,' Youssef added.

'Nadia, she *silly*,' Mohammed countered, dropping her hand like it had bitten him. 'She should to go 'otel for night – she should not go travel in... God know *where*. Somethin', it could 'appen... '

'She wanted to get home, Mohammed,' I cut in. 'She had the train tickets and remembered how to get back to Victoria.'

He snorted. 'Nadia, she know what I want, we speak on this before. She 'ave some English money. I worry she not listen for me.'

'Who knows what we'd all do in strange circumstances?' I said, finding myself welling up. Nadia sobbed, wiping her eyes. 'Shall I take this up with the police?' I asked.

'Uh? What you mean, Jeannie?' Youssef asked.

'What you say, Missus Jean?'

'You should've been allowed that phone call. It would've made all the difference to us – we'd have known you were safe.'

Mohammed snorted again.

'We could put in a complaint.' I looked around at them all. 'They were in the *wrong*. They should've— '

'No, Missus Jean. Me, I want... *forget* all these thin' now. I want 'aves my 'oliday with my wife, an' forget.' His face was dark with anger and fatigue.

'Okay Mohammed. If you're sure.'

'I sure.'

'I sure you were dead, Mohammed,' Youssef whispered. 'What for tell family? What to say? Really, if that happen, I never, ever be happy again.'

Mohammed shot him a look; he then grabbed Nadia's hand, pulled her off the settee, waved goodnight to us, and hauled her up the stairs to bed.

'You keep asking him, Jeannie. He doesn't want. Leave him now with this.'

'I asked once – just *once*,' I said. 'Is there anything I can ever do right for you, Mister Misery? Let me know if there is.'

'Uh?'

The Poke Police

Denton, East Sussex
July 1995

We had all cheered up by the following day. It was Saturday and Nadia volunteered to cook. Mummy and I were shooed out of the kitchen – we didn't mind that at all.

We sunned ourselves in the garden.

Later on, I was allowed back in to collect cutlery, glasses and paper tablecloth to lay the table on the patio outside. Nadia was stirring some kind of stew. Hot bread rolls were laid out on the work surface.

'I like 'ave *you* 'ere Jweenie.'

'That's good.'

'I not mind 'ave you 'ere – but I not want Mummy Soudia be 'ere.'

'Why not?'

'She... come to food, an'... ' Nadia, breathing heavily in exasperation, demonstrated what Mummy did by poking at the rolls with her forefinger.

'She pokes?'

'She poke. She do this to food in my 'ouse when she come one time.'

'She does?'
'I see she do other place with family. It very annoy.'
'I don't think she's done it here.'
'She 'fraid 'ere. She be good.'
'She's *always* afraid.'
'In Morocco, she not. She strong, very. Argue... thin' like this, lot of time. It difficult.'

Seconds later Mummy appeared in the kitchen. She went over to the stew in the pan, lowering her head to sniff at it. She grinned gummily at us both through her worn and broken dentures, moved round to the work surface and, with pursed lips, extended a finger and gave the bread rolls a good poking, each one in turn.

On Monday, Youssef and I returned to work. Mohammed and Nadia went out to celebrate his lucky escape and their reunion.

Mummy was in the house alone when someone came to the door. It was a man in a dark suit with shiny buttons and a peaked cap. She spotted him through the front window and fled to the bathroom, trembling, locking herself in.

Youssef got the full story when we returned home.

'She see police an' get afraid. She thinks he come to see her.'

'Why would he want her? It's more likely to be something to do with Mohammed.'

'What could it be?'

'I'll call them,' I said, heading for the telephone.

He looked worried. 'You call London?'

'No, Newhaven. London police wouldn't come here.'

On the phone I kicked off with my concern about Mohammed's rights when he hadn't been allowed a phone call. I wanted to get it off my chest. The officer was very sympathetic and agreed that Mohammed's rights had obviously not been adhered to.

'But we're letting it go,' I said.

'Why?'

'He's been through enough. We all have.'

'Oh.'

'And could you tell me why an officer come round to the house today?' I asked. 'My mother-in-law was terrified.'

'Oh, that. He was returning the photo your husband had given us – the one of your cousin.'

I laughed. 'Thank you. That explains it.'

I told Youssef what had been said.

'Mummy, still she worry. That man, he coming back again?'

'No, we can pick it up sometime.'

'Mummy, she worry always for see police. In Morocco, we see police an' it be trouble. Really, always she be this way.'

When Mohammed and Nadia returned, we told them the story of the policeman coming round to arrest Mummy. We all laughed.

Nadia wasted no time in cornering me in the kitchen. 'Jweenie, I know why policeman 'e come,' she said.

'Oh?'

'It was policeman *special*. 'e come take Soudia to

prison for... poke at *bread*.' She covered her mouth to suppress a giggle.

'I *see*.' I grinned, jogging her arm. 'Poke Police.'

'Yes, that it. I think... you know... 'e get to 'ear some'ow what she do.'

I looked into her young face and smiled. 'I think maybe you're right.'

She smirked, her Egyptian eyes flashing. ''Course.'

'Maybe it's the devil at work,' I said.

'Uh? Devil?' Nadia's face dropped. I bit my lip; I had blundered. Then her face brightened and a slow grin unfolded.

'Oh, Jweenie.' She fluttered a hand. 'That be... rubbish. Mummy Soudia, all this devil thin'.'

'Really?'

'Yes. Devil, 'e live in Morocco, not 'ere in England.'

'Does he?'

'Everyone, this they know. Soudia be jus' silly.' She sniggered. 'This place, it country modern. It not 'ave these thin' stupid anymore. Much more clever.'

Proper Love

London
September 1996

'I never thought you two were right for each other anyway,' Marta said. She exhaled, remembering at the last split second to turn her head to blow a smoke ring. 'But, at the same time, I didn't think you'd break up.'

She turned her cigarette packet over and over on the bar top, her long fingernails tapping against the hard edge... *Click-click...click...*

'You know, it looked like a proper love,' she added. 'And he seemed so genuine.'

'Genuine, maybe,' I replied, 'but single-minded.'

'Yeah? And now you're saying it's divorce?'

'Looks like it,' I said, picking up my drink. 'Might as well get on with things.' I took a large gulp of lager and replaced my glass on the bar. 'It's all slid away, that life. I always thought it would eventually.'

'Sliding away, eh?'

'Yep.'

'You look resigned, Juanita,' she said, peering at me. She dropped the cigarette packet and picked up her whisky. 'I know you worked hard at it, but he seemed to want it all. Just typical.'

'Yeah. He always was ambitious but it hasn't done him any good, has it? He could drop dead with exhaustion at any time.'

'Are you wishing he would?'

'No, of course not. But I can't help feeling bitter.'

'You bet, gal.'

'*She* might think it,' I said, 'but I don't think the new girl is going to... you know, reap any benefits from *him*.'

'What d'you mean?'

'Well, he might be *with* her, but his heart isn't with her. They're just using each other. She works for him, remember. Lives upstairs there now.'

Marta gave me one of her looks, then shifted awkwardly on her bar stool. '*Hey*,' she said, 'this *pub!*' She looked agonised, the way she always looked when she was about to make a statement.

'Juanita – it's a bit ropey, don't you think?' She huffed. 'Lyceum Arms? There must've been a better place to meet.' She sighed, running a hand over her face. 'Christ, we've known a few.' She gazed at the tarnished pewter tankards hanging in a row above the bar; the faded sepia photo memorabilia of London's theatreland pinned at every angle on the rough wooden posts built into the counters. All coated in dust.

She wrinkled her nose.

I didn't blame her; it wasn't a smart pub. I was conscious of the scuffed stool legs marked by a million flailing shoes and the padded seats flattened by unimaginable numbers of backsides.

'It has a few memories, this place,' I said.

'Of him?'

'No, not of him.'

'Nice part of London though. The architecture's interesting.' She sniffed. 'But this place, almost empty. Smelly ol' men. All we need is some ancient stinky dog or two.'

'It wasn't as bad as this before.'

'When?'

'I used to come in here with my workmates. Most Fridays.'

'Beer goggles, maybe?'

'No... I was never that drunk. Okay, the decor's a bit much.'

'Too bloody true.' She gave me that wordless look indicating her scorn.

I rolled my eyes.

Marta's attention was suddenly drawn to the swing doors as two suited young men came in. A muted bell *dinged* as the doors closed behind them. Her mouth curled into a smirk. She flicked ash, and straightened her back. She re-crossed her legs, the nylon of her tights crackling.

'She *is* gorgeous, though,' she said, looking at me.

'Who?'

'The girl. I know you're dwelling on it.'

'Am I? Well, yes, she is.'

'Brings punters into the café. Youssef isn't daft.' She pulled a face.

'Well... there's that. She's a bit of a trophy for him.'

'So, you really think no big romance there?'

'I don't reckon so. I liked her... but the bitch is welcome to him. I don't bloody want him.'

'Yeah!'

'Let's change the subject, shall we.'

'Okay,' she said. 'Are they still there?'

'Who?'

'The young men... ' she said, stretching her neck to take a look along the bar.

'I can hear them talking,' I said. 'Don't panic.'

'Well, yes, Juanita... I'm feeling so much better since I came back from Spain. Wouldn't want to live there again, not really.'

I laughed. 'No more chewed-down nails then.'

Marta grinned, flexing both hands, her scarlet nail varnish gleaming in the overhead lights.

'*And,*' I said, 'I found evidence.'

'Back to that, are we?'

'Yeah.'

'Go on.'

'On a table in *her* room.'

'Ha!'

'I was there at the café last week.'

'There? What, you actually *go* there?'

'Yeah, if I'm passing. They fall over themselves to look after me.'

'Yeah?'

'Yeah. On the young woman's table, right next to the bed.'

'Bleedin' cheek. A little sachet thingy? How fuckin' blatant was that!'

'I know.'

'Well, that just has to be proof.'

'Definite proof.'

'You tackled him?'

'Of course. But he blamed it on the Spaniards, that couple from Madrid who had that room for a while.'

'Right. So you believed that?'

I raised my eyebrows and waved a hand. 'He came out with that just a bit too quick for his own good. Believed him? What d'you think!'

'Fuckin' 'ell. Yeah.'

'I don't know why I bothered really. But he won't admit to it.'

Marta drained her whisky. 'Well, Juanita my poor ol' mate, I don't know what to say.'

'Say nothin'.'

'Ironic that you talked about him taking up with the café – like it's his mistress.'

'It might as well've been.' I moved my upper half backwards slightly to avoid another smoke ring. 'I never saw him. Ships in the night.'

'Where did she come from?'

'He filched her from Burger King.'

'You never really needed him.'

'True.'

'But he needed *you*.'

'Yep,' I agreed. 'He did.' I bounced the toe of my shoe against the wood-panelled bar. 'Funny... I found some old Home Office papers in the shed the other day,' I said. 'All *kinds* of stuff. I wrote to Lord Denning! Bloody Lord *Denning!*'

'He's dead now.'

'But he wasn't then.'

'We heard about it quick that day,' she said. 'His death. Chancery Lane an' all that. News spreads like wildfire.'

'Of course, *you'd* know... up to your neck in legal stuff there.'

'We hear a lot in my office – I think we might've been the first to know. You'd be surprised at what I've picked up on.'

'I bet,' I said.

'Drink?' Marta dragged out her purse, meanwhile looking through narrowed eyes along the bar towards the two young men; one fair and one dark, their backs turned to us. The dark one had curls creeping over his ears and was broader... he reminded me of someone I wanted to forget.

'What we having, Juanita?' She turned to wave a tenner impatiently at the barman. 'Bar person! Can we have some service up 'ere?'

'Just weren't interested, were they?' Marta said, holding onto my arm as we crossed the road. 'Not bloody interested at all. Now, if we'd been in Spain... '

'I know. But we're not. Wish we were though.' I drew up the collar of my coat, the night air had become chilly.

'They *appreciate* older women over there.'

I shivered. 'Or is it that our reputation precedes us, as they say?'

'A bit of each probably. But, fuck me, how wet are they *here*! Clueless. No idea at all.'

With Marta clinging to my arm, we were already halfway down The Strand and walking through London's litter. In some of the shop doorways, street people sat huddled in dirty blankets, silent, maybe too dejected in the cold night air to offer up their usual wavering call for some cash.

'And the bar staff were bloody slow too,' she sneered.

We were nearing Charing Cross, approaching the top of Villiers Street.

'You alright on the Underground, Juanita?'

''course. Done it a million times before.'

She stumbled a bit. 'Sod the bus, I'll take it with you. Fancy a coffee or somethin' first?'

'Yep, why not. Looks like you need it.'

'Me? No, I'm thinking of you, you silly cow.'

McDonald's was practically empty. We manoeuvred the narrow steps leading down into a semi-basement area. I ordered two hot chocolates. The staff looked tired and tight-lipped and there were signs they were getting ready to close up.

We took our cardboard beakers to a window table, pushed aside the clutter of debris from the previous occupants, and collapsed onto the split plastic seats.

'What'll *he* be doin' now?' she asked. 'Working still?'

'Who knows!'

'Seems to me, Juanita, his love was... '

'Don't... '

'... *suspect*. The more I *think* about it.'

'It's those papers that worry me...'

'What papers?'

'That stuff I found in the shed, the transcript of that first interview in Rabat.'

'Yeah?'

'Y'know, before he could come back. We were seen separately. Bit of a shock that.'

'Oh yeah?' She fumbled around, lighting up again, then threw her lighter onto the table. She looked exhausted.

'You don't really want to hear, do you... '

'Why not? You've started, you might as well— '

'Alright.' I looked down at the grubby floor, concentrating. 'Well, it kind of stayed with me a bit. I read through, you know, the interview *he* had with that cow... one of the officers, as it happens, and— '

'Go on.'

She was fidgeting. I ignored it.

'I'd already read it, when it was sent through to me, like, *years* ago... but really, this time I took it in properly.'

'Yeah?' The usual smoke rings wafted between us. I doubted she was listening, she was too done-in.

'D'you really want to hear this?'

'Yeah, yeah.'

'Well... remember me telling you about all the hoo-haa with him wanting to marry this *much older* woman? Me? Remember that?'

'Yeah.'

'They kept on about that, kept shooting questions.'

'Confusing him?'

'Possibly,' I said. 'He was interviewed in Arabic though, and the transcript was in English of course. His answers were... well, typical of what he'd have said really, but— '

'But?'

'He said we *liked* each other, we got on well, and he wanted a better life in England.'

'Daft sod. What was he thinking of!'

'Neither of us knew how to play it, but *blimey*, he could've done a bit better than that.'

She laughed. 'So what conclusion have you reached, Juanita?' She nudged me. 'Eh?'

'Possibly he was shy of the word— '

'What?'

'Well... *Love*,' I said. 'Know what I mean? Especially having to talk to a foreigner and being in a place like that.'

'Like what?'

'In the bloody Consulate, in *there*.'

'You know you're making excuses for him.' With her elbow on the table, her jaw cupped in her hand and her eyes half closed, she was squinting out of the window, up at the passing army of high heels, legs and sporadic noise: young women on the town.

'Maybe,' I said. 'But then, as you said, he was still a bit wet behind the ears. He may not've thought to use the word they were waiting to hear.'

She grunted. 'Who knows, Juanita, if there *is* a proper word for love in their language?' She yawned loudly. 'You know, as *we* would know it.'

'I know,' I replied. 'It's such a complex language.'

'Don't you know? Eh?'

'Well... how *much* of it did I actually pick up!'

'Love in Arabic. A proper word? But yeah, seems like he played it all wrong. No wonder that all went pear-shaped.' She stubbed out her half-smoked cigarette on a crumpled cardboard plate and let out a sigh. 'What do *you* think? Were you conned?'

'I don't know, I really don't. But I did believe in him, for quite a long time.'

Marta twitched and fiddled.

'The summing up didn't make good reading though.'

'Eh?'

'Something like... ' and I thought hard to remember the words, 'this... applicant does not appear to me to be... sufficiently fond of... or committed to, this... *much* older woman, his fiancée, and therefore... '

'Bloody 'ell. I don't remember you telling me— ' She was showing interest now.

'... and therefore... I recommend refusal of entry to the United Kingdom... blah-blah... at this time. *Something* like that.'

'Sounds like he just couldn't muster up the right word. Either that or he's a bit stupid.'

'Marta,' I said, feeling tears stinging my eyes, 'I don't think he *realised*. We were together all those years. If he hadn't been genuine, he wouldn't've stuck around, would he?'

'Yeah, but not very honest now, is he.'

'No, I suppose not,' I said, wiping an eye with the back of my hand. 'He wanted to make money, take care of his family in Beni Ahmed. I couldn't really blame him for wanting to do that. He loves them.'

'*Love!*' she jeered. 'It takes over.'

'I remember him telling me, some years back... there's a few words, four or five, for love in Arabic.'

'Yeah?'

'*Yeah*. There's... love for your fellow man,' I said. 'Then there's love for your family.' I was getting into the swing, counting them off on my fingers, and she looked up, her eyes sliding open, showing real interest. 'And love for a... lover.'

She cackled. 'Presumably that includes husband or wife.'

'Probably *only* husband and wife.'

She laughed out loud.

'That's the love word he should've used,' I said, 'the one that seemed to escape him. Silly bugger.'

'Yeah? That's a whole bunch of love there,' she said. 'Who would've thought it, eh!'

'And then there's illicit love; sex with someone you oughtn't. I'm surprised he mentioned that one.'

'Hanky panky? Must mean tarts.'

'... and, above all, love for Allah.' I pursed my lips. 'That's the lot. That's five.'

'Good bloody job.'

'What?'

'Better drink up, gal. They're about to throw us out.'

'Okay.' I picked up my beaker. The hot chocolate scalded my lip and I looked around for the plastic top, but the staff had cleared the table without me noticing and had taken it away with everything else.

'You're better off without him, Juanita,' Marta said, pushing her untouched drink into the middle of the table and getting up unsteadily. 'Twat.'

I laughed. But she remained serious.

'Any man who can't say the important things,' she said, 'ain't worth having.' Ignoring the frowning member of staff strategically positioned by her side, she pulled at the handle on the heavy glass door leading back onto The Strand. 'Christ, let's get *out!*'

By the time we boarded a westbound tube, Marta seemed to brighten up. She looked around our carriage attentively.

'There's my bloke!' she joked, half-rising from her seat, pretending to get up to join an elderly man who was slumped against the glass partition near the sliding exit doors; a dosser who was on his way to somewhere from wherever. '*Just* my type,' she sniggered. 'Let me get at 'im!'

I was afraid she might. '*Sssh*,' I warned, grabbing her arm. 'He might *hear*.'

She switched on a beatific grin. 'Like I would. Nah. Way too old for me.' She bashed my upper arm with her fist. 'Past his prime, that one,' she cackled.

A few people looked our way.

She collapsed back into her seat and became serious again. 'Don't know what I'll find when I get home,' she said, rubbing her nose vigorously, snuffling.

'Your mum, is it?'

She nodded. 'She's losing it now,' she said.

'Sometimes she thinks she's back in Poland. She's not lived there since she was in her twenties, before they came here. Thinks my dad is still around sometimes too.'

'Oh dear...'

'Yeah. She's kind of frightened that she's going that way, but she can't help herself.'

'Keep an eye open. Maybe let Social Services know.'

'It's scary, getting old,' she said. 'What's that song about dying before you get old?'

I had a sudden longing to be out of London, away from Marta, to be at home curled up in my bed; to be out of all this.

'Shoot me,' Marta was saying, 'if I end up talkin' to the neighbours the way she does. She's a mare, she just doesn't know it.'

On her face, genuine concern.

She slouched forward. 'My poor mama. It's a nightmare.'

Concern, and real, proper love.

'Hope I die before I get old,' I said. '*The Who.*'

She looked up. 'That's the one.'

'Don't forget to change at Lewes, Juanita,' Marta counselled as I got off the tube at Victoria, leaving her to travel on a few more stops before she changed at Earls Court; *she* was more likely to go wrong than I was. 'Bye!' she shrieked. 'Juanita, make sure *you* divorce *him*.'

I craned my neck to look back as I shuffled along the platform, hemmed in by the pack of boisterous

Friday night people. The tube train groaned and clanked into action, quickly gathering speed before disappearing with a blast of warm and choking air into the tunnel. I caught sight of Marta briefly; she looked worn and subdued.

This image stayed in my mind all the way up the escalator and onto the station concourse. I veered diagonally, half running, hurrying past the unmanned ticket barrier and onto Platform 17 to catch my last train home.

I took a window seat just as the insistent blasts of a whistle from platform staff started up. Tilting my head, looking through the smeary glass, I watched as a gaggle of last minute passengers hurled themselves into the train's carriages, slamming the doors violently just before we jerked into ungainly motion.

How do we know when it isn't real, when we've got it wrong?

How long before we let go?

It has to be a proper love.

I closed my eyes against the noise around me. I needed to blank out the escalating vision of the dark and drear railway sidings as they slid from view outside, unfolding into blackness. I drew in a deep breath.

I was still a long way from home.

The Devil Did It

Brighton
January 1998

A gust of cold wind and a rattling Coke can followed me through the door of Burger King in North Street.

There weren't many people around.

Youssef was already there, sitting at a table to one side by the wall. He had that familiar jittery look about him, watching me warily as I unwound my scarf and unbuttoned my coat. Once I sat down opposite him, he looked me boldly in the eye.

'Hello Jeannie. Nice see you.'

His hair was thinner, scraped back over his scalp, and his forehead more furrowed than I remembered. He reminded me of Daddy on my trips to Morocco when he had held my hands so tightly.

'Job okay?' he asked.

'Yes, alright.'

'How are Tess an'... ?'

'Tess and Teddy? Our little spy and her husband?'

'Yes. They— ?'

'They split up. Gone now.'

'Gone?'

'Yeah. Back to London.'

'Never I think that,' he tutted. 'Things they go change, eh?'

'They do.'

He looked worn out. Even though I knew he was wearing several layers of clothes against the January cold, his body seemed thicker than I remembered.

'How's Mummy?' I said. 'And the café – still doing well?'

'Café doing *very* well. I have a few little business here now… and property in Spain, and Morocco… '

'I know. I heard.'

'Devil, still he follows Mummy around. She thinks never he give up.'

We both chuckled.

'Give her my regards.'

'Always I do.' He scratched his nose, looking pensive. 'She worry for you in Denton house. She afraid for things come down from jungle.'

I laughed, alone this time. 'I'm alright. Tell her not to worry.'

He cleared his throat. 'Mummy, she says it be devil do this. Him, he come between us.'

'Us? You and me?'

He nodded.

'The devil?' I sneered. 'More like— '

I didn't go on. My instinct told me not to mention past misdemeanours.

There was an uneasy pause.

'So… how are they all?' I eventually asked.

'Uh?'

'The family. Mohammed, Nadia, everyone.'

'Oh, they okay. But Ya Ya, she's gone.'

'Gone?'

'She died couple month back.'

'I'm so sorry.'

'Mohammed, he has new baby. Another girl.'

'How many girls now?'

He pondered. 'They have... three. Three girls. And one boy, Omar. He speak good. Very intelligent that boy, very clever.'

'Like his dad.'

'Uh? Yes, like Mohammed.'

I thought back. This was an opportunity to clear something up, to finally know the truth. 'Youssef... ' I said, 'maybe... maybe you could answer this... '

'Uh?'

'Remember that time at Heathrow with the luggage mix-up?'

'What's that?'

'When Mohammed and Nadia arrived that day. You picked them up, when Mummy was with us. That time?'

He sighed.

'The luggage swap?' I continued. 'Mohammed's case ended up with someone else.'

'Uh?'

'Identical luggage. The day they arrived. *That* day.'

His expression changed. A muscle twitched at the corner of his mouth and both eyes darted sideways. His polite smile seemed to wash away.

'Remember – later on, we thought Mohammed had died, somewhere in London? Nadia found her way home. All that crazy carry-on...'

He pouted. 'Oh, that luggage was nothing.' He shrugged. 'Just thing strange.'

But I wasn't convinced. I felt he had given himself away; and he knew why I was asking.

His head was still turned away from me, eyes averted.

Another pause.

There were other things I could mention to him... the curiously late shifts at Burger King, that affair I knew about, the swiping of packets of veggie seeds and a cable at the local garden centre – the police presence and why he thought he could get away with it? CCTV doesn't lie – and neither does stuff poked up your jumper. From a conversation I'd heard, I suspected he'd also contacted most of the English girls he'd met in Spain before I turned up – and how clever was he to conceal that from me.

As if reading me, Youssef cleared his throat and tried hard to make eye contact. 'You know... that girl, we be friend now,' he said. '*Just* friend.'

'Which one?'

He let that remark pass.

There was a brown envelope on the table between us. Youssef's eyes drifted down to it.

'Long time since I see you. Must be one year almost now?'

'Thereabouts. Probably more.'

He was just about to crack his knuckles – the

horrible thing he did when he was pondering, but he caught my look and dropped his hands.

'I... don't know if you know,' I said, pushing at sugar grains on the tabletop with my fingernail, 'but Pablo died a while ago.'

'Oh!'

'Drugs,' I said. 'It was drugs.'

He flinched. '*Pablo*. How you know?'

'Marta emailed me. She picked up on the news from someone in Spain.'

'Shame. Always I like him. He was my best man – remember?'

'Of course I do.'

He took a breath.

'Yes, great shame,' I replied. 'He gave you fifty quid when you came here, to help you.'

He took another gulp of air.

'Well, Jeannie... ' He was struggling. 'I been to 'ove... er, Hove... this morning. I pick up this before they post to me.' He gave an edgy cough. 'It's our paper. Our divorce paper.' He reached out and took my hand across the grease-streaked table, stroking my thumb with his forefinger. He had a tear in his eye and to my astonishment, so did I.

'Mine's in the post?'

'Yes, in the post.'

Youssef smiled uncertainly. He cleared his throat again. 'Tomorrow, I leave early for ferry to north Spain. Go to Morocco from there.'

He freed his hand from mine and opened the envelope, taking out its contents. Then he waved the

Decree Absolute at me; it flapped around in his hand like a dying albatross, the absolute end of an era. 'See... me, I need this paper before I go.'

'You and your *papers!*'

I took it from him, noting the date: *15 January 1998* in very large print, but absorbed nothing much else.

I handed it back to him. 'Nearly eight years. Eight years of... what?'

'Good times, good knowing you. Learning different things, your culture... your friends.'

I said nothing.

I knew his plan.

He was going to find a new wife in Morocco; someone who could give him babies, have couscous on the table when he came home, and slippers – figuratively – by the fire.

'You're coming back?'

He grasped my hand once more. 'Of *course* I come back.'

When he married again – undoubtedly with gifts of gold and all the traditional paraphernalia – would he look back and remember *our* wedding day? The drama, the skulduggery to get into Spain, the brevity of our *luna de miel,* and the frugality and simplicity of it all?

'Well... it *was* interesting.' I looked him in the eye. 'Most parts anyway.' Then I dropped my gaze.

His grip on my hand tightened. 'Yes. *Yes.*'

'Remember that Christmas when it clashed with Ramadan?' I said. 'A big hoo-hah in our house if you remember.'

It'd been a grim day.

Youssef pulled a face. 'And remember that time my brother Ab'slaam ask on the phone on Christmas Day why so many turkey going over from Morocco to Europe in December?'

I laughed.

'Weird how he phoned me *that* day, he had no clue of Christmas, he never heard of it.'

And neither had Youssef at that time, before he landed in the UK.

Two tables along from us chair legs scraped and screeched. A baby howled. A piece of cutlery clattered to the tiled floor.

Startled, we looked up at the same time; we licked our lips simultaneously.

Youssef shifted awkwardly. 'Coffee, Jeannie?'

'Coffee? Here? No... thank you. Not the same here, is it. Much better in Morocco.'

'Always.'

Spawn

Denton, East Sussex
January 1998

Two days later it was into the weekend.

On Saturday morning, a weak but steady sun was out and I took advantage of this to make a little tour of the wintry garden. At the top end it looked mostly bleak, but clusters of daffodil shoots were already forcing their way through in the barren flowerbeds, and clumps of heather here and there were beginning to burst into colour.

I walked further down the garden towards the shed and the now abandoned pond. To one side, holding up the ivy-thick bank that was once my grassy slope, the breeze block Moroccan wall stood clad in its winter coat of glossy foliage and bright red berries. It was almost completely covered, the flimsy trellising beneath the denseness now splintered and broken under the weight.

In the flowerbed to one side of the wall, pushing through patches of frost in their usual spasmodic way, were the cuckoo plants with green heart-shaped leaves

Youssef had so eagerly planted everywhere. Spawn of the devil... as I'd once said; or, if not voiced, I'd certainly thought it. They became *Beni Ahmed Specials* – that was their former home, and were probably prohibited material at Heathrow when Youssef smuggled them in, carefully wrapped in newspaper. He insisted they looked like baby *minarets* and was so keen to see them grow in our garden.

However deep I'd dug my trowel I could never find a bulb or tuber attached; I'd given up searching. For all their sleek splendour, I'd concluded that these plants had no root system. No roots at all.

Squinting in the sunlight I peered more closely. I could see that all around the garden the plants were snaking their way up through the frozen soil, ready to unfurl their hearts and burst forth; the plants that I had tried systematically to destroy because they were so alien and seriously persistent.

An Accidental Woman

It was very foolish to get involved.

I've always known that, but I've never regretted it. Not once.

It had been a short acquaintance. When I think back, I'm astonished how quickly I became drawn in. She did resist a smidgeon longer, it's true, but it was all rather whirlwind; too intense to be workable, especially with children on both sides to consider.

Foolhardy for sure.

I didn't think of it as cheating, certainly not to begin with. I knew she was jolly wary, thinking of her very settled life in Surrey, her marriage, and then her considerable guilt. Such an attraction is described as *chemistry* in literature I believe. That's definitely one way of looking at it.

Her husband, seemingly an affable dullard, and her two small children, were a mystery to me. We never spoke about them. Quite frankly, announcing I was going off to work in Johannesburg was a good way of extricating myself from the entanglement when the situation became intolerable, but it was painful. And, in the end, I didn't go to Africa – it wouldn't have solved anything, and was more likely to confuse my life yet more.

How could I tell her my wife was divorcing me at that time? Taboo. It was totally unacceptable without a very good reason back then. What a long way we've come since 1945.

It wouldn't have helped telling her in any case; she'd have thought I was a scoundrel and not worth knowing – even though she said that she did love me. I needn't have worried, our relationship, such as it was, lasted merely weeks. It's no coincidence that I'm thinking of her now, the woman I met by accident all those years ago. She's still around.

I've seen her.

My wife, highly strung always, became convinced that I was about to leave her. Ironic, really – she was mistaken at the time, I was yet to bump into the remarkable woman who was to throw me totally off balance for that very short time. I'd been working hard in the surgery, partly involved in my research, and maybe too much so, which aroused my wife's suspicions. All I wanted to do was provide for her; and, if I'm really truthful, I enjoyed my time in the surgery away from home and domesticity. Eventually, my wife managed to take a very good share of what I'd built, and of course I needed to ensure that she and the boys were well provided for.

They've always kept in touch, my children. And I thank heaven for that.

I'd spotted her in London, my accidental woman, just a few months ago. But initially, I noticed her daughter. I knew it had to be her. I was walking through Covent Garden – just on the periphery of the theatrical heartland – after meeting a business friend for lunch at a little bistro in Charing Cross. It was busy, a hustle and bustle as always; so noisy, people milling around, yelling. Some broken cauliflowers were strewn in the gutter, and bruised apples in a heap at the corner of Neal Street. I still flinch at the sight of perfectly good food discarded. Earlier, I'd noticed that The Mousetrap was still playing at The Ambassadors Theatre, and pondered on how much longer it might run. I thought it was splendid that Agatha Christie was still so revered. Her books really are rather spiffing, certainly difficult to surpass.

The crowds had thinned out somewhat now.

Just past The Crown and Anchor, I stopped to light up a cigarette, and it was then I caught her out of the corner of my eye... my mind playing tricks, I thought.

A fleeting profile.

How could I forget, even now, the way she'd moved so gracefully, the set of her shoulders, the tilt of her head, the curve of her cheek. Then, as the two women walked on, I heard her laugh, that delightful tinkle. She would laugh a lot, I remember, once we got to know each other better during our time.

I felt my heart twinge, if that is at all possible.

I turned, and followed.

There they were, two women, side by side, their backs to me; one bigger-set and walking quite heavily.

I had to find out. But I already knew, of course.
What were they doing here?
I strode forward somewhat to stay closer.
I couldn't help myself. I called her name.
No reaction.
And then again... louder!

We had, on our last day, mused that we might just meet again – sometime in the far off future. I'm not sure that either of us believed it; we were just so bereft, so full of angst, brimming with tears. And then, anger, when that friend of hers, the chatter-jabberer, joined us at our table in the station buffet just minutes before I was due to catch my train.

There had been no proper goodbye. A real cause for regret. Our very last day together, in all our lives, spoilt. Shattered.

We'd always met on a Thursday. A blessed day. She had a quaint way of referring to past Thursdays as, for example, 'Last Thursday Week.' For me, each Thursday stood out brilliantly, etched in my memory. The everyday things we did: the one and nine-penny seats in the circle at the cinema, having lunch, taking tea, and out in the countryside... leaning on that charming little bridge over a stream watching the ducks; the innocence, the naturalness of being with one another.

I swallowed hard, unsure of myself.

They'd stopped walking. I crept a little closer.

I tried again, cupping my hands around my mouth; I didn't want others to look at me, the whole thing was extraordinary enough as it was.

One or two heads swivelled. *Why was this shouting man standing in the middle of the pavement, possibly on the verge of collapse?*

I felt a tear in the corner of my eye.

It was then that I noticed her daughter was wearing a baby sling on her front, making her stoop rather. The baby cried out – whether in glee or anguish, who knows.

She fussed over the baby for a moment or two.

I called again, trying to keep my voice level, but I faltered. I was almost ready to give up.

At last, the daughter looked round; she was taller, half-a-head above her mother. Good Lord, she really looked so much like her. They were both kitted-out in Swinging Sixties gear of course. Above-the-knee hemlines, and such bright colours. Females in their 40s and 50s – maybe even mid-50s, as *she* would be now – considered themselves still young. They could get away with it. It was nothing like the elegance of the fashion era in which we grew up – now considered old-hat – but times had changed. My hair is a tad longer than I used to wear it, admittedly, but through necessity now to cover up some hair loss.

She touched her mother on the shoulder, and she turned around too, but slowly. Both women stared at me. I was a little distance away, standing resolutely on the pavement with a trickle of people steering themselves past me, but I could see them clearly.

Her daughter, with the same slightly crooked mouth, tried an uncertain smile. Her mother showed no reaction, she was expressionless. She wore thick spectacles and appeared unsteady, and I noticed a walking stick in her hand.

Her dark hair, sparse now, was peppered with grey.

They stood awhile, and then turned away from me.

My heart was slamming.

Her daughter shook her head. I caught: 'How strange, Mummy. It's almost as if he was calling *you*, wasn't it!' She took her mother's arm, and guided her forward. 'A ghost from the past, eh?' And they laughed in that tinkling fashion, in unison, with her daughter shifting the baby on her front to position it more comfortably.

Still I stood there, wiping my eyes with my handkerchief.

My brief encounter with this woman, all those years ago, was excruciatingly, deliciously special. No woman I've known since has come anywhere near to the way I felt when I was with her. I've known so many women, been disappointed countless times, especially in these free-and-easy days where anything appears to be possible, and usually is. The war years were difficult, but we did have some fun then, it wasn't all calamity.

And then I met her, my own dear darling.

My head was swimming. I was in tatters. If I'm honest, it damn well served me right. How could I think she would look the way I remembered her? After all this time... with never any hope of rekindling our relationship – which wasn't a real relationship anyhow, not in the true sense. She was never going to run into my arms again. Was she?

She hadn't known me that day. Not a glimmer of recognition.

I crossed the road and walked onwards. I wept, my vision blurred, my legs trembling. I eventually took the Underground at Tottenham Court Road, then stumbled my way home. A foolish, ridiculous wreck of a man.

Bereft. Not only for the love that I'd lost so long ago – but for the shattering of a very dear, treasured memory.

Laura... how I loved you!

That encounter weighed heavily for weeks. Time dilutes most things, and ghastly feelings begin to evaporate. But we never forget. I knew I'd never forget.

Going through life now, as I get older and very much out of the loop as far as modern socialising is concerned, it's dispiriting to say the least.

I glance in my bedroom mirror, stroke my hair into place. I'm a grandfather for goodness sake, and with yet another generation soon to be born into the family.

We met by accident. We loved each other so much.

These days, I leave it to the young. It's too damn complicated.

This story portrays a 'what if' – what might have happened in later years: a nod to Noel Coward's famous play *Still Life*, a love story depicted in the 1945 movie *Brief Encounter*, the screenplay written by him.

Losing Him

A freezing night in November at the side entrance to Greenwich Town Hall; part of a lengthy snake of young people blowing on their fingers, coat collars up, some stamping their feet.

Winter had arrived as a blow.

Everything had changed. And I was losing him.

There'd been a shift. It was different between us now; unspoken, but obvious.

I felt wounded, helpless.

Over the summer months I'd learnt how it was to be a couple: meeting Ken's friends, enjoying live music, beer, discovering the Arts. My emotions had run haywire, and deliciously, and were up in the air still. Raw.

'Alright?' he said, pushing my hand into his jacket pocket. We hadn't thought to bring gloves. My friend from school, Annette, was with us; she was standing the other side of Ken.

He'd organised the tickets. Eight shillings and sixpence each.

Worth it?

Should I have come?

I couldn't stay away. I wanted to be with him.

'They're fairly new,' Ken said, 'to the general public. They did *Ready Steady Go!* earlier today. On the television tomorrow night.'

I nodded.

'Yeah,' he continued. 'They're getting known.'

'But,' I said, 'you're a Jazz person.'

'They're different, this lot. They draw from the Blues.'

'Strange name,' I said.

'What?'

'Strange name for a group.'

'It's from Bob Dylan's song, isn't it. Cool, eh?'

'What?'

'When he went electric. *You* know the song.'

I didn't.

He gazed at me. What did that mean?

It was nearly over.

The heave-ho was coming.

Maybe tonight, after the dance.

My eyes prickled...

Then, somewhere behind us – a scream!

And raised voices.

Top Twenty music was blaring sporadically from someone's transistor.

More loud yelling. Heavy footsteps now, as someone was running up from the back.

'Kennedy's dead!'

Ken whizzed round. '*What?*'

'*Kennedy!*' the voice blared again. 'He's been shot!'

The front of the queue was now moving forward. Heads bobbing, arms and legs on the go, conversations cut short, people thankful to be getting out of the cold and dark.

'Kennedy shot?' said Ken to me. 'Bloody hell. What's that gonna mean?'

I didn't know what to say.

Our section of the queue was now shambling towards an open door; shuffling along, inch by inch. After that shock announcement, the mood was subdued. We could still hear the babble of music and voices in the tailback behind us.

Our tickets were checked and we were in. There was a cluster of agitated people around the ticket office.

'They'll be lucky to get tickets,' said Ken. 'Popular, this gig.'

Onwards, into the hall.

The bright lights dazzled us. Annette hung onto my arm and we stood for a minute or two to get our bearings, then headed for some tip-up seats at the back of the hall. Ken went off to the bar to buy some beer.

All those people in the queue ahead of us had dispersed, scattered into small groups throughout the spacious hall, yet there was a palpable buzz; everyone seemed animated, excited. And someone, somewhere, was playing with the lighting – groupings of lights were being turned on and off – click click… click – until the overhead spotlights were diffused to something more comfortable.

We settled ourselves into the tip-up seats.

The seats, placed all round the edges of the hall, were now filling up quickly.

'Can't believe we made it here,' said Annette, easing off her jacket and smoothing her skirt into place. 'Managed to swing it with my dad. Easier than I thought.'

'All last-minute,' I said. 'Can't believe my luck either. I might not've made it here if you weren't coming too.'

'This Kennedy thing,' Annette continued. 'Our dads are going to be shocked.'

'Upset, too,' I said, 'if it really is true.'

'It must be.'

I stole a look at the bar area...

'You're a bit jumpy. What's wrong?'

'Am I?'

Telling her would make it too real.

There was activity up on the dark stage at the far end. Shadowy figures, heavy dragging, clanking, some muted heated words. Sparse curtaining trailed at each side.

'Seems a bit... haphazard,' I said. 'They're not ready yet.'

Ken materialised, juggling three plastic beakers. 'They'll only do half pints,' he said. 'Don't want a riot here.'

'Thank you,' I said, taking his offered beaker, feeling grateful as well as puzzled. What did he mean, a riot?

He handed a beaker to Annette, who took it with a

dazzling smile

'Back home by eleven?' he asked, turning to me.

'Yes. A bit of an extension tonight,' I said, pulling a face. 'Special dispensation.' I was glad to have got that last word out properly.

He'd be gone before too long.

I knew it.

He stretched his neck to gaze at the elevated stage. 'They'll be on soon.'

His profile... the way his lips moved; his curly hair creeping over his collar...

He caught my stare with, I thought, a stony look. Then, with the ghost of a smile, he squeezed my arm.

The groups of people standing had swelled to quite a crowd.

Floodlights lit the stage, bringing it to life. A drum kit, guitars, cabling and amplifiers littered the area. A face peered around the curtain at one side, followed by a good head of hair and a very slight body...

Bang!

Five young men leapt from the scant wings and onto the stage.

They seized their instruments, and one came forward to the mic stand...

Boom!

Got my mojo workin'...

We stood up, drinks swirling around in our beakers.

'Wow,' said Ken, but looking totally unmoved.

'Their *hair!*' I said.

Yeah – Got my mojo workin', snarled the frontman...

'They have this joke,' Ken shouted in my ear. 'They get asked why they wear their hair so long... '

'Oh?'

'Seems they reply... 'Oh, it's been goin' on a few years, mate. Really a shame for barbers – cos they're *starving* now."

It took me a moment to get it.

Ken gave me that look.

I stared straight ahead at the stage. 'Look at *him!*' I said, pointing.

'That's Bill.

'How d'you know?'

'I've read about them, haven't I. Bass guitar.' Ken liked to exercise his knowledge, validate his eighteen and a bit years of existence.

I'd gazed at Bill's ruffled white shirt and austere bearing, but it was the singer who really held my attention. He wore a simple t-shirt and jeans and commanded the stage, and not only because he was the frontman.

Ken spoke again. 'That's *Mick*, that is.'

The skinny one.

Mick writhed, wrapping his skinny body around the microphone stand. With his cavernous mouth so close, he looked about to eat the mic.

I exchanged a look with Annette. We didn't speak, the music was taking over.

Dancing was in full swing, obscuring the lower part of the stage.

I handed my half-full beaker to Ken and, gripping his

shoulder, tried to stand on my seat. I wanted a better view...

I wobbled...

Then I was face-down on the floor.

'Silly girl,' said Ken, trying to haul me up by one arm. 'What were you doing!'

Annette held my other arm, trying not to laugh. 'Take it easy,' she said, stroking my splayed hand. 'Take your time.'

'It's a tip-up seat,' said Ken. 'Didn't you know?'

Another nail in the coffin; another faux pas that didn't suit a worldly boy like Ken.

I shook off his arm.

He was laughing. 'Beer too much for you?'

But it was a mean laugh.

I was on my feet, groped for my handbag and sat back down, fingertips on my stockings, checking my knees for damage and for snags in the nylon. Ken was still on his feet, watching the group. 'Alright?'

'Alright,' I replied.

I was an idiot.

Mick exploded into *Sweet Little Sixteen*...

'Good song,' said Ken, swinging his hips. 'Chuck Berry. Sixteen. *Your* age.'

Not quite. A few more months to go.

Why did he have to mention it?

'Let's go down to the front,' said Annette. 'Just for a while, have a proper look.'

I looked at Ken, and he nodded, but stayed where he was.

We pushed our way towards the stage, struggling past twisting arms and legs and a few jivers; finally standing right by the stage edge. Mick was still making love to the mic stand, almost gnawing away at the perforated metal phallus on its stalk. We were close enough to see the sweat on his brow, his unruly, sodden hair, and already his pale t-shirt darkening in patches.

His complexion was bad.

'Pimply,' Annette observed.

An acrid smell wafted down like some kind of pheromone-laden gift.

There was a lot of shrieking coming from a group of girls nearby. I turned round to look. They were wearing bizarre outfits; skirts that were barely there, with tumbling mermaid hair, and kaleidoscope make-up. I didn't know whether to feel shocked or envious. Our knee-length respectability and bouffant hair suddenly looked out of place. I didn't know what Annette might be thinking.

Mick was snarling lyrics, wrapping one leg around the stand.

I'm a hog for you...

He seized the mic from its holder and moved away. In his plimsolls, he prowled the stage, free-form, end to end; slowly, rhythmically, all the while surveying the crowd. From time to time he flicked his head.

We were on our way back to our seats as they launched into *Come On,* their first record. The crowd went wild.

As I fought through, I listened. Mick was agonising

about parting with his baby; his girlfriend. Everything was wrong, nothing was right.

It hit a nerve.

I could believe his pain.

A harmonica wailed urgently, seductively. I looked back, consumed with the sensuality of their performance; heart racing, skin prickly. Hot everything. Never mind the lyrics, it didn't seem to matter what he was singing.

'Watch out for cigarettes,' Annette said as we pushed forward, just as I felt a stinging burn on my bare arm. Then, blocking the way, a girl with her head cradled in her arms, shaking, swaying. I had to barge by, knocking her sideways. She didn't look up.

Ken seemed okay to have been on his own. He stood with his arms folded in front of him. 'Good?' he said.

'Yes, good. They're all mad down there.'

He laughed. 'There's a song they do that's caused some trouble,' he said. '*Stoned*.'

'Stoned?'

'Wonder if they might do it here. Can't be played on the radio, not on the BBC.'

'Why not?'

'Why d'you *think! Eh?*'

I wanna be your man...

Another song we knew of theirs from the wireless.

'Written by The Beatles,' announced Ken through the commotion. I knew Annette thought he was a bit of a clever dick; and, yes, I suppose he was.

Mick skipped about, clapping to the side, his wiry frame in perpetual movement... then, pouting, he unexpectedly turned and presented his rump to the crowd...

Uproar.

'We're dancing,' Ken said, getting up. 'Let's go.'

We veered away from some lively twisters, and set to dance with barely space to move, reducing us to an inept kind of shuffling.

Ken, with such relaxed rhythm, was of course the better dancer.

The hall was full to bursting now. Ken said it was four-deep at the bar.

No chance of more beer.

And we'd lost our seats.

Cigarette smoke corkscrewed high above; caught by the upper spotlights, illuminating the swirls, and specks of dust floating in the vortex.

Ken looked on edge. The intimacy of the hall was blown, it was turning into something more than just a dance. We stood bunched together, hot and clammy, breathing into each other's faces.

The lights dimmed...

Mick was making an announcement, asking for some hush. 'New record,' he said. 'Out next year. Debut tonight. *Not Fade Away.*'

The crowd roared.

'*Our* version. Apologies, Mister Buddy 'olly!'

More roaring and applause. Shrill cat calls.

'So – 'appy Nineteen Sixty Four, everyone!'

Then, as an aside... 'When it comes! *If* it comes!' He grinned, looking slyly at Bill the bass player.

A guitar riff, the *shh-shh-shh* of maracas, a drum roll... and they were into the song.

I'd never heard it sung that way before; a pulse throbbed in my throat. Even stoic Ken seemed moved.

Mick strutted with the maracas, flicking them towards his shoulder, then up, up – eye level. He pouted, he grimaced. He pouted... he *screamed*. A sudden hop, skip and sideways scissors jump.

Groovy. He was fabulous.

I caught Ken peering at his wristwatch. 'Better get going soon,' he said, once he could make himself heard. 'Not sure how good the buses are.'

Annette had to leave soon, wait at the entrance outside. Her dad was picking her up.

The crowd had thinned somewhat. 'Just going into the toilet first,' I said, holding Annette by the arm and moving us both away, pushing through to find our jackets first.

'Don't be *too long*.'

'Bit harsh, wasn't he!' said Annette.

'You mean Ken?'

'Yes. Bit hard on you in there.'

I dabbed at the burn on my arm, and we smoothed our hair in the large wall mirror. It was hardly worth getting out the lipstick and perfume now that we were leaving to go home, but we did anyway. I washed my hands and glanced again in the mirror at our reflections.

More or less younger versions of our mums. Pretty – but was that good enough?

I turned to Annette. 'You know he's going to Goldsmiths after Christmas.'

'Yes, you said.'

'He'll be in with a different crowd. He knows some of them already.'

'Don't worry.'

'I won't stand a chance. Everything'll be different.'

'Not necessarily.'

'Yes, it will. Art students. You know what I mean.' I wiped an eye. 'I'm not mature enough for him. I don't know enough.'

'No-o...'

'There's too many flippin' restrictions, him being with me. *And* I'm still a schoolgirl.'

'Don't— '

'I'm just too young.'

As we left the toilets, buttoning our jackets and pulling up our collars, Mick had gone into a low growl...

Stoned.

It had to be the infamous song... slow Blues with, I thought, a familiar rhythm...

Stooon-ed...

'*That's Green Onions, that riff!*' snorted Ken, checking his pockets for his wallet then steering us out of the hall. 'Rip-off. They've bloody *stolen* it!'

Annette made a face, rolling her eyes.

Ken walked me back from the bus stop.

Was this the moment?

But he didn't linger outside my house. A freezing drizzle had started.

'Don't tell him about the beer.'

'But we only had— '

'I'll phone you,' he said, giving me a moist kiss on the mouth and striding away swiftly to catch his last bus home. I didn't know when I'd see him again.

I was losing him.

He was on the periphery of a new life. I knew my memories of him wouldn't fade away as quickly as his of me would.

Maybe this was *it*.

Ditched.

I went in through the basement door, straight into the kitchen. Through the dividing glass door I could see Dad in our living room, sitting in his green swivel armchair and looking stern. I assumed Mum was upstairs in bed.

I placed my handbag on the kitchen table and took off my jacket, dumping it on a chair. I crept in, trying to adjust the expression on my face. I felt shaky, my mouth was dry.

He didn't seem to notice I was twenty minutes late.

He was sitting watching the television, a mug of coffee half-way to his mouth, his eyes fixed on the screen.

'You should watch this, love. It's history being made.'

He put down the mug.

'What's that?'

'The American President's been shot dead. It's a terrible bloody thing.'

'We heard.'

The wall clock showed twenty-five past eleven. It always seemed to be set too fast.

The television screen was flickering badly, and the same scenes were being shown again and again. A cavalcade of cars... a long shot of a group of people milling around in distress, a despairing newsreader... then back to the fuzzy cavalcade. The commentary sounded scratchy, anguished.

'What?' He didn't move his head. I took in the powerful set of his boxer's shoulders, his awkward stance, all the tension he was feeling. I didn't want to bear the brunt of all that emotional strain if he turned on me; if he tongue-lashed, or shoved me...

'We heard when we were queuing,' I said. 'Someone had a radio.'

I was still standing by the door. I was waiting for his reprimand.

'Better sit down. Jesus *Christ*, this is serious stuff. We've lost him. God knows what's gonna happen now.'

He looked very disturbed.

Facing away from the wall clock, he wouldn't be able to see it without swivelling round. His forgotten cigarette was burning away to a crooked grey worm in the metal ashtray on his left.

'Good time?' he said.

'Yes, good.'

I didn't think he was going to swivel, but I could be wrong.

He was leaning forward. 'This really is history in the making, love. Just as things were beginning to... *improve*. Your mum doesn't want to watch it. Too upsetting.'

He reached for, and then took his mug of coffee slowly, bit by bit, to his mouth. His eyes were still riveted, with the hint of a tear in the corner of the one I could see.

I understood why.

As a serviceman in WW2, this came as a blow to his hopes of a new world of peace and understanding. I knew that much.

'Alright, love. Sit down. This really is terrible news. Appalling.'

Holding the mug with both hands, he gave his wristwatch a quick glance and looked straight back at the television screen.

'This won't go away quickly,' he said, puffing out his cheeks. 'Not this one. There'll be riots. *More* blood.'

He licked his lips, reached for his packet of cigarettes and lighter.

'Losing him now, like *that* – things might never recover. Not after this.'

On Mission Oeuf

'You're going into drift,' I said, and waited.

I thought those words inside my head too, just for good measure.

Ulysses was floating not far off, and was now safely enough away from our spacecraft; I'd made sure of that. With one swift thought I could have him scudding around the heavens at will, but never would. He's here to protect Glo and me. But I'm his controller, always.

'*Food!*' yelled Glo. 'Coming up *now*.'

Glo was always scornful of Ulysses; she was jealous of my relationship with him, and decried his name as ridiculous. Every so often I'd remind her of the reason why he, our own personal drone, bore this name... it was all to do with 'UASes'. A handy acronym – as near to Ulysses as you can get. *Unmanned Aircraft Systems.* Been around for a very long time now. Some of us become a little attached, it's true; but Ulysses is our guardian angel for sure.

For the time being anyway.

We're more than just trainees – we've proved ourselves. We heard the mission to collect seeds went very well, though Planet Saturn was tough to crack. Somewhere along the way some wires were crossed: the mission was that seeds were to be collected *from* Saturn, *not* to be taken to him – for, although Saturn is of masculine gender, it's a fruitful planet. We know that. That's what the report said.

Wish we'd been part of that mission.

Our sights were now on Planet Earth.

'Come get it, Voz,' Glo insisted, *'Now!'*

With a fingertip, I adjusted a sensor to ease the pressure in our craft, then left it totally on autopilot. Of course, it's perfectly okay without my intervention, but what man alive can't help fiddling with things?

I was bouncing with energy. Wired.

We'd been stuck in our cryo-chambers for so long, though four years went by in a flash, just as it's meant to. A timer sounded the first alarm, and I was out as soon as the technology would allow me, hazy and irritable. I dressed quickly. Glo didn't seem to want to get out – I had to tinker with her knobs and temperature control – easy does it – before she opened her eyes. I checked her over to be sure she was crystal-free.

She thawed quickly, grumbling all the way, then she found her space travel apparel already laid-out: we had to wear this gear throughout the mission.

Glo struggled into her stiff layered tunic, leg-kit and boots while I dealt with the mechanics of cryonics-shutdown and reset for future use. I was getting rather adept with super-cryo-tech procedures.

Outside, a piece of detritus moved by – and it looked like a frying pan. What the *hell!* – how long since anyone had one of those! I knew what it was, we had old-times-memory-banks at hand for our onboard entertainment. For me, a softy, it was often poignant – and unthinkable what was thrown up... barbarism, starving infants, disease, poverty, futile wars, mind-altering substances that also wrecked humans' bodies; and those smouldering paper sticks that they, for an alarming count of centuries, stuck in their mouths, turning themselves into desperate, rabid creatures, fiercely afire. Seems initially it was seen as a healthy thing. Ha!

Glo had given up shouting. I heard a door crash, so I knew she was on her way here.

For me, travelling on this mission had been excellent so far. Glo wasn't so keen. There were more craft out there doing just the same as us. We were to save the universe again. How many times did we have to rally? Shouldn't we be a perfect universe by now?

'He's drifting again,' observed Glo, stomping into the bridge area with our breakfast. I gave a quick wave to Ulysses, who immediately veered much closer to the craft... not really what I wanted. 'You treat that drone like a child,' she said, placing the usual two small metallic cylinders on a counter. 'Be careful you don't overdo it, you know that thing could kill us if you give the wrong signals.'

'Don't be daft, Gloria,' I said, using her real name to annoy her. 'I have everything under control. Just enjoy our mission, will you?'

She snorted. She was weary of our shiny new life, tired of missions, and ridiculously contemptuous of this assignment. She was keen to retire.

'It won't be long. Any time now, Glo,' I said. 'We'll be told when we're ready for descent.'

She was Auld School, she wanted back what she'd missed out on. Yearned for. She'd never actually had it in the first place – all that was many years ago, when Planet Earth was at the absolute zenith of turmoil, when things *had* to change. We had to survive, and survive we have.

'What's in the cylinders? Porridge?'

'You just stop taking the pee. As *if.*' She tried a wry smile. 'The usual. Tasty eggs and bacon. No black pudding today.'

We hooted with laughter.

I took one of the cylinders, tilted it, and slipped the contents into my mouth and straight down my throat. We *had* eggs and bacon, it tasted and smelt like eggs and bacon, but was the usual thick, gooey paste of substances we could rely on to keep us alive and healthy. 'Yum!' I said, licking my lips. 'Tempted, I was, to ask Ulysses to bring in that frying pan... '

'What frying pan?' She too tipped her breakfast down her gullet.

'It was part of the flotsam and jetsam outside,' I said. 'That's what they used before our time.' I loved rubbing it in that Glo really had missed her era, and there it *was*, no going back. We never had it, wouldn't really recognise it if it bit us on the brain. Or would we?

'I hate all this,' she said.

That frying pan quip did not help her mood. She looked extra irritated.

'Some mission this,' she said. 'Exciting? I don't think so.'

I needed to remind her: 'Of course it's sodding exciting! What could be more important than getting rid of excess lifeform? The Universe is bursting. Eggs means creatures, which means procreation, which means trouble.' I fixed her with my best glare. 'More than that – disaster!'

It was a mission to stamp out any form of egg production. For us, a really important one this time.

Glo turned to go. 'Eggs,' she said. 'Ironic, as it happens. We've just eaten some.'

'Not really,' I said, but seeing the funny side. 'It's gotta be done, Glo. Unearth egg-layers, any egg-type creature. All of 'em. Destroy.'

'So we're talking, mostly, about birds?' Turning back, she looked like she was about to weep.

'We know the score,' I said. 'We can't be sentimental.'

'That miniaturisation nonsense – how good was that!' she spat at me. 'Universal reduction in size, for us all, whether we wanted it or not. Took forever to get everyone shrunk by two-thirds. What good did it do!'

'Come on, Glo – you know it really helped. That was some years back. Things have to change, again, to ensure our survival.' I groaned, holding my head, shaking it from side to side. 'Don't you feel honoured that we're part of the chosen ones to bring about good change?'

She said nothing.

'And, anyway, that wasn't the first time,' I said. 'Seems every space inhabitant got chopped down by half, back in the year 2292. No one complained then.'

She huffed and puffed and stomped off further along the craft, disappearing into the nucleus of our temporary home. She was better off there, she could trawl old universe memories... memories that weren't hers, but enough to keep her dewy-eyed; and always fractious, of course.

From the corner of my eye, I could see Ulysses lurch again, shift course somewhat. I needed to send a message, a thought that would send him back on track.

Steady... Steady...

Mission Oeuf – our official assignment. Makes no sense to me, I don't know that word, or any of the old languages. Japanese? Italian? Why would I? We'd soon be landing on Planet Earth... our target, earmarked as one of those most in need of reccy and action. Our ancestral home, where Glo and me originally sprang from, through many generations long gone. We came from English stock, and we've picked up some understanding of that.

Our patch was the south-east area. There were more experienced cadets in the big cities, particularly in what they say remains of London. I wasn't to hold back on extermination, I knew the importance of obliteration of every living creature capable of producing an egg, and thus a threat; but not humans. Strictly speaking, humans don't lay eggs.

Humans... if there were indeed any left on such a

poisonous, stricken planet. I'd soon know. I didn't need Glo, she could stay aboard.

Ulysses was restless. I knew he'd soon be decommissioned; we weren't allowed to keep a drone for too long, they knew the perils of over-attachment – something that Glo feared, and moaned about all the time. I had to give him the *'you're fired'* instructions very soon. My heart was heavy with the thought; I tried to dismiss it. With all these thought processes going on, it was no wonder that Ulysses picked up things. What Glo said was true, I had to be careful.

I did a reccy of the skyscape. Drone Ulysses was drifting nicely, the correct distance from the craft. I sent him a mind signal that all was well. I swear his very slight swerve, almost a swagger, was an acknowledgement. If I concentrated, I could imagine a face on his smooth metallic sides; a phizog, a smiley countenance.

The air inside was thickening; something was coming, and I knew what it was.

It seemed too soon.

A booming voice: *'Cadet Voz. Time for descent.'*

I felt like snapping to attention at this command. 'Message received,' I said. 'Message understood.' I turned to the control panel; the back-up apparatus. Almost surplus to requirements now.

'Within five minutes. Mission Oeuf. Retain weaponry. Look sharp.'

'Of course.'

I'd had the brief a long time back, and had refreshed my memory several times since. It wasn't something I'd forget easily.

I allowed myself a silent farewell to what led up to this point: emerging from our cryosleep chambers, then a week or so to get into a routine; watching the flickering stars and the light receding, turning, reappearing; the colours fractured by bright spots of unknown elements. It tugs at the senses. I knew all about sun orbits, the beauty of the universe, the distinctive patterns of constellations even when we were so obviously close.

But we still didn't know all the secrets of our beguiling cosmos.

This was it. It was time to get moving.

'Glo!' I waited for the clomp of her arrival.

Again: *'Cadet Voz – operation slot imminent!'* This time roared directly into my ear.

It was the moment to instruct Ulysses. 'Okay,' I said out loud. It was an emotive time. 'This might be the last time I get to do this... '

Ulysses was rolling around... uneven, jerky...

'Can you hold still?' I said, more loudly. 'Drift again, one last time... then think hard.'

My petulant drone sensed it all. He was not pleased. Did he think he was more astute than our commander? Cheeky.

'Told you,' said Glo, now at my elbow.

'Time for descent,' I said in my head, moving my lips in sync. 'Time, trusty Ulysses, to obey and get us where we need to be.'

I sensed Ulysses listening; he knew what he had to do. And he did it.

We began to descend.

All the pertinent planetary data had been compiled; other cadets were out there journeying the same way to specific points on the same planet. Cadets rely on those with greater knowledge, but we have our own strengths.

I tried not to think of the possibility of someone bungling things this time.

The faint hum of the craft petered out. Silence.

I could feel power leaving us. We were almost in free-fall. Ulysses kept pace, his spindly antennae-limbs moving in step with the atmospheric currents.

On our way.

As the craft took the descent, we seemed just about to land directly on cloud formations... then we'd go straight through; how fragile those wisps of vaporous layers are.

Lower and lower...

Down... down... down...

The light changed. Strands of pink formed around the craft, whirled and lashed, then evaporated; and instantly reappeared. I stretched my neck this way and that, enjoying this brilliance.

Glo shrieked.

We dropped to the required height... and the craft shuddered briefly as it met with the new atmospheric conditions. Ulysses, still very close, jolted in sympathy.

Further still, and into a new world.

Touch down!

Glo clapped her hands to see sumptuous greenery, real old-fashioned plant life, gliding nearer, ready to envelop our craft. I've never seen her light up in that kind of way, ever. Bright flowers in borders, an assault of colour – and close enough now to see huge butterflies arching their intricate wings and doing their own kind of drift from petal to petal, fluttering from one frou-frou bloom to the next.

Glo shrieked again, taking me by surprise. 'Roses, and hollyhocks... and agapanthus!'

'*Shush*! This is serious stuff.'

My face was pressed to the porthole at fore, my breath coming hard and misting the thick pane's surface. Sweet flower fragrances seeped through the fissures of our craft's structure; I hadn't realised that possible. An oversized dragonfly shimmied and bustled nearby, reminding me of a baby Ulysses, if there was such a thing. Another feast for the senses. It wasn't difficult to see how our world had borrowed from previous incarnations of planets in the universe. Everything impacts on everything else.

I heard a *bok-bok-bok-bok-bok-begowwwwk...*

I raised an eyebrow.

'A chicken,' said know-it-all Glo. 'Listen to it.'

An egg-layer, of course. The first of those we had to annihilate.

The noise was sporadic but distinct. Glo smirked at me. She loved all this. 'There's a cockerel too,' she said, 'somewhere.'

Our descent needed all my attention. The craft, with Ulysses sticking close, now moved through a very large framed area, abruptly leaving behind all that leafiness and vibrancy.

'That's a window,' said Glo, awe-struck. 'Sure as eggs is eggs.' She sniggered at her own gag. 'With curtains! *Blue* curtains!'

'What?' I was too busy looking out for us.

There was a warm glow ahead. Our target?

A different kind of light.

Seemed we were now heading for a diverse sun, one contained on Planet Earth. It was distant, but unmistakably sunshine yellow. *This hadn't been in the brief.* Too late to check now.

Still a fair way off.

Was this possible?

What the hell was happening?

There'd been a period distortion! I was convinced of it.

'*Distortion!*' I reported. '*Target unknown! Request for instructions!*'

I waited, but our commander did not answer.

More time passed.

Earth's sun, ever brighter, ever nearer...

I knew some Greek mythology... Icarus' flight to the sun. I'd picked it up in the ancient-data-memory-banks onboard just last week when I had a thirst for some real, antediluvian history. The hope was that we didn't meet *his* cruel fate.

No, surely not.

We drifted onwards, into shadow now, and towards the unknown sun... nearer and nearer, with Ulysses, I thought, looking very unsure. I sensed movement, but could see nothing recognisable. It was as if we were back in the vast universe we'd already travelled through. We glided forward tentatively. I could smell food. It couldn't be from inside the craft, it had to be coming from outside. Glo inhaled appreciatively.

We landed.

An effortless placement. Ulysses stuck around, alighting on a flat surface nearby. I feared for him. 'Drift again!' I whispered. 'Drift. Be cautious. We don't know anything yet. Understand?'

I felt edgy. It could be hostile territory.

Then, from my commander: *'Cadet Voz. Disembarkation. Visor on. Weaponry at the ready.'*

This was it. This was what it was all about. First port of call. I was ready to show my true mettle.

What a journey!

Visor in place, I grabbed my bag of weapons; made for the craft exit area, waiting for the buzzing siren that told me I could now leap out.

This really was it.

Glo sat tight.

The door rolled back as smoothly as a lover's caress; I found that such a beautiful simile. Some image!

A voice from nowhere said: 'Eat your egg, sweetheart. I know you like it really.'

I flinched at the scale of the volume. It sure wasn't the commander speaking. I hesitated for a nano-second, and was then through the door, jumping into an area near the vivid glow of a radiant, natural Earth sun. I had no choice.

Ulysses took off immediately. Maybe he knew

too much. He sped, whirling back to where we'd come from, nothing drift-like about it. Full throttle. I watched him go, a tiny blur on the horizon, through the large framed area, the massive window with the curtains – back into the blue skies and lush vegetation we'd admired as we'd cruised through. Did I detect a slight judder of his glittery hindquarters as he deserted us?

Had he betrayed me?

Or maybe early decommission? *And without a word to me.*

That needed to be taken up with the powers that be, and *soon*.

Again, that breakfast smell; now overpowering, pungent.

Shadows rolled over me, yet the Earth sun continued to shine brightly very close by. I took a step towards it. I had to assume this was what I needed to do.

Dazzled!

I held my hand to my eyes. I really needed tinted goggles.

Damn! This wasn't going well.

'There's something on your plate, darling,' said the voice.

Deafening!

There was a perceptible shift in the gloom. I sensed rather than saw a looming presence – and had no way of knowing what it was.

My head rang with invisible bells, my bag of destruction weapons hung heavy. I looked around, above and behind me, my eyes rolling, panicky – but there was nothing to see except shadowy space.

Glo was gazing out of the craft porthole. She looked worried.

Orders *must* be obeyed. Where, now, do I start with finding egg-layers?

There was more movement above, rising and falling; shredding my nerves. I tried another step forward, still shielding my eyes...

I couldn't. I was caught in a swampy goo, some kind of quagmire. It was the colour of a rich sunset on Planet Mars. I felt heat through the thick soles of my boots and knew they were ruined with the yellow gloop.

'Can you see?' said the voice, sweetly this time. 'Here, on your egg? How *funny*... '

I struggled.

'Looks like a little man! He's wearing a *helmet thingy*.'

I was standing on an egg?

'Where did he come from, Mummy?'

I struggled some more...

'Oh, my goodness! He's *moving*.' A very loud scream. 'Get away... *quickly* – quick as you can! Get away NOW, Daisy!'

My senses whirled with the noise and the full-bodied reek of breakfast. I managed a gigantic leap onto the hard surface around me, hearing a spectacular r..i..i..p..p..p.. as the soles of my boots left the vile gloop.

A different voice: 'Get him! *Get him!!*'

That's when I knew for sure that the mission was a disaster. But without Ulysses, my erstwhile guardian angel, we were sunk. Glo's look of concern had been replaced by hysteria.

We were amongst humans. I knew that.

They'd grown in our absence. Developed. So enormous now, this terrified space cadet – me – couldn't see them; as high as the loftiest, most ancient craggy peaks on any planet in the universe. Or so it seemed.

Had everything on the planet gone that way?

In my ear: 'Mission aborted! Mission Oeuf terminated!'

'Yeah, too true Mr Commander. You don't have to yell.'

There was huge activity above me; the deafening, spasmodic clatter of crockery, scraping chair legs, shrill voices. And the smell of fear.

A bright white light from above swept over me.

What now?

I sensed a change – a sudden hush – then a faint whirring from afar.

Could it be...?

There was something approaching, going full pelt; not much more than an uneven blob, still far away. I threw my consciousness wide open: *Pick up, Ulysses... pick up!*

Help us!

More shifting, wavering shadows from above; it was anyone's guess what was going on there. They'd be after me once the shock had subsided – I was their target in plain sight.

They'd regroup, and I'd be squashed into a pulp.

Closing my eyes, I willed Ulysses to come. My buddy, my guardian angel… be loyal to me.

Please.

The oncoming speeding form was unwavering. Still too soon to be certain. Glo wailed desperately. The penny had dropped for sure.

Bloody mission. Damn the flamin' eggs!

I needed to get Glo and me back into the cryo-chambers. Then home, to retire. It was time for us to call it a day. Our commander really needed to hear this – if he was still on duty. Somehow, I doubted it. He'd finished with us, he'd foreseen the oncoming calamity, then snatched back Ulysses.

Leaving us to it.

Spiteful.

My vision was blurred with tears.

It was hopeless. Trying to pivot to shoot upwards, way above me, would be futile. And the heat of the bright light overhead was burning into my visor.

I didn't move.

That was it. It wouldn't be long before…

Then I heard a shout from our craft – it was Glo in the doorway, cupping her hands to her mouth. '*Look, Voz!*' I froze, fearing the very worst. '*Look!* There's more of them!' And she pointed.

I swivelled to gaze at the hurtling voyager…

'It's *him*,' she yelled. 'He's *back*!' If so, Glo would need to retract her harsh words from before – and I knew how grumpy that'd make her. Ulysses' familiar spindly gait was obvious now. I swear his metallic panels glinted in greeting. It was as if Glo had her own personal built-in radar system – he had company; there was a whole fleet of drones clustering around and scudding along behind him.

The cosmos had been listening.

But space was compressing above me; something terrible was coming my way…

Abruptly, Ulysses landed nearby, then swiftly zoomed upwards with a resounding *ROAR!* His allies, all his mates, followed on. Massed together, they'd cause the right kind of chaos.

I trembled as I stumbled across to our craft.

Then I smiled…

Seemed Ulysses knew better all along.

And we were going home.

Grade A, Grey Day

None of them were like me.

How *could* they be!

They'd never let their kid stay up until midnight and beyond to watch Dracula movies; or authorise ice-cream consumption on a 24-hour loop. Or agree to a ten-year-old painting his bedroom any colour he wanted, even if it turned out to be pitch black…

It looked marvellous, actually. I helped him.

And that lot definitely wouldn't allow the postman through the door to creep between their sheets at a time when it was most inappropriate. Oh, dearie me, no.

Ha! Well… is it ever appropriate?

I'm betting they certainly wouldn't harbour murderous thoughts about their husband either; making a list of all the ways possible to take him off the face of this earth.

Not like me.

I'd see them, standing at the school gates in their leopard-print onesies. Puffa jackets, lip-sticked up to the nines. Fag half-hidden, with hand pinned at hip level, nearly out of sight.

Swamp trollops.

Her with the carroty hair, posing like some version of Rita Hayworth in her scuffed stilettos. She might think she looks the part; a third-rate version of a glamour puss.

No style, no grace.

I know I'm mouthing-off here – and I don't care.

It's blowing a hooley outside. Time to settle down with *Days of Wine and Roses*. How achingly sad it is. They don't make actors like that now – it's all about super-heroes these days, blowing-up this and that, saving the world, and biopics of washed-up rock stars.

And weird sex.

After that, I'll be thinking of *Casablanca*.

Then maybe *The Postman Always Rings Twice*. That one always makes me snigger. How I identify with it! My postie did mention the kitchen table... but as I don't actually have one, it wasn't going to happen. Rick was out at the time. He works shifts.

The postman comes around nine o'clock.

What's it now? A quarter to eight. Some time to wait. He hasn't made an appearance for a while. I'll give him what-for.

The dustcart turns up just along the road – belching and snarling like an irritable and loathsome dragon from a Tolkien widescreen epic. I imagine it with flames erupting from its disgusting grinder... its jaws, or is it its belly?

Clank... clank... then silence.

This is where I foresee Rick ending up; if only I could

manage it. Sling him in there along with the decaying banana skins, coke cans, stinking cat food. And gawd knows what else.

It's just a dream.

I'm *still* talking out loud. Wish I wouldn't.

The rubbish guys have been coerced into that old lady's place again, the basement at the end of the terrace. She pushes mugs of tea at them, especially during the winter months. They come out with crumbs around their mouths, laughing, wiping their mooshes.

Silly old bat.

I can picture her screwed-up lips, like a funnel, in a graceless pout. And I can easily visualise her poisoning the whole lot of them, stirring in rat killer on a whim. Wouldn't that be sensational? Ha! Didn't some impoverished Northern woman do just that to all her husbands sometime in the murky past?

I yawn loudly.

Her with the teapot, the basement woman up the road. She's not like me.

She's being kind. I wouldn't be.

I look at the wall clock. A quarter to eight. That can't be right.

My boy has just slammed the door, hard, so that means he's home from school.

'Grade A!' he shouts.

Presumably this means good news. He's been taking some kind of mock exams. Not sure what that means either.

He's not like me. Not at all.

Okay, we share a love of Dracula, but he's inclined

to lethargy and laziness just like his father. But my boy is bright. He'll go far, with a bit of arse-kicking from me. If I can be bothered.

'Grade A?' I shout back, but it's futile – he's in his pit, and will have his own special music blaring out.

The postman is late.

Wine o'clock? I squint at the clock again. A quarter to eight. Time moves so slowly here; getting on for eight o'clock doesn't make sense, not if my boy has just come home from school. Does it?

And when did his voice get so deep?

When did everything change? I can't remember.

There's rumblings from his room and that high, squealing music. Sets my teeth on edge. Are his walls still painted black? I quite liked it.

In the background, the dust cart noise melts away. At least the driver is still alive.

Blurry days, if I'm honest. How long have I been sitting here?

It's quiet. The music has stopped. Was it ever there?

I feel the roaring of life... the rushing sound that I hear, every so often, that I have no explanation for. It isn't my heartbeat.

Is it?

I call out to my son. 'You there, sweetie? What you doing?'

No answer.

'What's with the Grade A?' I yell.

'What's that, Mum?'

'Exam results.' I cup my hands around my mouth. 'School stuff.'

'I didn't say *that*. I said—'

'Come in and *speak* to me,' I bawl. 'No good you being in there.'

He stands in the doorway and takes my breath away. He's changed. He isn't my little boy – he's a grown man with a beard.

'What are you on about, Mum?'

'You said— '

'All I said was it's a grey *day*.' He winces. 'Grade A?' He goes to the window. 'Look at it outside. It's bloody dreadful. That's what I meant.'

'Get back to school... or wherever you need to go, son.'

'I'm a working boy now.' He laughs. 'All grown up. Doesn't time fly, Mum!'

'What's that?'

'Time for dinner. Tuna steaks in the fridge. Are you ready to eat?'

I'm feeling a bit confused.

'It's a quarter to eight,' I say, looking at the wall clock again.

Time flying? I don't think so.

'It's wrong, that clock,' he says. 'Needs a new battery. I'll fix it. I'll get dinner going now.'

'You said two mistakes. What did you mean?'

'No. Tuna steaks. What's going on here?'

But he knows what's going on. He knows only too well what's going on.

Is he ever going to tell me?

I know I've been set up. I know. Just this last week or two.

I sometimes remember to look to see where the camera is installed. I zigzag my eyes around this room, when I think of it, to see if I can spot its sneaky snout.

The lens.

Or maybe more than one.

It's all a set-up.

They think I don't know. I'm not daft, of course I know. Even the stupid bastard clock trick was there to fool me.

Are they still filming? *Now?*

I can hear sonny boy clattering around in the kitchen. He thinks I'm going doolally. Far from it, son. The whole bloody world thinks I'm crazy it seems.

I turn to look out of the window, at least what I can see from here. There's a nasty sky looming.

Soon we'll have dinner. He usually calls it supper. We all grew up calling our main meal of the day our *tea*. I know... but that's what we said. That's what I said, and he said. And what Rick said.

Rick? Rick! Where is *he?*

'Son!' I roar. 'Where's your father?' Silence. '*Oi! Anyone there?*'

Complete silence.

Then I hear the back door slam, and footsteps. His voice. He's coming back from the garden gabbling into his phone.

Always on his flaming phone.

'She's such a prima donna,' I hear him say. 'Crafty. And deaf as a post. If she knew what's really happening, eh! Did you see her footage today? Did she mention Dracula? Or the dustcart?'

They've been watching me today.

'Hey, boy! What's going on?' I bellow.

'She's calling me. Hang on.'

I shout 'Where's the *tuna steaks*?'

'Coming soon. With a bit of salad. I just took the rubbish out.'

Yeah. And you'd better hurry up, sonny.

'I'm back,' he says into his phone, lowering his voice. 'Yes, just show the highlights. If she knew she was appearing on some channel somewhere, she'd blow a flippin' fuse. Whatever she does all day, it sure seems to raise a laugh with her followers.'

I shout *'It's burning!'*

'The fish is burning. *Jesus!* Nothin' wrong with her sense of smell.'

Silence.

Then: 'Yep. Yep, thanks. I know you have my account number. A barmy, feisty widow – we'll keep her performing.'

A widow? Me! So, Rick died? I remember now. When?

Heart attack?

He's still on that damn phone...

'*OnStageMumsDotCom* obviously love it,' he whispers. 'She's *always* enjoyed being the centre of attention. What's more, it'll benefit her in the end – when she needs more care. Cash in the bank. She wouldn't settle for anything modest, if you know what I mean. She'll want the best.'

He's a little shit, my boy.

'Okay. Better go now, she's hungry,' he says.

He nips into the kitchen, checks things, then comes back in here.

'Ready in a jiffy,' he says.

'Cooking up something, are you?' I ask sourly. 'In more ways than one?'

He looks aghast. Shocked.

'Look at the time! It's a quarter to eight already.'

He smiles uncertainly – and I laugh.

He's confused.

I cackle again, loudly. 'Criminal what you've done. You're a *villain!*'

And then he colours-up. 'You mean – you *know?*'

'*What* do I know?' I look him straight in the eye. 'Just get that clock fixed,' I say. 'I'm sick of it being a quarter to eight. If I'm on show, I want to know what bloody time it is. And tell them to get my good side as much as possible.'

I reach out and slap his wrist. 'Into the kitchen you go, fix our dinner, then you can get back to school when you've washed up.'

His mouth falls open. 'Mum— '

'Do you need telling again?' I despair with this boy. 'And did you take anything in for the nature table this morning? Eh? We left carrot tops on the work surface, three seagull feathers, and those two pine cones you like. Didn't we?'

The Embodying Spirit

He looked at me and raised an eyebrow. 'We know each other well enough, don't we?' He let go of my hand abruptly. 'Madeleine,' he said, 'you don't have to know every sodding thing about someone, *ever*.' He frowned. 'Nice to have *some* secrets left.'

'I guess so.'

'You should know so.'

He was doing it again. On his high horse.

I'd only asked him if his children knew. If *anyone* knew.

We needed to talk.

We walked on, buffeted by the Shaftesbury Avenue crowds milling around on the pavements. I felt my stomach growl, and I sensed my heart quicken with irritation. This was meant to be a special time for us. Of sorts.

The evening was sultry, sweaty. It'd been a hot day. Leaving our hotel room hadn't achieved much. Tom wanted a wander around before the day turned into dusk, and as always, he had his way. We were thinking of moving in together but, first, we needed that discussion.

He wanted to find a decent eatery, and to breathe-in his beloved city of birth one last time; one last time before his life changed – again. Seems he'd had a few of those over the years. So dramatic of him, yet nothing was certain with us.

'Mads... is Chinese okay?'

'Guess so, yes. Or Italian?'

He reconnected with me, squeezed my hand, giving me a tight smile.

I gazed at his handsome profile, at the way his dark curls coiled around his ears, how perfectly it sat on the back of his collar; the set of his shoulders, his smart casual jacket and his linen shirt, unbuttoned at the collar, suiting him so well.

He was the one making the sacrifice, if it happened. That seemed massive to me. But he didn't want to talk about it. I needed to *know* him more. Amazing sex was all very well, but we really needed to get in sync.

'*The Lion King* is showing at The Lyceum,' he said. 'Where's *Wicked?*'

'No clue. How would I know?'

He waved his hands around expressively. Beautiful, sensitive hands. He really should have been an actor, he was so flamboyant. What woman hasn't been totally entranced by a certain man at some point in her life? A man who was irresistible. Tom was ten years older, worldly, charming, so sexy – and in a marriage, with teenage kids. Now, six months down the line...

It was crunch time. He seemed certain. I wasn't.
And he was being strange.
It was making me feel edgy.

'There's a certain feeling in this area; the buzz... no – it's more than that.' He fiddled with his chunky ring, the one on his marriage finger. 'It's the colour, the bright lights, the roar, the pathos.' He smiled enigmatically. 'The Spirit of the Theatre.'

He was being more dramatic than usual. I remember loving him for it.

'And the smell,' he said finally. 'Magical. *So intoxicating.*'

'Do you think so?' I said, bothered by a nearby flickering neon, trying to shield my eyes. Dusk was gathering. 'I barely know it here, Tom. You know that.'

He slowed down his pace, looked deep in thought. 'The Apollo,' he said. Just along here. We've never seen it, have we? *Wicked?*'

'No.' *Please God, no last-minute ticket-buying shenanigans.*

We walked some more, and The Apollo came into view on the other side of the road.

'Damn. I got that wrong. The other Apollo, in Victoria, has it.'

He scowled. Then grinned. 'Seems the gods were laughing back in 2013,' he said. 'Part of the ceiling collapsed – did you know that? – during a performance of *The Curious Incident of the Dog in the Night-Time.* That one. The upper balcony got it all, of course. Calamity!' He chuckled. 'Someone – a few people – thought the clattering noise was part of the show.'

'The theatre here?'

'Yes, this one.' He threw his head back and laughed. 'Some people got hurt. Wonder if they ever went back there? It's a bloody old theatre, of course. 1901 I believe.'

'You love that so much,' I said, 'snippets of info, history. And especially when it's London.'

'Yep. All kinds of happenings. Fodder sent by the gods.'

I laughed. 'If you say so.'

'I'm besotted. We're standing here in London's Theatreland, knee-deep,' he whispered, drawing me into him. 'Such wonderful stuff, all of it,' he crooned. 'Madeleine, it's all around us. Full to the brim.'

'You'll miss this, Tom. If... we leave London, go out beyond the suburbs, or even— '

'Of course.' He paused. 'These nonsensical, bizarre delights. I'd like you to love it too, Mads. *Wonderful* London.'

I gave him what my gran would've called an old-fashioned look.

He released me, waving his hands around again. 'And the pubs. Ah – the pubs!' His eyes were shining. *Was he going to blub?* 'Particularly those cask ales in The Cambridge, back there. Classy place.' He half-swivelled, then he changed his mind.

'We could've eaten there?' I said.

'No. No, we couldn't.'

Ah, his cronies would be there.

'Let's keep an eye open for a decent restaurant,' he said. 'Friday night... not good timing with all these crowds.'

We walked on, my sticky feet sliding in my open-toe shoes as I tried to keep up with his long strides. Traffic fumes stung my eyes, acrid cigarette smoke drifted from the gaggle of people walking ahead, with no way to avoid it. They were shouting their conversation to-and-fro, in competition with the snarl of the ongoing stop-start traffic.

Masked cyclists, backsides up in the air, weaved in and out but cautiously. One or two tuk-tuks drifted along. A motorbike thundered by, mounting the pavement edge, the rider clad in full sweaty leathers.

We walked past The Lyric Theatre on the right, passing Denman Street, which took us straight into glittering Piccadilly Circus. Heralding nightfall, there were banners of red and pink across the mottled sky.

Time to eat.

Eros, the Greek God of Love – or was it Desire? – still there aloft, poised as precariously as ever. So high. Recent builder's cladding gone, as the *Metro* had proclaimed, and the fountain now subdued.

As if he was reading my thoughts, Tom piped up: 'Not Eros, y'know, as everyone thinks. It's actually Anteros.'

Bloody know-it-all.

The vast illuminated signs looked even more slick, with some additions. Over my left shoulder, huge moving images of impossibly expensive cars; smart clothes for attractive male and female executives, serene models gliding through empty, sterile rooms. Boots the Chemist shop was still there, snuggled beneath the massive, curved, animated billboard above.

It looked resigned, if an inanimate structure could possibly be able to do that. Tom might think so.

'What happened to Bovril and Schweppes?' I said.

Tom laughed. 'Long gone. And all *LED* now,' he said. 'Neon is history.'

Clever Clogs. This man knew everything.

Mostly young people packed the steps at Eros' site – standing, smoking, enjoying selfies, sprawling, laughing, maybe arguing. Where were they going? What would their evening be like?

'It's chaos here. What're we going to do?'

Tom pulled a face. 'I suppose a burger's out of the question?'

'Can't we do any better?'

'There's a Burger King not far away.' He winked. 'We can't sacrifice food for love, Madeline, can we.'

'Too many sacrifices to think of at the moment,' I said. 'We need to talk.'

He shrugged, turning away. 'Lighten *up* girl.'

I wanted this to end. I'd had enough.

I was just about to agree to burgers, but my eyes were drawn to something new. Tom too looked skywards, to the space above Eros the errant archer and the fountain below. Beyond, the sky was darkening, the red streaks already broken-up, with stars beginning to become just visible; outshone by Central London's dazzling brilliance. In that gap, I could see some kind of bulky creature slowly moving through the sky, unfolding from the direction of Haymarket. I screwed up my eyes, tight, and looked again.

Some publicity stunt?

Tom saw it too. Straight away, he knew.

'It's a chimera,' he said flatly.

'A what?'

'A hybrid thing. A chimera. I... I'm sure. It's decided to make an appearance tonight.'

I swallowed nervously. 'Tom – what's going on?'

'A she-goat. Greek mythology.' He gasped. 'She's *real*. Bloody hell – *she's real!*'

The chimera had gathered pace, she was floating almost overhead now. Shimmering, with strong beating wings. I looked at all the people hanging around on the steps leading up to the fountain and Eros, waiting for their reactions; but no one noticed it. Not one person looked up. Oblivious.

Was I dreaming?

Tom let out a breath. 'See it, Mads? See how it's made up?'

'It's... hideous!'

'It's magical! See the Lion's head? And that's a goat's body, with its head coming from the side. See the horns?' he yelped, his eyes rolling. 'And look at the snake tail swishing around!'

I looked, and I saw all those things. She seemed almost within touching distance now. As the tail lashed, red flickering snake eyes appeared to lock with mine. With a toss of her head, the lion part of the creature began spouting vapour, and then a sheet of orange flame shot across the sky...

Tom thrust his arms upwards, yelling: *'The Spirit of the Theatre!'* He was in complete awe, captivated.

She lowered her lion's head and flapped her elaborate wings a little harder, gaining height and veered in a disjointed, iridescent cluster of body parts towards Regent Street. I thought I heard a low snarl, followed by a hiss.

I sensed a hint of sulphur hanging in the air...

Dazed, I shook my head and looked around for Tom. I expected more words, some sort of explanation from him; there must've been more to say about what we'd seen – that sudden apparition, a monstrosity apparently embodying the spirit of greasepaint and the roar of the crowd.

Everything in Piccadilly Circus was normal, just as before.

But no Tom.

I gazed around – at the young people swarming over the steps, the tourists, day-trippers and workers clutching their iphones, all swivelling eyes and gabbling mouths. I gaped at the sky, then down at the grubby pavements, the blur of feet, the scattering of dribbling, scrunched-up beer cans; at the enormous LED billboards playing on an ever-changing loop those shiny, greed-induced, rich people's wholly excessive commodities.

Maybe he'd gone to buy burgers.

I turned, craning my neck. I thought I could see him pushing through the crowd at the junction with Regent Street but I couldn't be sure.

He might never come back.

Did I care?

Should I care?

Yes, it *was* him. It was Tom.

Above his agitated figure, and higher this time, the she-goat lion swarmed some way ahead – her side-on fuzzy goat head bobbing – breathing fire and wriggling her snake tail; perhaps on her way to Oxford Circus and beyond to spread more bewilderment, or delight for those who were attuned with the theatrics of her evidently unpredictable, alluring spirit.

The Other Me

I'm in a queue outside black wrought-iron gates, a stone's throw from Hades.

It's raining of course. It's always raining.

What'll I be given this time?

See, had I known what kind of mother she'd turn out to be, I'd have put in for a transfer – to a different time period, or something else altogether. I dragged it out for sixty years, and then I threw in the towel.

I reach the front of the wretched queue, and I'll soon know what my *something else* is going to be.

Blackheath Fairground. What's *that*?

I'm to mingle. I'm to pop up in different places. I'm to frighten the pants off folk.

If I'm good at it, I'll be on the path to better things. Promotion. I shouldn't have given up my previous assignment so readily, he says.

Ah, Blackheath. I know my history. That's where they buried so many plague victims. Should have suitable vibes.

I start with the jolly spotty teacups merry-go-round. Easy peasy. Without being seen, I can stop-start the going around process. The jolted kids shriek, the mums watching on are panic-stricken. The guys in charge look worried, shaking their flat-capped heads in disbelief.

Then I move on to the dodgems. Deafening Fifties music thickens the air. I make those dudes yell even harder when I seize hold of their steering wheels. The steel in the eyes of the men and boys shines bright as they pretend it's their own doing – daredevils, pumped with adrenaline.

Youth stalks the sloped walkway surround. Spoiling for a fight methinks.

Easy. I engineer it.

What a bloody ruckus. A veritable brouhaha.

On to the coconut shy. No actual coconuts now, we live in a modern world. Garish clown heads, scarlet lips agape, rotate from side to side inviting a coloured ball to hit them in the tonsils. Dads and young men aim carefully, sucking their lips, one eye on their woman to make sure they're watching. All-in-a-row teddy bears, gangly monkeys and hideous gonks for the winning. No goldfish in sight.

Yawnnn...

Time to find the Crooked House. There it is, a pale pink exterior, sporting thick painted green creepers; exaggerated proportions, roofing sloping drunkenly. A warped chimney. A lumpy walkway leads to a twisted front door; and an exit guaranteed to contain hollering teenagers on their way out...

Craaackkk!!

The chimney stack disintegrates, crashing down.

That'll do nicely for my report.

I'm ready to have a good laugh with the fortune teller – Madame Za-Za, in a turban covered in stars no doubt, and hunched over a crystal ball...

But I stop in my tracks—

A trick of the light? A mad moment?

At the attic window of the Crooked House, I see myself staring back at me.

Ha! Someone got that very wrong. Something adrift with their aeon files.

A spy, sent to monitor me.

Another *me!*

Me!

I snigger, can't help it. Flamin' Hades!

Sometimes Satan doesn't know his eras from his eyeballs; and, smirking, I scribble all that down.

To Know Seville

I'm booked in, I've inspected my room, and I'm settled in a snug corner in the hotel bar. The barman smiles at me and takes my order: a large Rioja.

It's time to relax.

I take out my phone and tap in Bella's number. It rings a few times, and then some more. I shut off the call and text her instead:

I'm here. Vino on the go. No León yet.

My head feels clear. I breathe in... the air-con is delicious. It's a different zone, just a few steps in from the scorching heat outside. I'd thought of wearing a silk scarf, but that encourages perspiration. Not today; no one wants a moist neck on a hot date. I love my scarves, particularly this turquoise sea life chiffon I'm wearing. I've counted the stylised fishes, jellyfish and crabs several times in the past. Thirteen – lucky for some.

The barman brings my drink. 'Aquí tiene, señora.'

'Gracias.'

León has organised his own room; we thought it best. We're not known here, but he worries he could bump into business associates – and that someone might look at the reservations register – but how likely is that? He insisted we book separate rooms, he couldn't take that chance. We've had brief steamy moments before, in bars in Malaga, but too many people know us there. It was my idea to come here. He's so good looking, so confident. How could I resist?

I have quite a crush on him. We need this private time together.

Hotel El Embajador, Sevilla. It's written everywhere: gold lettering on glossy coasters, in neon above the illuminated bar, on the ruby red velour *bienvenido* mat welcoming those that can afford to stay or drink in this establishment.

It translates as The Ambassador Hotel.

Chosen by me. I've always wanted to visit Seville.

The high ceiling of the large reception area is alive with glittering lanterns, in varying sizes and at different levels; and way below, a carpet the colour of jewels. This area merges smoothly into the bar. There's no one much around, there's a hush throughout; even the buzzing telephone behind the main desk sounds muted. Residents might be drinking in the local bars where it's much cheaper, and seeing something of Seville. Wish I'd thought of suggesting that, but it could've complicated things.

I wait.

I order another Rioja.

Something beeps: it's my phone. Battery is low. Damn! Better re-charge it. Could be a problem if I don't have my charger with me...

The barman is watching. He approaches, very dapper in his cream and gold uniform. He asks if I need my phone charged, I smile and nod. He doesn't have much English, and offers his name: Paco.

'Te gusta Sevilla?' he says.

'Ah, si!'

Yes – and I'd like to know Seville more.

He moves away.

I'm still waiting.

I order another Rioja and some *agua con gaz* on the side. Have to think of pacing myself; don't want to be accused of drinking like a fish.

Something occurs to me. I get up and stroll over to the reception area and speak to the receptionist, her charcoal eyebrows and dark shark eyes in conflict with her delicate features and impossibly blond hair. With a hint of impatience, she picks up her phone.

Paco brings my phone back to me fifteen minutes later and I immediately phone León. It goes to voicemail. I end the call, tap my fingernails on the edge of the table. I wait five minutes and try again. This time I hear his voice. '*Louise!* Where are you?'

'Waiting,' I say, 'for a couple of hours now.' I try to keep my voice level.

'In the 'otel?'

'Yes, in the hotel bar.'

'Reception, they tried your room number. But they say there's no one registered for there,' he says, clearly agitated.

'I asked them to ring your room number too,' I hiss. 'I kind of gave up waiting for you.'

'Uh?'

'León, someone else answered, a woman. Señora something-or-other. Then Reception asked me for your name.' I'm getting irritated. 'What's going on?'

'Your room number is thirteen, first floor?' he says. 'That is right? I went to bang on the door.' He draws in breath harshly. 'You're playing games with me?'

'*What!*'

'Number thirteen? It's right?'

'Yes, it is. What the hell's happening!'

'I was a bit late. You know I'm a busy man. Could there be... some misunderstanding?'

'What d'you mean?'

'Is the 'otel correct? I'm in The Ambassador.'

'Yes... that's where I am.'

I hear a wail of despair. 'Is it the correct *city?*'

'*Wait,*' I say. 'I'm in the Embajador, Seville. Could there... be... ?'

'*Dios mio!* El Embajador? Louise, that's a different 'otel!'

'What?'

'Yes, it *means* Ambassador. You went to the one with a Spanish name!'

'What?'

'You could've told me properly which 'otel you chose!'

'*Christ.* Sorry, León. I don't know what to say.'

'I come over. It'll take a little while. Stay where you are.' He rang off.

Breathe, breathe... calm, calm...

I text Bella: *Cock-up here. Can't even tell you how bad things are. Will text later.*

I order another Rioja. At this rate I'll be incapable of any kind of romance. The turquoise scarf slips from my neck; I drag it off, I'm hot. I wish I could leave – just go home, back to Malaga. But I really do want to see him.

It's going to be cramped in my single bed. León's room, he'd said, was a deluxe single; much bigger. He'd thought it through, but that was in the *other* hotel. How much more can go wrong with this tryst?

'First, I need a drink,' he says as he walks into the bar area.

It's gone ten o'clock.

He looks furious. He beckons to the bemused barman, the only one there: it's Paco.

'It's a fiasco, Louise,' León says, not meeting my eye. He doesn't touch me, doesn't kiss my cheek. I can see it's going to take some time. He pauses mid-sip and stoops to pick up something from the carpet. It's my scarf.

'This scarf, *typical tourist tat!*' He lets the scarf slip onto the low table by his side and carries on drinking.

He's tired. I sit tight.

I wait.

'I need another drink first,' he says, fiddling with his chunky gold rings. His eyes flicker to Paco, who immediately takes notice; some people have this gift of getting what they want with barely any effort.

He's livid. He must think I'm an idiot.

'Soon,' he says, 'I have to make a phone call.' He picks up my scarf and examines it. 'Fishes,' he says. 'Unusual.'

I feel pleased he likes my scattering of shimmering sea life. 'Are they?'

'Okay, but cheap.' He throws it back onto the table as Paco approaches with his drink on a small tray. 'Gracias,' he says, taking the glass without looking at him.

I try: 'Busy on the roads?'

He pulls at his tie, and huffs. 'Traffic? Bloody crazy. And you?'

'I took the train.'

This isn't going the way it should. He still won't look at me.

'Excuse me,' he mutters. He drains his drink, gets up and walks away with his phone clamped to his ear, casting furtive glances my way. There's no doubt who he's phoning. I know there is a woman in his life, but he says it's a relationship on its last legs.

Paco, running a hand through his dark curly hair, smiles a thin smile. I didn't plan for this rendezvous to be so public.

I gather up my wrap and handbag and wander around the reception area, pretending to read the tasteful posters and laminated notices pinned in place; the hotel name so prominent, almost as a deliberate derision, mocking me... wrong *Ambassador* booking, wrong move, bad decision.

I should leave, but it's late to get a train now.

And I want to be with him.

Señora Dark Eyebrows behind Reception is eyeballing me. She looks ready to pose a question but I give her a hard stare and she quickly looks away. She's probably seen it all from behind that tasteful, ornate barricade: arguments, breakups, kisses, maybe fisticuffs. Alcohol and much-anticipated weekend breaks can take their toll.

León is still talking.

I halt at a pinned notice, see there's a coach trip to The Cathedral; another to The Andalusian Centre of Contemporary Art. Both include snacks and wine. What I'd like to experience is a mosey through Seville's orange trees… but it's the wrong time of year: I've missed the fruits, and the white blossom. We're in stifling July, well past the fragrant Spring months.

I see that León is off his call now and looks more relaxed. I'd avoided listening to his staccato words, words of explanation and possible endearment. Not my business.

'Room thirteen,' he says, coming over to me.

'Yes. How ridiculous,' I say. 'Lucky for some, thirteen. What's the chances of that!' Then I want to bite out my tongue.

He looks grim and takes my arm. We head for the lifts.

Dark Eyebrows is staring at us. I don't look back.

A new romance. It doesn't feel like it.

We kiss awkwardly and then undress. I was right about the bed. He cradles me in his arms and seems to be somewhere else. Suddenly, he's on top, crushing me, his hands working my breasts as if they're two doughy loaves that are destined for the oven.

'I'm not flying,' he says regretfully, moving off. 'And you?'

'Take a break,' I say diplomatically. 'Have a breather.'

'I flounder... like a fish,' he says, chuckling at his own joke.

He nods off. I shift around quietly trying to get comfortable.

You berk, Louise. You idiot.

There's a clock built into the bedside cabinet. The fluorescent hands show it's nearly two o'clock. In the next beat I'm shocked by a shrill ring: his phone.

He's alert immediately, reaching for it. *'Diga!'*

I turn to face away, my heart thumping in my throat. He doesn't speak for long.

'Have to go. My kid, she's ill. I knew. Thought she'd be okay.' He slides into his smart trousers. 'My fault. I shouldn't be here.' He shakes his head.

He has a child!

I say nothing.

'Cariño,' he says, stroking my hair. 'We try again, yes?'

I move away.

'Another time,' he says, dragging on his jacket, 'perhaps.'

He picks up his belongings.

I pull on my top and walk with him to the door. He

touches my shoulder, then sprints down the corridor, looking back briefly... 'Adios!'

Goodbye. That's definitely right.

I thought we had something. I really believed we were at the start of something good.

But he has a child, something I knew nothing about.

Heartbroken isn't really the right word, but... it's more than my pride that's injured. Didn't we have *something?*

I'll have to tough it out.

Picking up my phone, I text Bella: *It's finished. Slippery moron. Will explain later.*

I go back to bed, eyes brimming.

What a fool I am. I really believed in him.

I was used. Hooked.

I leave in the morning, stepping carefully down the marble steps outside, tired, and still feeling an idiot. There's so many fish in the sea, and it's time I snared myself a decent, uncomplicated one.

I need to use the day ahead wisely. What is it I really want to do?

I hear footsteps behind me. It's Paco, already togged-up in his uniform. He holds up something blue; it has to be the turquoise scarf. He reaches me and tucks it into my hand.

I say goodbye. He wishes me a good journey... and do I need a taxi?

The rank is empty.

'Si,' I say, adding 'por favor.' I never forget my

English manners.

He's still standing there. I like his curly hair, his fine straight nose. I dip into my handbag, scrabble around, and hand him my business card:

Little Fishes
Pequeños Peces
Wine Importer / Importador de Vinos
London / Malaga
Louise Perez

'Our wine is *excelente*,' I say. Wine is my business, I'm good at it.

He smiles, and hails an approaching taxi...

I've always wanted to see Seville. Where shall I start?

He deposits my overnight bag on the back seat, and turns to me. He makes that clicking noise with his tongue, the *chasquido*, and grins. He has his eyes on me.

I don't take the cue.

'Gracias, Paco,' I say, tucking my handbag under my arm.

And climb inside the cab.

That Crazy Vibe

Sometime in the near future

I'd been shoulder to shoulder with a golden-eyed fellow in The Dog & Duck last week. We nodded, and after I bought him a pint, he mentioned that Mars will collide with Earth next Thursday.

I laughed.

Then I noticed he had six fingers.

I assumed he was in fancy dress that evening. The transformation of his eyes was clever, the facial prosthetics were ace. No revealing join lines, no caked panstick.

'I don't know you', he said, 'but I hope to get under your skin.'

I slurped on my beer.

There was a very strange vibe. Crazy.

He watched me. A quizzical scrutiny. 'Mars will come off far better,' he said.

When I caught his eye, he gave me a crinkly grin.

It seemed his presence sucked in the air around us. Music from the jukebox curdled, the faces surrounding us seemed suddenly grotesque. Yep, I thought, someone's slipped something into my drink.

That someone had to be him.

I needed to check him out some more.

His wife Geena joined us the following evening, this time in The Green Man across the street. I sensed I'd probably been wrong about him being dodgy; but I *was* feeling heady again. Crazy, weird stuff.

Geena, a tiny woman, had the same kind of eyes, but hid her hands in bulky black mittens. When she spoke, in monotone, her pink gums gleamed from the fairy lights strung around the bar. Her dull red hair matched the rawness of her scalp. A home dye? She held herself rigid, guarded.

This fellow explained that his wife had one central eye previously. All to do with family genetics, he said. 'There's nothing that can't be achieved with medical science now.' I thought that seemed a bit bloody far-fetched.

'I have more time to do less this time,' he said. 'If that makes sense.' Seemed he'd gone away and then returned.

We'd run out of politics chat, and what the weather was doing, and the price of everything under the sun. 'Where are you from? Originally?' I said. He didn't seem the type to have spent all his life in Greenwich. 'Are you on a mission? You said— '

'You know – what is it they say? Oh, I know, yes… I'm a Citizen of the Universe.'

'Does that mean you're travelling on?'

'In time.'

What did that mean? Soon?
Or actually hurtling through space time-zones?

The following afternoon I took him somewhere quite different. Greenwich Park.

Just we two.

He hadn't been there before.

This time, my head was perfectly clear.

It was late autumn, and there was a sense of decay; so many of the half-leafed trees were broken and some looked diseased, decidedly sickly. The sweep of grasses climbing the hill, up and up to the stately Royal Observatory, was wild and scrubby. We scrambled higher. The Observatory came into view: tarnished, neglected. I was aware of the ongoing abandonment of crucial repairs. I knew it was a nationwide lack of funds, a swing of inevitability, of decline. Too many national setbacks of late. The Government sticks to its reasoning that we're all lucky to still be alive.

From our new vantage point, looking down at the kids' boating lake, the end-of-season scenario looked pitiful. A couple of broken boats were half-pulled from the dark water, spilling chaotic rubbish of some kind. Where we stood, midway, beneath the lofty spreading branches of the horse chestnut trees, the moss-dank ground was littered with trampled, rotting once-spiky chestnut fruit. I thought back to my enthusiastic flint-hard conker fights in my boyhood: dangerous by today's standards. I felt a pang, a shift in my heart. How we'd hurtle down that hill on toboggans, or on our bellies – depending on the season.

Yet further on, to the north and beyond the ancient River Thames, the far horizon gave us thick clusters of fancy skyscrapers that'd been spawned somehow over the last fifty years. Intruders, certainly to those of my parents' generation. Progress and regression, all at the same time.

My alien looked around with interest. I wanted to tell him how lovely the Thames looked on a fine day, how it sparkled in the sunshine.

Instead, I asked 'What's Geena doing today?'

His eyes clouded. I caught the tortured lines of his ageless face: both old and youthful. 'Gone home,' he said. I was just about to ask him where home was, when he sat himself down on a low, heavily-graffitied bench, stretching his legs out in front of him.

'Which part of the universe are you *originally* from?'

'Zogg. I'm a Zoggite.'

'Oh, okay. I see.'

Abruptly, the autumn wind came in with teeth of glass.

The sky was a stormy grey. A spattering of rain was beginning.

He sighed, and wiped his eyes with the back of his hand.

'I should never tell,' he said. 'Normally, I wouldn't. See, this new exploratory scouting was interesting. I've seen a lot.'

'I assumed you were some kind of scout. I really did.'

I knew I sounded patronising.

'Geena is back home there now. In Zogg.'
'A long way to travel!'
'She needed to go.'
'Bored?'
'No, she's quite shy. Just that. Your planet – your home – is so beautiful. For us all on Zogg. I was looking in all the wrong places on my first visit.'

My eyes popped. 'Not so beautiful today,' I said. 'But, I suppose… '

'You've helped me see. *So* intoxicating.' He tried a feeble laugh. 'Just as I was when we met.'

'What? You seemed sober enough.'

'I spoke too much. Off my guard, you see. I gave away part of my mind.' He mused for a second or two. 'I presented, what you'd call, a bad vibe.'

So, that was it! Nothing more than a slip in decorum.

'Tell me,' I said. 'No invasion from Mars?'

'Not now. I've submitted my report.'

He stretched again, taking in gulps of freezing air. His broad back straightened to reveal the unmistakable outline of neat folded wings beneath his tunic.

'Too beautiful by far. Your home is safe, earthman,' he said, getting up and gazing skywards. 'You're placed bottom of the list, and it'll take multiple aeons for anything to be decided, dreadful or otherwise. Depends on the state of the cosmos.' He gave me one last crooked smile, shrugged off his tunic, and soared up towards the Observatory; onwards, and then over the distant rooftops of the large, opulent houses edging the green, gentle rolling plains of urban Blackheath.

In the Shadows

We wore porkpie hats to Mama's funeral, we knew it was the right thing to do. Smoky Joe's was at an angle – him, he always wanted to be different. Nutcase.

The priest intoned, committing Mama to an eternal life, and carried on with all the usual mumbo-jumbo. I just sat there trying to hide the rawness.

Someone wanted to say a few words; she stepped up, a thin, untidy old woman, and read her piece:

> *When I come to the end of the road,*
> *and the sun has set for me...*
> *Why cry for a soul set free?*
> *It's all a part of the universal plan,*
> *a step alone on the road to home.*

It was one of Mama's chums.

I thought her words seemed fair enough. I tried to take it in, but it didn't stop the hurt. Nothing could.

Smoky Joe did the eulogy. He didn't say much, he just spoke about Mama's existence being a life well lived. I said later, I wasn't so sure about that. She'd lived through tough times; she'd come from a family of ne'er do wells. 'What you saying?' he retorted. 'She rose above all that. And then we came along, Jimmy. Don't forget that. We two looked after her best we could.' He was right.

Rita the Righteous. She ruled us with a rod of concrete. We grew up with more than the occasional swipe around the ear 'ole, but it was her way; her shining resolve to keep us under some kind of control. She'd snaffle a tanner from the big glass bottle at the back of the larder and press it into my hand once in a while, with a warning not to tell Joe. I was aware she'd plundered *special* money; it was hoarded, bit by bit, to go towards the rent and the household bills. She was always short of cash back then, those times were so hard. Pa was hardly ever in work and we barely saw him anyway.

Useless git, to put it politely.

One of the last things Mama did was to remind us to keep to the shadows; she never really approved of our activities but went along with it. We suspected she liked the excitement on the quiet. It's a bloody business, or it can be.

Another thing she always said: 'Never make an enemy by accident.' I took great heed of that. Every person I met was a potential enemy.

I don't mind saying, my heart was the most tattered. And I was the one to go and collect the urn. Mama's urn. Smoky Joe drew on his ciggie and gave me that look, the one that said he was handing that task over to me, even though he was a couple of years older – and so the one who should be taking most of the responsibility.

I was barely nineteen years old.

Smoky Joe spent years in the slammer. Long stretches. His face was too well known to be able to disappear for long. He never grassed on me, I'll say that for him. 'Keep your head down, Jimmy,' he'd said. 'But you *are* the sensible, savvy one. Make Mama proud.'

He'd always hated Johnny Foreigner, that was the problem with him. That, and dealing drugs and violent warehouse heists. He always forgot we have Italian blood, the nearest thing to Sicilian you can get. Not so much an open mind as an open mouth, that's him.

It's been quite a few years now. As he grew older, Smoky Joe's mouth, and fists, got in the way of his brain too many times. Just like our old man, it was the same kind of pattern. A ciggie was always in his mahogany-stained fingers; burning a hole in someone's flesh to get what he wanted was common enough for him. He had a habit of making enemies.

He wouldn't know it, but Oscar Wilde had got there before him, in Pentonville, briefly, in 1895. John Christie, the notorious serial killer, perished there in 1953. These things interest me. Mama always said I had an enquiring mind.

I stopped going to Pentonville to see him; not that I'd go very often in any case. Someone quite recently described that place as 'the most dramatic example of failure' within the prison system. It sounded impressive.

As Oscar might've said... *the last talons of light creep through the window, a dying sun edging the horizon.* Time to switch on the lights, I need to put my books away for now.

The house closes around me like a warm embrace.

I always kept to the shadows. I always kept my guard up. That's how I've survived. Being a gangster is a tricky business. Families should stick together – but not all members are willing, or able. Smoky Joe gave up on himself.

I close the curtains, grab a beer from the fridge, and sit back down to watch EastEnders. Up on the mantlepiece I have my family, or what's left of them. There's photos of me and my brother over several decades – nippers to late teens, cocky as hell. Some aunts and uncles sitting in deckchairs, and a few of Mama in her prime, looking gorgeous, especially with her wartime coiled hair. Lost far too soon. Her porcelain and silver-plated urn stands in the middle, directly under the big wall clock. The crystal chandelier throws a very pleasing, dappled light in that direction. My cleaning lady comes in twice a week, she dusts everything in sight. Sometimes she puts things back in the wrong place and I have to check.

I use the smell test.

During a soap punch-up on the TV screen, playing out a familiar scenario, I go and check. The glinting urn in the middle smells faintly of *Le Train Bleu*, Mama's perfume; the almost identical urn towards the end of the mantlepiece smells just as you would expect – it's Smoky Joe's resting place. Somewhat smaller.

At the other end – an old wooden box. That one smells of nothing. It's Pa, our old man.

I swear they tremble when they know my eyes are on them; just a little bit.

It's the truth. But I welcome it. My family.

I've learnt well. The outside security is faultless. My super-strong safe is well hidden in the house, no one would ever know it was there. The basement area is considerable and very useful. I've thought of everything.

Nothing succeeds like success.

I clamp-on my ancient porkpie, sling my coat on, seize the dog's lead from a hook near the front door, and out we go, Oscar and me. He's a sizeable hound. Shadows move in the darkness, my eyes dart from left to right and back again. Oscar stiffens, then snuffles – he knows what we might encounter. Whispers drift from the swaying trees, night creatures pulse and frisk in the grasses.

We stick to the shadows.

Still tough times, but in a different way.

And I'm ready. Always.

Party Piece

Nurtured throughout the summer
for a really special occasion.
Now autumn chill, bonfires, golden leaves…
I was ready for the knife, nicely glinting under the
kitchen fairy-lights. She began work, caressing me, but
soon released me into the sticky hands of her young
child, whose scratchy attempts failed abysmally.
He kicked me into a corner.
I was never going to hold a welcoming light.
Morning brought new hope.
She bathed me, cut me into chunks.
Boiled me.
As a pie I sat, wretched, next to the spicy Devil's-
food cake and giant sweet eyeballs on the party table,
imagining a broad toothy smile still intact.

By Magic

I've lived close to the port all my life. I've seen what seems like the whole world trooping by: the tourists, the workers; and the arrival of souvenir shops crammed with nests of colourful matryoshka, the wooden babushka dolls that seem to represent our country for foreigners. They're loved so much. I laugh when I think how far these tourists have travelled only to drool over pieces of hollowed out, painted wood with rosy-cheeked faces.

Would they know the real significance of these items in our culture? Not a chance.

They have the magnificence of Russia to explore – they have money, they have opportunity. What do I have?

Vladivostok is a very cold city. The icebreaker vessels come into port regularly; cold, dry winds from polar areas blow south from Sakhalin Island, and the winter snows surge up from Japan. We rarely feel any warmth on our skin. I yearn to move on, somewhere. Anyplace.

April will bring better temperatures, but not for long.

I *have* to get out of here.

Most of the Mafia has gone now, so the travellers feel safe. As safe as they possibly can. They arrive in unsuitable clothes and complain about the freezing temperatures. Didn't they know what to expect?

They still want to know about Gagarin the cosmonaut. That's a long time ago. Now, we look to the future.

I do. I'm young.

And I keep hoping, secreting some roubles when I can.

I need some good fortune: some magic.

I married someone once. It was a low key wedding. We wanted to travel abroad, get away from all the oppression and the freezing air. So we needed to save up.

We lived with my auntie. But it didn't work out; I found out he was already married in any case. What was going through his head to hook up with me?

How could that have happened so easily? Now he's a criminal – though it's unlikely anyone really cares.

He hadn't helped himself by coming home one evening with an armful of roses. It was my birthday. I was putting them into the largest vase I could find and counting them – and there were ten. How could he not know how unlucky that is? Everyone knows! He said he didn't know, but I found that hard to believe. One fewer, or one more, would've been okay. Auntie wasn't impressed. I don't know how it is in the rest of the world, but *everyone* knows you don't give even numbers with flowers. Unless someone has died.

I don't see anything of Oleg anymore. It wasn't long after the roses fiasco that we parted company. He trundled off with the rucksack he'd arrived with.

My Auntie Svetlana said I'd been foolish. She said, 'There's ten million – or more – women in Russia than there are men. Are you mad, Irina? I know you're educated, but don't you want to settle down and have babies? You're twenty-three, and you're not getting younger. You'll lose your chance, just you see!'

'Oh, Auntie. There's plenty of time for that.'

'You *should* marry again. What would Baba Yaga make of you?' She wiped her sticky hands on her front, and then splayed them on her rump: such broad, sinewy hands. She was busy making *peljmeni*, her dumplings. 'She'd sort you out, my girl.'

She'd disapproved of Oleg. He enjoyed vodka too much for her liking. If he'd stuck with kvass, it wouldn't have been so bad.

No one knows how this has come about, this swell in the number of women; maybe there's some kind of scientific explanation for it. Surely not still a consequence of the loss of so many men at war in the last century? There's been rumblings that dark forces have engineered this for a specific reason. When I heard that, I shivered.

I'd laughed at my auntie for her concern. 'Marry – again?' I said. 'And what about money?' But her words stung me.

Things do need to change.

In so many ways, our people are stuck in the past.

In Slavic myths, Baba Yaga is the wild woman or dark lady of magic and in Russian folklore we have so many stories about her. She lives in a hut in the forest, is often described as a frightening old witch with a terrible appetite for eating people. But there's also another side to her: she can determine a person's fate. My auntie says Baba Yaga will assess someone, face to face, and then come to a decision on the course of the rest of their life – or their death; she stands for the dark side of wisdom and can choose to appear in a variety of forms.

She's not all bad.

Do you know, the word witch once meant wise?

That's what they say.

But do I believe all that? Of course not. It's a load of *der'mo*. A crock of it. I laugh about it with my chum Elvira – but not too hard, and especially not in front of my auntie. Elvira works with me, we're good friends. We think alike.

We were all brought up with these stories, it's part of us. Auntie says, if I ever meet with Baba Yaga, I have to talk my way into her good books – and not to take it lightly. Ha!

People say we're the largest country in the world. I don't doubt it, but there's still so much more to see. The whole, entire world. I'm modern minded. I'm patriotic too, even if I don't always agree with the political stuff.

But I have to get out. I need to leave Vladivostok.

I yawn as I crawl my way out of my bed and grab my thick hooded robe. It's bitterly cold. I fasten my robe and try to stop my fingers trembling.

I should never have stayed up so late watching *Mosfilm* movies. So cheesy.

The TV set conked out twice; a bit of a slap sorted it out.

The frozen air and the bleak blare of today's icebreaker outside the port sets my teeth on edge. We hear it loud and clear from here. They have nice little communities on those vessels, the crew live far better than most people do, and they're travelling the world – or, at least, part of it. *Top of the World People* we call them.

Auntie Svetlana is in the kitchen making *borscht* for later. Hers is the best. The beetroot juice gets everywhere but she doesn't care. Up the walls often and inside the cutlery drawer, sometimes pooling into the spoons.

Soon she'll be making fresh bread and different

types of *blini*. She'll give some to the neighbours. She never stops working.

I'm late.

I grab a slice of black rye with cheese to eat before I wash and pull on my outdoor clothes.

I go back into my cubbyhole bedroom to move a few treasured books, all swollen now with the damp coming from the crumbling wall at the side of my bed. We'll have mushrooms sprouting soon. I have to get away – and before too long.

I try to save, but there's not much in the moneybox under my bed.

Now ready for work, I leave the flat.

I walk into the centre in my heavy duty, fur-lined boots, crunching along the main road. My hot breath creates clouds of steam dancing in the icy air.

I'm just going past *Jimmy! Jimmy!* – our local Indian restaurant – what a name! And then there's the ice cream parlour as I cut through, but that's closed – and has been for some while. My workplace is round the back. I can smell the grease and muck, always, before I can see the unimposing building, a rundown takeaway unit tacked onto the end. If I have to work with burgers, why can't it be in a more salubrious area, not to mention better premises with decent decor! From this distance, I'm certain I can see a blur of midges fuzzing over the filthy garbage bins outside; they're there for a bacteria feast, even in this diabolical climate.

There's no one around yet. It's still too early for most people. The mournful sound of the horn from the icebreaker vessel punches its way through the rundown streets of the neighbourhood. The *Ekspress* from Moscow will be in soon, roaring into the railroad terminal, spilling out today's weary, dishevelled travellers.

Seven days of draining incarceration across Siberia.

I think of being in Moscow... the famous Big Golden Arches, the ultimate in burger joints – everyone knows the Double Arch logo. Moscow's premises is the biggest in the world. I'm told they pay well.

Now I hear the *Ekspress* in the distance...

I've never been inside our beautiful railroad building; with its parapets, pinnacles and grand entrance. It looks so incongruous in its setting, with streets of dreary tenement buildings and worn cobbles not so far away.

I've never travelled anywhere.

Not yet.

A blast of freezing air hits as I round a corner; I pull up the collar of my *shuba* – tatty rabbit, definitely on its way out, and clamp my fur hat on tighter.

I spot something. It flutters.

A bird?

Attracted by the scraps of rotten food no doubt, competing with the greedy gulls.

Is it hurt?

I slow my pace. The bird stands its ground and looks straight at me. It's the most peculiar bird I've ever seen; obviously lost somehow during migration. It's crested, with a long forked tail, and with plumage of every colour you've ever seen. It has big gnarled feet, skinny legs and a yellow pointed beak. I move forward to shoo it away, but something stops me.

I step back.

'Irina,' says the bird, now approaching me. 'Irina. It's time to tell your tale.'

My heart jolts.

It speaks! But no words are actually spoken. Am I still asleep? Have I frozen to death in my sleep and ended up in an alternative, icy hell?

My auntie's words come back to me:

Tread carefully.

Do not take things lightly.

Is this really happening?

The bird is still looking at me with its piercing red eyes, a scornful look about it. Or – am I just imagining this? I'm stunned.

And I swear this bird is increasing in size...

Then I hear a shout behind me. 'Hey! *Dobroye Utro!*'

Good Morning!

It's Elvira. She's still a fair way off.

'I know your story,' says the exotic bird. 'You dream of the Big Golden Arches.'

'Yes... I did,' I say. I explain that I had wanted to go to Moscow to work – but that was before I decided to see more life, to travel the world. Somehow.

I hope I come over as humble and polite. And, of course, I know I'll wake up fairly soon. Dreams can be so weird.

'I've had enough of burgers. Sick of it,' I add.

Tread carefully. Do not rock the boat. Auntie

could've been standing at my shoulder prompting me.

It's all *so* real.

'*Dobroye Utro*, Irina!' says Elvira, out of breath, exhaling her own clouds of vapour. 'Didn't you see me?' She stands next to me, her mouth falling slack at the sight of Baba Yaga. The enigmatic old sage has properly materialised now. She's whole. She's as the picture books portray her, but even more extraordinary.

Still she regards me with that penetrating look.

'It's not advisable to be too greedy, Irina,' she says disparagingly, then gives her whole attention to Elvira; her red eyes gleaming, her mouth twisting into a knot.

'And you, young female. What'll become of *you*?'

I hear Elvira gasp. A death sentence?

'You knew you'd find us here, didn't you,' Elvira says, and I nudge her hard for her risky impertinence.

'I know everything,' says Baba Yaga.

A prickle runs up my spine.

She points a knotty finger... then spreads her arms like wings, as indeed they were just a moment or two ago. In an instant, she envelops us both in a vivid kaleidoscope of warmth, exhilaration and terror.

'My time is precious,' she says. 'I heard the call. Listen to me now.'

I'm used to the reek of burgers, of sweet drinks and strong coffee, the clatter of pushchairs and high-pitched voices. Here, the worst thing was metal chair legs scraping on the hard floor; but before too long I didn't hear them.

I'm supervisor in a burger joint. Not Moscow's Big Golden Arches, but Big Golden Arches nevertheless. The sign outside says it all.

It's a busy city eatery.

There's no icebreakers here.

Only crushed-ice containers for chilling drinks cans.

The English are quite different to us, but interesting just the same. They're actually quite a noisy nation. And my English has improved amazingly.

My life is on course.

Yet another espresso machine hisses, following on with a brain-numbing blast, and then a *clunk*. There's always a clunk, that's when the jug is tapped on the counter. All those buttons to grapple with. And remembering the grinders settings, and the precise timing needed. There's a science behind the creation of Espresso – small and large – and Espresso Macchiato, Americano, Caffe Latte, Cappuccino, Caffe Mocha...

It's a hellish job. I'm not part of that now.

I take out my phone.

'Auntie,' I say, 'I'd give anything for a taste of your *peljmeni!*' I laugh, smacking my lips. 'I'm taking my break now, it's time. How are you?'

The ongoing commotion level goes up a notch.

I smile at Elvira as she races by with a loaded tray. I have to press the phone to my ear to hear what Auntie is saying, then I nod. 'Oh, good! *Chudesno!* We'll organise that for you,' I say. 'Can't wait to see you. That's *so* good to hear.'

'Tread carefully,' she says. 'Irina... it's all very *strange.*'

McDonalds is just a stone's throw from Brighton beach with its famous pier. We go to sit on the pebbly sand often, spreading our towels near the sea edge. We love the feel of sun on our bare arms and legs.

And on our faces.

We're so many, many miles from Vladivostok.

We know it doesn't have to end here.

And Auntie Svetlana arrives soon.

Very strange indeed.

It's as if by magic.

Shiny-Eyed

From Christian Dior's *New Look* onwards, she'd taken great care with her appearance: neat stockings, polished shoes, a svelte two-piece or chic dress worn with gleaming pearls.

Hair styled fashionably, lipstick a juicy plum red.

Discreetly rouged, delicately perfumed.

Shiny-eyed.

People remarked what a pretty woman she was. She'd tilt her smooth, round face appreciatively, smiling.

Yet... always aloof.

No real friendships.

Now, drowsy in her chair in Greenhavens, she tweaks her cardigan, sweeps her hand across her wispy grey crop, and turns misty eyes to the closed door.

Proud, always.

Certainly refined.

Forever hopeful.

But no one ever comes.

Printed in Great Britain
by Amazon